Animan

By

Michael K Chapman

Animan

Harry, a normal university lecturer is spending a quiet Sunday. Rising late in the morning, Harry makes the short journey to the local shop for the Sunday papers. Life for Harry is predictable and safe, his only concerns in life is to survive each day attempting to teach a class of teenagers the rudiments of science. His only pleasures involve the local pub and a microwave meal. Nothing exciting ever happens to Harry, until this day.

On the walk back from the shop, Harry encounters a small jade box on the pavement in front of him. Curiosity leads him to pick it up and take it back to his small flat for further investigation. Once alone in his kitchen, Harry opens the box . . . .

When Harry awakes, he is no longer in his flat. He is no longer on Earth. He is no longer human.

Animan

Copyright © Michael K Chapman 2017

The right of Michael K Chapman to be identified as the Author of this work has been asserted by him in accordance with the Copyright, Designs and Patents Act 1988.
All Rights Reserved. No part of this publication may be reproduced, stored in a retrieval system, or transmitted in any form or by any means, electronic, photocopying, recording or otherwise, without the prior permission of the publisher.

All characters in this publication are fictitious and any resemblance to real persons living or dead is purely coincidence.

ISBN: 978-0-9927317-5-5

Cover Image by Tamsin Chapman.
Editing and proofing by K Njoh.

Other titles by this Author.

Animan ll
Animan: Evolution

Humour
A Fly on the Ward
A Fly on the Garden Wall
A Nautical Novice (A Fly on the Boat)

Children's
Billy the Hero
Sally to the Rescue

Non-fiction
Humanology

Table of Contents

	page
Chapter One: The Box.	7
Chapter Two: Awakening	18
Chapter Three: The Journey	53
Chapter Four: The Sage	79
Chapter Five: A Kill	116
Chapter Six: Band of Brothers	133
Chapter Seven: A Demon before Us	152
Chapter Eight: Science	167
Chapter Nine: Defero	183
Chapter Ten: Burning Water	203
Chapter Eleven: Trapped	241
Chapter Twelve: A Warning	269
Chapter Thirteen: A Friend in Need	301
Chapter Fourteen: A Plan	329
Chapter Fifteen: The Palace	349
Chapter Sixteen: Face to Face	368
Chapter Seventeen: The Green Jade Box	390

6

Chapter One: The Box.

The constant beep from my alarm clock signalled the start of a new day. I surfaced reluctantly from a world of snug warmth and wonderful dreams, into the harsh reality of a cold wet morning. I decided for the thousandth time that I hated alarm clocks but resisted the powerful urge to throw the damn thing out the window again. I had done that before and immediately learnt my lesson, first open the window! This day the clock survived with only a slight dent as I flung out my arm to turn off its annoying shout, knocking it to the floor in the process. The hated sound was silenced and, with a sigh, I crawled out from the only form of luxury I had in my life at this time. With wobbly legs, I stumbled to the bathroom to complete those necessary morning duties that I assume all living things have to perform. I tried to avoid looking into the bathroom mirror, no point in making the day any worse.

Following a quick breakfast of tea and chocolate, I left my small flat in the city and made my way to work. More accurately I made my way to stand forlornly at the bus stop to await the rattling, smoking monster that would transport me to the university where I lectured in the sciences. I had returned to the academic life after a short spell in business and with hopes for an easier life, but I was now into my second year of a headache. Knuckling my eyes red and with head bowed against the constant British rain, I walked the hundred yards to the bus stop and stood in line with others of my ilk.

No one spoke other than the odd grunt as one recognised another, otherwise our small group of seven travellers simply stood hunched against the elements and waited for the bus. I did own a car but chose not to use it, not for any environmental consideration but rather laziness. I hated having to force my way through morning traffic before spending an eternity seeking a parking space. The public transport system is quite good here. Buses run past my flat approximately every ten minutes and soon we would have the Metrolink option as well. So instead of battling other grumpy drivers in the daily rush hour, I climbed aboard the bus and relaxed, letting the bus driver take the strain. It was only a fifteen minute journey and I was soon entering the college campus, a place of doom, gloom, work and – students.

The day progressed uneventfully, I attempted to teach groups of late teens and a few mature students the delights of environmental and natural science, some chemistry and a whole lot of physics, which I hated almost as much as my bored students. It was not until I had to perform an experiment and nearly set the classroom on fire, that many of my students actually woke up. I must state that my various groups of students were not normally so disinterested, however on this wet Monday morning, many were suffering from a weekend at the Glastonbury Festival.

Standing before a class of twenty yawning, sleepy and hungover students, I often wondered what they thought of me. Taking stock of myself, something I had not attempted for years due to my weak constitution. I was in my early thirties, with short untidy dark hair, brown eyes and clean shaven, most of the time. A slightly hooked nose sat in the middle of an average face that appeared somewhat older than it was. I stood at five foot eight inches tall on a good day and my waist was fast developing a paunch. Normally fit due to regularly attending martial arts classes and occasionally lifting weights, I still had some bulk to my upper body and arms but age and sloth were beginning to take its toll. Nothing special to look at I admit, I did not care as my life seemed to be on hold and any romance or excitement was so far over the horizon it was truly invisible. My employment path had been uneventful since leaving school, college and university. I had experienced several employment occupations before falling reluctantly into teaching.

I cannot in truth state that I was any more than fair to middling as a practitioner of education, though I tried. From my student days, I remembered spending many lessons, seminars and talks fast asleep at the back of the auditorium because the speaker had so little charisma. I did not want my students to lapse into a similar state of unconsciousness. As I stood in front of the class I attempted to make each lesson as interesting and often as humorous as possible, in a habitually futile effort to penetrate the reluctant brains of the modern educational traveller. Sometimes I hit the mark and a lively and enthusiastic class ensued. Today though, nothing I said or did would combat the after-effects of a raucous weekend.

At last, all the classes of the day were concluded, with varying degrees of success or failure. I found myself back in the staff room examining the students' assignments and trying desperately to find gems of intelligence within the contents of these demonstrations of learning. Marking was never one of my most favoured chores, hours spent examining items of work that some poor student had sweated over, and others that were flung together hastily in the forlorn hope that the coffee stained document would gain a merit or distinction.

A couple of hours later with glazed vision and an even worse headache, I decided to vacate the building and head home to a microwave meal and the television. Mine was such a thrilling existence. Deciding I required some cheer, I considered the possibility of visiting a local attraction or maybe even a weekend down in London. Perhaps someplace new and exciting to add a dash of colour to my dreary life. I pondered the matter as I returned to the bus queue and awaited my rumbling, smoking chariot home.

That evening, following the less than eager consumption of a microwaved beef platter, I came to a decision. On Saturday I would visit a Zoo. I have always loved animals and enjoyed animal parks and zoos since I was a child. I had not been to one for years so a quiet stroll around looking at the animals seemed a charming idea. Maybe a pint and a sandwich for lunch, if my funds would cope with tourist attraction prices. It would be a pleasant change to view the members of the animal kingdom instead of animals of the human variety. So the weekend was planned and I eagerly awaited the conclusion of the working week.

Saturday duly arrived and I set off to my chosen destination. I still did not use my car; the poor thing sat rusting away in a parking space allotted to me as a resident in my block of flats. In fact, I was not even sure if I could find the keys, it had been so long since I'd used it. So instead, a combination of trains and buses took me to my grand day out. Eventually, I stood within the grounds of the zoo, wondering which unfortunate animal I would gaze upon first. I say unfortunate not because they were in any form of distress, I meant simply because they were in captivity and that can't be fun for any animal. No fun perhaps but zoos today help to keep declining species on our planet, their planet. So many animals are becoming extinct around the globe, at least the bars and cages of the zoo kept these animals in existence.

I meandered along, caught in a tide of fellow visitors, allowing the flow to carry me to the destination that always drew me in fascination. It was not long before I found myself outside the tiger enclosure. I loved tigers and considered them to be the real kings of the animal world, so it was not surprising that I arrived there first.

I stopped and peered into the securely fenced off area, absentmindedly pulling a small snack from my pocket, some form of granola bar I think. As I stood and stared in wonderment at the magnificent beasts, one of the animals rose to its feet and slowly, somewhat timidly, approached me. Coming to a halt just a few feet away on the opposite side of the fence, the mighty tiger stared right into my face. Its eyes boring into mine with surprising intensity. Moments or eons passed as we held each other's gaze, the man and the animal. After a minute or so, I recognised I was being challenged. In defiance, I firmly locked my gaze onto the yellow eyes of the magnificent big cat. I felt the urge to mutter, 'Here kitty, kitty,' but decided against it. The strength and intensity of the whole episode struck me as the most important battle of wills I had ever fought, cracking a joke was simply not appropriate.

At last, the spell was broken as the tiger slowly lowered its head, possibly in acceptance or recognition but certainly not in defeat. The magnificent animal did not look up again as it turned and moved silently away. I remained in place for several minutes, too dumbfounded to move, unwilling to let that moment become just a memory. An eternity seemed to pass before I broke the mood and moved off to see the other sights and animals I enjoyed whilst visiting the zoo. I refrained from returning to the tiger enclosure. I felt too guilty to see those fabulous animals caged. I was also concerned that a specific tiger would do more than just stare at me if I ventured near it again.

Around four in the afternoon, my appetite for the animal kingdom sated, I retraced my journey home and relaxed with my newspaper for an hour before heading out to my local pub for a pint and a meal. I could not face yet another frozen microwave dinner and required the company of non-academic types.

Sunday morning dawned bright and I leapt from my slumber at the crack of noon. Delaying the consumption of breakfast, I rushed down to the corner shop to obtain a Sunday newspaper before the shop closed. My mission accomplished, I began flicking through the newspaper, dropping all the supplements into waste bins as I wandered home. I found an actual news story of interest hidden amongst all the celebrity hype and my concentration on where I was walking floundered, I felt myself trip on something. Once I had regained my balance and quickly glanced around to ensure no one had witnessed my minor bout of acrobatics, I looked down to see what had caused my stumble. I prayed the cause of my trip did not involve the residue of a dog's dinner. Cleaning one's shoe before breakfast failed in its appeal.

This time however, a lowly mutt was not to blame. There in front of me on the pavement was a small box. It appeared to be constructed of a green material, possibly jade I thought. I picked the item up and placed it in my pocket for examination later after I had breakfasted and finished reading the newspaper. Succeeding a quick check of my location to make sure no one was actively searching for the dropped box, and more importantly, no one had seen me pick it up, I continued on my way.

The pavement was now beginning to get busy as the Sunday morning rush for a pub lunch entered its initial stage and soon I found myself struggling home through random parties of middle-aged persons who now discarded the historic tradition of a home cooked Sunday roast. The mystery of the little box was instantly forgotten as I played human dodgems with the mass of humanity also passing through my tiny space on this planet. No one looked at me as I sidestepped, swerved and avoided those human obstacles, no one spoke. City life can be extremely unfriendly even on a Sunday as each city inhabitant makes their own way in life, and many had chosen the same time and space on the pavement as me.

Home again safely following the game of street rugby, I remembered the box as I patted down my jacket to ensure I had removed my keys, my mobile phone and any spare change from my pockets. I placed it on the kitchen table along with the other items before switching on the kettle for a morning, or early afternoon coffee and whatever I could find for breakfast come lunch. Picking up the newspaper I began to read while waiting for the kettle to boil in my small kitchen. My flat was laughingly termed an apartment by the renting agent who obviously saw me coming.

My 'apartment' consisted of one bedroom containing a double bed, a wardrobe and a small chest of drawers which took up virtually the whole sleeping space. Stubbed toes were a frequent hazard. One bathroom without a bath, instead it possessed a tiny shower cubicle, so small that when I bent to pick up the soap I either banged my head or pushed the door open with my rear. A toilet and washbasin nestled beside the shower. The only other room consisted of a small kitchen area located at the opposite end of a tiny lounge. I could if I wished, turn over the bacon in the frying pan on the cooker whilst at the same time removing eggs from the fridge and switching channels on the television. The renting agent described the 'apartment' as compact, I described it as a damn rabbit hole. We agreed to differ. Anyway, it was all I could afford at that time and to be honest it suited me fine. I live alone, I'm not an untidy person and I live by frugal means, keeping my small flat and my few possessions clean and tidy was a doddle.

Reaching the sports pages in the newspaper was my cue to add it to my recycling pile. I am not a fan of football; I think cricket is good only as a cure for insomnia and I have never understood rugby, so I seldom bothered reading the sports section. These days, if one was not fascinated by the antics of celebrities, shocked at the subtle dishonesty of politicians or following footballing prima donnas, it rarely took long to read a newspaper.

Relieved of the adult comic laughingly termed a newspaper, the small green box once more caught my attention as it sat unobtrusively upon my kitchen table. Curious rather than intrigued, I picked it up and held the box in my hand, peering closely. It was quite small, maybe only three inches wide, two inches deep and two inches high and, as I had already concluded, appeared to be constructed of pale green jade. Two dainty hinges were attached to one side of the lid, securing the lid to the box. Opposing the side that held the hinges, a small hooked clasp held the lid and the base firmly closed. Both the hinges and the clasp were of a gold colour. I did not consider them to be actual gold as such workmanship was rare these days. I also considered gold hinges far too expensive to adorn a small green box lost on a city pavement, though I could have been wrong. I turned the box over in my hands as I searched for a makers label or shop signature but found nothing, it was completely unadorned. Lifting the box closer to my eyes I opened the clasp and made ready to cautiously peer inside. As the lid became fully open I leant my head slightly towards the box in curiosity and then, blackness!

Chapter Two: Awakening.

I appeared to wake almost instantly. Opening my eyes carefully, fully expecting a mugger or a little old lady to be looming over me. But no thug, mugger or policeman blocked my vision, instead I found myself looking up at a clear pale blue sky. What the hell had just happened? I asked myself with no small hint of trepidation. Was I dead? Had I wandered outside and some boy racer or maniacal bus driver flattened me into the road? Was this Heaven . . . ? I quickly decided it was not Heaven; I knew my track record. Sadly I was more likely to be somewhere much warmer. I had always tried to be a good person, however, my human nature often took over and I have done, seen and wished for things I should be ashamed of, but was not. To survive anywhere in this world overpopulated with humanity, one did what one had to, and some things purely for fun of course. I did not identify myself as a sinner, but likewise, I was no saint either.

Then another fact concerning my predicament struck me. I was lying on untended grass in what appeared to be a municipal park. Tall unkempt grass stretched out on all sides with small clumps of trees in the distance. If it was a park, then it was a damn big one I thought. What had happened to my little apartment? I expected to be lying flat on my grubby carpeted floor in my tiny flat, not staring up at a blue sky!

Confusion hit me like a hammer as my startled gaze flashed about me, where the hell was I? Was I dreaming and if so when did I fall asleep? The world around me was strange yet familiar; I recognised some of the trees, many of the birds fluttering across the sky and certainly the wasp that was buzzing about my head. Nope, I did not have a hangover nor had I partaken of any strange substances that could easily be found on street corners. What the heck was happening to me?

I am no expert in flora and fauna by any means but even an idiot like me can identify familiar trees or a clump of brambles and of course the green grass on which I lay. All these things I recognised immediately but still the world seemed strange, different in an indefinable way. The air tasted clean if that is possible. There was no hint of vehicle exhaust fumes or other such delightful aromas I normally associate with city life. Nor were there any sounds to be heard other than the birds singing, and there were a lot of birds. A gentle breeze rustled through the grass but otherwise, the world was void of manmade sounds. No automobile engines, no aeroplanes flying over me and absolutely no drunks singing off-key in the distance. I had no idea where I was but one thing I was sure of, I was no longer in the city. I could only assume I was still somewhere in Britain but where, I had no idea. Things looked the same but there were many subtle differences.

Laying there on the grass my mind was filled with total confusion. There appeared to be no one else in the vicinity so maybe I should do some exploring; to determine whether I could find a landmark or point of reference to establish my location. Quickly I flexed all my muscles to check for injuries. I did not know how I got here so I considered it wise to identify any broken bones, bruises or any of the other myriad of miscellaneous breakdowns that can befall the frail human form. Firstly though, I reached to my back pocket to check my wallet was still on my person, the possibility of a mugging remained a possibility. It was still there and I gave a small sigh of relief, its presence at least discarded that explanation. I continued my personal examination. After just a few moments I realised with astonishment that not only was there no apparent damage to my person but my body felt great! Never had I felt so healthy or strong in my life. Whatever had happened to me had certainly been a cause of improvement. I felt I could spring to my feet and run a marathon. I decided not to spring up and run off at that moment, besides where would I run I wondered.

About that time I realised my clothes were constricting me. Following my muscle clenching and wallet checking, I felt it prudent to do a visual examination of my body. I could have been lying in a cow pat, or worse. I peered down at my body. I had been so absorbed in the landscape and the mystery of how I had arrived at this strange location, I had not taken stock of myself, other than the mental scan to ensure I still possessed all my limbs. Peering down I saw my clothes had shrunk, no wait; I had grown. What the hell was going on, who was I? Had I mistakenly swallowed some magic beans or some of Alice's strange drink?

Cautiously I rose from the ground, taking care over each movement in this weird and unfamiliar body. First I lifted my hands to my face, ripping my shirt as I moved, and received an even great shock. Not only were my hands huge, but looking closely I could see they were covered in what appeared to be fuzz. It resembled a teenage male's first growth of maturity, but on closer inspection, I decided it appeared to be – fur!

The back of my hands were covered in a faint, light brown hair to be precise, with faint patches of a darker hue running through the brown. My fingernails were thick and so dark they were almost black, while my accompanying fingers appeared rather short against the wide palm of my hand. I was delighted to see I still owned four fingers and a thumb. While short and somewhat stubby; my digits could still be classed as fingers, though I would never play the piano. Following through I saw the fur continued up my arm. A very muscular arm with the shreds of my shirt hanging from it. No wonder my clothes were taut, I was far too big and my garments had all but completely ripped apart. Visions of the Incredible Hulk sprang to mind but from what I could see, I was the wrong colour.

In frustration, I tore the remains of my shirt from my torso. Lo and behold I was covered in fur-like hair. Taking the risk that I would not be discovered and arrested as a furry streaker, I peeled off my jeans and stared in horror. From the top; my upper torso consisted of wide strong shoulders, narrowing down to a slim waist. Arms that radiated strength and were definitely not the arms I recognised hung down to what, in my opinion, were not my hands. The fur covered all I could see, from my shoulders and arms, down my stomach and loins and on down my – wow! My long furry and very strong looking legs. The fur on my stomach and loins I noticed, was a cream colour, not the same as the brown that appeared to coat the rest of this strange body. The fine almost invisible fur did not resemble the normal human hair found on many gentlemen (and some women) with hairy backs, arms and legs. No this appeared to be genuine fur, smooth and silky to the touch. In places the brown colour was interspersed with black, from what I could see of myself, the black fur ran through the brown in an uneven pattern.

As I stood there with the gentle breeze a pleasant sensation on my body, I knew I needed to seek help. My scientific brain could not analyse what had happened to me, how I had changed into this alien being? I knew all the tales of vampires and werewolves but what the hell was I? The incredible Furry Man? I gave up, my head hurt and my body had begun to shake, I was slipping into shock. Okay, I thought, get moving and see if I can find help, a doctor or perhaps a veterinarian may be better, possibly including a *peticure*. Picking up the remnants of my shirt, I wrapped it as best I could around my waist to form a makeshift loincloth. I was afraid my underwear was way too small for me now and I did not want to get nicked for indecent exposure on top of all these other new problems. Off I set, at first at a walk but soon I was running, where? Who the hell knows!

I decided to head south, I had no real reason for this decision and I trusted that the sun shining in the azure sky moved in the same pattern as it did yesterday. I ran, I ran through the endless grassland, relieved to be doing something, anything to keep my body from going further into shock and inject a purpose into my struggling mind. Thirst began to make itself noticed as I ran so I determined to seek out water, or preferably a pub, but whichever came first. For some time I ran, surprised at the ease and speed at which I ran. I had never been a runner before, in fact,

I hated running. If I needed to be anywhere fast I simply jumped in my car or onto a bus, I never ran.

The pace I was managing ate up the miles and the physical activity quickly became routine, allowing my mind to dissect the recent events. But my thirst was growing and I feared I would soon collapse in a heap. Surely I could not keep up this pace for much longer but I still felt great. No tiredness or aches and pains were evident so I just kept on running. At last, I came to a small lake and halted my headlong rush to nowhere. Crouching down at the side of the lake, I dipped my paws - sorry, I mean my hands into the cool water and drank. The refreshing liquid tasted clean and delicious as it flowed down my throat. Suddenly I stopped. What the hell was I doing? The land I was familiar with held lakes, ponds, rivers and streams that no health conscious person would even consider drinking from. Pollutants, rubbish and assorted human waste often outweighed the actual water content in my world. This water looked so clean and clear that I gave up my worries and continued to drink.

As I drank I noticed something strange in the water right before my eyes. The sight caused me to leap back in horror, not sure what I had seen and absolutely certain I did not want to find out. I had covered some ten foot in my leap, again a surprising feat of agility for someone who could barely drag himself from an armchair to make a cup of tea. Cautiously I edged forward back to the lakeside, I could see nothing out of the ordinary from where I now stood, primed in the fight or flight mode of human existence. I knew I would choose flight if anything ventured from the water in front of me, super furry man I may be but underneath my new body, my main interest remained self-preservation. Closer now to the water's edge, I knelt down low and peered vigilantly into the lake and at once saw a strange face looking back at me. Another rapid retreat from the lake ensued as I realised with shock and horror that the strange thing I had seen in the water, was me!

Gasping and on the point of a mental breakdown, I steeled myself and approached the crystal clear water once again. Looking down I saw reflected upon its surface a face, a face that was not mine. Long flowing brown hair topped a wide face with inhuman features. My eyes were elongated lengthwise and the pupils therein were yellow with black irises. My normally slightly hooked and often running nose had vanished. Instead, there appeared an almost triangular shaped shorter, stubbier thing sitting conspicuously above a long philtrum that reached down to a thin-lipped mouth. Both my nose and mouth appeared to protrude slightly from my face, not enough to call myself the Elephant Man but no longer did my face have the flat features of a human being. Unwittingly I opened my mouth and immediately cried out in fright as large canine teeth came into view. Bloody hell I thought, I look like a damn cat! Quickly I spun around, expecting to discover a long tail to add to my transformation. I found only a short stump at the very base of my coccyx. I have never felt such relief!

I rocked back onto my (tail-less) rear and sat in confusion at the lakeside. Bram Stoker had devised Dracula and Mary Shelley had written the story of Frankenstein but who had created me? Was I now just a figure in fiction? Had I been secretly exposed to some unknown radiation or chemical concoction that had caused this? No that cannot be right, I must still be dreaming. What I had seen in the water was a physical impossibility by all the laws of biology that I understood. I held my head in my hands and wept in fear and horror at my transformation into what I could only describe as a feline creature, a big magnificent pussy but a feline all the same. How was I ever going to get a girlfriend looking like this, maybe I could join a circus or a freak show? Would I start chasing mice and purring?

Finally, I cracked up, jumping to my feet I screamed and shouted, stamped my feet and threw my arms around. If there was anything near I would have hit it but there was nothing other than grass, a few reeds and the water so I began pounding myself. In my state of utter bewilderment and mental collapse, I bent to the ground and grasped a rock and with all the self-destructive force I could muster, I battered myself into unconsciousness and escaped from the animal that was me.

I regained consciousness and some sense moments later. Nothing had changed aside from a very sore head and a smear of blood on my forehead. I had returned to a form of sanity following my plunge into madness, though I think I could have chosen a less painful method. Gathering what remained of my wits about me, I decided to continue searching for some form of civilisation. I warned myself not to blunder into anything before I was certain of my safety, or at least hopeful of my safety. If I went strolling up to strangers in my present state, I had no idea what reception my appearance would have on the local population. One thing was certain, I did not want to encounter a gang of back street youths looking as I did. It gave a whole new meaning to the saying, scaredy-cat! I prayed that like a cat, I too had nine lives. So with my mind made up, almost, I set off once more at a fast walk.

It was not long before the elation of a strong and healthy body, performing amazingly under the warm sun and blue sky encouraged me to again increase my pace to the ground covering lope I had experienced earlier. Over rolling hills I travelled with ease, avoiding small clumps of trees as I wished to remain out in the open. I realised this action could go against me if I was seen, but with my new found strength and speed, I was confident I could out run any pursuers, unless they were in a vehicle of some sort of course.

An hour passed before I saw any signs of life bigger than a bird or rabbit. The undulation of the land had increased but I ran up and down the gentle hills and valleys with ease. Finally, I could see I was nearing a deeper valley. I had not noticed it at first for a small wood surrounded the valley rim, effectively almost hiding it from view. I headed towards it, the night would be upon me soon, judging from the lowness of the sun on the horizon. I began making my way down into the valley, hoping for something, food possibly. I would certainly need some form of shelter, even a tree would offer some cover.

Below me in the valley, I glimpsed in the distance a herd of what looked to me like deer, though I was not sure, nor did I have any knowledge of deer species so I just hazarded a guess. Living in the city, the only wildlife I normally encountered wore baseball caps or hoodies and roamed the streets in gangs. Suddenly, I stopped in my tracks and dropped to the ground. I had caught sight of a large figure off to one side of the deer herd. The figure appeared to be shepherding the herd towards a rough track virtually hidden in the undergrowth of the valley. It was not a deep valley, it was more of a dip in the landscape. I remained crouched down whilst inspecting the area before me. In contrast to the grassland, the valley harboured an abundance of shrubs, small trees and other flora.

I made ready to shout and wave my hands in an attempt to attract the attention of the shepherd, but halted my actions swiftly as reasoning and caution stilled my enthusiasm. I did not know who the individual was or how my presence would be received. Moving away from the skyline to avoid being seen, I decided to follow the herd and the shepherd. I concluded he may lead me to some form of civilisation, even if just a farmhouse. I had been in this strange land and alien body for several hours and I was hungry. The shock of waking up in the middle of nowhere in a feline form had taken all thoughts of food from my mind, until now. At home, I would have suffered the delights of a frozen ready meal or perhaps enjoyed a pint of beer and a meal at my local hostelry by now. I might have forgotten but my stomach certainly had not, my body may have changed but my belly still required sustenance. Perhaps I could beg a tin of cat food? No, I thought, be serious! Wherever and whatever I was, I could be in grave danger so quit the wisecrack thoughts and concentrate.

Carefully I began following the shepherd, praying that my rumbling stomach would not give me away. I moved slowly down the slope, keeping low and dropping flat into the grass whenever the shepherd showed signs of looking behind him. I may now have the appearance of a cat, but I had not yet acquired the skill of stalking like a cat. The sun was now low in the sky and I began to dread the prospect of spending the oncoming night out in the open in this unfamiliar land. I remained convinced I was still somewhere in Britain but doubts had begun to invade my mind. I had not heard of deer being farmed in Britain before but as I said, I was a city boy and had no knowledge or experience of farming livestock.

Gradually I neared the herd but now I made sure I kept upwind of the animals. I had watched a nature programme on telly so I knew all about animals smelling scent on the air. Now I was actually putting the knowledge into practice. My sense of smell had changed immensely with my regeneration, as I now thought of it. I could smell the animal odour of the herd. Strangely I could not identify the scent of the herder, most humans have a recognisable smell, pleasant or otherwise but I could detect nothing familiar. There was a different odour amongst that of the herd, but I could not identify it. Until now my only contact with wild animals stemmed from visits to a zoo or wildlife park. I had never been on safari or even on a farm for that matter. However, living in close proximity to fellow humans in the city gave me the experience of a wide variety of human scent, smell and awful odours. I could detect nothing familiar in the herd before me, though I could clearly see the figure shepherding the deer through the valley.

A mile or so along the track what I took to be a small farm came into view and obviously, it was there that the shepherd was heading. When he drew close several more figures came out from what I assumed to be the farmhouse, though surprisingly it was shaped like a dome, and positioned themselves to direct the herd into a fenced off area to one side of the track. I noted it appeared to be a family unit. Two adults including the farmer and two younger members, children I judged from their size in comparison with the two adults. No movements were hurried and the herd of deer was efficiently driven into the enclosure where hay lay in piles about a head high for the animals to eat. Hiding behind a small shrub of what species I knew not and cared even less, I watched the family make their way back to the house after securing the animals in the pen.

From where I lay, the farmer's home appeared solidly built and made of stone; the 'house' formed a dome, resembling a stone igloo but much larger. Windows were placed high around the walls and thick curved wooden shutters stood hinged to the side of each window, hanging in readiness to be closed against the elements. Or perhaps from attack, I didn't know. A sturdily built door raised up on several steps secured the entrance to the house, while a stubby chimney stood on top of the structure, barely protruding above the apex of the dome. Why a dome? I wondered as the door closed and I was alone.

The animal enclosure was situated to the right of the building, I could see at least two other buildings of similar construction to the left, a short distance from the house. The outbuildings were also domes but with gates rather than a door and again the gates were placed up off the ground, forcing the animals to scamper up wide ramps to enter the sheds or barns, whatever they were. A wooden fence surrounded these two sheds as I began to think of them, possibly one was a barn but what the hell did I know.

I edged my way a little closer to the farm hoping to reach one of the outbuildings in which I might spend the night. I was still utterly confused and my thoughts were a mess. I still had no idea where I was, how I got here and, most of all what I was? Fear accompanied my confusion and I desperately needed a quiet safe place in which I could consider my situation. Crouching low, I moved perhaps a hundred yards towards the farm, almost reaching the courtyard en route to the sheds. Suddenly the farm door opened, spilling yellow light onto the courtyard. I sidestepped behind a bush and watched in trepidation as the shepherd exited the door and began walking straight towards me. What the hell do I do now? I could not run as I would surely be seen and I was already hiding behind the only bush available to me. Hopefully, I would not be discovered, the daylight had faded and it was almost completely dark, only the light from the doorway offered feeble illumination and silhouetted the figure. I lowered myself flat to the ground, hugging it tighter than I've ever hugged a woman. The shepherd drew nearer and as he did so I noticed he held a vicious looking hand scythe, a farming implement that could easily part limbs from a body, namely my body.

'Well? If you are here to rob me or harm my family then I will stop you,' growled the shepherd in a deep voice. 'If you are lost I will offer directions, if you are hungry I can offer food. If you come with peace in your heart then you are welcome.' The shepherd paused, waiting for my response. 'So, what is it to be?'

What? What was he saying to me? As a city boy, I was not familiar with kindness and I was dumbfounded for a few moments.

'Well?'

Terrified but hungry and confused, I slowly rose to my feet and looked straight at the figure in front of me. What I saw almost caused me to jump back behind the bush in fright. Clenching my fists and buttocks, I managed to control my fear and my instinct to run. I did not know where or who I was so no matter how frightening the shepherd looked, I still needed help.

'I wish you no harm sir, I'm lost, I'm hungry and this land is strange to me,' I finally responded, adopting what I hoped matched the strange shepherd's form of speech.

'Then please, follow me and I will offer shelter and food. However should you intend doing harm, I will kill you. Is that understood?'

It was fortunate I had not eaten for many hours otherwise I am sure my furry buttocks would now be loose. 'Thank you Sir, I would be grateful for any sustenance and perhaps any information you might give me.'

Without another word, the shepherd walked back to the farmhouse. A moment of misgiving on my part was swiftly ignored and I followed a short distance behind. I had no idea what to expect, my only experience with farmers and their families came from television programmes. Would I find a plump welcoming farmer's wife and a ravishing daughter I wondered? Or would I be trapped in the abattoir of a murderer? Was I on the menu for the evening meal? Still, I had no choice, I needed shelter and food and more importantly, I was desperate for information.

My God! My appearance, I had forgotten how strange I looked. Would it frighten them to violence, would the local police come screaming down the farm track at any moment with sirens wailing? I had stated I meant them no harm but he not once answered that he would not harm me. Then I recalled how frightened I had been upon my first clear sight of the shepherd, and likewise his lack of reaction when seeing me. But my doubts remained, looking down I realised I must resemble someone with severe mental issues along with one or two health considerations. I was basically a huge cat walking upright in a makeshift loincloth. Surely once in the light, my appearance would result in loathing and revulsion. Oh crap I thought, there's nothing I can do about it now as I stepped over the threshold and into the house.

The light blinded me for a second or two; it was not bright and did not appear to originate from an electric bulb. Once my eyes were accustomed I realised some form of oil lamps provided the illumination. It appeared to be a single roomed home, not unlike a cave I realised. These thoughts took but an instant before I was faced with the inhabitants of the house. I stood trembling in my state of shock and fright as the farmer turned to look at me. My fear increased tenfold as I stared back at the creature. Standing six foot tall, though surprisingly much shorter than myself, stood a figure with a huge powerful upper body on top of a rounded waist supported by short bowed legs. The face that stared back at me was the like of which I had never seen. The eyes were a deep brown, set in a wide face while the nose and mouth extended slightly, giving the impression of a snout. Beneath the 'snout' a double chin sat atop a thick neck protruding from the heavy shoulders. Like me, his body or what I could see of it under the cotton shirt and blue dungarees, was covered with a very fine dark brown fur. Despite his kind countenance, his build and appearance suggested menace, his huge hands lay down by his sides like shovels and his smile showed a healthy set of fangs that could rip me to shreds. Other than those terrifying characteristics, the farmer's eyes showed what I hoped was a gentle soul and his offer of help demonstrated he may not eat me, least I hoped so.

Still shivering in the doorway, I forced my gaze away from the farmer and turned to study his family. All had the same brown fuzz, short legs and powerful stocky bodies but their height and clothing gave me a clue as to who they were. If women wore dresses and men wore trousers then the group consisted of what I assumed to be the farmer's wife and two children, a girl and a boy. The wife was staring back at me while wringing her hands with fear etched upon her face; her young daughter clung to her apron while the older boy peered at me with a slight snarl on his face – er, muzzle.

'Hi,' I began hesitantly, 'My name is . . . . umm, er . . .' I realised I did not know my name; I could not recall the name I had used my entire life! Not only had my whole world vanished and my whole appearance changed but now I could not remember my name.

'I'm sorry, I can't remember my name. I don't know who I am or where I am. Am I dreaming? Is this a nightmare or am I going mad? I just can't remember.'

These words came out in a sob as realisation finally hit me full in the face, the stomach and the bowels. The enormity of my situation flooded my mind, I was utterly and totally lost!

In a calming voice, the farmer answered softly, 'Well you're not dreaming nor do you appear mad. And we can't tell you your name, only you can figure that out. But we can offer you food and rest and give you directions to where you are heading . .'

'That's the point,' I interrupted, 'I don't know where I'm supposed to go or where I am or what I'm doing here. I don't know who I am.'

Tears began to flow down my face despite my efforts to hold them back, my mental state was on the point of collapse and I could feel my mind closing in on itself. Without being asked, I slumped onto one of the wooden chairs that surrounded a large wooden table in the middle of the room. My head lowered into my hands as the enormity of my situation struck home.

'It's ok,' said a gentle voice as a huge arm circled my shaking shoulders. 'I am Mrs Opilio and this is my family. We are of the Ursidae Cast and I can tell from your appearance that you are of the Felidae Cast. You are a warrior, a Tigris and the first we have ever seen. My name is Jōan and this is my husband Harron. My two little ones are Cinzz and Aulzz. As you don't know your name, we will call you . . ., let me think. A tall strong but lost Tigris warrior, we will call you Grandiz, it means full-grown and tall. What do you think about that, eh?'

I looked up at her with a tearful smile. 'Thank you, though I still need to discover who I really am, if I'm anyone at all.'

Gathering myself together I looked closer at those around me, the initial shock of their appearance was quickly wearing off, if someone could speak my language, I saw no reason to hold their looks against them. Anyway, regarding looks, I too appeared monstrous to my eyes so who was I to judge.

'That's good, now how about something to eat, you look starved. We were just about to have our evening meal and I invite you to join us if you wish,' said Jōan as she withdrew her arm from me and began fetching dishes for the table.

The rest of the family immediately found a chair each and also sat down, though their eyes still watched me with some misgivings. What do I do? I wondered, do I make small talk or just come straight out with the questions I need answers to? Harron took the decision away from me.

'So you don't know who you are or where you are and judging from the startled look you gave us, you have not encountered an Ursidae before?'

'No I admit this, you are all strange to me, in fact, I myself am strange, a few hours ago I was a normal human being going about my daily life. Suddenly I end up here, in the body of a cat and in a world I do not know. I am from a city in England and . . .'

'May I stop you there Grandiz, what is a Human Being? From what do you descend? We've never heard of such a thing, not in all the Animan Kingdom have I heard of a Human Being. What is a Human Being?' interrupted Harron with a frown.

My mind began to spin uncontrollably; the world consisted of human beings, all trying hard to destroy nature and themselves in their endless search for wealth and fame. Who could not know of humans, we were everywhere, we had even reached the moon for crying out loud. Who was this guy and more to the point what was this guy? I glanced around the table to ensure I was not the victim of a humorous windup, to ensure that no one was making me the butt of a terrible joke, but all I saw were faces as confused as mine. Even Mrs Opilio had paused in preparing the meal to await my explanation. The words, "*from what do you descend,*" completely threw me. How do I answer a question like that I thought. Okay in for a penny, in for a pound, as they say, I'll start at the beginning just in case I am surrounded by aliens.

'By descend, do you mean family history or evolution?'

A look of either sympathy or frustration flitted across Harron's face. 'By family of course. We all know our family descents as they dictate what Cast we will belong to throughout our lives. But what did this Human Being creature descend from? This is not known to me.'

'Fine, I'll start at the beginning. The human race evolved from the apes, or so we think. Progressing on through the Caveman to the Neanderthal and finally to the modern human being. So I am - was - a human being.'

Silence greeted my brief explanation as all stared at me in disbelief, moments later the family roared into laughter. Nudging each other and pointing at me, they laughed themselves to tears. I could not understand what I had said that would result in such mirth. I had stated a fact I had known all my life, a fact backed up by science and by fossils, remains, cave drawings and who knows what other proof. I knew some folk still wished to believe we were conceived by Adam and Eve but science had proven evolution and this fact was now common knowledge around the world. So what the hell were they laughing at?

'I'm sorry but what is so funny?' I asked, 'Humans populate the entire world, you can't miss them, they're everywhere and into everything.'

'From apes!' gasped Harron between laughs, 'I've never heard the like. How can you descend from apes? They are lowly creatures, not people like us. None of the Simia family or apes as you call them, have ever shown any more intelligence than a base animal. The Simia is regarded as a lowly beast, amusing to watch but that is all. Simia have no descents. You are obviously one of the Tigris Cast and I would warn you to be wary whom you tell this tale. Any member of the Tigris Cast would slay you instantly for uttering such blasphemy. The Tigrismen are a fierce and proud warrior Cast, matched only by the Leomen, who like you are from the Felidae Cast. So be told my friend, take care in what you say. There are no Cast descents from Simia and there is no such animan as a human being.'

Harron's words struck a chill to my very bones. Where and what the hell was I? Where were my fellow humans, my friends? Before I could reply, Jōan began to serve the evening meal. I was not sure what to expect but in front of me, I found potatoes, cabbage, carrots and some form of meat, all covered in rich dark gravy. My stomach went wild; I could not have cared what I was eating as I dived hungrily into the food. Jōan must have caught my very brief expression of concern but I was already tucking in before she managed to put my mind at rest.

'I hope you like the meat, it's from our own herd and was killed and hung last week.'

Through a mouthful I replied, 'It's lovely, thank you.'

'Good, good. I like to see a grown animan with a healthy appetite. Besides, I think you may need your strength soon. Being a Tigris, I expect you'll soon find reasons to practice your skills. Will you be searching for others of your kind or are you on a commission to someone important?'

'Huh? My skills? What skills? I was a science lecturer in my other life; I have no skills as such. What form of skills will I need?' I asked in between mouthfuls.

'Hah so obviously you've forgotten what being a Tigris is about? However, it is not my place to instruct someone of your standing, your Cast is much more important than a lowly Ursidae. I'm sure you'll find out as you journey.'

'Now I'm confused. What journey?' I enquired.

'Enough for now Jōan, let the animan eat and then rest. We'll have a long chat after he's refreshed. Any more information now will only confuse him further.'

I cast a grateful eye at Harron for coming to my aid. My mind was in turmoil and the meal was threatening to rise to the surface. Not a good practice for a guest to offer back his food.

Suddenly a thought struck me and I asked, 'Why is it I can speak your language? If we are in Britain fair enough, but if I'm somewhere else I would expect a different language, French, Russian or Chinese even, there are many languages from many lands.'

'Silly, we all speak one form of words here. Our ancestors migrated right across the land so our words moved with them. You have many lands? We only have the one here, a huge land that stretches from the ice regions at the top of the world right down to the ice at the bottom. We call our land Totus-Terra,' explained Jōan with a laugh. 'Everyone knows that.'

With that statement signalling the end of the conversation and the meal, Jōan led me to a curtained off section of the room that hid an area consisting of large cushions covering the whole floor with woollen blankets piled off to one side. Jōan indicated where I should sleep and handed me a blanket. I felt some trepidation as I realised everyone slept in the same room upon the cushions. I was used to a bed to myself, apart from the very odd occasion when I got lucky, which to my shame did not happen often enough.

Surprisingly the bed of cushions and the woollen blanket proved comfortable and I grew drowsy. It had been an extraordinary day, I still remembered that I had bought a newspaper, I remembered my flat and that I spent my days in the university, lecturing to a bunch of society's latest hopefuls but even as I thought them, the words began to sound strange in my mind. Like my name, it seemed details of my normal life were fading. How much would I remember in the morning I wondered? Exhaustion took its toll and I fell into a deep sleep, not even stirring when the Opilio's came to take their rest. Soon my mind began its attempt to organise my thoughts and my memory cleared. Perhaps the shock of all that had happened had forced my bewildered brain to shut out the past because the present was so alien. Whatever the reason, in my dreams I was once more an academic lecturer and my name was – my name was, Einstein. No wait, that's not it, my name is Harry, that's right, Harry Petoverum.

Morning arrived all too quickly and although awake, I forced my eyes to remain shut, hoping to hear the sounds of traffic outside my flat in the city, to hear a mobile phone ringtone or a police siren screaming its way through the rush hour madness. There was nothing, no familiar sound reached my ears, only dishes clattering and someone humming a disjointed tune that I failed to recognise. In resignation, I finally opened my eyes and found myself face to face with the creature called Aulzz.

'Morning Grandiz,' he said, all too cheerfully for my liking, 'mum says breakfast is ready if you wish to eat.'

It was obvious that he wished to eat because immediately after giving me the message, he scampered off eagerly through the curtain. There were no other rooms in the house, only the sleeping section was separated from the rest by a thick curtain. This fact caused me some concern, after the food and drink of the previous night; I desperately needed to relieve myself, but where? Climbing from my cushions, I tidied my makeshift loincloth and pushed through the curtain to be greeted by the rest of the family.

'Morning Grandiz, I hope you slept well and are refreshed this fine day?' asked Harron with what I assumed to be a smile.

'Yes thank you, I slept very well and it seems I've remembered my name. My name is Harry.'

All the Opilio family looked at me for a moment or two before wide grins spread upon their faces. Harron was the first to speak with a question.

'Har-ry, that's a strange name, I have not heard the like before.'

'That's okay; I haven't heard names like yours before. So there's no need to call me Grandiz anymore. My full name is Harry Petroverum.'

Harron and Jōan glanced at each before Harron gave a sigh, 'Ahh that we understand, the second part of your name I mean, Har-ry is still strange to us.'

'What? Are there others called Petroverum near bouts?' I asked in surprise.

'Oh no, it's not a name we know but we understand,' replied Harron, but that was all he would say on the matter because at that moment he noticed I was standing somewhat cross-legged and jigging about.

'I'm sorry, I expect you need to toilet first. Come, I'll show you where you can mark.'

With that Harron opened the door and gestured for me to follow him. I was still pondering what he meant by *mark* but I assumed he understood my need and I was right. We walked around the house to the rear where I discovered yet another dome-like structure but much smaller than the house and barn. I understood, it was an outside toilet. Okay, I'll give it a go I thought. Once he was sure I understood his implication, I entered the small dome, desperate now to relieve myself. Inside I found a familiar looking object, a large unadorned clay bowl with a hole in the bottom sat upon the floor. It suggested the toileting arrangement, least I hoped so, and I completed my toilet. A bucket of water stood nearby and as there was no evidence of a flush, I poured an amount of the water down the orifice of the bowl shaped seat and watched in curiosity as the water and my bodily fluid disappeared. Where it went I knew not and in truth, I cared even less.

Back in the house, I sat down to a breakfast of cold meat and berries, slightly unusual as a breakfast but who was I to complain. Trying not to gulp down the food, I ate as much as I could while my mind pondered on what to do next. Surely I could not stay here forever, the Opilio family were perfect hosts but it was apparent they were not wealthy. Another mouth to feed may push their meagre lifestyle to the limit. I had to move on, but where to?

Harron was of a like mind as he finished his meal and peered across the table at me. With a glance at her children to leave us alone, Jōan tactfully collected up all the dishes and moved away to a large sink that resembled half a beer barrel situated in front of what even I recognised as a water pump. Turning her back on us, she began to clean the breakfast implements without another word.

'So Harry, what are your plans now? Where will you go?'

Harron sat with his elbows resting on the table and his chin in his hands as he gazed at me across the table. His look indicated this was going to be a man to man talk, or perhaps an animan to animan talk, if I refer to his language. I sat and thought, I had no idea in truth. I was still trying to come to terms with what had happened that resulted in me sitting at a kitchen table, facing a creature that was not a man, not a human I should say, but realised then that Harron resembled a bear. A bear with intelligence and a kindly soul. What was I to say to him, my mind was blank concerning my next move. I didn't even know where I was. How could I know where to go and what I should do when I got there?

'I really don't know,' I responded after several moments. 'I have no knowledge of where I am, if I am still in my world or if I am caught in a fabrication of my mind. What do you suggest I do?'

Harron didn't reply immediately, instead he scratched behind one ear, adjusted his dungarees and appeared to frown, if indeed a bear could frown. Finally, he began to speak.

'I know not why you are here or what your reason, however in the far south others of your kind are known to dwell. Perhaps you should seek them out? Possibly they are better informed than I. There is a Sage of sorts some distance from here; he too lives to the south of us, so mayhap it is he you should appeal to first. I can give you basic directions but I cannot for sure tell you where he abides. You may ask at the next village, someone there will know how to reach the Sage. If you travel south I hope you will either encounter the village, the Sage or eventually other of the Tigris Cast. Personally, I would suggest the village first, you will need work for funds before you continue. I assume you have no funds of any kind?' he asked with a glance at my homemade loincloth.

I shrugged my shoulders and replied that I had nothing, Harron continued.

'And remember, if you do encounter one of your own Cast, Tigrismen are all too inclined to attack first and ask who they are attacking afterwards.'

'What do you mean, attack? If I'm one of their kind or Cast as you say, surely they would not offer me harm before hearing my tale?'

'That is the problem; you must not repeat your story to any of the Felidae race. Better that you claim a loss of memory due to an injury in battle, which they may believe. And be sure not to speak of the Simia or these human beings, a Tigris would surely not understand. I recommend you attribute your lack of knowledge and strange ways to the result of a fight or battle, nothing too heroic please. Perhaps fighting off bandits or a wild beast, this they will understand and may not question.'

The apprehension and fear on my face clearly showed Harron what my thoughts were on travelling alone to meet other beings I knew nothing about, and the dangers that might assail me along the way. In order to allow me a few minutes to ponder his advice, I looked down at my ill clad body, though my mind was in such turmoil I was not really seeing it. Harron however, did see my downward glance and immediately stood up from the table.

'Of course, I forgot. You can't travel like that; you will need clothes and a weapon, also supplies. If you are of a mind to travel south, I'll provide you with as much as I can, I fear it will not be much but we'll see.'

'Thank you,' was the only response I could give because I felt my mind would fall apart in fear of what the future may hold.

How I missed those reluctant and ungrateful students now. Within the hour I found myself dressed in an old pair of Harron's work trousers and a woollen homespun shirt that itched like crazy. Neither the trousers nor the shirt fitted as I was not nearly as broad but stood much taller than Harron. My legs protruded way out from beneath the trousers and my arms did the same in his old shirt. Harron provided me with a cord so I could tie the trousers around my waist; I did not wish to suddenly display my bare bottom to this strange world.

Now as decent as I could be, under those circumstances, Jōan hung over my shoulder a leather pouch filled with a water container, bread and a hunk of meat. A few hard biscuits and a form of candied fruit made up the total of my provisions. A warm looking woollen blanket had been tied to the bottom of the pouch. I didn't know if this strange land had cold seasons, but at least the blanket would help me avoid any night chills. Harron appeared again accompanied by his wide-eyed children. In his huge hand, he held a heavy staff made of aged hardwood with metal bands located along its length and metal caps attached to each end. The staff was as hard as iron and would withstand all but the hardest blow from the sharpest sword. Without a word he demonstrated a few moves of defence with the staff. Then to my surprise, Harron pressed a small button, hidden on one of the metal bands and out from one end of the staff, a blade appeared, about nine inches in length with both edges honed to an almost perfect sharpness.

'It can be used as a spear or a staff,' he explained, 'depending on what enemy you may face. There are many wild beasts that would consume you, such as the Hyaenidae that roam these regions. Do not lose it or you will die!'

I muttered some thanks though I knew in my heart I was taking from them more than they could afford to give. With a lump in my throat, I hugged and thanked each of the little family that had already done so much for me. Harron pointed the way for me to travel, adding a few hints on how I should recognise the way south. He suggested I fill up my fluid bottle whenever I encountered a water source as there may be long stretches in my travels when water would not be available. Harron gestured towards some hills far in the distance and told me to head for them first, from there I would be able to plot my next route. And then it was over, I could not say another word and it was obvious that Harron had helped as much as he was able. Standing with arms around each other, the precious members of the Opilio family waved as I turned and began walking along the track and out of their lives.

'Beware the King's men as you travel,' called Harron behind me. 'A dark cloud is gathering over the land and soldiers are everywhere, so take care.'

Okay I thought, bandits, Tigris warriors, wild beasts and now a King's army to watch out for. Could things get any worse! Ah well!

Chapter Three: A Journey.

I walked away from the small farm in absolute confusion and dismay. I had no thoughts or plans. I was still reeling from the shocking events of the last twenty-four hours, shock at my transition from a normal boring human academic into a wandering alien. Standing beside Harron I had been surprised to discover that not only had my body changed into a feline creature, but I was now much taller than my previous height. I stood over seven foot tall with muscles in places I never knew existed. The strength of my limbs, the ease and speed at which I moved could only be dreamed about as a human. Whatever I was now, the overall sensation of power and health gave me a level of confidence I had not experienced before. I still didn't know where I was nor did I truly understand what I was. However, as I strolled through the long grass I began to feel at home in my new body, although with no peace of mind as I was scared witless to be honest, but at least I felt at peace with my body. I walked on over the undulating landscape under a warm sun and clear blue sky. I was certainly not in my home county, where was the rain? I had never seen the sky so blue nor smelt the air so fresh as my long strong legs carried me to . . . somewhere.

When the sun had climbed directly above me I finally decided to take some rest, not that I felt the need to stop but my empty stomach demanded attention. As I rested beneath a clump of trees and munched on some of the rations supplied by Jōan, I began to notice other differences in the landscape around me. There were no hedgerows or walls and thus no fields, all was open and vast. I was of course more accustomed to fields being surrounded by some form of boundary, but here there were none. No man-made barriers stood between me and the hills in the distance, apart from obvious natural barriers such as streams, trees, gorse and bramble patches. As far as I could see the land stretched away from me in rolling waves with no sign of inhabitants. Wide open space covered in long grass and interspersed with clumps of trees and things with thorns. I could see hills on the horizon but could not ascertain the distance. All this wonderful panorama laid out under an azure sky.

I had noticed several tracks earlier as I walked; wheel tracks I assumed although not as wide as I remembered from home. They showed no indication of tyre tread, most likely wooden wheeled wagons I concluded. I began to notice small animals such as rabbits, squirrels and tiny rodents. I didn't always see them but now I could actually smell and hear them. It was all very weird.

Lunch over I set off walking again, taking visual reference points along the way to help maintain my southerly journey. It appeared the sun moved across the sky in the same direction as at home, so I had no trouble remaining on course. After a few hours in the sun, my heightened sense of smell became aware of another overriding odour. However, this one I did recognise, it was me. I admit my bodily hygiene had slipped my mind during the last day or so, but I was not about to start licking myself clean as cats are prone to do. I was sure I could never reach the body parts that a cat could. Nor would I want to in all honesty. With this in mind, at the very next river I came upon, I topped up my water bottle before removing my clothes and jumping in the water. Funny, I always thought cat's hated water, but here I was splashing around happily. A brief rub down in the cool water refreshed me greatly and I was soon on my way again.

The day was waning and my thoughts turned to the night. Looking around as I walked, I hoped to see some form of shelter, a hotel if I was very lucky or perhaps a cave within some trees, anything that may provide me with a secluded spot and some degree of defence. Alas, there was nothing, the landscape continued with grasslands interspersed with small groups of trees, but no cave in evidence. With no other choice available, it was in one of these groups of trees I would spend the night.

Very quickly I discovered there were indeed brambles, hidden amongst the tall grass in the vicinity of the trees. I managed to escape with only a few cuts and scratches so counted myself lucky. I finally settled down with my back against a tree surrounded by the long grass and brambles. The darkness of night fell as I ate sparingly of my rations, having no idea when food may come my way again. Although Harron had supplied me as best as he could afford, I realised I had no way of initiating a fire. It was going to be a cold night. I made myself as comfortable as possible and willed sleep to take me.

Unfortunately it did not, even though I knew it should be pitch dark, my cat eyes could still see quite clearly. Instead, I sat gazing at the world around me as my spinning thoughts verged on madness. Forcing myself to remain calm, I had no idea where I was but I was here and I had to deal with it. In an effort to quiet my mind I began experimenting with my new found senses. I say newfound even though I had all the same senses as before, smell, sight and hearing but now all three were vastly improved. I listened to the night animals scurrying about in the undergrowth, I watched the occasional deer wander past, oblivious to my presence. I smelt all kinds of new scents beneath the stars and tried to identify all that I discovered. Finally, when I was confident I had made myself aware of my surroundings, I drifted off into an uncomfortable sleep. I slept alone in the wilderness of a strange world with my back resting against the rough bark of a tree, my bedroom provided by the vegetation, the sky my roof.

My eyes snapped open and I was fully awake. Not the groggy wakefulness brought about by a bleeping alarm clock but wide awake and poised. My whole body was tense and the fur on my neck and back was standing to attention. Something had awoken me, but what? A different scent had drifted on the air currents and I didn't recognise it. What was that new smell? Stealthily I reached out one arm and grasped my staff while otherwise lying perfectly still, all my senses on high alert. Something was approaching, something big, something with a scent that poured fright into my soul. I didn't know what it was but I sensed it was in attack mode and I was the target. Suddenly I heard it run, footfalls running straight at me. Then I saw it, a huge shape leaping through the night air towards me.

With little thought, I quickly spun a few feet to my left before lightly springing to my feet. The creature landed on the exact spot where I had been sleeping; if I had still been there I would have had no chance of escape. The creature rallied itself with lightning speed, spinning round to face me and now I could see its glowing evil eyes and salivating mouth, filled to the brim with long razor sharp teeth. For the longest moment I have ever experienced, we crouched glaring at each other. Fear gripped me tightly as the creature's head dipped to attack. Lowering its hind legs it made ready to leap again. Its eyes focused intently on me, eyes full of malice and the desire to kill. Thinking rapidly, as it leapt I too leapt, jumping swiftly sideways while bringing my staff down upon its head with all the force I could muster. It was as effective as swatting a fly with a feather. The beast stopped, shook its head and sprang at me again. Once more I dodged from its path and brought my staff down, this time striking it on the neck. I had intended to aim for the base of the skull as this is often the weakest part of the body, yet the creature possessed thick fur along its neck and back so once again my blow had little effect.

With amazing speed the creature turned, ignored the blow and, as its teeth caught on my right leg, its jaws slammed shut. I found myself thrown violently to the ground with the sheer strength of the attack. I howled in agony as the beast began to shake its head in an effort to tear off the hunk of flesh held in its jaws. The power of its attack and the sheer weight of the creature threw me about like a rag doll. Using all my strength I fought to twist onto my back so I could attempt to defend myself. Again and again I struck with the staff but the beast would not let go, I could feel its teeth working into my leg as it growled in a strangely familiar way. At last, I remembered the hidden blade and quickly sought the button to release it. I began to stab frantically at the creature. My first attempts met with failure, my poorly angled blade skimming off the thick fur that covered the beast. Eventually, I stabbed down my spear into the shoulder of the thing that was striving to eat me alive. This worked and with a grunt, the creature let go of my leg, blood now evident from the stab wound as it ran down the beast's fur. Quickly I regained my feet and stood, favouring my torn calf. For a moment we faced each other, me with a bloody and wounded leg, the creature with a bloody and wounded shoulder. Panting, I stared back at it, I was scared out of my wits, I was sure in its next attack I would die. I did not want to die, especially in this strange place. I wanted to get home, not become the creature's supper. Intently I watched for signs of another attack, my heightened visual ability allowing me to see the animal clearly and I could see it resembled a canine of sorts. Just my luck I thought, here I am face to face with a vicious dog and what am I? I'm a bloody cat!

Suddenly the beast tensed, warning of a new attack. I also tensed and held out my staff in front of me like a lance, ready to stab with the blade. It leapt at me, a huge doglike creature that would have made the Hound of the Baskervilles resemble a Yorkshire terrier. As the creature took to the air I lunged forward, ignoring the pain from my leg, I leapt forward and to one side with all the speed and reflexes my new feline body could muster. My actions caught the beast unawares and surprised the hell out of me. With both myself and the beast in mid-air I thrust out my spear, aiming for the area just behind its shoulder where I prayed I would find its heart. I missed, my blade simply raked along the creatures rib cage, enraging it further. The huge animal twisted in its leap, causing me to jump back away from its snapping jaws. Again we stood for a moment staring at each other. We were both now panting heavily and spraying blood with each movement. My mind raced as the creature and I circled each other in the long grass, both seeking an opening that would conclude the battle. My experiences in martial arts in a past life were no use against this huge creature, I needed a new plan. Still circling, I began jabbing at the beast, hoping to spur it into an action I could use against it. Each jab of my spear was met with snapping jaws in an amazing display of speed.

Suddenly I saw the tell-tale shoulder muscle bunching and I knew the creature was going to strike again. Almost instantly the beast leapt at me with a ferocious laugh ripping from its throat, its jaws wide in anticipation of a kill. Up into the air it leapt, its body releasing its powerful tension, all its strength focused on me. I reacted on instinct. I dived forward to the ground beneath its leap, pushing my staff and blade up above me as I landed. With all my new found strength I stabbed up at the creature's underbelly as the momentum of the beast carried it over me. Holding the end of my staff firmly, the blade tore through its hide and into its soft belly, ripping a huge wound from its ribcage to the groin, slicing it open like a rabid surgeon performing an appendectomy. The whole action lasted but a moment, so rapid was the manoeuvre that not a drop of its blood spilt on my face. The now mortally wounded beast landed with a thump and lay wide-eyed and panting. Ready for another attack I shot to my feet, still favouring my torn leg but with my survival instinct dimming the pain. The creature did not stir but I waited a moment or two before moving warily over to the prone creature. The mortally wounded creature still did not move other than its eyes that followed my actions, its rib cage heaved as it lay, its blood flowing into the ground. A long tongue hung limply from the gaping mouth; the mouth filled with teeth, teeth that had sought to tear my flesh and crack my bones. 'Bastard!' I shouted as I drove the blade down into its eye with all the strength I had in my powerful arms. The beast was dead.

I stood over the corpse for some moments before the shock of my sudden fight for life took its toll on my body and I collapsed to the ground gasping for air. I stared at the prone creature and realisation dawned on me, it was a Hyena. Least that's what it resembled, though its size appeared to be thrice that of those poor animals I had seen in zoos. As my mind focused and reason returned, I remembered those parting words from Harron; he had warned me about wild beasts, including some creature he called a Hyaenidae, perhaps this unfortunate dead creature was one of those. It certainly resembled an overgrown hyena, so hyena – Hyaenidae? Was it possible the two were the same? Well not entirely the same obviously, the deceased creature before me was huge but apart from its size, it did resemble a hyena. But where was the pack that Harron spoke of? Crap I thought, I had better get moving in case the rest of its mates appeared. One I've dealt with but a pack of the bastards could be troublesome. I gathered up my pitiful belongings and limped off into the night.

Morning found me sat atop a boulder amongst a cluster of rocks on a small hillock. I had decided to stick to high ground for a while so I might retain the advantage of height. My body felt sore all over but my leg was worse, it was agony. Blood poured freely from the bite wounds and I guessed I had left a trail behind me even a blind pig with a cold could follow. I knew the loss of blood would weaken me, perhaps even into unconsciousness, so I had to stop the flow somehow. I attempted to stem the flow by clasping my hand over the wound while I sat and surveyed the landscape, but to no avail, the blood continued to pour freely. I needed a doctor, though in truth I felt positive there would be no ambulance rushing to help me with its sirens wailing. No hospital where I could spend many restful hours waiting in a queue. Not even a Girl Guide with her First Aid badge to care for my leg and mop my fevered brow. Okay I concluded, my brow was not fevered and I still felt fit and healthy, apart from my ripped leg of course. Now in daylight, I caught sight of a lake a mile or so in the distance and decided to head there to wash my wound. I had realised earlier that my body was covered in minor cuts and scratches gained from my fight against the vicious and terrible brambles hidden in the thicket, plus a few from the Hyaenidae. These stung but my leg was by far the worst and I desperately needed to attend to it. Leaning heavily on my staff, its blade retracted once more, I began hobbling towards the water.

Following a journey of increasing pain, I finally reached the water's edge and, disregarding any form of caution, I simply walked out into its depths. The cool water instantly began to numb and ease the pain. I continued out deeper into the lake until the water reached my shoulders, soothing all my abrasions. Drinking deeply of the water in which I stood, I slowly began to relax, but my moment of relief was not destined to last long. A sound reached my ears, a sound I really didn't want to hear. In the distance I could hear the unmistakable sound of a hyena pack, laughing merrily as hyenas do. They must have picked up my scent, not difficult as I had leaked enough blood to act as hors d'oeuvre to the main meal – me!

Peering about me, I could see the lake was intermittently surrounded by small deciduous trees and other low shrubs. I knew from a lifetime of watching nature programmes that the pack would most likely attack me from the cover of these bushes. I peered intently at each bush, each branch, each leaf, searching for the most likely location of a strike. I could hear the pack drawing closer and made the decision to remain in the water. I deduced the water would be the safest place, I certainly could not outrun them in my present condition. Hiding chin deep in the lake may give me a slight chance, that and luck was all I had aside from my staff. I threw my attention into watching the shoreline so intensely that a moment or two followed before I registered something else.

To the left of me came another sound, one I could not yet identify as my main attention was still centred on tracking the progress of the hyena pack. Keeping my ears alert I risked a glance in the direction of this different sound. At that very moment other figures, what appeared to be a band of horsemen, emerged from the trees and headed nonchalantly for the water. Shit! I thought, talk about being between a rock and a hard place. Were these riders another threat? They didn't appear to be farmers, shopkeepers or city bankers for that matter. Each rider was armed to the teeth with swords, knives and other assorted sharp implements, all showed signs of hard use. So far they hadn't seen me as they gradually moved towards the water, obviously to allow their mounts to drink. I lowered myself even deeper into the water so only my eyes and nose remained above. Perhaps they would not see me; no one would expect to see a bodiless head protruding from a lake, least that's what I hoped. There was a bonus to the riders appearance however, their presence would surely frighten off the hyena pack, for a while at least. Perhaps long enough for me to make a hasty escape, I hoped.

    Silently and as motionless as possible I watched the riders dismount, allowing their horses to muzzle the water and drink. I was quite relieved to note that horses remained identifiable in this strange land; however the same could not be said for their riders. Watching from the relative safety of the lake I stared at the strangest collection of horsemen I had ever seen. There were six of them, two I saw resembled Harron so possibly they were from the same Cast, the Ursidae I think he called it, bears to you and me. Another looked similar but larger with more aggression in his actions. Of the remaining three, one had the resemblance of a cat-like me but his colouring was different; pale brown and no dark stripes or patches on his fur. He was taller than the Ursidae and his bearing indicated he was perhaps the leader of the group. Powerful shoulders cloaked by long thick golden hair, a muscular body adorned with what appeared to be a gold necklace and gold rings around his huge biceps. The last two riders were the tallest of the bunch and looked identical to me, possibly not as big as me but in almost every other aspect they could have been my siblings. Harron would have called them Tigrismen I thought, so very probably they were of my kind. I declined the urge to run with open arms and greet them as brothers.

As the horses drank, each of the riders crouched at the water's edge and began to fill their water bottles. All was quiet, even serene as both riders and horses refreshed themselves at the water's edge. Suddenly the horses' ears pricked up and the leader sprang to his feet, the rest followed immediately. They had heard the laugh like bark of the approaching hyena pack. Without apparent haste, the group drew their weapons. It seemed swords and spears were the main armaments and I noted no guns of any form.

Surely a gun would be a much better form of defence and with such a mean looking bunch I wondered why they had none. I admit the scene itself emerged straight out of a western movie so the lack of guns as the main weapon puzzled me. I knew guns were illegal in Britain but as I didn't have the faintest idea where I was, I could not answer my own question. I watched as one of the Ursidae type riders grasped the reins of all the horses and moved behind the others, as they formed a half-circle facing the direction of the nearing pack, their stances indicated they knew what to expect and were ready.

Abruptly the pack burst from behind a clump of trees and raced towards the riders. The riders held their ground to the last moment before launching into the most ferocious attack I have ever witnessed, in life or on television. Meeting the pack head on, the riders slashed and cut at the beasts, killing two of the eight strong pack of hyena-like Hyaenidae almost immediately. Though the Hyaenidae were at least three times the size of the species I was familiar with, the riders themselves were also huge, and the scene before me could have been described as men fighting a pack of vicious wild dogs in a city park on the shoreline of a lake. But I was not in my city, the dogs were massive hyenas and the men were not men. After the initial attack, the Hyaenidae backed off and began prowling back and forth while glaring at the riders, searching for a weakness or an opening that would instigate the next assault. I watched in fear, not knowing which of the two opponents would be victorious. I certainly did not want to be faced alone with the pack and I was still unsure about the riders. However, reason concluded that my best chance of survival in this strange land would be the men, or animan as Harron would say.

The Hyaenidae attacked again, driving between the group and centring their gaping mouths and flashing teeth on the two Ursidae. Instantly the other members rushed to their defence and once again swords and spears fought with bone crushing jaws and slashing teeth. Within a moment, one of the Ursidae went down under the ferocious combined efforts of three Hyaenidae, ripping off flesh and crunching bones in a frenzy of bloodlust. The other riders could do little to help as they were kept busy by the rest of the pack. Soon all that was left of the unfortunate Ursidae was a bloody stain on the ground, then the three unsated Hyaenidae turned to rejoin the attack against the remaining riders. I had made a decision and slowly began making my way back to the shore; fear froze my heart as tightly as I gripped the staff. Two of the Hyaenidae had now managed to separate the leader of the riders and were forcing him back towards the water's edge, near to where I was silently emerging. The leader's sword flashed in repeated blows at the two hyenas as the other riders frantically increased their efforts to reach him. Desperately trying to keep both creatures at bay, it was obvious that the leader would lose the battle. Coming at him from opposite sides, the beasts made ready to pounce, the leader unable to defend two sides at once. Suddenly both Hyaenidae leapt in a perfectly synchronised assault. With speed and accuracy born of desperation, the leader's sword slashed at the face of the hyena attacking from the left, unable to defend his back and leaving himself exposed to attack from the other animal. Certain death awaited the courageous leader until my staff and blade slammed into the second beast with all the force I could muster, penetrating its body just behind the forelimb, cutting through hide and ribcage and on into its heart.

The hyena immediately collapsed, dead before it hit the gravel shoreline. With unbelievable speed, the leader spun to face the remaining beast. He had followed up his slash across the face of the beast with a stab to the throat and now it too lay dead at his feet. Up flashed his sword as adrenaline coursed through his body, overcoming reason in his fight to survive. I realised the danger as the sword descended towards my head. The sword crashed down, only to be halted by my staff as I blocked the blow with a speed that equalled the attack. A heart stopping moment passed as the leader stared in shock, first at his deflected blow and then at me stood face to face in front of him. Yellow eyes stared at me, finally in recognition that I was not a Hyaenidae, and understanding I had certainly saved his life.

With a barely noticeable nod, the leader turned and rushed to the assistance of his fellow riders. Having made my decision, wise or not, I followed him and entered the fray against the remaining Hyaenidae. Faced with six armed animan, the hyenas chose to retreat and the pack fled, disappearing into the undergrowth and away from the steel death that stood exhausted and bleeding beside the lake. In the fear and adrenaline of the fight, I had forgotten my injured leg and now collapsed to the ground, no longer caring what reception I might receive from this odd group of riders. At first, no one took notice of me, apart from the leader who cast a curious glance at me before going to the aid of his group. Most were only suffering from bites and cuts, a much more desirable position to be in than the sixth member of their band whose blood stained the shoreline.

After checking all his men were in one piece, the leader approached me, his hand still on his sword and his posture alert. I wondered why he still considered me a threat, if I had wanted him dead I would have simply stayed in the water. Noticing my wounded leg for the first time he bent and, none too gently, grasped the limb for a closer inspection. Again he stared thoughtfully down at me before calling to one of his group to bring dressings and bind the wound.

'So who are you? What are you doing out here alone and without a horse?' he questioned in a deep rich voice. 'I see you are of the Felidae Cast but you are unknown to us.'

Remembering Harron's advice I replied, 'I met a Hyaenidae earlier when it killed my horse. I think I must have hit my head in the fight. Now my memory is lost,' I lied. 'I think my name is Harry but that's all I can tell you.'

'You've tackled the Hyaenidae by yourself?' he asked incredulously.

I tried to shrug, 'There was only one and I managed to kill it but not before it killed my horse and did that to my leg.'

'Well, that's no mean feat, killing a Hyaenidae by yourself. What did you use?'

I showed him my staff, though I had remembered to hide the blade after killing his attacker. It was not due to lack of trust, I just felt I needed to keep an ace up my sleeve, or in my staff at least. Before he could say any more, one of the animan that looked like me came over and began examining my leg. Without a word he pulled a small bottle from his pack and poured some of its contents over the wound. Suddenly, my leg was on fire and if I had not been trying to portray a strong face, I would have shot up into the air with a howl. Instead I clenched my teeth.

'What the hell is that?' I growled.

'That is something I should be drinking and not wasting on you!' muttered the animan darkly. 'It's Vinum flavoured with honey, a strong drink that will fade your memories, but also good for stopping badness, but not the pain,' he concluded while searching for and finding a long strip of cloth with which he began to bandage the wound on my leg.

'So who are you all? Where do you come from?' I asked through gritted teeth.

'Not now,' growled the leader, 'wait until the wound is bound. We have to move on.'

None too soon for my liking, the first aid was complete and I slowly and very gingerly got to my feet. The leader was still watching me as were all the members of the group now, hostile curiosity in their faces. Leaning on my staff I stood and stared back at them, meeting the eyes of each one as I adjusted the staff and my leg and found with relief that I could stand unaided.

'So what happens now?' I asked.

'That's up to you friend Harry, we've some travelling to do and can't remain here any longer. We'll give you the horse that belonged to that heap of gore over there,' he said gesturing towards what remained of their dead comrade. 'What you do or where you go is your concern, not ours.'

'Thank you for the horse, I accept gladly as I'm not sure how much walking I can do on this leg.' I replied with a slight bow before continuing, 'I'm seeking a Sage that lives somewhere in the southerly direction. Do you know this person? Would you point me in his general direction please?'

'What in Totus-Terra do you seek him for? He's completely mad and may be treacherous. A sage my arse! More like a villain and a cheat and very likely a murderer. That's what I would call him. In answer to your question, yes we know him.'

The leader of the riders laughed, shaking his mane of golden hair as he turned to his fellows with a grin. They too began to laugh, it seems the Sage was somewhat of a joke to these men, or animan as I was beginning to describe them. I certainly could not continue identifying them as men because they clearly were not, nor was I any more.

'You will find him a short distance over those hills,' stated the leader as he pointed to the south, 'Do not trust him as he will surely do you ill. Are you armed? Other than that piece of wood you call a staff?'

Stating that I carried no other weapons, one of the Ursidae went over and began to pick through the remains of their fallen member. Finding what he searched for, the rider walked over and presented me with two knives and their sheaths, one knife was large and lethal, the other smaller and more ornate. I muttered my dubious thanks, wondering if it would appear impolite to wipe off the blood that covered the blades first. I decided I would wait, just in case. I had no idea of local customs and for all I knew it may be counted as an honour to receive a weapon already blooded.

'You have a horse and you have weapons to aid your travels. I am also aware that you did me a great service in the fight against the Hyaenidae. I would hope to repay my debt, but perhaps in the future. For now, I have other matters to attend to and must leave you in your search for the madman. If you wish you may accompany us, but we are heading towards what may be our deaths and it is not yet your fight. So find your sage and mayhap we'll meet again. My name is Janiz Fastus, remember my name but do not speak it. My friends and I have been deemed as outlaws in this kingdom, so the mention of my name could be hazardous. Go now friend Harry, and find your way. We must leave. Farewell to you.' Returning to their horses, the riders moved off with no more thought to my plight.

I was again on my own in what was rapidly becoming a very deadly land, very deadly indeed. I simply stood for a few moments and pondered on what had just happened. From a city boy to a Tigris warrior in no time at all, so what next? Would I awake to find myself sat on the moon or in the arms of a delicious beauty? Huh! Most likely I would wake up in a small room with white padded walls and restrained in a straitjacket. With a sigh, I shook these thoughts from my head and began to take stock of my situation. I now owned two knives along with my staff. Judging from its size and design, the smaller of the knives was for use as an eating implement. I determined to ensure it received a thorough clean before I considered using it as cutlery. The larger knife had an evil appearance and a very sharp edge on its fifteen inch long blade leaving no doubt as to its purpose. I also now had a horse. I had ridden a horse when I was a child, and I didn't like it. How the hell does one ride a horse these days? My prospective form of transport was presently munching on the grass with not a care in the world, totally unconcerned about the horrible death of its previous master or the ignorance of its new owner. I decided to call it Fred. I always called things Fred, it is a name I can easily remember and never upsets anyone, so my horse is now Fred. Wonder if the horse cares what it's called, I'll soon find out I thought ruefully.

Deciding it was time to make a move, I steeled myself to check over the remains of the fallen rider in case there were any further useful items. Not a wise move. I had never seen a ripped apart corpse before and have no wish to see one again. My search was brief before I eagerly retreated, leaving the body to its eternal rest. I had noticed the rider's sword some feet away from the body but declined to retrieve it, what the hell was I going to do with a sword? I hadn't even held one before, I was certain I would be more likely to hurt myself than any opponent. Nothing of use remained intact on the body so I moved to the horse; perhaps it carried something that might assist my plight.

Hah, approaching a horse is not easy. Every time I neared it, the damn thing took a pace away. Even when I managed to grasp the reins, the beast realised I wasn't its usual rider and decided to be as obstinate as possible. So I began talking to the animal, saying nothing coherent but simply using the new name I had given it while patting its neck and trying hard to hide my fears. Horses did not have engines, I understood engines. Finally, after what seemed like an hour, I managed to get the thing to stay still long enough for me to search the saddle. Keeping the reins tightly grasped in one hand; I used my other to quickly examine the blanket roll and a leather satchel that hung from the pommel. I found nothing significant in my initial search other than a pouch containing some flints and dry wool, obviously for making fire. I discovered more water which was always useful and some scraps of dried meat that looked less than appetising. At last, deep down in the satchel, my hand found what I assumed were coins. Dragging one out I was amazed to find they were indeed coins and gold coins at that. Obviously, the deceased outlaw had led a profitable life until very recently. I had no idea of the local exchange rate for gold, but let's face it; gold is gold in any language. At least I should be able to purchase provisions if I succeeded in locating any form of community or village. I pushed the coins back down into the satchel with a lighter heart, until I realised I would have to ride the damn horse. Hah! A cat riding a horse, whatever next.

I had watched many cowboy films and dodged hundreds of young girls on horses along the road, so I had a rudimentary idea of how to mount and ride a horse. But as they say, the proof of the pudding is in the eating. Still clinging to the reins I grasped the saddle pommel and placed one foot in a stirrup. I was mounting from the left side of the horse, hoping this was the right way to do it. I remembered that the Native American Indians only mounted from one side but I prayed that rule was not followed in this land. It was. As soon as my foot touched the stirrup the damn horse shied away, causing me to almost split myself in half. The horse had moved away from me a couple of paces. Damn thing! Freeing my foot and keeping a hold on the reins, I walked cautiously around the horse, avoiding the teeth, and attempted to mount from the right side. This worked and within moments I was sitting nervously on the horse's back.

Again, my hours spent watching westerns on television provided me with a few options on how to get the beast moving. 'Giddy-up,' I called, but the animal didn't move other than a twitch of its ears. Next, I tried nudging it with my heels but again nothing happened. Frustrated now, I kicked harder with my heels. The damn thing took off so fast I nearly fell head over horse's rear. Regaining my balance and clinging on tightly to the reins I suddenly remembered I didn't know what to do with them. I pulled back on the reins but the horse simply stuck its head forward and kept going. I pulled harder but still no response. Finally, I jerked the reins back with all my strength and just managed to stop myself flying over the horse's head. It had stopped so abruptly it surprised the hell out of me. Regaining my posture and, after checking my bowels were still secure, my temper began to flare. 'Move!' I shouted and was again surprised as the animal began to walk forward, no headlong dash, just a walk. The next ten minutes were spent attempting to reach a median between a headlong dash and a standstill. Eventually, I gained enough control to get the cantankerous beast moving at a reasonable pace and in the direction I wanted. I was on my way south to meet a sage.

Chapter Four: The Sage

Situated precariously on a four legged form of transport, I was eager to put some distance between myself and the lake. The bloody remains would inevitably attract carnivores and I didn't want to meet the surviving members of the Hyaenidae pack. No doubt they would be angry at losing me as a meal and the demise of several fellow pack members. I rode for the rest of the day, stopping every hour or so to allow the horse to chomp on grass and drink. It was apparent that in this part of wherever I was, finding water would not be a problem. These short breaks also allowed me time to recover; riding a horse is definitely not as easy or as comfortable as the film heroes portray. My legs ached, especially the wounded one, my butt felt battered and my back verged on the point of breaking. Getting back into the saddle grew harder and harder until I decided only the threat of bodily functions or death would drag me from my perch until nightfall.

The landscape still consisted of grass covered low hills and shallow valleys, interspersed with small woodlands and scrub. The scenery was beginning to get boring, but I rationalised that if it were a tundra or savanna, maybe even a prairie, then this was to be expected. Continuing at a sedate plod, I allowed the horse to make its own way across the countryside, correcting the direction occasionally to ensure I remained travelling south. Even this leisurely ride on horseback tortured my inexperienced muscles and caused the day to proceed in misery. My body was sore and the sun beat down on my head, not in enough strength to present a risk to my health but as the hours wore on, it too became increasingly uncomfortable and eventually forced me to seek out shade for both myself and the horse.

Heading into one of the numerous small groups of trees, I guided the horse into the shade and dismounted. Actually, in truth, I fell off. My legs and butt appeared to be fixed in the riding position. For the first few steps I resembled a bow legged drunk as I tried to return life to my aching limbs. Not trusting the horse one little bit, I tied the reins to a low branch, leaving enough slack for the animal to graze on the flora that flourished beneath the trees. I wondered if I should remove the saddle but I didn't know how. I decided to leave it in place and just remove the deceased rider's blanket. This I placed under the one donated by Harron and there I lay. I was amazed to find I could finally lie down; I had begun to suspect I would be stuck in the riding position for hours. Eventually, the aches eased and function returned to my joints. My wounded leg still hurt the worst but at least there was a reason for that. Sporadically I sipped at my water and nibbled on of Jōan's rations, I was not eager to face the dried meat in the dead animan's satchel just yet.

I must have nodded off for a short time as the sun was lower in the sky when a sound awoke me. I could hear singing. What the hell? Who would be singing out here in the middle of nowhere? Unless the singing was an attempt to frighten away any strange and vicious beasts roaming the vicinity. Suddenly, like a bolt of lightning searing through my tired brain, I realised I knew the song! It was a song I had grown up with, a song I could even sing along with, a song from my past. It was a Beatles song I could hear. I knew the song very well, it was called, *"I saw her standing there"* and it was coming from the opposite side of the trees under which I rested. Leaping to my feet I quickly rolled up and stashed my blankets on the annoyed horse. Carefully, very carefully I remounted and began walking the horse, newly christened Fred, round the perimeter of the trees to discover who or what was murdering a Beatles song.

Abruptly the singing stopped. When I reached the far side of the trees there was no sign, or sound, of the singer. It hadn't taken me long to round the small wood but even so, there was no sign of a Paul McCartney wannabe. I pondered the possibility that I had imagined hearing the song but soon discarded that. I knew many strange things had happened to me recently, not least waking in an unfamiliar land and in an alien body, but I was convinced I had heard someone singing. I paused for several moments scanning the trees and surrounding area but to no avail. With no signs or song to follow I decided to continue south and see what happened. Either way, I would find the Sage or encounter the village Harron had mentioned.

With a numb butt and a tired mind, I continued to plod through the open countryside, all the while keeping a wary eye and alert ear. I didn't want to be caught napping by any more Hyaenidae or any other such unknown beasties. Several more miles passed and now my thoughts began to mull over prospective sleeping arrangements as the sun sank lower on the horizon, signalling the approach of night. Once again I sought out a suitable copse where I might rest in relative safety. Another mile or so travelled before I reached what seemed a suitable spot. Thoughts of a hot cooked meal filled my head and my stomach began to growl in agreement. Thinking I might try to build a fire tonight and stew some of the dried meat and rations. My hunger grew strangely intense as I searched for a suitable site in which to make my camp, a moment later I realised why. I could smell the tantalising smell of cooking meat. I didn't know what to expect on my travels in this strange land, but one certainly doesn't expect to encounter the aroma of hot food wafting across an empty landscape.

My newly acute sense of smell indicated the direction of this appetising fragrance and I nudged Fred in that direction, scared but hungry and painfully saddle sore. As I rode deeper into the trees, the strength of the aroma indicated the source was near. Fearful of what or whom I may encounter, I slipped from Fred's back and, ignoring my squeaking limbs, I led him quietly towards the alluring smell. My fears were almost overridden by my desire for a hot meal, but I remained in stealth mode, for want of a better description. Soon I could make out the flicker of a small fire ahead of me. I decided it would be prudent to proceed alone. I could travel with all the furtiveness of a cat even with a torn calf. Unfortunately, Fred cared not a jot and clumped through the undergrowth, his hooves smashing twigs and stamping the ground with a volume that would awaken even a teenager. It seemed wiser to leave him secured to a tree limb within reach of enough grass to ensure his silence.

I crept slowly towards the fire and eventually saw a camp set up within the warm glow. One small figure sat cross-legged near the fire, stirring at a pot hanging from a makeshift tripod. The little chef did not give the impression of danger, but I was taking no chances. I remembered from the cowboy films and books there was a courtesy one was supposed to follow when approaching a stranger's camp.

Rising from my crouched position I called, 'Hello the camp!'

The response was spectacular. The small figure leapt into the air with a cry, a spoon shot sideways and a tin plate flew in the other direction. On landing, the figure whirled; one hand grasped a long dagger that was already pointed threateningly towards me.

'Whoa steady on. I announced myself so you wouldn't take fright, no need to get all defensive.' I said in what I hoped was a calming voice.

'Who the fuck are you and want do you want of me?' snarled the little figure.

'I would like some company and possibly share your fire. That is all.'

'Come closer then, but not too close, I want to see you in the firelight.'

I edged closer, keeping a firm grip on my staff as I searched for any signs of hostility. Once within the circle of the fire's feeble glow I stopped, remaining watchful as I took my first real look at the figure who in turn peered back at me.

'You're a Tigris!' exclaimed the figure, 'What are you doing in these parts? Are you an outlaw?'

'So I've been told, whatever that is, not an outlaw and I have no idea what I'm doing in these parts. Now are you going to let me near the fire or do you want my life history?' I replied still in a calm voice.

'Alright come forward, but be warned, trying to harm or rob me will have dire consequences. I have the means to defend myself, so no tricks.'

I moved slowly into the camp and finally stopped within range of the fire's warmth. I held my staff firmly but made it appear it was a walking aid and not a weapon, I didn't want to lose any defensive advantage I might have. The figure before me was noticeably smaller than I was, standing less than six foot in my estimation. Much of his features were obscured by the night but with my heightened vision I could easily distinguish certain traits. Again the extended nose and mouth gave a hint of a muzzle and amber eyes flicked over my body, examining me as I examined him. I could see from areas not covered by the rags which the figure wore, a type of fur-covered the body. It appeared all animan had a fur-like covering upon their person and I was no exception. In the feeble illumination of the fire, I thought I could see a grey colour to the fur but placed no significance on it. His body itself lacked my muscular build, instead it appeared lean and wiry, like an athlete with strength but no bulk. The figure's appearance was dirty and dishevelled, although personal hygiene was not high on his list of importance.

'What do you mean, you have no idea why you're in these parts, either you want to be here or you don't, which is it?' enquired the scruffy creature before me.

I decided that there was no point in pretending that I had answers. I considered I could overpower this creature with relative ease, thus I saw no harm in being honest. Harron had only warned me against voicing my confusion to others of my ilk.

'I know it sounds weird but I don't know who, what or where I am,' I replied as I stretched my hands out towards the fire. 'I have been told I am a Tigris but in all honesty, I don't understand what that means. This land's very weird to me, I don't know where I am or what country I'm in. To say I'm confused would be an understatement.'

'Umm. Alright, can you remember where you are from before you arrived here?' he asked thoughtfully.

'Yes. But you won't understand and I've been warned by a friend not to speak of it to anyone.'

The figure peered at me for long moments before muttering softly, 'Try me.'

'Manchester!' I stated bluntly and waited for the confusion.

'Umm – Liverpool.' Came the unexpected reply, sending my mind into perplexity as the realisation of what he had said pierced my brain.

'What?'

'Yeah, I know Manchester. I come from the home of the Scouser - Liverpool.'

'So it was you singing that Beatles song I heard a while ago? I went to look for you but you disappeared. What's going on here?'

'Ah I heard someone or something heading in my direction so I took off. This place is deadly and I wasn't about to hang around to find out. I survive by remaining alone, avoiding any strange animan and certainly staying away from any creatures with big teeth. But if you're from Manchester, how the hell did you get here?' asked the figure with as much surprise on his face as there was undoubtedly on my own.

'I don't honestly know. I woke up here, that's all I remember. I was at home and the last thing I did was to open a . . .'

'Jade box!' interrupted the figure.

'Yes! How the heck did you know that?' I exclaimed.

'The same thing happened to me, that's why. About ten years ago I think. I'm not sure of the time in this place. I found a small jade box and of course I opened it. The next thing I knew I was here and I had become a kind of wolf. From then on I've simply survived.'

'Well have you any idea where we are? And what the hell are we?' I pleaded.

'Okay, sit somewhere, I'm hungry and the food is ready. There's not much but you can share and we'll discuss this new life after we've eaten,' suggested the figure.

Sitting myself down near the fire I offered, 'I have some food I can add to the pot if you wish? I managed to obtain food from a farmer who helped me when I first arrived. I'm sure we can make a decent meal by combining our food items.'

I wandered over to Fred and untied the satchel, taking it back to the fire. We both sat and rummaged through my rations, adding some things to the bubbling pot and laying aside some of my bread to accompany the stew when it was ready. I didn't let the odd creature near my bag, I wanted to hold onto the coins hidden at the bottom of it, pulling out just the items of food for him to see. Mostly the figure had selected the dried meat as a supplement to the stew and I agreed, the thought of chewing on that black shrivelled meat didn't appeal to me one bit. However adding it to a stew, well that was a different matter entirely. While the added ingredients cooked, I went off to retrieve Fred and brought him nearer to the campsite. I tied his reins with as much length as possible to allow him to reach the long grass that carpeted the ground. I retrieved my blankets and laid them as close as safety would permit near the fire and sat. I still kept my staff at hand and the comforting bulge of that vicious knife in my waistband added to my sense of security.

Finally, as darkness covered the land and with a plate of steaming stew in my lap, I began to relax. I had found someone who knew my world, who was in fact from my part of the country. Surely no animan would know of Liverpool and the Beatles unless he had been there. If the figure was lying, why would he come up with Liverpool of all places? Why not chose London or somewhere more exotic like Paris or Rome. The fact that he had also linked Liverpool with the Beatles and he knew the words of a Beatles song convinced me I was no longer alone. For good or bad I had yet to decide, but for now, I was in the company of a kindred spirit and I was at rest.

The astonishingly delicious meal over, we both settled down on our blankets and the discussion continued. It turned out that my campfire companion had been in this land for some time. He thought it had been ten years but when he named the year in which he disappeared, we worked out it was more like twelve years. A long time I thought to be wandering this place alone. As an afterthought, he finally introduced himself as Dave Johnston but added that the animan people called him Sophos. He was considered as a Sage of sorts and because of this, the animan seldom bothered him. It seems that the knowledge from our land was far above what they knew in this place.

He had been a consultant psychologist in his previous life and had discovered that his skills were ideal as a mediator or adviser amongst the animan. He soon became regarded as a wise man or shaman by the local inhabitants and now possessed the valued title of Sage. However, it was not all a bed of roses. Many animan were suspicious of Sophos, distrusting his different thought processes and his ability to see beyond the spoken word, a talent we humans were used to. Psychiatrists, psychologists and sociologists abound in the land I knew. Those who did believe him and trust him, those who sought out his advice or opinion, paid for his services in food or work and thus he now owned a small house some miles from where we sat. He had prospered in this new place, though he still resembled a vagabond. Dave admitted he kept his appearance scruffy to reinforce the belief that he was a gifted shaman; it may ruin his reputation if he cleaned himself up. As good an excuse as any I thought to myself.

Interrupting this meeting of mutual minds, Dave stated that he was going to fetch his horse nearer to the camp for the night and off he went, returning moments later with his own mount. I wondered why he didn't retrieve his horse when I brought Fred to the camp. His muttered comment suggested he was still suspicious of me at that time, I may have been a horse thief for all he knew. His horse had the look of a blue dun, I only know this because many of my family kept horses. I just avoided them, until now. Dave immediately began removing his saddle and I asked if he would show me how. He agreed and I learned then how to saddle, unsaddle and hobble my mount, lessons I considered very important for the comfort and health of Fred himself. Once both horses had been attended to, Dave and I returned to the small fire and our blankets.

'OK, so we both come from Britain but back to the here and now, where are we and more importantly, what are we?' I finally asked. I hoped that Dave or Sophos as he was now known would have answers to my long list of questions.

'Well as far as I can understand, we are in the general area of Africa or maybe South America. However in this world, the continents did not drift apart, no plate tectonics scattered the continents. I think we are in what historians call Pangaea. The animan call it Totus-Terra, meaning I think, the Whole Land.'

'Yeah, I've heard that name before but didn't see any significance in it.'

No wonder Harron was mystified when I had mentioned there were many lands where I came from; here there was only one huge landmass. Weird!

'Okay, so we're still on Earth then?' I asked as my mind attempted to assimilate these new facts. In truth I didn't know what to expect, I secretly still hoped it was a dream and that my annoying alarm clock would drag me back into the real world at any moment.

Settling himself on his blankets with his feet nearest the fire and propped up on one arm, Dave continued, 'Well I think we are on a version of the Earth as it was millions of years ago but it's clear this is different, the same but somehow different. Perhaps we are in another universe or even dimension, I don't know if such things exist, and perhaps by some means, the jade box acts as a doorway. We could be in the past or in the future, there's no way to tell. But we are here and I don't know how we got here but I'm sure it's linked to that damn jade box. I've searched all my years here for another jade box in the hope that I can return home but to no avail. I've heard tales that the king possesses one but that's out of my reach. It would be simply too dangerous to approach the king and ask to see his jade box. Even a normal monarch would decline my requests but here it's even worse. Rumours suggest the king appears to have gone mad lately; he's no longer the king he was. I've heard he's increasing his army and making all kinds of threats to the neighbouring kingdoms. Anyone who disagrees or stands in his way is either exiled or decapitated immediately. Even his only son has been exiled. It took a plea from the queen to stop the king killing his child in a bout of fury when the prince attempted to reason with him. Sadly the queen died not long after the banishment of her son. This loss helped to drive the king further into madness. What chance would I have of getting the box from him? None! All I would achieve is the loss of my head. Anyway, the king is safely guarded in his fort-like palace in the city of Urbem Regiam. Unreachable to lowly animan like ourselves. But let's return to the question of where we are.'

Taking a moment to sip some water and adjust his position upon the ground, the Sage from Liverpool resumed his narrative.

'From what I've seen, what I've learnt and from what little I know of Earth's geological history, I think we are on a different Earth, where or when I don't know but I'm sure it's still Earth. Clever huh?' concluded Sophos, while twirling his finger near his temple in the age old sign of madness.

'Yeah. So it's not a dream then?' I asked wistfully.

'No.'

The evening was wearing on and nature, whichever nature that is, demanded I head off behind a tree. Once relieved I returned to the fire and pulled my blankets over my prone body, as the evening air had begun to chill, before continuing my questions. I still had much to discover, outlandish theories or not, Sophos had more time to consider the problem of where and what we were and I would need his knowledge to survive.

'So we may or may not be in an alternate universe in a different time, space and dimension. We may or may not be on a single landmass similar to Pangaea on our Earth. But we are definitely not in England.

So the next question is what are we? What am I?' I asked.

'That's an easier question to answer,' replied Sophos, 'in this place, humans didn't evolve from apes, in fact, apes have not evolved at all.'

'Yes, I've heard that before, from the family who helped me when I first arrived. They thought it was highly amusing that I claimed to have evolved from the apes.' I interjected.

'Yeah okay, so if man didn't evolve that would have left a huge hole in the evolutionary process. In this place, four of the top predators evolved instead. The lion, the tiger, the bear and, like myself, the wolf. Basically, you are a tiger. No longer human but a descendant of tigers, probably a Bengal tiger judging from the size of you. I am a wolf of the Lupus Cast, descended of wolves. The land we are in is ruled, oddly enough, by a family of Leomen, or perhaps a pride of lions, of the Leo Cast. Very appropriate really as we have always considered the lion to be the king of beasts on our world. The lions consider themselves to be the superior Cast and have managed to wheedle themselves into all the highest positions, like politicians, bankers or high ranking army officers. The Leomen are not quite as big and strong as the Tigris but tend to be leaders.

The tiger or Tigrismen are mostly warriors or mercenaries, happy to sell their fighting prowess to the highest bidder. Many Tigris have gained the status of royalty but remain few in comparison with the Leo Cast. The bears or Ursidae Cast are more peaceful and are often farmers; shopkeepers and tradesmen, the workers of this land, though vicious fighters when they choose to be. We wolves appear to have no stable role in life, some farm, some fight, some trade and some even frequent the king's court. The Lupus Cast have integrated themselves into all levels of society, including that of government. We're the clever ones it seems. Individuals from all four Casts form the king's army and all his subjects are expected to be loyal unto the point of death. Charming really.'

'Huh. What about the Hyaenidae? I've had a couple of meetings with them since I got here. What part do they play in all this?' I managed to get in before Dave/Sophos continued in what was notably his favourite pastime, talking.

'It's obvious isn't it? With the four main predators reaching higher degrees of intelligence and leaving the plains and forests; progressing through evolution as man progressed from the ape, other predators have stepped up to take their place. A Hyaenidae is the evolution of the hyena. All the new predators have grown huge and a very dangerous threat to life and limb. The Gulo gulo I think has evolved from the Wolverine, a nasty creature and you would do well to stay the hell away from one of those. It'll rip you to shreds in a moment! The Lynx is another animal that has been promoted to the upper ranks of top predators. We don't see too many of those around here but they are now the size of a full grown male lion on our world, so run and hide if you encounter one. Finally, scattered throughout the land, there are the Vulpes. This is a very clever predator, a descendant of the fox family. Never seen one myself but, to be honest, I don't really care to. Lightning fast, intelligent and vicious I've heard. Many other animals that you know are different here, some have grown much larger, some smaller and some not at all. The main rule here is if it looks like it will eat you, kill it before it does. There are no animal rights here, self-defence and staying alive count highest of all.'

'Ah, I think I have read a theory by Soulé describing a process where medium sized predators such as the fox, the weasel and the raccoon became more prominent predators when larger carnivores declined. Predictably, with the evolution of the tiger, lion, bear and the wolf, other smaller carnivores moved into the vacant positions. Hence the Hyaenidae. A bigger, meaner version of the hyena from our world.' I theorised.

'Sounds about right,' agreed the Liverpudlian.

I snuggled further under my blanket and pondered this new information. So I was in another world where man does not exist and animals in the form of animan rule the planet. The main large predators that roamed the wild or sulked in zoos back in Blighty have evolved into sentient beings and have ascended the evolutionary ladder to the top rung. The world consists of one land, a land split into kingdoms, kingdoms ruled by creatures who call themselves animan. Bloody hell, I thought, what in God's name had I gotten myself into? One thing is for certain, the next box or strange object I see lying on the ground can stay there. I remained wishful that this was all just a dream and I would re-enter my world upon waking, but in the meanwhile, I would have to accept what I saw about me. Talking animals in an era that had yet to devise the gun or invent the combustion engine. Sleep approached my tired body and addled mind, the gentle sounds of steady breathing informed me that my companion was already asleep and moments later I too drifted off into a dream filled sleep.

All too quickly dawn urged our bodies awake. I had slept well, perhaps comforted by the presence of a fellow Englishman. I shuffled from my blankets as Sophos stirred the fire back to life; the morning was cold, the sun not yet radiating warmth. Imitating Sophos's actions, I rested one of my blankets around my shoulders as the fire gathered strength to radiate its warmth. We shared a cold breakfast of what remained of last night's stew and my rations in silence. My thoughts were still very confused and I had no plan or direction laid out in my mind for the day. I knew I would soon need to replenish my supplies so the discovery of the village Harron spoke of was swiftly becoming a priority. However I wondered what Sophos intended, I found myself reluctant to leave his company.

Finally, with breakfast over, Sophos offered to re-educate me in how to saddle and prepare Fred for the day's ride. The lessons were given with the skill of someone who understood my limitations and were repeated constantly throughout the demonstrations to reinforce my knowledge and ensure I would cope with the tasks on my own. Fred took it all calmly, occasionally eyeing me in such a manner that I could have sworn the damn thing was laughing at me. It was then I realised just how big the horses were, certainly bigger than I remembered and when I pointed this fact out to Sophos, he gestured to my own huge size and reminded me that many animals were different here. Horses had become taller and stronger here, evolving past what I considered a normal size because most animan were quite large and heavy. Finally, we sat astride our mounts and contemplated our next move. Sophos stated that he intended continuing south to his home and as

I too was travelling south, the ideal solution would be to journey together. I agreed happily so we both got our mounts moving, Sophos more successfully than me, and began the trek south.

I spent two days travelling in the company of the Liverpudlian, learning about this new world and its inhabitants. Most of what Sophos told me continued to bewilder my brain. Although I understood what he was saying, my mind would need to see for itself before it properly understood. Sophos told me about the king and some of the surrounding kingdoms, listing them by proximity and potential threat as he understood them. I was reminded of ancient England where assorted kings vied with each other for territory and wealth. Unlike England though, the individual kingdoms here were massive. What I still considered to be Britain was, according to Sophos, part of a kingdom that included a small part of the landmass I knew as North America, along with a section of Greenland. No sea or ocean divided the many kingdoms so war was common across the land, each ruler battled to either increase their boundaries or stop others from taking theirs.

At present, the land through which Sophos and I rode was ruled by King Fastus and the kingdom was named Regnum. Sophos was not sure of the names given to the surrounding kingdoms. He had never felt the need to travel the huge distances involved to visit neighbouring countries. He considered this land of Regnum large enough for any man to survive, and hopefully thrive. Sophos saw no reason in exploring a world that consisted of one huge landmass surrounded by an even larger ocean. I had to agree, I was having enough trouble understanding this kingdom without needing to increase my horizons more than I had to. I was content to roam the land called Regnum and be ruled by a king called Fastus until I could find a way home. Why did that name seem familiar I wondered, for a very brief moment before concluding that I didn't give a damn and promptly forgot it.

The land we rode through had begun to change as the miles passed. More woodland appeared but also signs of the land having been worked, occasionally we came across areas that had been sown with crops. Animals that still resembled cattle and goats roamed in the distance. Sophos assured me that the animals were indeed cows, goats and sheep. He explained that most herbivores were the same as I remembered, a fact I was grateful for. Following our nighttime conversations, I now expected rabid rabbits, ferocious frogs and killer ladybirds to descend on me at any moment. Knowing that the majority of the animal kingdom still existed as I knew it and that a six foot tall Guinea pig was not about to leap from the bushes and savage me, calmed my fears somewhat.

On the second day of travelling, small farms became evident about us, most seen in the distance but some were situated within half a mile of the track on which we rode. Despite the signs of inhabitants we saw no one, either the locals were keeping their distance from the two strangers that rode past their homes, or Sophos and I were in need of soap and water. Riding beside him, I could vouch for the fact that Sophos certainly needed to pay his personal hygiene some attention. His odour had attracted his own personal swarm of flies that buzzed about him almost continually. However, thoughts of personal hygiene would have to wait a while longer so my attention returned to my surroundings.

'Why do they build their houses like that?' I asked as a sudden thought struck me.

'Like what?' murmured a sleepy Sophos.

'Well, like domes instead of the more usual square shape structures. Why has every building I've seen here been dome shaped?'

'Hah I see. Well, there's no rule to say that buildings must all be square, like at home. I suppose the shape simply evolved from the cave, I don't know but maybe that's possible. I think it's a better design myself. No roofs to blow off, no need for guttering and easy to keep clean inside and out. I like them. I know that domes are about the best shape for surviving high winds. In this land, we get some terrible storms, winds stronger than anything you've known before. Suburban homes in Liverpool would be flattened in an instant by the winds they get here. Possibly that's why the buildings are domes, I don't know for sure. But whatever the reason, the trait has followed the animan through the years, even the huge buildings of the city are round domes,' explained Sophos. 'And wait until you see the King's palace if you ever do of course. Now that is a dome!'

'How come the trees still stand then? Surely they would be the first things to be destroyed in hurricane strength winds?'

'Yep, that would be true on our world. Here the tree roots are incredibly strong and travel much deeper into the soil. The trees and plant life here have all evolved methods to cope with the extreme weather. Trees here have three times the root base to those in our world. In fact, all the flora of this land anchors itself tightly to the ground to combat the wind. One other fact is that leaf and foliage regrowth is rapid here, trees regularly shed their leaves during a bad storm, again to help protect them from being torn from the ground. But once the storm has passed, the trees reproduce leaves at an astonishing rate. These storms can appear and disappear quite rapidly, so seldom pose too great a threat, but once in a while, a storm can rage for weeks. Not nice then, not nice at all. It's not the same across this world, just here for some reason. It must be something to do with the climate conditions. On that point, make sure you are never caught outside when such a storm hits. Head for shelter or even underground if you can. You will not survive a bad storm here so don't try comparing the weather here to that of home, because you have no idea, no idea at all.'

As if to reinforce his weather forecasting skills, Sophos peered up at the clear blue and cloudless sky, before nodding in satisfaction and urging his horse to pick up the pace slightly.

As we rounded a bend in the track, Sophos pointed to a small dome dwelling set away from the track on the edge of a wood.

'That's my home,' he announced and steered his mount towards the building.

As we neared the building I could see it was much smaller than Harron's home, and much less cared for. What I assumed to be junk lay scattered about the place, old rusted weapons, animal bones, pots and pans and feathers, feathers everywhere. When I questioned Sophos about this he reminded me he was supposed to be a Sage and so he felt it important to set the scene. Like me, he remembered all the television shows about Native American Indian shaman, African witch doctors and voodoo priests. All appeared to place importance on strange or useless items, especially feathers. All he was doing was copying their example. I nodded in understanding and widened my area of inspection and noticed a smaller, if that were possible, dome structure at the rear of Sophos junkyard. This was obviously for his horse, I didn't know if Fred would fit in there as well.

'Here I've just had a thought,' I stated suddenly, 'how do the animals in the wild survive the wind?'

'In any way they can. Don't forget they have survived here since creation, they find ways and places of safety. If you walk through the many small thickets and woodlands, you'll find evidence of depressions in the ground, many burrows and holes that the wildlife use to shelter. Some of these holes can be the size of caves. Also because trees themselves have evolved strengths to cope with the wind, they act as a natural shelter for the animals. Perhaps that's why there are so many clumps of trees across the land. Of course, a few of the animals are now so big, they need only lie low and let the wind fly over their bodies; providing they are on low ground, it is these animals that create the many depressions which they dig to lower themselves from the wind. Luckily the strongest winds only occur once a decade or so, otherwise nothing would be able to survive. I've not seen a real strong wind yet, in all the time I've been here,' muttered Sophos as he pushed hard at his front door and entered the dome.

Sophos gestured that I should follow him so I entered the building he called home and stood in amazement. The place was tidy, nothing like the junkyard outside. Wooden furniture consisting of three chairs and a sturdy table, a shelf unit of sorts and off to one side was a wooden slat bed, covered with homespun blankets and an animal fur resting over the end. Woven rush, reed or straw, I couldn't decide, mats covered much of the earthen floor and a hazel broom stood sentinel beside the door. A large metal bowl served as a sink and was accompanied by a hand levered water pump. A fireplace was sunk into the wall near the bed with its chimney reaching up and exiting halfway up the wall. In truth, the house contained many of the comforts of home I recognised, but without a television or personal computer in sight, thankfully.

Without haste, Sophos began to unpack his bags and bustle around, refilling the stove with kindling and logs before using a flint gadget similar to the one I now owned to light the fire. That done, Sophos filled a pan from the water pump and set it upon the stove to heat. Gesturing for me to make myself at home, Sophos continued to move about the dwelling, doing all those tasks we all do when returning from a holiday or spell away from home. I sat on one of the chairs and waited, not wishing to get in the way of my host. Once satisfied with readying his home, Sophos suggested I join him in taking both horses to the barn and ensure they had enough food and water for the night. Fred appeared to be delighted at the prospect of a rest and real food in the form of oats and mash. I had no idea what mash was and didn't ask. Surprisingly both horses did fit in the small barn, then, care of the horses complete, Sophos and I returned to his abode to rest. I sat down on a wooden chair and stretched out my legs. The pain of constant riding had begun to subside as my body became accustomed to the torture, and I was able to sit on a chair without painful spasms shooting up my back.

Sophos had plenty of food and supplies stored in his home so the remainder of the day was spent eating, drinking and resting. Possibly I should amend that to, I spent the rest of the day doing almost nothing. Sophos turned out to be the perfect host and catered to my needs with all the pleasure of a domesticated and fully trained husband. At this realisation, I ventured to ask if he had a wife waiting back in our world. His face split into a wide grin and he replied that he did have a wife back home but he doubted that she had waited for him, least he hoped she hadn't. If he ever managed to return home he would seek a new life. A domineering wife was certainly not part of his plans. The rest of the day continued quietly, a fact I was grateful for and the night followed the same. Sheltering under a roof with a full belly and warmth made up for the hard floor on which I slept. We had talked most of the day, about our homes, our past lives and the new world in which we found ourselves. I learnt much but Sophos warned there was still more I would need to understand, but time itself would teach me what he could not, if I survived.

The following morning Sophos offered to guide me to the village. Luckily it was only a few miles away. When I commented on this, Sophos gave me a pitiful glance before explaining that in order to make a living as a Sage, he needed customers, and customers mostly lived in communities; hence his proximity to the village. After a good breakfast, we set off on the now fully rested horses. The day had dawned bright but black clouds could be seen gathering to the west. Sophos repeatedly glanced up at the sky and I could see the concern on his face. With a gentle nudge he urged his mount into a faster gait and I followed, or in truth, Fred decided to follow. By the time we reached the boundaries of the small village the sky had blackened further, a blanket of dark clouds covered the land and the wind was noticeably growing in strength.

'We need to get to shelter I think,' muttered Sophos with yet another glance at the sky before pushing his mount into a full-on gallop into the village. I followed but at more of a headlong rush as I held on tight and gave all my strength over to staying in the saddle. It was the first time I had ridden a galloping horse. Into the village we sped before slowing and finally coming to a halt outside what I took to be a stable. Sophos walked his horse straight in and Fred followed. Once inside we dismounted as an animan, whose appearance told me he was of the Ursidae Cast, came to take our horses.

'You got here just in time Sophos, a few more minutes and the storm will howl,' greeted the stable owner, 'What made you venture out in this?'

'Hello Equester, I didn't expect the weather to turn bad today. How long do you think it'll last?'

'Not long I think, there's clearer sky over to the west, you'll be home again today. Anyway, what can I do for you and your companion?' Equester the stableman enquired as he began to unhitch the girth of Fred's saddle, his hands moving with a surety of experience.

'Good, we don't want to be laid up here for days. Just take care of our horses for the duration of the storm, please. We'll head over to the publican and wait it out. Is there any news from the king or elsewhere?' enquired Sophos as he passed over a couple of coins to the stableman.

'Nothing much. Soldiers are appearing everywhere in an attempt to reduce the problem of bandits. I don't think they'll have much success; the bandits tend to hit and run long before the soldiers can catch them. I've heard rumours about the king though, seems he's searching for one particular group of bandits, no one seems to know why. The bad news is he's forcing all able-bodied animan into his army. I'm hoping his conscript party doesn't reach our village, I'm too old for the army but my son is not. I don't want him being forced into some insane war for a king we never see and who does very little for us common folk.'

'Huh! Much as I thought. I'll try and stay away from those conscript groups as well. You too should keep a wary eye open for small groups of animan in uniform Harry. They won't be interested in how you got here or who you may be, so take care,' warned Sophos before turning back to the stable owner.

'Have you any idea why the king is after this one particular bunch of bandits Equester?' I interjected.

'Nope, not a clue. Whoever the bandits are or whatever they have done, it's obvious they've upset His Majesty. I wouldn't like to be in their skins when he does eventually catch them. Anyway, you'd better head off to the publican, the wind is getting forceful now and if you stay here any longer you'll be stuck with me and the horses for company.'

'You're right. Thanks Equester.' With that Sophos and I hunched against the powerful wind and ran for the shelter of the publican.

The village was not large so it didn't take us but a few moments to dash across the hard packed and rutted road that separated rows of dome dwellings. All the buildings were constructed as domes but one could still distinguish between private residences and places of trade and commerce. Signs attached to outside walls or propped in windows vied for custom just like any other village or town. I noted a bakery and a hardware store as we ran towards our destination of sanctuary. As we ran past, I noted many of the domes were enclosed in stone walls, marking off gardens and individual properties exactly the same as the garden fences in suburban Britain. For some obscure reason, I felt comforted by the sight of little houses surrounded by little gardens in such a familiar manner. At a glance I could see that both sides of the street were lined with either private homes or places of business. But I could linger no longer as the wind had reached a strength that threatened to take me off my feet, head down I pushed forward into the publican behind Sophos.

A wash of calm flooded over me as I forced the door closed behind me and turned to take stock of my surroundings. A small smile crossed my lips as I surveyed a scene that in any language would be called a bar. I admit at first I expected a Wild West style saloon, with dusty floors, small tables surrounded by poker playing customers, a honky-tonk piano tinkling in a corner and a stout barkeep wiping glasses with a dirty rag. But no, this bar resembled the lounge of a posh hotel. I was standing in a large semi-circular room of luxury. The floor was laid with polished stone, granite I assumed, with thick woollen rugs scattered about, giving pools of colour in a stone grey sea. Sturdy dark highly polished wooden tables were accompanied by chairs covered with heavily padded upholstery in a dark rich satin that gave temptation to a saddle sore butt. Cabinets and shelves ringed the walls and supported ornaments and curious objects and to my surprise, even books. Above my head several oil lamps hung from the ceiling giving warm illumination. A set of stairs set against the curving wall beside the bar proved the building to be at least two stories. Finally, the bar itself formed a semi-circle of shining nut brown wood, deliciously carved with representations of wheat, barley, grapes and honey.

There was no sign of the stout barkeep, instead two dainty Lupus females tastefully attired in cotton smocks smiled a greeting as Sophos and I made our way through the room. Even though both bar girls had the distinct characteristics of the Lupus Cast, I will admit here and now that both were stunningly attractive. Now I was becoming accustomed to the light fur and underlying animal features, I realised I was seeing the animan as people.

To my disappointment, Sophos kept on walking, ignoring the gleaming bar and its two eager attendants and headed straight for a door situated at the end of the lounge. Through the door, we passed and into another room, not as big as the previous one and certainly not as elegant. We had entered another bar, but this one lacked the gleam of the lounge though it too was clean, tidy and welcoming. The room was identical to the lounge but less expensive, less luxurious and this time behind the bar stood a barkeep. The bartender was a burly Ursidae male in a white shirt and black trousers. He was not wiping glasses with a dirty rag but his appearance suggested he ought to be. A broad smile belied his façade as he greeted Sophos warmly.

Outside I could hear the wind and rain howling with a ferocity I had never encountered before. I wondered if it would rival the hurricanes and tornados that savage the American states. I was certainly not inclined to stick my head out the door and find out, a fact reinforced as none of the other inhabitants of the bar showed any eagerness to leave the safety of the stone walls. I mentioned this to Sophos and he muttered a reply that this was nothing compared to the really bad storms that can strike, this is just a flash storm and it would be gone in an hour or so.

I hadn't noticed many customers in the lounge, but this bar was obviously for the more raucous or boisterous drinkers. Customers sat at tables conversing and drinking while surreptitiously watching us, or more specifically me, over their glasses. Sophos chatted with the barman and ordered us both drinks. He didn't bother asking me what I would like to drink because justifiably I would not know any of the beverages available. After a moment or two, a glass was placed in front of me with a muttered explanation that the substance inside was quite safe. Picking up the glass I sniffed at the drink before taking an experimental sip . . . . then my throat caught fire!

'Bloody hell Sophos,' I gasped, 'what the hell is this?'

'Ahh, thought you'd like it. It's their form of whiskey I think, though it's probably more akin to Tennessee moonshine than scotch whiskey. Take your time and drink it slowly, it's – er – an acquired taste so to speak.' Sophos then demonstrated by taking a sip of his own drink before slamming the barely touched glass back on the bar and gasping for breath. 'Lovely!' he croaked as soon as he could breathe.

We remained standing at the bar while Sophos gossiped idly with the bartender. I took no part in the conversation and covertly studied the other customers. There was a cross-section of Casts in the bar, Ursidae, Lupus and Tigris but I noticed there were no Leomen. From what I had learned so far, I assumed if any Leomen did frequent this publican, they would not venture from the lounge. The thought had barely passed through my head when I noticed there was one Leo in the room. A huge Leo sitting alone at a far table away from the bar. I stared in interest until I found his hostile amber eyes staring right back at me. Not wishing to instigate trouble I turned away and made a pretence of interest in Sophos's conversation. A sideways glance from Sophos indicated he had also noticed the look I received from the Leo, and, with a twitch of his hand, he warned me not to turn back around.

After an hour or more, the roar of the wind decreased and several customers began to stretch in their seats as they too became aware of the wind's dying ferocity. I continued to sip very sparingly from my glass though I observed Sophos had managed to swallow three glasses of the battery acid. There was now a slight glaze to his eyes and his speech had gradually increased in volume. The bartender watched Sophos knowingly, with the familiarity of a vendor well versed in the antics of his customer. In the interests of self-preservation, I had decided not to anaesthetise my reactions or brain, tempting though it was. A shuffle of furniture drew my attention as a few of the customers made ready to leave the premises. Sophos also took his cue from the quiet of outside and the strong rays of sunlight that brightened the windows. Sophos said his goodbyes to the barman and turned to me with the suggestion that we make a move and venture out into the village. To be honest, I was glad to do so, we had been in the publican for some time and standing virtually alone in a bar and not being able to drink properly was not my idea of fun.

Chapter Five: A Kill.

Sophos and I left the publican and wandered through the village, taking care to avoid the large puddles of water that were even now beginning to dry in what remained of the wind. We set off to visit food stores and a hardware shop to replenish supplies, mine mostly as I had nothing left of my rations from Jōan. I was delighted to discover that Sophos shopped like most men, into the store, buy what he wanted and out again without lingering. Sophos was well known within the community and all those we met treated him with respect. Not bad for a lad from Liverpool I thought. I received many strange looks as I passed, the animan appeared to accept me while I accompanied Sophos, but I considered their reactions may differ if I was alone. I wisely decided to let Sophos do all the bargaining and bartering as I was a complete novice, unfamiliar with the methods of trade in this strange land. I need not have worried, all appeared to be the same. With the waving of arms and cries of ruination from the sellers interrupted by similar pleas of poverty and misery from Sophos, a deal would take place. Though fascinated by one of the most surreal shopping trips I have ever undertaken, my eyes and ears remained alert.

During one of my frequent glances about me, I noticed the Leo from the publican also appeared to be browsing goods, though I also observed he had not yet purchased a single item. Once or twice I perceived him staring in my direction; looking away quickly each time he was detected, making me highly suspicious. I mentioned the Leo to Sophos but aside from a slight frown, he made no comment on the matter and continued his harassment of the hardware trader. Finally, our shopping completed, Sophos suggested we head back to his home and decide my future over some refreshments. Returning to the village stable, we collected our horses and headed off.

Soon we were sat in his cosy little dome, munching on sweet cakes and sipping mead. Sat at the table, Sophos asked what I intended to do. He had been in the land sometime and thought I would be also, so some form of employment was in order. It was hardly likely, he said, that a Tigris would find work in this rural area and that I should travel to the city. There I could sign up as a soldier or mercenary in one of the king's local militia unless I had a skill that I could sell or barter. I hadn't told Sophos about the coins I had in the satchel from the dead rider back at the lake. Somehow it seemed prudent not to.

'Nope, I have nothing to offer here as far as I can tell, I'm not that good with my hands, only my head. I haven't seen any places of learning where I could ply my trade. Anyway, what would I teach? I sincerely doubt my level of knowledge would have much value in this land. As for joining a militia, what do I know about fighting? I've never held a sword and would most likely only hurt myself if I did. Besides, I have no weapons,' I lied.

'I wouldn't worry too much on that score. You'll find most animan have retained their survival instincts and for you as a Tigris, fighting will soon seem second nature. Besides, you've already fought a Hyaenidae and triumphed, so it would appear you are already quite capable of fending for yourself.'

'Huh, I'll hold you to that when I'm dead and eaten or worse,' I replied with little conviction. 'Is there anything else I should watch for, apart from huge evolved animals, armies of animan and the odd bandit or three?'

'Well, I personally have never seen one but I have heard tales of sorcery. I believe the king himself has the aid of a powerful sorcerer . . . .'

'Oh hang on there; you've got to be kidding me,' I interrupted. 'A sorcerer! What next? Witches and ghosts, demons and other assorted nasties? Nah I'm sorry but as a man of science I can't believe in such nonsense as sorcery.'

'Scoff all you wish. But don't forget Harry, you're in a different world and many things here will appear strange or even ludicrous to you. Don't be fooled,'

'So what do I do if I encounter one of these sorcerers then? I asked with a smile. 'Is there a magic amulet or sword that will help me combat these evil wizards like in all those sword and sorcery books people read?'

'Nope, nothing. Just keep out of their way if you find one. As I said, I have never encountered one and from the rumours that pass this way occasionally, I don't want to meet one.'

Sophos held up his hand to silence my next derisory comment and continued, 'However the fact still remains that there are many other dangers here, without including a sorcerer or two. Firstly you must be aware of the animan; many that roam the land are either bandits or murderers who will kill you for your horse and the contents of your bags. Then there are the animals themselves, you've already met the Hyaenidae so you know what to expect from them but in this land where there are no physical barriers such as oceans or seas, you may encounter anything. Remember, although many animals remain as you know them, others have changed, grown larger more vicious and deadly.'

'Okay I understand, though I still don't know how I'm expected to survive for long. A classroom does little to prepare one for life or death survival.' I muttered as fear grew sharply inside me.

Sophos was beginning to lose patience with my whining. 'I don't know why the jade box sent you here, nor do I know why I'm here. But perhaps there's a reason, my ability with people has turned me into a Sage and I survive. You are a Tigris so somewhere in your destiny will lie the reasons for you being here. Whatever, you're here so you'll have to learn to cope, somehow or die. Rely on your new instincts and your strength, it's all you can do until you find your true path.'

That statement led to Sophos suggesting that it was time I went out in search of my intended destiny and I should leave the next day after a full nights rest. No more was mentioned on the subject, instead, the talk then centred on memories of home. Sophos was desperate for news of Liverpool and their football team. I could not help much there but to lighten the mood, I informed him that Liverpool were league champions though I didn't have a clue. Other snippets of information included how the country had changed and who was Prime Minister when I left. He asked about the street where he lived but I had no knowledge and could not comment. Further conversation took us into the evening and supper before tending to the horses and turning in for the night.

The next day dawned warm and bright and began with a large breakfast. Sophos had insisted on this, food may become scarce during my travels. With misgivings weighing heavily on my mind, I saddled Fred and packed my bags with supplies. With heartfelt thanks to Sophos, I duly set off in the direction of the next city. Following Sophos's instructions, I was heading towards the city of Fulgeo several days travel south of Sophos and the village. Seems I was destined to always travel south, I wonder where north, east and west led to? Fred seemed eager to be on the move after his rest, even though he was loaded down with supplies. Sophos promised I would find many sources of water on the route so we saw no reason to add more water to my load, a fact for which I was grateful. I had become accustomed to riding now and my butt had recovered, though I expected to still ache at the end of a day's ride.

Small farms and all signs of inhabitants soon faded from my proximity as I rode further from the village. On my travels, I had encountered no other large animals but the land teemed with small creatures and birds. Had birds evolved I wondered? Sophos had made no mention of killer birds, but I kept a wary eye on the sky. Mid-day arrived and I rested on the edge of a copse perched on a low hill. I preferred camping on higher ground after my recent escapades, height provided points from where I could survey the land about me and watch for impending threats. I paced to and fro while Fred nibbled at the grass and I devoured some bread and cheese. I found I had no desire to sit so I walked life back into my legs as I ate and let my eyes roam. A small black dot in the distance caught my eye and I pondered on its existence. It had the look of someone on a horse but I couldn't be sure. I decided to keep watch on it, more out of curiosity than concern at this stage.

With my butt and legs refreshed by the pacing, I remounted and continued my journey. For the next hour or so I maintained a watch on the black dot, seeing it grow slowly larger in the distance until I could clearly see it was a horse and rider. As yet the rider was still too far away to worry me so on I plodded. The day wore on and I dozed in the saddle, Fred appeared to be happy heading south so I had little to occupy my mind. I had forgotten the rider but now as I climbed a small hill to check on my surroundings, I remembered although the land was empty once more. Perhaps the rider had chosen a different direction I thought. Nonetheless, there was no sign now of the rider and horse. Evening follows day as it does, and I searched out a place to make camp. I chose a spot near a stream and refilled my water bottle, still amazed at the clarity of the water here. I would not even contemplate drinking from a stream at home. Stamping down an area of undergrowth for my bed before building a small fire, I hobbled Fred before setting about heating some food and settling for the night.

At dawn I awoke, vaguely surprised that I had slept the night through without being attacked or eaten. The morning held a slight chill so I teased the fire back to life and ate a chunk of bread. A drink of fresh cold water from the stream and I was ready, ready for what I had no idea, even so, I was ready. Once Fred was saddled I mounted to resume my journey towards the city. I felt fearful of what I may find but eager to find it all the same. However, as my leg swung over the saddle I noticed something odd. There were footprints in the ground around my campsite. Clear footprints that I was certain were not there the night before. Doubt assailed me, not being an expert tracker or boy scout, I had no way of knowing if they were fresh or not. They could have been there for days, I couldn't even be certain they were not there last night. I might have simply not noticed. The faint depressions, clear to my new eyes, appeared to be similar to mine. Long narrow footprints with short stubby toes, indentations from nails dotted each toe mark. I had already noted the animan didn't wear anything on their feet and judging from the leathery pads on my own feet, I could understand why. Pushing the image of the footprints to the back of my mind to a draw marked labelled imagination, I continued my journey. The sun shone brightly in the east and the sky was a fresh pale blue. Birds twittered and flew, small animals scurried through the undergrowth and I felt at peace.

Until an armed figure suddenly loomed up from the tall grass in front of me. Fred reacted with fright and reared up. I struggled to remain in the saddle, fighting to calm Fred. I felt very lucky not to be thrown to the ground, I was still an inexperienced rider nonetheless I clung on limpet style until Fred had all four hooves on the ground again. Furiously I stared down at the stone faced apparition standing before me.

It took my mind a moment to register that the apparition was the Leo I had noticed back in the publican. As before he was dressed in a woollen smock belted at the waist from which hung an empty scabbard. Dirty leather trousers completed the attire of the powerfully built Leo. Lank lifeless brown hair rested upon his shoulders and fuzz of lighter brown fur covered his body. Most of my attention was centred upon the wicked blade, three foot of sharp steel glinting in the sun. As Fred became still, I grasped my staff tightly and met his stare.

'Well if it isn't the Tigris friend of Sophos,' he growled, 'get off that horse and bring me those bags.'

Judging by his threatening stature and the tone of his voice, I reached the conclusion that he was not here to wish me well on my travels. Sitting higher in the saddle whilst grasping my staff tightly and my buttocks tighter, I stared back at him and in my best Manchurian accent, I made a simple statement, 'Fuck you mate!'

Suddenly he lunged at me; his movement so fast I was caught completely unawares. Leaping forward he grasped my foot, tore it from the stirrup and heaved me over and off my horse. With a thump I landed on the ground, scrabbling immediately to my feet as the Leo darted around Fred, his sword held poised to strike. Down flashed the sword in an attack aimed towards my shoulder. I whipped up my staff in both hands to block the blow. The speed of the attack was astounding, before I could retaliate, another blow aimed at my head forced me to block again. I knew I too had great speed but no matter how fast my body reacted, it still relied on my brain to make the decisions, and it was not doing too well. The shock of the attack and the fact that one rarely encounters a lethal duel in academic circles slowed my actions. I knew I would lose. A thought pierced my frightened mind and I changed my tactics to something more familiar.

As the sword came down once more I leapt sideways and away from the blade. I blocked again with my staff before lashing out with a straight *Mae Geri* front kick to his solar plexus. I felt instant gratification as the breath whooshed out of him. Immediately I followed with a *Kin Geri*, a kick to his groin with all the force I could muster. As he bent over in pain I brought my staff down on his exposed head with a mighty crack. Quickly I stepped back and released the catch on my staff that ejected the hidden blade in its tip. Holding the staff like a spear I moved in for the kill, only to be met with the sword pointed right at my throat. While I concentrated on readying my staff, the Leo had taken the advantage and with blinding speed had moved in for the kill. Crap!

'Nice tricks Tigris, but not enough. Now you'll die!' rasped the Leo.

'Hold!' The sudden command ripped from behind us.

I did not move but the Leo jumped back in fright, staring over my shoulder. With one eye still on my assailant, I slowly turned to discover a group of animan, each heavily armed and flanking another golden haired Leo. My body trembled with fright as I realised how close I had come to death, it took me an age before I recognised Janiz and his riders. Neither I nor my opponent had heard the riders approach but I had to admit I was pleased to see them. The expressions on their faces nevertheless caused me some concern, had I gone from the frying pan into the fire?

'Applying your trade as usual Praedo?' questioned Janiz.

'No Janiz, I was just giving this animan some lessons in swordsmanship. Honest!' stammered Praedo.

'Not bloody likely! You were going to rob me, you bastard!' I retorted through clenched teeth.

'Thought so. I suppose you caught him unaware? That's your normal trick, catch an animan in surprise to give you the edge, isn't that so?'

Praedo cringed and quickly dropped his sword to the ground. 'No Janiz. Honest! I meant no harm.'

'Well let's see how you get on now. Pick up your sword Praedo. You,' said Janiz as he pointed at me, 'make ready and we'll sort this here and now.'

I looked at the leader of the riders in horror, 'What?'

'Animan to Animan. You will both finish your fight. I'm eager to witness your skills and the demise of that creature will do the land no harm. However, I suggest you don't lose.'

With that command, Janiz and his animan formed a rough circle with me and Praedo in the centre. Praedo looked at me in hatred, the gleam of anticipation for an easy kill glittered in his eyes. Turning to face me he dropped into a crouch, his sword retrieved and once more held tightly in his right hand. Slowly he began to circle me as I too raised my staff into a defensive hold, its blade still protruding from its tip. I was ready, this time I knew what to expect. This was going to be no pub brawl or back street mugging, this would be a vicious fight and only the one still breathing at its outcome would be the winner. I did not circle like Praedo, I was too afraid that I would wet myself if I moved at that moment. I remembered someone once telling me during my karate classes that defence was the best form of offence. Fighting with deadly weapons was certainly new to me, but martial art combat was not. I turned slowly where I stood, keeping my body turned partially to the right as I watched him, waiting for him to make the first move. Praedo held his sword in his right hand but I paid no attention to the weapon, instead I glued my gaze to his eyes, hoping for the tell-tale signs of attack. Praedo continued to move around me, feigning blows and dodging away, he was attempting to intimidate me.

I saw his eyes narrow a fraction as he lunged at me, his sword held low for a stomach strike. I blocked the sword thrust easily with my staff and pushed him back. Several more attacks followed and each time I either dodged away or blocked his blows but did not retaliate. Finally, Praedo stepped back and stared at me in confusion, why did I not attack was the question in his expression. With a roar Praedo rushed in again, aiming to finish me once and for all. This time he grasped his sword in both hands high above his head with clear intention to cleave my head in two. Now I moved with all the feline speed I possessed. As his arms reached up I leapt forward and stabbed my blade into his exposed belly, pushing the blade in hard before rapidly withdrawing it in one smooth motion. Praedo staggered but the wound was not fatal and again he sprang at me.

My mind was now clear, I knew what I had to do and was fully prepared to do it. As Praedo stepped forward I also advanced, moving rapidly to his left, opposite to the sword arm, making use of his weapon difficult. He turned to meet me but I had moved again. I kept my opponent's body between myself and his sword. Anger lined his face as I nimbly manoeuvred around him until his temper snapped. Howling in fury, Praedo rushed forward, throwing his whole body at me like a rugby prop forward. At the last moment, I stepped to his left and thrust the base of my staff down between his feet, allowing his forward momentum to do the rest. His feet tangled on my staff and off balance, Praedo stumbled forward as he attempted to right himself. His arms shot forward automatically to brace his fall; he had no chance to recover, gravity had taken over. Before he hit the ground, I whipped up my staff and drove the blade deep into the side of his neck, just behind the ear. The blade faltered for an instant as it forced its way through bone but my grip was strong and a further push ensured the blade broke through the skull and entered the brain. Praedo dropped to the ground like a stone, no sound, no agonised cry so often seen on television and films, no reaction at all, he simply dropped and there he remained, motionless.

'Withdraw your weapon,' commanded Janiz behind me.

With a start I realised I had been standing over Praedo, holding my staff with its blade still firmly planted in the head of the corpse at my feet. Gingerly I pulled back on the staff, wincing as I felt the blade grate against bone as it exited the skull. Slowly and with some disgust, I bent and wiped the blade clean on Praedo's smock before retracting it back into the staff. I had never killed a man before and even though the prone body was that of an animan, the feeling of dumb shock was the same. With my staff held limply in my hand, I turned to face Janiz, sure my life was now forfeit for the killing of Praedo.

Janiz and his riders stood watching me as the shock caused trembles to ripple through my body. My thoughts were wild and confused. I felt shame at taking the life of another sentient being, no matter that he was a robbing bastard who had tried to kill me.

In resignation, I looked up into the face of Janiz and simply stated. 'Now what?'

'That is for you to decide, not us. You've won your battle with Praedo and it was a fair contest. He sought to harm you so the just cause was yours. You appear proficient with that staff but your fighting style is unfamiliar to me, I'm intrigued.'

My fear was diminishing as my mood darkened, why me? Why was I here with strange creatures all out to kill me? My reply to Janiz was a little terser that I intended. 'My fighting style is unfamiliar to me as well and I'm surprised I'm still standing. But that's in the past, so I repeat my question, now what?'

The other riders began to wander back to their horses, all interest lost now the fight had concluded. Janiz alone remained, peering at me with a puzzled expression. 'I require nothing of you, what you do now is entirely your choice. Do you have a destination or someone to meet?'

My shoulders slumped and I sighed, 'I'm heading for Fulgeo to seek some form of employment but that's my only goal, I have no one to meet and no home to go to, so Fulgeo is my destination.'

At that point, I remembered I was standing over the dead body of Praedo and decided I wished to be gone from here and moved away to where Fred stood unconcerned by the recent events.

Janiz continued to stare at me until at last he appeared to reach a decision. 'You're strange to me but I need animan, animan who are ready to fight for their beliefs or reward, I care not which. Would you join with me and my riders? I will offer protection, to a degree, and a share of any wealth we find or take. We also travel towards Fulgeo so ride with us and ponder a while on my offer. Upon reaching the city I'll expect your answer.'

What did I have to lose? Travel alone and risk dangers that would reduce any Health and Safety official to a state of comatose shock, or ride with Janiz whose life I had once saved. Huh! The decision was easy. This land and its inhabitants scared the crap out of me, so journeying with a band of tough companions to a destination I was heading towards anyway made perfect sense to me. I replied to Janiz that I would ride with him, but I made no comment on the offer of actually joining his band of merry animan. I did wonder what he meant when he offered protection - *to a degree!*

Chapter Six: Band of Brothers.

Leaving the lifeless form of Praedo for the local scavengers, I mounted Fred and set off in the company of Janiz and his band of . . . ? I realised I knew the answer to my own question, I had heard about these bands that roamed the land, bands of outlaws. The riders chatted idly between themselves but none yet spoke to me. Even Janiz appeared to forget my presence so I remained silent in my thoughts while Fred ambled along, following the other horses. We rode on for an hour before Janiz dropped back alongside me. After a moment or two, he attempted small talk but it didn't take long for him to realise I had no idea what he was talking about or, I was an imbecile.

'You are strange Harry, you walk the same land as I, yet you appear to know little about it. You have the appearance of a Tigris but little knowledge of yourself. So, I wonder. What are you Harry?'

I didn't reply immediately, pondering on how much I should say. I remembered Harron's words, words that had served me well thus far so I saw no reason to change now.

'Ever since my fight with the Hyaenidae my mind has been confused, much of my past has disappeared along with the knowledge of who I am. I'm like a child, having to learn over again. I don't remember the land on which we walk or this world. I no longer know even myself. In truth, I can give you no more explanation than that. I'm sorry.'

I had spoken more truths than I realised in answer to Janiz. Long moments passed like the path on which we rode before he replied, his frowning brow an indication he was considering my words. Finally, his mannerisms suggested he believed me.

'That's a fair story Harry, filled with misfortune but fair I think, and it would explain your distance from the land and those who live upon it. Perhaps we'll find someone who knows or remembers you as we travel. We'll see.'

We rode together for another mile or so without speaking, each of us alone with our thoughts. Janiz gave no impression of being a social being, I had not noticed him being overly interactive with the rest of the riders. Perhaps that's simply the way of a leader I thought. Perhaps he has to distance himself from the pack to maintain authority? Either way, I felt comforted by this noble Leo riding beside me.

Small talk gradually increased between us, and I used this time to gently probe information from Janiz about his life, how did he end up riding with outlaws? What underlying events had turned him away from the straight and narrow path of a law abiding citizen? After some thought, he began answering my questioning. He started reluctantly, mainly about his animan and some of their adventures, though little about himself as if fearing I would ridicule, or perhaps betray him. However, with much flattery, encouragement and offers of sincere understanding, this reluctance was soon overcome and Janiz warmed to his tale.

'I was not always an outlaw,' he began slowly, 'I am in fact, the king's son but alas no longer his heir.' Here Janiz paused, waiting for and receiving the look of incredulity on my face. He waited, gauging my reactions, perhaps waiting for me to deride his announcement. But what could I say? I had no knowledge of this land, its rulers or its history. As far as I knew, Janiz could have been from another planet. Let's face it, I never expected to be having a conversation with a lion riding a horse. Once my facial features had returned to normal, I gestured for Janiz to continue with a gentle nod in recognition of his statement. I wanted to know about this scruffy outlawed heir to the throne. Janiz continued his history, but the depth of his words and the emotion that came forth surprised me.

'My father and I loved each other and drew comfort from each other's company, until the arrival of that cursed sorcerer. Then my life began to change, my father became distant and showed little signs of love for his only son. Within months it was as if he didn't know me at all, his manner became hostile and quick to anger. I didn't know what was happening and had nowhere to turn. It was a difficult time. The sorcerer remained cold and aloof towards me but close to my father, constantly whispering in his ear. I finally became suspicious that it was the sorcerer who was behind the changes in my father. I had no proof of course but made it my quest to discover the truth.'

Janiz paused in his narrative, his brow heavy as his thoughts grew dark with memories. The other riders seemed to be uninterested in our conversation, they knew the story and chain of events that led to our present position. Janiz and I were politely ignored as the riders chatted quietly between themselves. I took this break in the tale to scan the landscape, still very nervous after the recent attempts on my life. Although I faced the threat of muggings, theft, pollution and sullen students each day of my life, the threats here were very real, deadly real.

Janiz took a swallow of water and then continued. 'By this time my father had banned me from his presence, leaving me despondent and alone. Others in the palace tried to console me with whispered words, to be discovered talking to me could result in punishment. So I was alone, but instead of crying like a lost child, I grew angry. I resolved to both confront my father and the cursed sorcerer and gain answers, or I would kill the sorcerer.'

Janiz paused at this point for my attention had wandered. I was sniffing at the air, my new enhanced senses brought smells and fragrances on the air that I had never experienced in my world. But this one I recognised, I could smell sulphur! What the hell? Sophos had told me there were very few mountains as this was one very large continent, therefore reason stated there should be no volcanos. I could not be sure as I was no geologist but I reasoned that without tectonic movement between the continents, there should be no subduction as one continent forces its way beneath another. I had seen no sign of any orogenic processes that push mountains and volcanos up through the land in the immediate vicinity. So where was the sulphur coming from? I was far from being an expert and could be way off the mark, but I had to find out. I was a scientist after all.

'What is it?' questioned Janiz as he grasped his sword in readiness, 'What fills you with unease?'

'That smell, I recognise it but it shouldn't be here,' I answered as I turned Fred into the direction of that distinctive and unpleasant smell.

I guided Fred through the grass, searching for any evidence of what I considered to be impossible. Shortly I found myself on an area of bare soil, no grass or shrubs grew, only a few hardy weeds lay low on the earth. There in the middle of the region I saw a small hole. I began to move forward towards it but suddenly Janiz dragged me back.

'What are you doing?' he shouted. 'That is dead land. You must not go near the yellow rock, its spit will harm you!'

Realisation hit me in a blast from my academic days. I became cautious and, brushing off Janiz's grasp, I carefully ventured closer to the hole. Suddenly a spout of gaseous vapour shot up into the air. The smell was overpowering. It was sulphur! How the hell could sulphur be erupting from the ground that was otherwise devoid of all geological features? The fountain of gas disappeared as rapidly as it had begun, and now I could see traces of yellow sulphur encircling the hole, or vent as I now knew it to be.

'What is wrong with you Harry? Why does the yellow rock fascinate you so? It's not unusual in this part of the land.'

'What?' I exclaimed. 'You mean there are more of these?'

'The demon's spit holes stretch across the land and spew yellow rock from holes similar to this one, strange rock that bleeds red blood if set alight. Everyone knows this.'

Hah! I sighed as an explanation came to me in a *'light bulb'* moment. I walked back to Janiz and remounted Fred, my mind whirling with this new discovery. Sophos had told me this land had few mountains, it had never divided into continents. But even if no plate tectonic actions had taken place, magma would still flow beneath the crust, and volcanic gases would still require release. I concluded that tectonic plates still existed but did not or could not move. Nevertheless, some friction still remained, though much less violent than on my world. Perhaps instead of huge volcanos, the boundaries between the plates created a series of small vents that released pressure from below. What a weird world, I concluded in wonder.

Janiz and I returned to the waiting group, I could hear some sniggering as whispered jokes were made concerning my lack of knowledge about the ground demons. I was happy to let them continue. I feared I would be cast out as a mad man or worse if I attempted to explain my deductions. I kept my discovery to myself, the only other I could possibly relate my theory to would of course be Sophos, and it was unlikely I would ever see him again.

The rhythmic plod of the horses' hooves provided a muffled background as Janiz concluded his tale. 'Following my failed attempt to rid myself of the cursed sorcerer, my father flew into a rage, rejected me as his heir and banished me from the kingdom, to be caught here now would mean my death, and yours. That is why I felt you needed the whole story. Most are fully aware of the risks in riding with me, it is obvious you are not. Riding with me could be the death of you.'

'What? Why me? I'm no one's enemy.'

'You ride with me, that is enough to ensure your death,' explained Janiz with another sideways glance to see my reaction.

'Oh, I see. Is that what you meant about protection? To a degree?' I asked with feigned indignation.

'Yes, sorry, but is anyone's safety guaranteed in this land? No, so what does it matter to what degree you will be protected? We live and we die.'

'Yeah but it's how I die that interests me. But I understand your meaning, please carry on with your tale. I need to understand what I'm letting myself in for.'

'Very well, I will if you wish.' Janiz settled himself further into his saddle and resumed his story.

'I don't know how the sorcerer has my father under his control, maybe some potion, possibly a spell of sorts. I don't know but it is evident the sorcerer now runs the kingdom. As for me, since banishment I have wandered the land, hiding and surviving the best I can. Most of my men were also banished for remaining loyal to me, others we picked up along the way, like you.'

He smiled at me as he spoke these words but I wished he hadn't. I was still not quite used to a lion smiling at me. Any moment I expected him to lick his lips in hunger.

'So what do you propose to do?' I asked in an attempt to remove that unnerving smile.

'Hah! Now that's a question that has burned my mind ever since I was forced from my home and my inheritance. I have no real plan other than getting into the palace and ridding the land of that cursed sorcerer. He seems however, to know my plans before I even devise them. At every step I am assailed by traps, assassins, demons and forms of dark magic. I . . .'

At that point I interrupted Janiz, to me it seemed he was talking absolute rubbish. My modern academic mind would not accept what I was hearing and I exclaimed: 'Hang on, hang on. What magic? What demons? Assassins I can understand, but magic? Surely no such thing exists?'

'Hang on to what? I have nothing to hang on to.'

'Oh sorry Janiz, it's just an expression from somewhere I don't recall. It simply means wait a moment. That's all. Sorry, but what magic?'

Janiz glanced at me, I'm sure he was uncertain about my mental state, after a pause, he began the explanation.

'We didn't have any potent magic here until this sorcerer arrived. Yes, there have been some forms of magic around since the dawn of time, but mostly the practitioners keep themselves to themselves and seldom bother us. Anyway, we have the ultimate defence against troublesome sorcerers, magicians and so-called wizards.'

'What's that then?' I interrupted.

'We remove their heads.'

'Oh!' was my only indication of understanding.

Janiz continued: 'But this sorcerer is different. He seems more powerful than those we know. He can cause water to burn, demons to rise and can kill with fire. I don't know if you would call this magic but how else could he achieve these things if not through sorcery or magic? There is a darkness upon this sorcerer.'

I already had some ideas but the limited knowledge about the world I found myself in caused uncertainty. In my world, we had guns, tanks, missiles and politicians that could all kill from a distance. But here? The technology I had grown up with did not exist here. Still, my scientific mind refused to believe in any form of magic that did not involve pulling rabbits from top hats. What I did believe in, nevertheless, was the king's jade box. If I could get into the palace with the aid of Janiz and his outlaws, possibly I could steal the box. Maybe I could get home? Though I did not know for sure. But it was a plan.

We made camp, or whatever groups of lawless riders do when it's time to eat, at the edge of a gently flowing river. Two of the group retrieved some form of fishing tackle from their saddlebags and threw lines into the water. I was impressed at their resourcefulness, and the thought of a fish supper interested me. I looked at my cold supplies and wished them success. As usual, a fire was built and we all placed our blankets in a circle. Sleeping on the ground was not a habit I had gotten used to, so I decided to take my time setting up my bed, while watching how the others did theirs. Surprisingly, each rider laid out their bedding with their feet towards the fire. I questioned a rider and received a sympathetic look. As if instructing a child, he informed me of two reasons. Firstly, it is wiser to keep your feet towards the fire as it's more efficient at warming the body than head first. Secondly, if one has to wake and move quickly in the night, eyes accustomed to the dark may keep you alive. It is unwise to stare into a fire at night and lose one's night vision when out in the open with wild animals, bandits and assassins wandering around. Made sense to me so I followed their example.

It was not quite evening, but Janiz had decided this location was suitable and it had been a long day. There was no rush he stated, we all knew where we were going and how long it would take us. At this, I almost interjected that I had no idea how long our journey would be, but remained quiet. It was clear the gang considered me to be one step away from a moron, I was not sure if that was a step up or a step down in status compared to a moron, but I stayed mute. Campsite activity is the same where ever a fire is lit. Sleeping blankets were set, weapons placed near to hand and everyone contributed towards the evening meal. I was no exception and handed over some of my rations. Our two anglers had managed to catch a few fish and this was a welcome addition to our menu.

Food consumed and the fire stoked up, it was time to settle for the night and get some sleep, least I hoped I would sleep. This world and its inhabitants were all very scary, far worse than a Boogieman under the bed. I followed the others and kept my hand wrapped around my staff and my evil knife ready under my blanket. My horse Fred was hobbled along with the other horses. I had removed the saddle, then I followed the example of the group and placed my saddle under my head as a pillow. I remembered cowboys doing this in films back home, yet no one mentioned just how uncomfortable this is. But I persevered and with many wriggles, shuffles and cursing, I finally made myself as comfortable as possible and drifted off into sleep.

A furry hand over my mouth awoke me with a jolt. 'Shh!' whispered a voice in the darkness. When I had gained control of my wits, and my bowels, the voice instructed me to, 'Arm yourself and be ready but stay down.'

I tightened my grasp on the staff and placed my other hand on the ground, ready to push myself up and out of my blankets, just as soon as I knew what the hell was going on. I didn't know who woke me, a furtive glance around the now low fire informed me everyone was in place and appeared still asleep. A moment later the faint sound of footsteps treading lightly towards the campsite reached my ears. Still none of my companions moved. Dark shapes loomed out of the darkness and moved quietly towards the prone figures of the sleepers, but no one moved. I began to fear for my bladder. I knew I must not move until at least one of the others did. Someone had woken me so I prayed everyone was also alert. If not, I was in deep trouble!

The creeping figures were only feet away from our horizontal bodies when abruptly the 'sleeping' forms rocketed into action. All the riders sprang to their feet with weapons already slashing towards the intruders. I was a second behind in reacting but my Tigris speed shot me out of my bed in a blink of an eye. No intruder had attacked me so I flew at the nearest one as he engaged a fellow rider. Between us, the intruder stood no chance and within moments he was cut to pieces. My adrenaline was flowing, my reactions were quick and surprisingly, I was eager to fight. Now there were two of us with no opponent so together we moved to assist another rider. A sword and a bladed staff joined the weapon of the defender, giving the intruder a swift trip to hell. Then out of the darkness, three opponents rushed us and for the first time, it was a one-on-one fight. I found myself facing what I could only guess at being a Lupus, not as tall as me but nimble and cunning in his attack.

For a few swift moments we danced around while sizing each other up, my dance steps were still hindered slightly by my injured leg. It was healing but movement remained awkward. The Lupus held his sword forward and away from his body, its tip following my gut as we sidestepped and manoeuvred in an attempt to find an opening. He made the first move, lunging forward with blinding speed. Narrowly I avoided the stab, leaping to one side and bringing my staff down on his shoulder, a strike that failed to bother my opponent. Again we danced, the Lupus grinning as he realised my lack of skill. I too was worried that I would soon be a deceased pussy. Certain of a kill, the Lupus darted at me and with a swipe, he raked his sword along my knife hand. I sprang back in alarm. The attack had been so fast and so calculated I had been completely surprised. Again the Lupus struck, this time I received a small nick on my right thigh, not deep but enough to force me back again. I realised he was toying with me, having sport before the final blow.

The Lupus lunged, his blade aimed at my stomach. This time, I spun as he lunged, spinning round with both my arms held out straight. Centrifugal force added weight to my staff as it struck a blow across his shoulders. I continued to spin round, dragging the evil long blade from its sheath as I turned. My staff remained outstretched in my right hand, giving balance to my form with my left hand also fully extended. All this happened in a blur, my actions resembling a lethal ballet dancer. My momentum carried my left hand round as I spun. I needed only a slight adjustment in the height of my arm as the evil knife slashed deeply across the neck of my opponent. My spin continued and immediately following the knife, my staff struck him again. I halted my spin and leapt aside before turning back to face the Lupus, my staff blade slashing out before the Lupus could regain his balance ready to attack or defend. A look of pure surprise appeared on his face as his throat opened with a fountain of hot blood. In a vain attempt to stem the blood, the Lupus dropped his weapon and reached up both hands to grasp the bloody wound. He sank to his knees in front of me as his life seeped through his fingers and soaked into the ground.

I stood watching him die, my hand still tightly grasping the weapon that killed him. I stood, my breath coming in gasps and momentarily I was frozen by a mixture of shock and fear. I felt no remorse for my opponent, if I hadn't killed him, he would have certainly killed me. I watched as he finally collapsed on the ground, curling up into a foetal position as his last drops of life gushed out, then he was still. I remained standing there until a voice from behind brought me to my senses. Quickly I turned, expecting yet another attack, my staff and knife held ready to strike. It took me a moment to register the battle was over, what remained of the intruders lay scattered about the camp fire's faint red glow. It was over and I was alive.

Janiz walked slowly over to me, warily avoiding the bodies scattered about the campsite. The other remaining riders were all in similar stances, some like me standing in shock at what had just happened, others followed Janiz and made their way to me. I thought I had suddenly become popular as Janiz came close, until I realised I was standing right beside our feeble fire. They didn't want me, they wanted the comfort of the fire as they all came to terms with what had just happened. I was not the only one feeling disbelief and relief at surviving.

Soon all had gathered around the fire and one of the riders added fuel, prodding it back to life. For long moments nothing was said as our brains attempted to analyse the recent attack. A quick headcount showed we had only lost one rider, though all the intruders were dead. I could not understand why the riders still appeared fearful, we had won the fight and we were alive, so what was the problem? Finally, my curiosity overpowered my confusion and, turning to Janiz, I asked why everyone seemed tense and worried.

'Ah, I forget you have no memories Harry and I'm sorry. These animan,' he said while indicating the dead, 'would not risk attacking a large group of riders, unless simple robbery was not their reason. Bandits would not seek a fight with others of their ilk, especially one with superior numbers. So the questions I'm asking are; who are they? Why did they attack us and for what reason? At this moment I can't answer these puzzles for certain, but I think I can guess their purpose.'

Janiz ordered his riders to search for any clues amongst the bodies, hoping for answers, it was not long before he got them. The search had only just begun when one of the riders called out, followed rapidly by shouts from the others. Each rider had discovered a large purse of coins on each body. Far too much coin for a ragged band of bandits.

'The coin proves my guess correct,' sighed Janiz, 'these are paid assassins, poor ones of no quality, but assassins all the same. It would appear they have been paid to rid us from this world. I suspect the sorcerer is growing impatient in his desire for my head. Hiring such inept reprobates was a mistake, perhaps one he will rue. From here on we must increase our guard, we cannot know who or what he will send against us next. Nonetheless, with this increased risk, if anyone wishes to go their own way and perhaps save themselves, I will not be offended.'

This last comment was made with a long stare in my direction, certainly, Janiz knew the loyalty of his band of animan but although I had proved myself in a fight, I was still a stranger in their midst. I shrugged in reply, indicating I would stay. I did not add what was on my mind. If I left, where would I go? I knew no one, had no idea where I was or what I should do. It seemed wiser to remain with this capable group rather than on my own. Janiz read the meaning of my shrug and appeared pleased with my decision.

The bags of coin were distributed amongst us and for myself personally, it felt good to have the extra coin. I still had much of the coin retrieved from the rider eaten by the overgrown hyena, now my purse was definitely gaining weight. Great, I thought, I can now afford to buy things, if there were things to buy out here. Somehow I suspected it might be difficult to find an Asda, Tesco or Harrods in this land. However, the increased weight of the purse comforted me all the same. Any other useful items found on the bodies were also distributed among the riders, with satisfaction I noted Janiz only took an equal share. A reassuring discovery, proving Janiz to be a fair leader to his animan outlaws, which now included me.

As our campsite was now compromised by unsightly dead bodies lying around, Janiz ordered us to collect our possessions and move on to another site. The scent of fresh meat would certainly attract every carnivore for miles around, and none of us wished to be added to the menu. My horse Fred was decidedly unhappy with being re-saddled in the middle of the night and rode to a new location a mile or so away. Once we reached our new campsite, I treated him to an extra handful of grain as an apology. Within a short time, we were all wrapped in our blankets once again, trying to catch the last hours of sleep before dawn.

Chapter Seven: A Demon Before Us.

The morning was young and the sun gave a hint of its intent to provide a hot dry day. My butt was now toughened to the rigours of horse riding and long hours in the saddle. I could now gaze about me in reasonable comfort, taking in the landscape while Fred ambled along behind the other mounts. I stared in wonderment at the wide open space of the land, no houses, factories or columns of smoke bridged the divide between ground and sky. I stared out across a huge area of grassland. Again I was reminded of a tundra, the gently undulating land stretching out before me under a perfect sky. In the far distance, I could see the blue haze of hills bordering the tundra.

These were the first real hills I had seen since arriving in the land. The crystal clear blue of the sky puzzled me for a moment until I realised no aeroplane vapour trails formed long thin white clouds against the blue background. Of course, there were no planes, I had discovered no trace of the dreaded infernal combustion engine here. No vehicles belched out toxic fumes while carrying people forward to wealth, wellbeing or car wreck. Up to this moment there had been no indication of petroleum fuelled mechanical contraptions existing on this land, a fact I was rather pleased about.

We rode throughout the day, hiding from the occasional traveller but otherwise encountering no further threats. My mind eased and I grew content with my new life. The days spent in dreary classrooms, pubs and my little flat now just a memory as I rode across this beautiful country. I had desperately wanted to return home, but now I asked myself; why? It was dangerous here, that was certain, but it was exciting and I had friends. Did I really wish to return to my previous life? In all honesty, I could not decide. The day wore on while I weighed my recent adventures against my past unadventurous existence. I did not reach a conclusion. We had stopped several times to rest the horses and allow both horse and animan refreshments. It had been quite an uneventful day and I was content. I should have known better, but prophecy was not high on my list of life skills.

Evening was falling when Janiz ordered we make camp, it may have been a peaceful day but our bodies were weary and we all felt the need to rest. A small clump of trees was chosen as our backdrop for the night, fallen branches providing fuel for the fire, leaf covered branches formed a canopy over our heads. Not a large canopy but enough to give the illusion of shelter. The horses were tended and left hobbled so they could feed. Then it was our time to eat and again we all pooled some of our rations; I didn't see who the cook was, but was thankful it wasn't me.

Several of the riders foraged for plants and roots, berries and anything that may make our uninteresting meal more palatable. One rider had discovered some mushrooms and offered them around. I have always been suspicious of any form of fungi so politely refused. They must have been very special mushrooms because upon discovery, the rider had beckoned the others over to see them. Very strange! Why would a bunch of mushrooms require such investigation or attract such fascination? I could hear the riders muttering in low voices but could not make out what they were saying. Personally, I was not fond of mushrooms so my curiosity waned. After a period of dark whispering, they all returned to the campfire, the riders now oddly subdued. Spirits soon returned to normality as we sat around the fire chatting quietly as we waited for the concoction of ingredients to cook. Even without the added mushrooms, I enjoyed my makeshift meal and soon felt the comfort of a full belly. The meal over, our bedrolls were unpacked and placed in a position of choice upon the ground and the fire was set. Myself and my companions lulled around after eating, night had fallen and it was soon time for sleep. It was a dry mild evening and the stars could be seen twinkling through the branches. Sounds idyllic, doesn't it?

I had barely settled in my blankets when I noticed the riders begin to show signs of unease. Many riders were casting furtive glances about them, others peered constantly into the darkness. Even Janiz seemed ill at ease, a fact that grew apprehension in my mind. I nervously peered into the trees surrounding the camp but could neither see nor hear any threats approaching. In readiness, I grasped my staff tightly while ensuring the big knife was loose in its sheaf. I lay quiet, unsure of what was bothering my companions. We were all animan so our senses were as acute as our original species, a tiger in my case. I could smell nothing out of the ordinary, I could hear nothing other than the natural sounds of the night, and nor could I see any shapes moving in the darkness. Why did a sense of unease emanate from the others, what was wrong? I lay still, trying to keep sleep at bay until I decided I was safe. Nothing happened, my blanket was warm and my belly full and in moments I had fallen asleep.

Shouts of terror and screams of horror ripped me abruptly from my sleep. The screams and shouts came from voices I recognised. Pure fright was evident in the throats of my fellow riders. Quickly I rose from my bed, weapons held ready, and my eyes peering into the darkness in an attempt to discover the source of their fright. None of my companions lay beside the fire, empty blankets were strewn about but I could see nothing, even with my great vision, nor could I smell or hear anything that resembled a threat. Wondering what the hell was going on, I followed the shouts and rushed to the aid of my fellows. Some distance away on the other side of the wood, I found them gathered in a semicircle amidst a tiny clearing in the trees. Each member of the ferocious animan riders had weapons drawn, all were crouched in a fighting stance, shouting in fear as their weapons flashed, thrusting their blades forward into – nothing!

'What's wrong?' I shouted at the nearest rider, 'Where's the attacker?'

Wild and frightened eyes darted quickly at me, 'Can't you see it?' he screamed.

'See what?' I shouted back.

'The demon!'

I quickly spun around, peering into the surrounding darkness, anxious to finally get a glimpse of a mythical being. But I saw nothing, nothing other than the trees and the animan stabbing and slashing at thin air in front of an old gnarled oak.

'Huh? What demon? Where's the demon? I can't see anything. What are you talking about?' I peered about me once again but still could not detect any form of threat. I began to get angry, I concluded I was the subject of a prank by the riders, designed to scare the wits out of the newcomer.

'Defend yourself! We are lost, doomed! There is a huge demon in front of us, can't you see it? Are you blind?' screamed the rider while stabbing at something he clearly thought was in front of him. Janiz himself then shouted at me to fight, but fight what? I could see no enemy.

Around I spun, staring in all directions for this supposed demon but all I could see were terrified riders, whirling their weapons frantically and an old tree. It was no good, I simply could not see what was scaring them almost to death. I could see nothing but darkness. I decided to stop, look and listen, as my mum used to tell me, and analyse what was happening around me. As I watched, one of the riders turned and fled from the 'fight', soon followed by another. Riders were screaming, imploring me to join the battle, eyes wide with fear as they fought empty air. Even the brave Janiz portrayed a vision of terror. It was as if they were having a nightmare, a collective nightmare. Finally, my twenty-first century science brain took control and I began to understand what was happening or thought I did. If not I was going to be breakfast for some demon that I couldn't see and didn't believe in anyway. My mind refuted this possibility, mindless physical violence I could accept, but not some supernatural monster. I had an idea what was happening and it seemed to be the only scientific answer to the mayhem I was witnessing before me.

Taking care not to be stabbed, gutted or slashed, I ran to the front of the group and stood in their path, away from the flashing blades but with my back to the old misshapen oak tree. Screams of, 'Get out of the way' and, 'Run you idiot!' were directed at me as I stood there, stationary in the midst of their fright. Laying my staff at my feet and sheathing my knife, I slowly raised my empty hands to the night sky. Still I did not move or speak until I saw confusion battling with fear in their eyes. Remaining perfectly still, I began to hum a lullaby, it was the only thing I could think of doing. I began quietly, gradually raising my voice in an attempt to break through the fear without instigating further panic. My low singing of the lullaby eventually brought frightened eyes towards me.

'Stop!' I finally cried, 'You are bewitched! You are under a spell! There is no demon here, it's in your heads! Calm yourselves.'

Some riders repeated their calls for me to get out of the way or run, but I could see Janiz pausing, puzzlement on his feline face. I remained standing in front of them, quietly singing and unafraid. Slowly he began to lower his weapon, his eyes glued on my face. Gradually his hesitation spread to the other riders and weapons grew still, though muscles remained taut. When all eyes were fixed on me

I slowly turned around, keeping my hands held far above my head.

'There is no demon!' I repeated in a softer pacifying tone. 'Can you see me? Am I a demon?'

The group struggled to regain their senses as they continued to stare with wide eyes at my solitary figure standing before them in the night. Slowly I lowered my arms, very slowly. I did not wish to be mistaken for an apparition and receive a belly full of steel. At last, the group began to regain their senses, the horror of moments before still visible on their faces but all weapons had been lowered, and the group of frightened riders became still. I coughed nervously and was suddenly faced with a barrage of sharp steel things pointed at my stomach before calm returned once more.

'What happened?' asked a subdued Janiz, 'How did you banish the demon? What were you chanting? I thought we were dead for certain, lost to a creature of the darkness. How did you do it?'

All eyes were on me now, each believing I was a saviour, a mighty sorcerer who had battled a demon for them. The accolade was nice I admit, but not true and I had to devise a method of making them understand.

'I did nothing, there was no chant, I sang a child's song to ease your minds.' I responded. 'It was all in your heads, there was no demon, there are no demons, only tricks of the mind. The demon was a thought in your heads, each one of you, but it was not real. Believe me. I'm no demon slayer, there was no demon.'

Disbelief flickered across their faces at my statement, it was obvious they had no faith in my explanation. One could not break centuries of superstition with a few words of science. With a sigh, I turned away, 'Come on. It's late, let's get back to camp.'

I knew they didn't believe me but they followed anyway. I offered no explanation at first, I needed to think this thing through. Back at the camp, I began rebuilding the fire, more for the light it gave than the warmth it offered. Finally, all the riders, including the two that had run away, returned to the fire and sat in shock on their blankets, all still silent. Once the fire was burning brightly enough for illumination, I began to search the campsite. I didn't know what I was looking for but I felt sure there was a logical reason for their night terror. The riders all watched me in silence, hints of awe on their faces proof that they thought I had singlehandedly banished a powerful demon. I didn't want to be a false hero and so I determined to find the cause of their collective nightmare or hallucination.

My search found nothing suspicious and I even began to doubt myself, without proof, my scientific mind could not explain the demon, to myself or the riders. It was then that I had a *'light bulb'* moment.

Turning back to the still shaken riders huddled around the fire, I questioned the mushroom collector, a stocky Ursidae named Firmus. I asked if he would show me where he found them but was surprised by his reluctance. Fear returned to his face as he stated he would not go near that place. Others began to show similar signs of apprehension but I insisted I needed to see where the mushrooms had grown. Finally, Janiz plucked up courage and agreed to show me the place. I could simply not understand the reluctance of the riders or the return of fear upon their faces. Janiz remained anxious as he grasped a brand from the fire and led the way to where the mushrooms had been gathered.

In moments we stood facing a perfectly ordinary tree and Janiz gestured at the small mushrooms growing at its base. The area was dark and dank, perfect for fungi to flourish. Still, I could not fathom why this spot should be so scary, it was no different to all the other trees in the small cluster. I took the brand from Janiz and stooped to examine the mushrooms in its light, noticing Janiz remained still staring at the tree itself. Once I had recognised the fungi and discovered nothing unexpected, I straightened and glanced at the Leo who still stared at the tree, apprehension on his face and in his stance. Baffled I asked Janiz what was so special about this tree?

'Look at it, it's a warning,' whispered Janiz, still with his eyes fixed on the tree.

'It's only a tree, how can it be a warning? I don't know what type of tree it is but it's only a tree.'

For the briefest of moments, Janiz's eyes darted to mine. 'It's not the cursed tree, it's what's on it! Look closer Harry, look until you see clearly.'

I peered at the tree, seeing only what I expected to see. Bark, small branches, the odd insect, rodent and bird skulls, small bones and . . . What? What the hell was all this stuff? I saw resting on a low branch, all kinds of animal bones, snail shells and weeds, flowers perhaps but weeds to me.

'What's all this about then?' I asked the still fearful Janiz. To my surprise, he was no longer standing at my side. Turning around, I found him stood several paces away from the tree, wildness beginning to light his eyes.

'It is a demon tree. It warns us away from this place. Come, we must leave now before the demon returns.' These last words were spoken over his shoulder for Janiz had already begun to walk away.

Quickly I caught him up and together we returned to the camp. I thought I knew what had happened but I needed all the riders calm before I tried to explain. I had to be careful, I did not wish to trample all over their beliefs and superstitions. Even in my world, people have been known to lose their heads for criticizing someone else's religion or faith. I continued standing while Janiz sat down on his bed blanket. A rider passed around a flask of something I suspected was alcoholic. I turned down the offer politely, not wishing to offend but not wanting to dampen my senses either. I would need to keep my wits about me as I was about to use science to explain away a demon.

When all was quiet, I took a deep breath and asked, 'Can you describe the demon you saw?' Immediately all the riders spoke at once, giving descriptions of all manner of demonic features, but none saw exactly the same thing. This fact soon dawned on them.

I continued, 'I don't think any of you saw a demon, not in reality, you only saw it in your heads. It was an unreal apparition.' The riders rose, each one shouting that I was wrong, I was an imbecile and an unbeliever. I held up my hands in a gesture to quieten them and eventually managed to continue. This at least was something I felt familiar with. For years I had startled young students with facts about science that destroyed their lifelong beliefs. Amazing statements such as Batman was not a real person and potatoes really did from the ground and didn't grow in chip shops or supermarkets.

'The mushrooms you all had with your evening meal, I recognised them, I think I remember we called them 'Magic Mushrooms' and used them as a potion to er . . make us happy I suppose would be the best description.'

At this point, several of the riders nodded in agreement and Janiz stated that they were aware of the mushrooms' potential. I nodded back in agreement and continued speaking.

'The mushrooms alone would not conjure up a demon in your minds, least not strong enough for you to believe what you saw. However, when eaten whilst in a fearful mind, then that something really can appear real. Am I right in thinking the bones laid out in the tree had some significance to you all?'

Nods and muttered agreement came from the seated riders at this question, though most remained puzzled at my rationalisation. A rider spoke for the others and replied, 'It's a familiar sign to us. Bones placed upon a tree indicate a demon is near, the flowers tell us the demon lives in that tree and by gathering the mushrooms from around it, we awakened the beast and it sought revenge for our disturbance.'

I continued. 'I understand, I noticed on your *demon tree*, all the bones and weeds appeared fresh. Unless it was a new warning, someone had put them there recently. I think it was deliberately chosen due to the proximity of the mushrooms. Someone knew you were coming this way, knew that you would gather and feast upon the mushrooms. An unknown person placed the demon warning there as a deliberate trigger to your waking dream, they wanted to play tricks on your minds.'

Growls from the riders confirmed they followed my reasoning, nonetheless, it was apparent I had not conquered their ingrained beliefs.

'You all suffered from what is known as a mass hallucination or mass hysteria. There was no demon, but someone wanted you to think there was. Someone wanted to scare you, frighten you away.' I concluded quietly.

Silence. Not one rider spoke, they simply stared at me as though I was the demon. I considered I had said enough and needed a reply to assess what to say next, that's if words were enough. I might need to run for my life at this point. It was Firmus, the rider who had picked the mushrooms stood up and reached for his saddlebag. Digging inside he pulled out what remained of his mushroom supply and threw them into the long grass, grunting with effort as he threw them as far away as he could.

Janiz looked round the group and then stood to speak, I sighed in relief.

'I have heard of these tricks or enchantment of minds, we have all seen the mad animan who view a world different to ours, considered harmless but best avoided. Are we now the same mad animan?'

'No,' I replied, 'once the effect of the mushrooms wears off, you'll all be fine.'

'Hah, that's good. I feared we would all be cursed with losing our minds. I'm interested in why you would think someone had placed the demon symbols for our benefit though. Who would do such a thing? Who could know we would pass this way?'

'That I can't answer Janiz, I'm new to your group. Only you can know who may have done this. Do you have any ideas?' As I spoke, a culprit sprang to mind, but it was only a random assumption.

Janiz did not reply at first, instead he looked at the ground, his head bowed in thought. The others remained quiet and still as they watched their leader contemplate. I simply watched all, both fascinated and curious about the outcome of our leader's concentration. Dawn had arrived and I realised I was very tired. Sleep had been short due to the events of the night, however as none of the riders showed signs of fatigue, I hid my tiredness. A burst of bird song as they greeted the dawn appeared to awake Janiz from his thoughts. He straightened his back, eased his legs and then looked at each one of us full in the face for some moments.

'I know of someone,' he said simply.

I and every rider present battled the almost overpowering urge to shout, 'Who?' But we waited, we waited for Janiz in the dawn.

'My father's sorcerer!'

Chapter Eight: Science

No one offered a comment on Janiz's conclusion regarding who may be behind their little fright with the non-existent demon. No one spoke, including me. We ate a meagre breakfast, saddled the horses and returned to our journey. I remained as silent as the others but I knew questions would spew forth soon, not least from me. I also wondered about the so-called sorcerer. I didn't believe in magic, strange potions, chanting, magic books and certainly not sorcerers, wizards, witches or magicians. Tricks, illusions and drug induced hallucinations I could accept, but demons? Engineering a fright in a wandering group of outlaws would not be difficult scientifically. Scientifically, last night's events had a simple explanation.

In my world, chaos and destruction had often grown from a simple seed, a suggestion that evolved into a belief. I considered it no different here. The bones had been used to induce a fear of demons, the hallucinogenic properties of the Psilocybin or magic mushrooms had provided the visualisation. Most likely one member of the group had imagined he saw a demon and, like in other known cases of mass hysteria, it rapidly spread to the others. I was safe for two reasons, I had not consumed any of the fungi and I did not believe in demons. But the question remained, was it pure chance that the mushrooms were growing in the exact spot that contained superstitious artefacts? I did not believe this coincidence, in my mind, skulduggery was afoot!

We had ridden several miles in silence before Janiz spoke. The riders drew nearer to hear his words, myself included. 'I think Harry is right, there was no demon or friend Harry would have been shredded, standing as he did right in front of the apparition. Therefore it could only be one of two things, magic or trickery. Magic we cannot fight, but if it was a trick, I know of only two people who could do such a thing.'

We all awaited his conclusion eagerly, I was wondering who the second person could be, I thought the sorcerer was the chief villain in this kingdom. Did he mean there was another?

'There are only two who would have the knowledge to create a trap such as we faced last night. Sophos is one of course, but I cannot believe he would undertake such a plan, and if he did, then why? Sophos is harmless, we all know that. He's strange and maybe slightly touched with madness, but not malice.'

We all nodded in agreement with this statement, though in truth, one could never know what went on in the mind of a Liverpudlian.

Janiz continued. 'The only other I know of would be my father's sorcerer. He has long wished to be rid of me, my very presence on this land represents a barrier to all his plans. He intends to gain control of my kingdom; that much is obvious to all bar my father, and for him to succeed, I must be removed. We have faced assassins and now, if what Harry says is true, an apparition of a demon. It appears to me that these events have been placed in our way deliberately, and I fear we can expect more obstacles as we near the palace. We all must be aware that these attacks can come in any form of malevolence that can be conjured to falter our path. They will try to kill us. They are trying to kill us.'

Oh great! I thought, where was my boring but safe classroom now? How the hell had I ended up in this strange land and in the middle of a battle for a kingdom I never knew existed. I was beginning to feel very homesick, though I didn't have anything to go home for. However, here I was, a giant cat in a world where the Human Race did not exist. Possibly one may consider that a good thing, but human traits exist in all forms it seems. The animan still fought for land, for possessions and wealth. Like humans, they did not shy from underhand tactics, murder and theft. On the other hand, I had met some good animan, Harron and Janiz, possibly Sophos, but was he really an animan? Was I? My head hurts!

'I don't think we can prevail alone, perhaps it is time to seek assistance,' spoke Janiz after a short pause, 'perhaps it is time to rally our allies, our friends and supporters. We can raise an army if all answer our call. It is time to regain our kingdom and be rid of that cursed sorcerer. We will send the word on its travels at the next village. Do we all agree?'

A chorus of agreement came from the riders, some still shaken by the night's strange events. I remained quiet, I didn't know how I was to achieve my plan to obtain the king's jade box, would more riders help or hinder? I sighed quietly, whether I agreed or not would make little difference. I had no inkling of what to expect, oddly enough I've never attacked a palace before. Not much call in Manchester or Liverpool for a palace, though I'm not sure about London. With all those politicians down there, it will not be long before one of them puts in an expenses claim for a palace or two. I decided there was no point trying to make any plans of my own until I see the palace for myself. I would need to devise a plan to enter the palace, find the box and escape alive. Sounds easy I thought, but the notion failed to convince me.

On we rode, across a land that now appeared to have more trees dotted amongst the long grass. I was having some difficulty in coping with such flat land, it was akin to being on the ocean and having an uninterrupted view to the horizon. This land may have no huge mountains or large volcanos but the land itself must still move, just not much. While Fred plodded and I pondered, I discovered myself riding alongside an Ursidae rider I did not know, but a question supplied me with his name. He introduced himself as Secuutus and appeared to be a friendly individual so I initiated a conversation, hoping to gain information that might help my plans. Beginning with the subject uppermost on my mind, I asked him about hills and mountains.

'Yes there are mountains, but so far away, I have never seen one. Big lumps of rock aren't they?' I nodded in affirmation while hiding my grin at his description. His reply answered that question, so I switched to hills and other such geological interests. His response to these questions brought both an explanation and some relief. 'Of course there are hills! What are you talking about?' he exclaimed.

'It's just that ever since I awoke from my fight with the Hyaenidae, all I've seen is flat ground.'

'Hah!' said Secuutus, 'Well that'll explain it I suppose. We're travelling across a mighty plain, one of the biggest in this part of the world. It can take weeks to cross and let's face it; we've had the odd interruption along the way, what with bandits or assassins, whatever you want to call them. Then there was the demon you banished, and your fight with Praedo, it all adds up to wasted time you know. We're nearing the end of the plain and then you'll see all the hills you want. You really must have received a hard knock on your head if you've forgotten hills and valleys!'

I nodded my head in agreement, not bothering to explain again that the demon was not real. I was also chiding myself for not recognising a plain. I had wondered about a tundra but hadn't thought of a plain. I've never actually been to one, but I've seen lots of wildlife television programmes. And I'm supposed to be educated. Huh!

'Anyway,' continued Secuutus, 'once we're off this plain, the ground becomes hilly with forests, valleys and all sorts of things that make you climb up, climb down, climb under or climb over. So no, this land is not all flat. A pity because it's much easier to travel across the plains. So you don't remember anything then?'

'No, this could be a foreign world to me, I don't appear to know anything anymore,' I answered with tongue in cheek. Of course it seemed a foreign land, that's because it damn well was! I had no idea where on Pangea I could be. If the continents did not divide, then lands could not be identified by fauna and flora. Animals and plants would have no barriers to prevent them from migrating to all parts of this huge continent. That point made me wonder, kangaroos, koalas, polar bears and other such animals evolved in their individual ecosystems, separated from other countries by oceans and mountain ranges. Did they exist here? Are there new species that have evolved to cope with the huge distances and one singular landmass? Certainly, there were a few I already knew, in fact I was one of them. Tigers, lions, bears and wolves had evolved to become the dominant species in a world without human beings. What else had changed, what no longer existed and what was new. Were Dodo birds alive here?

All the time I had been lost in thought, Secuutus had continued to talk, I was to confirm soon enough that talking was his favourite pastime. I didn't mind as he readily answered all my seemingly childish questions without ridicule. Amongst the many random subjects and topics Secuutus rambled upon, his past and some of the local history proved interesting. Secuutus informed me he had not long been an outlaw. He was once a member of the king's guard like most of the other riders, and he had followed Janiz into banishment for his loyalty. I asked him what the king was like.

'Ah the king was a great fellow, that's before that sorcerer bloke arrived. He was always fair and treated us well. We had warm barracks and three good meals a day. Our training was fierce but we were well supplied with weapons, shields and tough leather armour to protect us from all but the most persistent sword thrust. I relished the routine of the day, I always knew where I should be and what I should be doing. Out here in the wilds it's confusing. I know why we are here and I know what Janiz plans to do, but surprises have a tendency to happen here on a regular basis. I don't like surprises. Tell me what to do and I will do it, happily, but demons and assassins coming at me in the night is not my idea of fun.'

'Nor mine,' I agreed, thinking back to the dull routine of the academic life I once enjoyed, no, endured. I wonder what Secuutus would think of that lifestyle? Probably as much as I thought of it. Tedious as my previous life had been, I meant it when I said I agreed with him, hallucinations, bandits and strange beasties were shocking enough, but to find oneself in a different world? That will take some beating. Dragging my chain of thought back to the present, I asked Secuutus where the so-called sorcerer had come from.

'No one knows,' he began, 'he just appeared in the city, made a name for himself and rapidly climbed the social ladder until he was invited to the king's court. Once there he somehow wheedled his way near to the king and before anyone knew it, he was announced as the king's personal adviser in all matters of the supernatural and magic. That was something different, totally unexpected because sorcerers are not generally held in high esteem in these lands. Good for party tricks and amusing children, but not at the king's side. Not as the king's adviser. It was unheard of. But then peculiar things began to happen, the sorcerer knew things and could do things that we had never known or seen before. We all began to believe he was a real sorcerer, not just a trickster. More and more animan began to believe in demons and magic until fears grew across the land. Now we all know that demons and supernatural beings do exist and it frightens us. Once we only worried about invading armies and roaming bandits, but now we fear the unseen and unnatural. The sorcerer claimed to have the power to protect us from such beings and he even convinced the king, who has had the sorcerer by his side ever since.

    At this point Secuutus paused and I made the mistake of glancing over at him. As my vision centred on his features, he sneezed. The volume of detritus that shot from his muzzle like nose was astounding, but what he did next turned my stomach into uproar. Catching the ejected nasal muck in one hand, Secuutus proceeded to first sniff it, then give it a tentative lick before finally smearing it all down one trouser leg. I had seen many gross sights during my teaching years, teenage boys can exhibit some truly disgusting behaviour but this spectacle revolted me. It did not, however, revolt Secuutus, for as soon as his hand was wiped, he continued to talk, taking up faultlessly where he had paused.

'Soon after the sorcerer's admittance to the king's side, everything changed. The king no longer spent time on the practice fields with his soldiers, he stopped being seen amongst the good people of the city and even began to shun his own son and heir to the throne, Janiz. Things got even worse, taxes rose, more and more animan were conscripted into the army to fight an enemy no one yet knows. Troops by the thousand have been sent to guard our borders for no apparent reason except paranoia. Any who spoke out were imprisoned, many were hung as traitors or judged to be possessed by evil and burnt alive. None of us could understand why the king had changed. Whenever Janiz tried to reason with him, he was ignored or the king would fly into an uncontrollable rage. In the end, things got so bad that Janiz and his most loyal guard were banished from the kingdom on pain of death if we returned. Janiz thinks the sorcerer convinced the king that Janiz and his loyal supporters were a threat to the king's reign. But as you can clearly see, we have returned.'

'That's some story,' I interrupted before he could ramble on, 'but could you not find out where that sorcerer bloke came from then? Surely that would give you a clue to his history?'

'Nope! He simply appeared one day, walking out of the wilderness. Funny though, he too claimed he'd lost his memory.'

Secuutus gave me a sideways glance, suspicion almost rearing in his eyes. I say almost because Secuutus appeared to be one of those solid and dependable people that never made assumptions, he would need to be told I was suspicious before he would consider the possibility.

    I ruminated on what Secuutus had said but with much scepticism I must admit. I was a man of science and held no belief in magic, sorcery or wizardry. Yes, I enjoyed the Harry Potter stories but that's what they were, stories. Superstition had reared its head in this otherwise sane land, and its birth was somehow connected to the arrival of the sorcerer. Once superstition and fear begin, they will quickly spread and become truth. When a true explanation is not known, superstition fills the void, supplying a reason where knowledge and common sense fails. I suppose everyone has to place their faith somewhere and if an event or situation arises that fail explanation, then the supernatural or religion are the easiest choices. Superstition itself can lead to all sorts of beliefs and fears. Humans and Animan alike willing to accept supernatural deities and demons, myths and Gods to explain the unknown. Myths that become truths, truths that become religions, religions that breed followers and more believers. The mysterious activities of this mysterious sorcerer had stirred the subconscious minds and allowed fear and superstition to gain control of this kingdom.

In this land, as all through my own history, devils, ghosts and assorted nasties receive blame for anything that defies the present level of understanding. We all now know that the Earth revolves around the Sun, but if we had not discovered this fact with the aid of science, what then? We know droughts, floods, ice and storms are products of nature and our weather, but it was not always thus. At times in our history, catastrophic weather conditions were placed at the feet of Gods or spirits. These days we know Britain has the odd drop of rain, we know that on occasion the sun will shine, we understand this is a natural weather pattern and not simply the whim of Zeus, Freyr, Indra, Jupiter or a certain BBC weather forecaster.

We know these days that wounds, sickness and injury can, in most cases, be healed and repaired with modern medicines and simple hygiene. But although the human being, again I'm referring to my world as I still think of it, has been around for several thousand years, treatments such as antibiotics are very recent. Before then, people thought the devil or a demon had taken possession of the sick person and a witch doctor or shaman would be required to remove the offending entity. So believing in magic, sorcery and all things supernatural is a common trait, but not for me. I needed proof,

proof that I could evaluate, grasp or verify. Did I arrive in this place by magic? Of course not. That damn jade box must act as a portal or key, there had to be a scientific explanation. That much I was sure. I did not believe in magic.

So the king had been a grand fellow before this sorcerer person arrived on the scene, loved by his army and his citizens. But now it appears he has been subjected to the will of this Merlin type person who appeared from nowhere. Now the animan are no longer happy under their king's reign, now his army grows and his son has been banished. Ok, I admit I'm still not sure of who I am or where I am, but even I understand that something needs to be done about this magician fellow.

'Why has no one assassinated him yet?' I asked my informative companion.

'Oh many have tried but the king protects him rigorously, the sorcerer even has his own personal guard that follow him about like shadows. Janiz was the only one to come close to ridding the land of this evil but even he was thwarted.'

'So if not by the blade, why not use poison or slip something nasty into his bedroom? Surely someone has considered that possibility? Killing a person is usually relatively easy I would have thought?' I asked in contemplation of the many, many ways human beings instigated the demise of their fellows, even genocide.

'The sorcerer is very cunning,' muttered Secuutus, 'he has his rooms searched by his guards before he enters and the king has provided a food taster. It's impossible to get near the creature, it's as if he outthinks and outmanoeuvres all who plan against him. He is very clever.'

The day was passing quietly, a pleasant relief from the recent attacks by assassins, hallucinations and wild beasties. There were animals in the distance, some form of antelope or deer I thought, and numerous small furry creatures rustled in the tall grass. Birds flew above our heads and insects buzzed annoyingly about us. It would have been classed as a peaceful sunny day at home. I could have been travelling through a nature reserve or safari park. I saw no sign of hungry Hyaenidae and any other predators lurking in the long grass remained clear of our group. I still had no idea what animals existed here or if and how they had evolved, being honest I admitted I was in no hurry to find out.

At midday we halted beside a small muddy lake and rested, eating what remained of our supplies. I had become hardened to life in the saddle but it was still a relief to climb down and stretch my legs. Our two anglers come hunters disappeared, pursuing small animals to supplement our dwindling food stocks. I concluded the pair were the experts and everyone felt content to sit back and reap the rewards, if there were any. Hunting food is somewhat harder than a visit to the local supermarket.

Talk rippled quietly between the riders but as yet few had spoken to me, other than Janiz and Secuutus. I didn't mind, my brain was exhausted from all that had happened, small talk was not high on my agenda. I pondered upon the infamous sorcerer, still totally convinced he was a charlatan. I had to admire his apparent rise to fame and fortune within the kingdom. Compared to myself at least, here I was sitting on the ground beside a lake and surrounded by outlaws. Soon, the rest period came to an end, signalled by Janiz holding up a hand for quiet. As he was the leader, our next move was his decision and it was obvious he was about to give instructions. When all conversation had ceased and all attention focused on the Leo, he began outlining his plan for consideration by the rest of us. Janiz was a born leader, always bouncing thoughts and ideas off his riders and taking counsel or guidance in reply. Everyone could comment it seemed, and Janiz was very willing to accept advice and suggestions. Now he explained his thoughts about our future, including mine.

'Tomorrow we will arrive at the town of Defero which many of us know. For those who don't, it is a tough town with tough animan. They can be suspicious of strangers and suffer no fools. Harry . . ?' he called looking in my direction, 'Best keep quiet and let others speak, I'm not sure what the residents of Defero will make of you. You look like a Tigris warrior, you fight well but there is something else, something different about you I can't identify. So if you wish to continue walking this land, consider your words and actions carefully. Any others who don't know this town, you should also tread carefully, it's not your average community. That's it then, mount up and we'll be on our way.'

Chapter Nine: Defero

True to Janiz's word, we eventually approached a small town nestled in a slight dip in the landscape. We had travelled much of the day through sparse woodlands and even encountered several small hills, much to my relief. Flat ground rapidly loses its appeal and boredom is let in by the lack of visual stimulus. Miles and miles of long grass interspersed with the odd clump of trees quickly rivals a long running television soap opera for the tedium awards.

The town called Defero, where Janiz hoped to gain recruits, grew in size as we neared. It was larger than the town I had visited with Sophos so long ago, but not by much. Around the outskirts, small farms were scattered with fenced in animals, and I was delighted to recognise cows, sheep, pigs and goats as the main livestock. I had wondered if these too had changed. Other farms were surrounded with fields of crops stretching out over the land. Thin trails of smoke rose from countless chimneys and I was surprised, though I didn't know why, to see several lines full of washing blowing gently beside rounded houses. Apart from the dome shape of all the buildings, everything else indicated a normal hard working community.

As I drew nearer, I could make out shops amidst the domes, stalls and a few larger domes that I suspected were bars and though I couldn't see one, possibly a hotel of sorts. Of course, all I saw was rationalised by my human civilised brain. I wondered if my assumptions were totally wrong but I would have to wait until we entered the town before proving either way. Riding past the farms and into the town itself, I noted how quiet it was. Entering the town there were domes scattered everywhere, but the main street appeared to be the central hub of business and commerce establishments. Shops selling foodstuffs and groceries, others offering clothing and hardware. I was surprised to see a baker's shop with bread and cakes displayed for sale. After days, weeks? I forget how long it has been, living on rations and shared food, the thought of a sweet cream cake filled my mind. I did discover a hotel of sorts, an inn would be a better description and yes, it was larger than the myriad of small shops and homes ranging about it.

As we walked our horses slowly along the street, a blacksmith could be seen, and heard, battering away at his forge, sweat dripping from his brow and down his Ursidae features. Massive arms swung a hammer in rhythmic time, not missing a beat, as he watched us approach. Not far from the blacksmith's stood a stable, a thoughtful arrangement I concluded. The place possessed all the attributes of a small town found anywhere in Britain, maybe not so much the blacksmith's and stables, but otherwise it was all very familiar.

It was about then I realised there was indeed something different about the town, something was wrong but I could not at first identify my concern. Banishing thoughts of cake from my mind, I realised the problem. Other than the blacksmith, there was not a single soul to be seen. No animan walked the streets, no children played, even the shops seemed vacant. Looking around I sensed we were being watched, but nary a curtain twitched or a whisper heard. The town was empty apart from the soul blacksmith. The whole town was deserted. Our group rode our mounts quietly and slowly, no one spoke but eyes darted nervously around, watching doorways and windows, side streets and especially the blacksmith. We had reached what I considered the centre of the town and there was still no one about, what the hell was going on? Where was everyone? All the visual signs suggested this was an active living town, but no one appeared.

We halted the horses near the blacksmith's forge and remained still. Janiz held the gaze of the blacksmith for several moments before slowly raising his empty right hand high into the air. Not a word was spoken as Janiz kept his hand above his head and remained perfectly still. Both continued to stare intently at each other while remaining mute. The suspense of the moment was astonishing, I felt my throat tighten and my heartbeat thudded in my ears, I could feel the tension in the other riders as a physical wall around me. Then there was movement. The blacksmith smoothly reached down with his hammer and gave a resounding blow to a cauldron shaped iron pot lying on the ground near his feet. A bell like chime echoed out through the town, resonating back and forth between the buildings. Within minutes the town came alive. Animan began appearing from behind doorways and buildings. Some even emerged right beside our group, where the hell had they hidden, I wondered in surprise. Children burst into the street, laughing and screaming, their games and play continuing as if nothing had happened. The blacksmith began hammering at his anvil once again, finishing whatever it was before the heat of the metal faded. Still, he and Janiz had not spoken.

'Good day Janiz,' the blacksmith finally greeted as he straightened from his work. 'I see you've some company. What can we do for you?'

'Good day blacksmith, it's good to see you again.' Janiz finally lowered his arm.

'And you Prince Janiz, but I ask again, what can we do for you?'

It was the first time I had heard someone refer to Janiz as a prince and was momentarily taken aback. It was obvious the two knew each other, however I was not inclined to use the word, friends.

'At this moment all we require is rest and to restock our supplies blacksmith, we have been without comfort for some time and it would be a welcome change to rest upon a real bed. That is all, we seek nothing else at this time.'

The blacksmith looked uncertain at this reply but chose to ignore any misgivings. He took a long careful look at each of the riders, his eyes resting on me for longer than I liked. A nod of his bearlike head signified all was well and our presence would be accepted. But not without a warning.

'You are welcome here Janiz, this time. But we want no trouble, if anyone from the king's forces shows up, you must be gone immediately. I don't want you and your animan seen here, it will only bode trouble for us. You may use the stables and the facilities of Defero providing you can pay, and be welcome. But heed my words Janiz.'

The blacksmith uttered the final sentence with what could only be described as a growl. Janiz agreed, turning round in his saddle to ensure we had all heard the blacksmith's warning, waiting for a nod of agreement from each of us before turning back to the blacksmith. Then with a curt word of thanks to the blacksmith, Janiz led us all off towards the stables. It appeared we may be staying for a while I thought as my mind deliberated on cake.

With the horses secure and being cared for, we all headed towards the inn. I wondered how a small local hostelry would cope with our numbers but no one else appeared to care. Inside the inn I was immediately surprised by the interior, I was not sure what I expected but, like the publican I visited with Sophos, this establishment shouted luxury. A small waiting room circled with soft comfortable chairs and a tiny bar welcomed us in. It rapidly became crowded with riders as the proprietor appeared behind the bar. He had my sympathy as he stared in horror at the large group of filthy riders invading his premises, however to his credit, he put on his best welcoming face and got down to business.

Janiz began by stating how many animan he had with him and confirmed we would all need a bed, a bath and a meal. Ah, I thought, let's see how the Lupus innkeeper deals with this. Again I was surprised as the innkeeper produced a large book from beneath the counter and began to organise each and every one of us. It came to light that although he could provide for some of us, he had an arrangement with some town members to cope with such large groups. Janiz and his closer riders would stay at the inn. For myself and the others, rooms would be made available in the homes of the townspeople. Now, this was an arrangement I had never encountered before and I was eager to discover how exactly it would work.

In ones and twos, the riders not staying at the inn were given directions to private homes within the town. We were informed that any costs occurring from our stay would be paid straight to the householder. We were assured we would receive the very best accommodation with clean beds and good food. We were warned that misbehaviour of any sort would not be tolerated. Any animan being rowdy, ill-mannered or troublesome would be evicted onto the streets immediately. Janiz reinforced this instruction, growling that he would personally deal with any wayward rider. I felt not one rider wished to incur the wrath of the Leo leader, I certainly didn't. So within a few moments, those riders being housed in the town each made their way to a designated billet.

Following my instructions, I walked to a neat dome house situated not far behind the inn. Once at my destination I paused to take stock of my location, ensuring I could find my way back to the inn for the meeting Janiz had ordered for that evening. My bearings firm in my mind I turned to the house where I would be staying. Looking at it I first noticed a little wooden fence running around its perimeter, enclosing a garden of sorts. Not exactly suburbia but the attempt was there. As I gazed about me, the door opened and a huge Ursidae stood glaring at me. I told him I had been sent by the innkeeper and he nodded. I remembered Janiz warning of the tough residents of this town and decided I was looking at one right now. Without a word, the homeowner stood aside and again nodded for me to enter. Not sure of my reception I quietly did as bidden. As a Tigris I was not small in any shape or form, I was tall with a body encased with hard muscle. However, as I squeezed past the resident I felt the pure strength emanating from his large solid form.

Once inside I found myself in a normal home, chairs, tables, pictures on the walls, the lot. Though all the walls were curved as is the case when living inside a dome, the main features of a domestic abode were evident everywhere. I had entered a living room of sorts, hidden from other rooms by thick curtains. There I stood, just inside the door, unsure of what to do or say so awaited further instruction from my host. Before he could speak, a curtain slipped aside and in walked another Ursidae, a female and I assumed it to be his wife. I now took little notice of what Cast the animan originated from, nor did I recoil at their appearance. I had become so accustomed to the appearance of my fellow animan that I no longer saw a female bear walking towards me, I simply saw an attractive woman and wife. She smiled at me kindly and offered me a chair at the table, brushing the seat off first with a small cloth she held in her hands.

'Hello,' she said softly, 'I am Pulchellus and this is my husband Taurum. Welcome to our home. And you are . . . . ?'

'Harry' I replied quickly, 'Harry Petroverum. Thank you for allowing me to stay here, it's very kind of you.'

'We're not being kind, you are going to pay us for our hospitality!' Growled Taurum from behind me.

'Yes I know. But still, I offer my thanks for sheltering me. I'm a complete stranger after all.' I was not going to be bullied or intimidated after all I had gone through lately. I hope my tone conveyed this fact to the hulking Taurum.

'Take no notice Har-ry,' laughed Pulchellus as she rearranged the table items in front of me. 'Petro Verum, that's an um . . . , unusual name but it sounds right.' I didn't correct her pronunciation of either of my names. Who was I to judge how others speak, not me.

'Matters not being kind. You will pay us,' demanded Taurum.

Oh hell I thought, even in this world there are miserable bastards. I dug into my bag and pulled out a few coins then held my hand out to Pulchellus and suggested she take want she needed to cover my stay. I didn't offer the coin to Taurum, I'm not that stupid. With a smile that could disarm an army, Pulchellus took several coins from my hand.

'This will do,' she said, 'we don't know how long your stay will be but this will do for now. Thank you.'

'Hummph!' was Taurum's response.

Finally, I was shown around their home, it was certainly neat and tidy though I could not help but notice two huge swords propped not far from the front door. The sleeping area had been divided into two, sensibly, Taurum did not want strangers sleeping next to his attractive wife, and I could understand this choice. My bedroom section was small, enough for two animan at a squeeze, and as at Harron's home, the floor was scattered with large cushions while woollen blankets were stacked to one side. Pulchellus then showed me the outside of their property, including the external toilet. Understandably, indoor plumbing had not reached the average animan yet. Once my basic needs were organised, Pulchellus showed me briefly what their trade was. Remembering the size and manner of Taurum, I was quite taken aback to discover the pair raised chickens. Hundreds of chickens roamed a fenced and secure field sized back yard. I have nothing against chickens and I was delighted to see yet another familiar animal that had not evolved into feathered monsters, least not from what I could see. Furthermore, I would never in a million years have written chicken farmer on Taurum's curriculum vitae.

At the conclusion of my tour, I was given notice of mealtimes along with a growl from Taurum as to the consequences if I returned to his home the worse for too much ale. I assured him I was not inclined towards over excessive drinking but from his manner, I could tell I hadn't convinced him. Then he strongly hinted that I should occupy myself for a few hours until the evening meal was ready. I could stay in my room if I wished or go and explore the town. It was clear which option he preferred me to take. So I stored my meagre belongings in my room and set off to see the sights, such as they were.

The town offered little in the way of bright lights, gambling halls or lap dance clubs so I decided upon a stroll back to the inn, looking for the company of fellow riders. I was bored, after all the recent adventures, I was bored. I realised with shock just how much I had changed in myself, in my view on life and even in my new confidence. I was bored because I was safe, relatively, no animal or animan was trying to devour or slay me and the peace and quiet of the town began to unnerve me. In my past life as an academic, I would never have dreamt in my wildest dreams, or nightmares, that I would find peace and safety tedious. My thoughts were in a reflective mood as I walked past quiet dome houses in a surreal suburbia. Several townsfolk were about, rushing on with their lives, paying scant attention other than to cast suspicious glances at me. I did not mind their avoidance as small talk and pleasantries would be strained and false. I reached the inn and discovered several of the riders lounging about outside, most leaned heavily against the walls but one, and I saw it was Secuutus had made himself comfortable upon the ground.

'Hi, what's happening?' I asked as I took up my position with my shoulder against a wall.

'Nothing yet. Seems the townsfolk aren't too happy about joining us in our fight. Janiz is still trying to persuade some of the young animan at this moment.' replied Secuutus as he turned towards the sound of footsteps nearing us from the street. We all turned with him and saw a large group of armed animan striding purposefully towards the inn. I could see Taurum amongst the group and made to speak before deciding to remain mute. The expressions on the faces of Taurum and the other town animan strongly suggested they were not here for a social evening. Without a word, half of the town animan shouldered their way into the inn, the low growls and emanating hostility causing each of the riders to finger weapons nervously. It was evident the tough folk of Defero would not take any rebuke from we riders as the remaining armed town animan formed a semicircle around us, hands held ready at their weapons. Not a word was spoken between the two groups, the riders wisely remaining in their resting pose, feigning nonchalance under the glare of the Defero animan.

'Think Janiz has got a fight on his hands in there,' muttered one of the lounging riders as more grim faced animan arrived and gathered around the inn.

I remembered Janiz had warned all his riders about this town, how tough and hostile it was and now we were seeing the evidence. Soon small spats of shouting interspersed with low growls issued from the inn as a heated discussion ensued. Outside the inn, myself and the others straightened our positions and focused all our attention on what we could hear from inside the inn. The waiting Defero animan did likewise, craning their necks forward in an effort to hear. We knew Janiz was not alone in the inn, some of the more senior riders were with him, but that did not ease our worries as they were now vastly outnumbered by the aggressive townsfolk. My boredom disappeared as the voices grew in crescendo. Suddenly the inn door burst open and out came the sullen town animan, including Taurum who still refused to acknowledge my presence. Off they stomped, back to homes or places of work, all the time muttering between themselves. Those animan gathered around us also dispersed, but only after Taurum and his group were safely away. This doesn't look good I thought.

Finally, Janiz called us inside and instructed us to find a seat. The inn was not quite able to cater for all of us so me and a few others simply made ourselves comfortable on the floor. We could tell from the expressions on the faces of Janiz and his lieutenants that the meeting had not gone well, but we already knew.

'Our plan to raise an army may require more thought than I first considered,' began Janiz once we were all settled. 'None of the townsfolk here in Defero will aid us in our fight, not even the young animan of fighting age. They say they do not wish to face the king and his armies in a fight that cannot be won. I can't blame them, it's not their fight after all. We are the outlaws here, not them. I had hoped to gain fighters from this strong town but it seems we must seek support elsewhere.'

'Could we not speak to them again? We cannot begin to build an army on a defeat,' questioned Fidelis, one of Janiz's lieutenants.

'No!' replied Janiz, 'They have made their position very clear and any further argument could put us at risk here in this town. We will stay another day to rest ourselves and our horses, but then we must seek other towns and try our luck in them.'

As a total stranger to this land and its inhabitants, I could not form an opinion on what had just happened. I knew Janiz and his riders planned a rebellion, I also knew Janiz wanted the throne, but in truth I didn't care much either way. I had my own plans and those involved the possession of the king's jade box. I would follow Janiz only as long as his plans coincided with mine. If not, then I would have to devise something for myself. How I would achieve this I had no idea, but I knew my needs must come before any uprising or rebellion. Perhaps I could discover an ally amongst the riders who would help me obtain my own goals I thought, but without conviction.

Janiz and his riders remained at the inn for the rest of the day, speculating on past and future events. I remained quiet during most of the discussions and conversation, after all, I was still new here, a human in the body of an animan. Plotting and scheming I left to those whose home this land was. The day was waning towards evening when I returned to the home of Taurum and Pulchellus, anticipating a home cooked evening meal. Later that evening I found myself sat beside a real fire, no gas, electric or other new scientific gadget designed to warm a home. Nope, I was enjoying a real log fire. I was correct in my assumption of the meal, it was delicious. Now I sat with my two hosts, warm feet and a very full belly. I had that Sunday afternoon feeling again, something I hadn't had since leaving home and my mother's Sunday roast dinners.

Small talk slowly increased between the three of us, initiated of course by Pulchellus.

Much of the talk was centred on gossip and news relating to the town and meant little to me. But then things turned slightly awkward when Pulchellus began to ask questions about my past and family. Here we go again I thought as I repeated the story suggested to me by Harron. I explained how I had fought a Hyaenidae which resulted in a blow to my head and consequent loss of all memory. At this statement, Taurum gave a slight smile and a nod of understanding but Pulchellus gasped in horror.

'You fought a Hyaenidae?' she questioned rapidly, amazement showing upon her face. 'Did you kill it? How did you kill it? They're very dangerous, why was there only one? I thought they always attacked in a pack?'

The questions bombarded me in a rush, shocking me into silence for a moment or two while I gathered my scattered wits. Taurum slowly rose from his seat and moved off to a cupboard in the room. A minute later he returned and handed me a cup of something that smelt familiar but in a strange way. I took a sip and remembered. It was the alcoholic drink I had experienced at the publican with Sophos, though there were some differences. This drink was smooth and warming, calming my nerves rather than blowing them away. I muttered my thanks, took a breath and told my tale, some of it anyway.

When I had finished, I sensed a different atmosphere in the room. Pulchellus watched me with large eyes, shock and sadness in her expression. Taurum surprised me the most, his whole demeanour changed from aggression and arrogance to someone who understood and valued what I had gone through. He offered me another drink, which I accepted, and when served, he sat and suddenly began to talk. I didn't realise Taurum could string a set of words together, so far all I had received were grunts and growls.

In a quiet voice, Taurum began to explain some of his town's history. I suspected he might be offering an explanation for the refusal to assist Janiz, I was right. Taurum told of how many years in the past, a grateful king had presented the town to his most loyal and most ferocious soldiers, a gift for services far beyond the call of duty. The town grew on its fame and over the years, numerous kings had drawn upon the young Defero animan to fight in defence of the realm. The legends grew around Defero, tales of their ferocity in battle and lack of fear in the face of an enemy were whispered across the land. Whenever a rival power attempted to invade the land of Regnum, the call went up for Defero.

Taurum sipped his drink and I noticed Pulchellus had begun to gently doze, she obviously knew this story. It had probably been ingrained into her very soul since birth.

With a glance in her direction, Taurum continued his tale in a voice so quiet I was forced to lean towards him in order to hear.

'We all felt pride in our reputation, our fighting skills and our valour,' continued Taurum, 'However, over time we realised our young animan were not returning from battle. Some sought a life elsewhere, but many never left the field of battle. Soon our numbers began to decline, no longer was Defero a town of soldiers, a town of fighters. We were growing old and times were changing about us. The military history of Defero was becoming a thing of the past, our young were dead or gone, and those who remained grew old.

My father refused to send me off to some battle or fight, as did many other parents. He did not wish to lose the few remaining young animan from the town and his feelings were shared among the other residents of the famous Defero. So our young animan no longer go to war. If war comes to us then we will face it, but no one from Defero will fight for another ever again. Now you come, you and Janiz, seeking our help to overthrow the king, a king we in Defero are still bound to, whatever the outcome. That is why we refused your plea. The animan of Defero will no longer fight and lose our young strong children. We teach our young the skills of a fighting animan still, though now it is for defence, for protection against any who might move against us. We will no longer leave home to face the call of war. Our children will stay and Defero will grow once again. No more lives from Defero will be lost to a cause, justified or otherwise.'

A silence fell between us then as I digested his words, words that made perfect sense to an academic alien. However, I could see from his manner and his expression how much this statement hurt him. His ancestors and his very life had been tightly interwoven in combat, in the art of violence, warriors for years stretching into past centuries. Now Taurum and his neighbours were learning to turn the other cheek for the sake of their children. He could not see the honour in this, but I could. I now understood why Defero refused to aid our plight, and I agreed with the reasons.

Things became quite civil between Taurum and me over the time I remained as a guest in his home. I felt it was the very first time I had truly relaxed since spending time with Sophos, although I admit the food and comfort were far superior here, Taurum accepted me and Pulchellus spoilt me. I loved it. But the time came for me to follow Janiz once again, I had to follow him for the time being. I was sure I would need him and his riders as my own plan was far from being fulfilled. After two days in Defero, our little group of riders set out to face our destinations. Janiz to reclaim his kingdom, me to find the jade box and return home. At that moment I felt sure only one of us would achieve their goal, and it probably wouldn't be me. To boost my sagging spirits, I rationalised that if Janiz was successful, surely he would be inclined to grant me a small wish and allow me access to the box. If not, then I would have to make plans of my own. But for the present, the safest place for me to be in this strange land was in amongst a group of tough and capable animan.

Chapter Ten: Burning Water

We left Defero as the sun rose, heading south again, I had no idea where I was in this land of Pangea but guessed we travelled through its centre. Nothing in this landscape indicated where we rode, I pondered on the landmass that encompassed all of the major continents. How would the characteristics of those lands I knew merge in this singularity? I gave up and went with the flow, I followed Janiz and his riders south and that was the limit of my knowledge. I could see tree covered hills stretching before me and I felt eager to experience the change of scenery. Janiz and his animan chatted idly as we rode, the day was warm and bright and for that moment at least, the world was at peace.

    We rode on for several days, seldom encountering any animan along the way. Wildlife, however, was in abundance and we regularly sat to a campfire meal of fresh meat. Piscator and Ventor, our two hunters were also competent at finding roots, berries and assorted plants to add to our menu, though I admit I received some puzzled looks when I munched happily on a fresh salad. A Tigris warrior enjoying a salad perplexed some of the riders until I stuffed a hunk of meat into my mouth. All this abundance came from a change of scenery, the grasslands were behind us and we now rode through wooded areas, some sparse while others were thick with trees, only a faint path led us onwards. The trees flowed over hills and down into valleys where streams ran clear and cool. After such a time on the flat grasslands, seeing hills again gave me pleasure, I don't know why, but they did. Hills and rocky protrusions now made up the bulk of the terrain, adding some unexpected trials for an inexperienced horse rider such as myself. Fred on the other hand, cared not a jot. He plodded on behind the others with only the occasional flick of his ears against the irritating flies to indicate he was still awake.

The temperature had fallen by a few degrees and nights were spent sat closer to a campfire, the days bright and clear. Personally, I relished the fresher air that circulated through the winding valleys. The air was clear and clean and vast numbers of birds sang their songs and soared across the sky. Their ease in the clear blue sky fostered a feeling of envy as I watched them fly effortlessly through the air. Exactly the same way as the arrow that flew past my nose!

I barely had time to register the fact that my life had been within an inch of ending before the world turned into chaos. Suddenly shouts filled the air, accompanied by the scrape of swords being rapidly drawn from scabbards.

'Scatter and find cover!' screamed Janiz as soldiers burst from the trees, descending on our group of riders as we stopped at a stream to drink.

I dismounted so fast it could only be described as falling. Scared witless at the shock attack in the beautiful landscape, I desperately scanned the area for something large to hide behind. The stream bed and its banks were littered with rocks of all shapes and sizes, my feet sliding as I scrambled over to some large boulders, sinking low to the ground behind them and tightly clutching my staff. The ground here made fighting from horseback useless, riders leapt from their saddles in a blur, each seeking either cover from the arrows or a defensive position from which to fight. The horses were left unattended and with animal wisdom, they ran from the battleground, coming to a halt some distance away.

Shouting intermingled with howls of pain, fury and fright echoed along the valley as both riders and soldiers came together. Still confused at this swift turn of events, I heard footsteps running towards my position. I dared not be caught face down in the mud and defenceless so with a bound, I leapt to my feet, searching for my opponent. There in front of me stood a Leo in a soldier's uniform, surprise showing on his face at my sudden appearance. The shock did not last more than a heartbeat before his training and skill took over. With almost a bark, the soldier swung his heavy sword at my head, which luckily was not there anymore. I had darted to one side, released the blade in my staff and turned to jab at the soldier in one flowing movement. It constantly surprised me how fast one can move when terrified. The soldier moved just as fast, blocking my staff thrust with his sword before bringing it to bear on my midriff, ready to stab. I took a rapid step backwards to avoid the blow, swinging my staff at his head in a wild and clumsy counterattack. Shock still clouding my brain.

Noting my feeble attempt, the Leo soldier paused, staring at me with huge yellow eyes, he snarled or grinned, I was in no shape to ponder. The soldier changed his stance and began moving slowly towards me, his sword held out in front of him. I realised then that he didn't consider me a threat and anticipated the easy kill. For a moment I too considered me dead, but as my feet pressed down on the rocky ground I vowed I would not die here, not now. Taking a large step backwards while feigning fear, I moved just out of reach of his sword. Switching my staff to my left hand, I bent at the waist and grabbed a rock from the ground. Straightening up in one swift movement, I threw the rock as hard as I could at the soldier's head, darting forward as soon as the rock was released. As I expected, the Leo saw the missile coming and his attention momentarily focused on the rock. His sword arm raised to knock it away and as he did so, my blade pierced his gut as I rammed the blade forward, using the superior length of the staff. Surprise widened those yellow eyes as comprehension of my trick hit home. Taking the advantage, I withdrew the blade and stabbed again, and again. Blood poured freely from the soldier's torn stomach, his sword dropped uselessly from his grip as his knees began to buckle. Once more I stabbed my blade forward, this time I struck directly at his throat. As the blade penetrated, I twisted the staff, ripping his throat apart. The fight was over and the soldier collapsed to the ground, already dead.

I did not waste time, my adrenalin was pumping as I searched for another opponent. I could hear Janiz screaming at me but failed to comprehend his words until another arrow slit my cheek. Immediately I sank to the ground, sheltered by the boulders and the soldier's body. Raising only my eyes, I scanned for the archer and found him. Standing a short distance from the stream and hiding behind the trunk of a tree, a lone archer reloading his bow. I took the opportunity to move towards him before once again diving for cover behind rocks nearer to the archer's position. Just in time, my chin slammed the ground as an arrow slid through the space my head had just vacated. Again I leapt and ran to more cover as another arrow was strung, all the time I was edging nearer the archer. It became almost a game, I moved nearer while the archer strung his bow, sinking behind cover as he drew back the bowstring. It was all down to timing, if I failed to reach cover in time, I would be dead, and the archer knew if I reached him, he would die. Timing and speed were our weapons and the loser would be the slowest. The next arrow whistled over my head, too close this time. A new approach was required; I was now only paces away and he could not miss at this proximity. Shooting to my feet, I pulled and threw the evil knife at the archer in one smooth movement as he bent his bow at me for the killing shot. The knife flew true and covered the ground between us faster than I could leap. The satisfying thud of the blade striking home was one of the most wonderful sounds I ever heard. I followed the knife at a run, stretching my powerful limbs to the utmost of my ability, I closed the distance between myself and the archer with dazzling speed. The knife had hit his shoulder, throwing off his aim and loosing the arrow harmlessly into the ground. His eyes turned to the knife handle protruding from his body before snapping back to me. That was the last thing he saw. With one last bound, I thrust forward my staff and sunk its blade into his chest, twisting it across his body as my momentum carried me a pace past him. There was no life left in the archer when I freed my staff and pulled out the knife. The killer craze was now pumping furiously inside me.

Wrenching the knife from the body, I dropped into a crouch and prepared for another attack, my staff held high in one hand, the knife low in the other. My breath panted as my body coiled in readiness, an eagerness to kill filled my mind with hate, my desire to tear and render consumed my body as I searched for another opponent. My next victim. A moment of frenzy was replaced with realisation, there were no more soldiers to rip apart with bestial ferocity. The fight was over. Janiz stood surrounded by bodies, his sword and clothing dripping red. Riders were slowly converging on him, stepping over the dozen or so carcasses of the soldiers. My legs collapsed and I fell to my knees as shock and exhaustion hit me. Confusion and relief fogged my mind as I stared dumbly at the scene beside the stream.

'You hurt Harry?' called Janiz when he caught sight of me on the ground.

'No,' I gasped in reply, 'I was lucky.'

'Lucky my arse!' quipped Secuutus as he rose from checking on one of the few dead riders. 'Fought well from what I could see. Pity you can't remember much because you fight like you were well trained in the past.'

I nodded back at him in thanks, though I had no idea if I was being complimented or ridiculed. I certainly didn't feel like a skilled fighter and certainly not a killer. I put my success down to dumb luck, I could think of no other reason. Then I remembered my pleasure, my delight at killing and shock lanced through my brain. What had happened to me? Revulsion drenched my body as I looked upon the bodies littering the ground and the riders standing numb with shock. What the hell had happened? It was all so fast. One moment we were riding peacefully through a beautiful valley, the next we were fighting for our lives.

'Quiet!' called Janiz urgently, 'Don't think this is over yet.' Silently he began to study the bodies of the soldiers, his brow furrowed in thought. 'Time to go I feel. Firmus, go round up our horses, we need to get away from here now. This was just a scouting party or vanguard, I suspect there are more troops in the area and they will certainly discover these bodies soon. We don't want to be here when they do. Let's move.'

Fear rose again in my chest as I went in search of Fred, my horse. Some of the riders were having problems with their mounts of a more skittish nature. I had no such concerns, Fred simply continued munching on grass as I approached. Swinging into the saddle almost expertly, I turned to follow Janiz. All the riders still held weapons and cast watchful eyes about them as we moved off. The rocky stream would now have to be avoided so we moved up into the trees, hoping to remain unseen and unheard, the horse's hooves muffled in the leaf litter under a canopy of green. Janiz led us up and away from the steam for about half a mile before turning ninety degrees back to the direction we had been travelling before the attack. Still no one spoke and amongst the trees the tension built. I began to grow very nervous, since arriving on the land, my surroundings had been vast and open, my visual aspect of the land unobstructed. But now I felt claustrophobic under the ceiling of branches amidst the thick woods, my field of vision reduced down to mere feet. With a shock I realised I was sweating, beads of moisture ran down the back of my neck and fell from my brow. I had no idea I would sweat in this form, do tigers sweat? I didn't think so. But here I was, sweating like a teenager with his hand edging up a girl's skirt for the first time. I was not alone, looking quickly around, I could see perspiration glistening on several of my companions. Perhaps the ability to sweat had evolved when the animan began wearing clothes? I didn't know the answer and the thought soon left my mind as Janiz gestured us to a halt.

I could faintly hear sounds of movement heading towards us. Janiz was scanning the area for a suitable escape but as yet we could not ascertain the direction from which the sounds originated. Each one of us listened with all the skills of our animal ancestors, ears straining to catch each sound, trying to pinpoint its location. Finally, Janiz gestured us further up into the woods, halting in a small heavily wooded basin. The basin was only fifty or so paces in diameter and not very deep, but hopefully just enough to lower our outline amidst the trees and undergrowth. Quietly, each rider slid from his horse while keeping a firm grip on the reins. Janiz caught my attention and indicated that I should copy the actions of the others and place my hand gently over Fred's muzzle. I did so while remembering all those cowboy films I had watched in younger years. By placing one's hand over a horse's muzzle, it reduces the possibility of the horse catching the scent of anything unfamiliar thus avoiding any whinnying or snorts that could give us away. I had no idea if this was really true but I followed suit and laid my hand over Fred's flaring nostrils. I don't know what I had on my hand but Fred was not amused and stamped a hoof in irritation. Immediately all the others turned to glare at me but Fred had made his point and became quiet.

Within moments voices could be heard, growing louder as they neared. Snatches of conversation from the oncoming soldiers drifted across the still air. I felt the ambience around our group thicken with fear. The very air seemed to become stale and heavy, catching in our throats and bringing the urge to cough, an urge that was swiftly swallowed as we remained desperately silent. We had no idea of the number of soldiers but from the sounds reaching us, the troop was certainly larger than the one we fought at the stream. If discovered, we would face the same slaughter, our band of riders could not triumph against the number of soldiers now searching, probing the forest. The voices grew very close, it seemed that within a heartbeat they would be upon us. Fear rolled down my spine and my knuckles grew white with the force of my grip on the staff. I dared not even breathe, perchance my time had come and I was about to be torn asunder, ripped from life, alone in a strange land. With a hand covering my horse's muzzle, I shrank lower, crouching as best I could, wishing the ground would swallow me up and hide me from the terror that surrounded us. The sound of undergrowth being slashed and tramped grew close as the soldiers investigated every bush and briar. Suddenly a flock of wood pigeons flapped noisily into the sky somewhere deeper in the wood, their cries and the beat of their wings cutting through the heavy air. Riders and soldiers alike froze, transfixed until a shout from elsewhere in the woods instigated a flurry of activity amongst the soldiers. I held my breath as we all listened to the sounds of the troop moving off in the direction of the shout. I realised I was still holding my breath in fear, my hand ached from grasping the staff, my other hand wet from Fred's nostrils. Moments passed in silence as we listened to the soldiers' trampling feet fade further into the distance. I did not know what had distracted them, but I was thankful for it.

'Mount up but keep it quiet!' called Janiz softly, 'let's get some more distance between us and the soldiers. It won't take them long to find our path again, then every soldier in these woods will be seeking our blood.' Forcing myself to remain calm and breathe, I led Fred on behind the group as we made our way through the woods. In the distance behind us, I could hear the shouts and commands of the officers as they gathered their troops once more. One particular officer could be plainly heard above the rest, giving orders and spurring his troops to find us. But it was one name that registered on our minds, one name shouted by the officer, one name whose head he demanded. Janiz!

We rode for the rest of the day, taking no breaks for food. Any rider needing a toilet stop had to do so at his own risk, catching the rest of the group up as best he could. Not a very pleasant experience, being on one's own in thick woods with soldiers baying for your blood. I have never urinated so fast in my entire life! Though we did not stop, we didn't rush either for fear of creating too much noise. Horses running can be heard for some distance, even in a forest. Instead, we kept up a steady walk, avoiding sound at all costs. Each rider nibbled on rations and sipped at water bottles in the saddle. I felt sorry for Fred but our pace was not sufficient to tire him and it even allowed him to swipe at any clumps of grass we passed, not that there was much on the forest floor. Finally, after hearing no further sounds of pursuit for some time, we moved back down the valley and again followed the course of the stream. Pausing just long enough for our mounts to drink, the riders climbed a safe distance from the stream and pushed on as silently as the terrain would allow. When evening approached, Janiz finally called a halt in a small clearing at the base of a craggy outcrop of rock. With that wall of stone behind us, we only had to watch our front for any signs of danger approaching, a small but welcome concession.

Wearily we made camp and cooked our evening meal on a small fire. We built a tiny wall in front of the fire so its light would not glare out over the landscape, giving our position away. Little was spoken, exhaustion weighed down our bodies, the fear of the day weighing down our minds. Hot food in our bellies helped revive our spirits though, and it was not long before muted conversations grew. There was plenty of speculation on why a troop of the king's soldiers were in this mostly uninhabited part of the land. Why would a full troop be required in an area that lay nowhere near a border, a military base or even a village? The answer was plain, we all knew it but we waited patiently while discussing idle theories we knew were false, we waited for our leader to speak.

The meal over, Janiz rose to his feet and the talking stopped, each rider now keenly interested in what the prince had to say. We all knew what he would say but we needed to hear him say it, for Janiz to give voice to our thoughts, and fears.

'We have just fought a small group of my father's soldiers and we have run from his troops. We all know, possibly not Harry, but the rest of us know that soldiers don't patrol this forest, no one of significance lives here, no bandits roam, no traders come here and this area has no strategic value. So why were the soldiers here? They were searching for me, plain and simple.' Janiz paused to turn and looked at each of us in the eye, holding our gaze for long moments before continuing. 'It is clear that the sorcerer wants my head. That I understand. It is also clear that the lives of each of you are in danger because of me. That we all understand.' Janiz held up a hand to quiet the muted calls of support from the group of animan.

'What I did not understand, what I could not explain, was how the king knew we would be here? Travelling through this very wood on this very day. That I did not understand, but now I know.'

Silence greeted this statement. There could be only one explanation, one of us was a traitor! As each rider assimilated this information, all eyes slowly turned to me. I was one of the newcomers, the strange one in their midst. I was the obvious suspect. Oh crap, I thought, what do I say? How can I convince them that I am not a traitor, who would I trait to? I didn't know anyone, hell I didn't even know who I was! Low growls began to issue from the throats of the animan, hands reaching for weapons as their eyes burned on me. I began to rise, ready to run for my life, I knew there would be no reasoning with them as I clenched my buttocks and tensed my frame. I would not kill anyone I decided, they were, or had been my friends, my only friends in this land. If I died, so be it, but I would not fight.

'Steady down, I have not finished!' barked Janiz, cutting through the tension and stopping the riders from committing murder, namely mine. 'Rest your hands and stay your weapons. Harry is not at fault, nor are anyone of you. My answer came when I remembered a nagging suspicion that has bothered me for days. We are being followed. I began noticing a furtive shape that always appeared to be in the same vicinity wherever we rode, never coming too close but never completely out of sight. I believe this shadowy animan is our betrayer. I believe he works for the king, or more likely, the sorcerer. We travel closer to the palace with each day, and although we are but a small group, I suspect we offer fear to the sorcerer and he will inevitably increase his efforts to thwart us. He wishes to stop me gaining access to my father and confronting the sorcerer himself. I believe he will stop at nothing, nothing at all to stop this from happening. He will try to frighten us off or kill us if we get too close. We all need to consider the possibility that we may be defeated, we may die. The shadow that follows us acts as the sorcerer's eyes and ears. We are a threat to his plans, so he now takes steps to ensure our demise.'

A silence followed his words before erupting into a babble of voices, each rider giving vent to his anger and offering promises to gut and render this elusive spy travelling in our wake. I was now completely forgotten and hopefully, forgiven. All the attention was on who it was that followed us. How we could trap and kill him. As the indignant voices grew around the camp, Janiz raised a hand and spoke a few words that quietened all mid voice.

'He may be listening now,' was all he muttered.

Immediately all the riders fell silent. Each one understanding that they may unwittingly inform the spy of their plans, the trees have ears was a phrase that sprung to mind. As silence descended on the group, Janiz caught my eye and gestured for me to speak. Suddenly I realised what he intended. If the spy was close, our lapse into silence would warn him of our suspicions. We needed to keep him unawares. I began to talk, I rambled and chatted, about nothing and meaning nothing, I simply gave vent to my voice. The riders all peered at me as if I had lost my mind, Firmus even growled at me to shut up and be quiet, but I kept talking. I could see Janiz signalling to Fidelis and another rider, instructing them to stealthily search the area around the camp and locate the spy if he was near.

At last, the remaining riders caught on to Janiz's subterfuge and a low but largely nonsensical conversation grew, each rider giving voice to his own random thoughts. Eventually, as is always the case, a real string of conversation began to emerge, and it was centred on me. First Secuutus and finally all the riders expressed their apologies for doubting me, some were more believable than others I admit. I replied that I understood their fears, I was strange to them after all. It was one of the weirdest conversations and apologies I had ever had. Each rider was attempting to rationalise their suspicions and make an apology without giving away any information to prying ears that may lie in the darkness.

Finally, I had endured all I could of this form of talk, I felt as if I was back in the classroom, attempting to make sense of modern teenage speak. I decided it was time for some direct questions, so turning to face Janiz, I asked him to tell me more about this alleged sorcerer. What was he like, how he acted and what he was called? The other riders fell silent as Janiz considered my questions.

I was not sure he was going to reply at first, but with a frown, he began. 'I do not know who the sorcerer might be, he appeared as a stranger, much like you although when found, he rambled and screamed so much, we considered him damaged in the head. However, within some weeks, he began to show wisdom, he became quite a communicator, offering advice and guidance to all who sought it. Animan would pay him for advice on a range of topics, from health to matters of the heart. He had an answer for all. The word quickly spread of his gift, his ability. Animan began calling him a wise animan or a Sage. In just a short time he became powerful and his fame reached across the land. Animan whispered his name in fear and awe, his wisdom attaining acclaim that soared above that of a simple sage. But that was only the beginning.' Janiz paused, collecting his thoughts before continuing.

'Soon the words that spread spoke of magic and sorcery. We had not known the like before, animan believed his words and fear grew. He warned of demons, spirits and devils that roamed the land and preyed on animan, stealing their life force. Many would have doubted the sorcerer but he could make things happen that we had no knowledge of. Demons appeared at his command, fire did his bidding and he controlled all through the strength of his magic. He became rich, dangerous and so powerful, all were afraid to challenge him but all still sought his counsel and paid well for his words. Inevitably he came to the attention of my father, the king. The sorcerer was summoned to the palace for an audience with the king. And there he stayed and is there to this day.'

Several riders nodded in agreement at Janiz's description of the sorcerer, they, of course, all knew of what Janiz had told me, it was old news to them. It was me alone that had no knowledge of either the sorcerer or the king, hell I didn't even know what day it was. All the riders had fallen quiet, sitting on blankets or nibbling on the remains of their meal. We all knew the dangers we faced, we all knew many would not survive our attack on Janiz's home and palace. I could not imagine what the others were thinking but it was a safe guess they were as troubled as I. However if there was one thing I had learned about these animan, it was the fact that they would not falter. They would not deviate from their path, a path set by Janiz, the rightful heir to the throne, an outlaw.

A shrill scream ripped through the air, startling everyone into diving for their weapons. The scream curtailed abruptly, the silence of the night falling once again. The riders edged backwards towards the fire, forming a tight circle. I followed suit and soon we had eyes on every inch of the surrounding area. I realised this may not be the wisest move as the fire illuminated the circle of riders, sending silhouettes out like spokes on a wheel. But then I considered our defensive circle further, with the fire behind us we would easily see anyone coming into its light. All a potential attacker would see would be black shapes against the light of the fire. Perhaps this wasn't such a bad move I decided. We waited, the fire at our backs sending flickering shapes across the ground. We waited silently, swords, knives and a staff bristling from the circle like a crown of thorns.

'We're coming in!' called a voice from the darkness. Sounds began to emanate from the trees and soon after, the two riders sent off by Janiz returned, dragging a body between them. The defensive circle broke up as everyone moved to inspect the corpse. A couple of riders even prodded it with their swords, just to be sure it was dead. Janiz ordered every one of us, including me, to examine the body in case anyone could offer an identity. No one could, the dead animan was unknown to us. Janiz indicated Secuutus search for clues on the body, but other than a few coins and a package of dried meat, nothing of use came to light. Whoever the spy was would remain a mystery, and that in turn sparked a new question. Were there more like him? Were there more shadows following us, more spies lurking? We all agreed it would be safer to assume that there were and take all necessary precautions on our journey. With the body of no further use to us, it was dragged off into the trees, well away from our camp. The scavengers would see to its disposal, but we did not want them coming too close to our camp that night.

Morning came and we set off once again, still travelling south, still destined to follow the path set by our leader, Janiz. The loyalty given to Janiz by his riders was indisputable, as for myself, I still had plans of my own and Janiz was simply an aid to my own goal. My thoughts were divided, yes my personal goal was important to me, but Janiz and his animan were also very important to me. I would do all I could to help him on his quest. I liked the company of the riders and Janiz had proven his ability to lead. I was happy to follow, providing his goal did not impair the achievement of my own. I still sought to return to my own world and my 'normal' life and for that, I needed access to the king's jade box. However I had to admit, this life with the animan held more excitement and more camaraderie than I had ever experienced before. I pondered if I sincerely missed my previous life that much? I was not so certain. Nevertheless, I desperately needed to be sure, and that would not happen until I held that green jade box in my hands. Then I would decide, then I would choose to open it, or not.

We travelled for several days, stopping at any towns or villages that we encountered.

In each place we received the same negative response to our plea to raise an army. Our cause was supported, but only with good wishes. None of those in authority in each of the communities would offer their young strong animan, always giving the same reasons as we received in Defero. Janiz was hugely popular with townsfolk and farmers alike, wherever he went, but the threat from the king was too powerful. I understood their reluctance, apart from paying royal taxes, most communities lived in peace and all believed their king would protect them. If it were discovered they had assisted Janiz, their peace and safety would no longer be assured. There was a faint light at the end of the tunnel however. Young animan are as strong minded and hot blooded as any human male, and as we left each town, village or farm, at least one young animan would defy his elders and sneak out at night to join our group. In just a few days, the number of riders had swelled to more than thirty. Not an army agreed, but thirty riders can make an imposing sight.

    The new recruits were assimilated into the group as quickly as possible, one was sent home due to a strong spirit but very poor health. Janiz feared he would not stand the strain of riding long distances day in and day out. But in the main, the new riders were fit, eager and useless with a blade. It fell on Fidelis to teach them how to fight without amputating their limbs. Some of the other experienced riders offered to help with the training. When I asked Secuutus why they were keen to help, he answered that it was in everyone's interest when it came down to facing an opponent. I had to agree, I was still only learning myself, though my inbred instincts as a Tigris seemed to cope quite well. Nonetheless, bearing in mind my lack of experience in slicing and dicing other beings, I too joined the training sessions, learning what I could while I could.

As yet we had not come face to face with any more soldiers, but the signs indicated a definite increase in military movement in the area. On several occasions we were forced to make time consuming detours to avoid patrols, simply hiding amongst the trees was difficult with a large group. On a couple of occasions when caught in open ground, a rapid flight was our only option, but mostly we kept to the safety of the trees. All of the original riders kept a wary eye out for solitary figures following us, but our fear was wasted on the newcomers. A threat is never taken seriously by the young until they have experienced the presence of their own mortality. At least they had the sense to watch for soldiers, but a lone shadow failed to dent their newly found confidence. It was not long before a new shadow had been seen, it was clear the king or his sorcerer was keeping abreast of our actions. At this point, we were still too far away from the palace to warrant sending out the troops in force, but in war, intelligence is everything.

Our plan to raise an army was not going to happen so that night, as we all rested in camp, Janiz spoke of his disappointment. A full discussion followed with many riders offering suggestions and plans. Most would need a miracle to succeed, but in my opinion, one or two of the ideas appeared within the bounds of possibility. However, I was at a disadvantage on the subject. I had never seen the palace, the land was alien to me and I did not believe in sorcerers and magic. I had never experienced armed hand to hand combat before arriving in this land, certainly not mortal combat, and I had only just gotten used to riding a damn horse! So I could contribute little to the discussion, but I did listen and I listened intently. The talking continued late into the evening, sometimes heated as one rider considered his plan to be the best, other times the talk dried up as each rider attempted to use their mental abilities to find a solution. Not successfully, it became evident, as we finally settled into our blankets without reaching any conclusions.

The journey continued the next day, the monotony was beginning to tell on several of the group, including me. There was only so much interest to be gained from staring at the scenery around us and, in my case as I rode towards the rear of our group, no interest in staring at a horse's arse all day long. I began to wish for some excitement, strange as I would never have considered myself as an action person, but now the tedium of the journey was getting to me. This came as a genuine shock, realising I actually missed the violence, the do or die thrust of combat, the adrenalin that coursed through my body as a result of pure fear. I had been a peaceful science lecturer in my past life, the only danger I had experienced came from hooded figures hanging around the streets at night. Now, here I was, experiencing true terror, true fear, and I loved it! I've finally lost my mind I rationalised. Nevertheless, some of the young newcomers shared my feelings and began to give vent to their frustration, bickering and verbally sniping at each other. Janiz ignored this for a while before snapping at them to be quiet and remain watchful. A peaceful landscape did not guarantee there was no one hiding in ambush. That shut them up for a time, but not totally.

Noon arrived and Janiz called a halt, more to give his riders a break than necessity. We had not seen any sign of soldiers for some time and even our shadow had disappeared. I knew this was not necessarily a good thing, he could simply be hiding more effectively than before. Whatever the reason behind the unexpected rest, I was thankful. My bladder was becoming increasingly uncomfortable being constantly bounced up and down on my horses back. Slipping from the saddle, I took time to straighten and stretch the various limbs that ached before securing Fred to a low bush, allowing him plenty of room to graze. Eventually, the urge became overpowering and as all was quiet I sneaked off behind some trees to relieve myself. From the sounds of splashing water around me, I knew I was not the only one eager for relief. Finished, I wandered back to the group hoping to grab a short nap. Many of the riders were taking the opportunity to refresh their drinking water from the pond and I decided I should do the same. I retrieved my water bottle and followed the others over to the pond or small lake or whatever. Remember, I was a city lad and so had no real concept of ponds or lakes, puddles on the pavement were my sole area of expertise.

    I was behind the group, just about to take my place at the water's edge when something caught my eye. I heard a slight rustling in the trees and instinctively reached a hand down for my knife. A flicker of movement caught my eye as something flew through the air and landed in the opposite side of the water with a faint plop. I relaxed again, naturally taking no notice, assuming it was a bird or a very talented frog that had dived into the water. I had not seen it clearly and was not concerned. I reached the edge and sank to my knees to submerge my bottle under the surface, carefully filling it to the brim. I had replaced the stopper when I noticed something was creating ripples in the water. A sound came from the pond, one I could not identify but assumed it was the local wildlife. The fauna of this land held little interest for me at that moment and I looked no further.

'The water boils!' came the cry from one of the riders at the water's edge. I sprang to my feet, knife in hand and scanned the trees around the pond, fully alert for danger. Certain that no threats came from the trees, I finally focused on the water itself and received a shock. The rider's cry was correct as sure enough, the water's surface was bubbling as if boiling. I could see something white skittering about on the water. Venting what I thought to be steam and moving like a skater on ice, it slid rapidly across the water in random directions, leaving a wake of bubbles and steam behind it. All the riders were glued to the spectacle before them, myself included. Hands began reaching for weapons as animan eyes widened with fear. A memory attempted to be known in my mind as I watched the events on the surface of the pond. Vapour began to rise higher from the blob as its speed across the water increased, giving the appearance now of actually hovering a hair's width above the surface. Suddenly the white blob began to burn, spitting sparks into the air, resembling a water wraith in fury. Then in a bright burst of flame, the blob exploded, sending a column of white cloud into the air.

All the riders at the water's edge leapt away in fright at this new phenomenon, they had never seen the like before and their wide eyes and cries gave evidence of their fright. All this had taken place in mere moments, the spectacle was over, leaving a few small ripples on the water's surface. I stood peering at the water as it calmed and became still once more. I had not leapt away from the water's edge, curiosity now had a firm grip on my mind. I realised what I was seeing was not a jet powered fish, or a water nymph, though at that moment, I could not identify what I had witnessed. Somehow it struck a chord deep in my mind. I knew what it was but could not recall, a fact which infuriated me. I knew I should remember but in these strange surroundings and amidst all the recent changes and events in my life, straight thinking was a step too far.

With my mind attempting to combat senility and regain its memory, my eyes registered a second flicker of silver fly through the air and splash into the water. My brain fired into gear and I realised what was happening.

'Run!' I shouted at the stunned riders as I bounded away from the water, not stopping to see if they followed. I knew I did not need to run far, as long as I was away from the water. I flung myself to the ground and turned to watch the spectacular show being performed on the pond's surface. I took a brief glance to see where the riders were. I need not have worried as they were already some distance from the pond, standing rigid as statues in fear at the sorcery of the pond, fear of a foe they could not see.

Instantly there came a loud hissing followed by clouds of white vapour streaming from a grey object that skidded over the surface of the water. Suddenly, flashes of lilac coloured sparks lit up the area around the pond, bright flashes resembling a cheap firework display. Then the sound of an explosion tore through the air. It seemed the very air over the pond ignited, joining with the water spout shooting up from the surface as the light from the explosion faded. A burst of lilac flame, an explosion and pond water erupting upwards into the sky against the backdrop of the trees. Pandemonium broke out amongst the animan, hands were thrown up to cover ears and swords were snatched from scabbards while other riders dived to the ground. I was unharmed as I knew I would be, though I was splattered with pondweed and slime. I rose from my prone position as the echo of the explosive bang disappeared off into the distance and turned to check the riders. All but one had run back to the camp and Janiz. The remaining rider stood transfixed with what had happened. I could see he was not physically hurt but pond water dripped off him like rain. A direct result of pond water thrown into the air and landing on the slow reacting animan. Should I laugh I wondered, but then realised it may not be a good idea as the terrified sounds of panic issued forth from the riders now standing in shock around the campfire.

I realised all the riders were terrified by this strange event, I suspected they had never seen water explode before, it's not exactly an everyday occurrence after all. I decided I would have to calm things before panic set in full. Words would not suffice, that I knew, so it had to be an action or a gesture. Bearing in mind, the focus of their fear lay with the exploding pond, so it was the pond I had to begin with. I walked calmly over to the edge of the now quiet pond, knelt down on the bank and peered into the darkness of the water. What I expected to find I had no idea, but I felt sure I knew what had just happened. I hoped to hell that my theory of what happened was correct, otherwise my next actions could be my last. Glancing back I could see the riders clutching their weapons, darting eyes searching for dangers rising from the water. Janiz alone, stood watching me, though fear lined his Leo features. Deciding on a plan, I slowly dipped my cupped hand into the water and lifted it to my lips. Immediately shouts of horror and shock issued from the riders as they realised what I was doing. I drank amidst cries of warning.

'Get away from the water!'

'Are you mad? The water is cursed!'

'Run Harry, run! A demon must reside in that pond, run!'

I ignored their shouts and drank, turning to face them as I did so, hoping like crazy that I was right and they were wrong. I don't believe in demons and such, but if one rose from the water now, I would die of fright long before it got its claws into me. Nothing happened of course and after drinking, I carefully stood up and walked towards the camp and its terrified riders. I noticed several drew back as I neared, clearly suspicious of my actions. I raised my hand to wipe my moist mouth and gave the loudest satisfying sound I could make, showing all I had enjoyed my drink of pond water. Pond water! What the hell was I thinking? I would never have even placed a hand in the pond waters of home. Heaven knows what I would have found lurking in the water, shopping trolleys, discarded condoms and a wide range of assorted plastic, not to mention chemicals leached from the surrounding land, and the old favourite, human waste!

'Calm yourselves!' I commanded as I reached the circle of riders, 'I feel our sorcerer friend has been up to his tricks again. There was no demon, no sorcery, just clever tricks to frighten us from our intended path. Something was thrown into the water just as we began to drink, someone else was here. It was a trick used to create fear and panic. Calm yourselves and look at me, I'm alive and well.'

'Did you see who it was?' asked Janiz.

'No, I didn't, all I saw was something being thrown into the water, but I didn't manage to see the thrower himself.' I replied, realising what Janiz was thinking.

'Appears our shadow has caught us up,' was the response that proved my assumption correct.

Any further discussion with Janiz was drowned by a flood of cries and questions from the riders. The next few minutes were spent attempting to answer the rush of questions while trying to overcome the superstitious fear that gripped them all. When relative quiet was achieved, I racked my brain to find an explanation I could give that would make sense to a group of animan scared witless. Unfortunately, I failed, their beliefs and fears were too strong. My explanations were shouted down, I could not persuade the animan that what had happened at the pond was not sorcery, not magic but trickery. I could not say what I knew because there was no way in hell these animan would understand a chemistry lesson. I resorted to terms they may grasp, hopefully. I explained what we all witnessed was a simple trick, probably by one of the sorcerer's agents. I told them I had seen something thrown into the water just before all the spectacular effects burst into the air.

Still, I could not make them believe, instead of registering my use of the word trick, they focused on the fact I had accused the sorcerer, thus what happened became a magic spell in their irrational minds. Only Janiz appeared to grasp what I was saying, he, after all, knew the sorcerer better than any of us. The day had waned by the time all the questions and hysteria had quietened, and it was too late in the afternoon to continue our journey. As evening fell, an uneasy calm returned as each rider began readying their blankets, building a fire and collecting rations for a meal. The muttering about demons, the sorcerer and my eccentric actions continued but now subdued. I noted that many riders sat with their backs to the fire again, obviously not reassured that the danger was past. The fire was built higher than necessary in an attempt to drive off the night and its horrors and eventually, the camp lay to rest.

As for myself, I could not rest. I knew what I had seen and recognised the reactions from my previous life as a scientist. School children would delight over these chemical reactions. Young men would try to impress the pants off young girls with their feats of daring, performing these reactions on a larger scale in ponds and lakes across the land. There were no demons nor was it the result of sorcery, it was chemistry. From what I had seen, my scientific experience deduced the first substance thrown into the pond was a lump of sodium, judging from the orange colour of the flames. Sodium reacts with water and so does potassium, and I suspected potassium was the second substance lobbed into the water. Potassium has a greater reactivity with water than sodium and burns lilac. The whole episode was planned to have the maximum effect on minds, beliefs and superstitions on a par with the early medieval times in human history. Maybe the king's sorcerer was not such a charlatan after all? Perhaps the so-called sorcerer had knowledge of alchemy and used such tricks to gain his lofty position at the king's side? I could not be certain but remembered the recent occurrence of hallucinogenic mushrooms and mass hysteria resulting in the riders seeing demonic apparitions. The use and knowledge of chemical reactions certainly pointed at a formidable foe who may be more than just a clever trickster. I eventually fell asleep while pondering how the sorcerer managed to isolate sodium and potassium in a land that still used swords, spears, bows and arrows.

The next day dawned bright and we breakfasted lightly from our supplies. Not much was said about the events of the previous night, but I could almost taste the mood of suspicion, fear and uncertainty directed at me. Few of the riders spoke to me, most appeared to be surreptitiously avoiding me. I gave a mental shrug, there was nothing I could do or say that would calm their fears and place them at ease. These riders were accustomed to bloodshed, comrades dying hacked to pieces in front of them, being torn apart by wild animals and all kinds of violence in their lives. But fear of the unknown mastered all, untouchable, invisible fears based on superstition, belief and even religion, these were the worst.

We broke camp and continued our journey, the riders remained distant from me for most of the morning until Secuutus manoeuvred his horse alongside me once again. Secuutus and I had become good friends during my time spent with Janiz and his riders. Perhaps it was the fact that I didn't mind his constant chatter, I learnt more from him than I could have hoped for from any of the others. Secuutus was a huge animan, not as tall as any Leomen or Tigris, but he was certainly built like a bull, or a bear to be correct. From the odd glimpse of him during a fight, fear was not high on his list, brute force and blood lust along with superb swordsmanship made Secuutus a deadly opponent. But when not attempting to tear someone's head off, Secuutus was just a genial and talkative companion, very talkative most would say.

'You've frightened them Harry,' were the first words Secuutus spoke.

'Why? Why would I frighten them? I'm the one who should be frightened, I have no idea who I really am or where I am, what is there to frighten anyone? Do I frighten you Secuutus?' I replied after a moment.

'Yes, I suppose you do, in a way. You do not fear demons or burning water, you know things that only someone of power should know. Yet here you are, riding with us to fight a king you have never seen or heard of until recently. You are a Tigris warrior but your fighting skills are outlandish, though effective it must be said. You have no memory and little knowledge of this land, but you show no fear in the face of sorcery. Yes, you frighten me Harry, because I do not understand you.'

I paused to ponder his words, wondering if I should confess just how terrified I have been ever since I awoke in this place. Everything frightened me, the animan and especially the wild beasts that had evolved into a whole new level of nightmare. Even the very odd fact that here I was, a tiger riding a horse called Fred while chatting to a huge bear called Secuutus. Yes, I was frightened, terrified of all I saw in this land. A thought struck me, this land was decidedly alien to me but as yet I had not considered time. I had categorised my surroundings in a period that resembled the medieval era on my world, but was it? Was I in the future or the past? Had this land existed before or after my time, or did it run parallel? Swords and horses, kings and sorcerers all indicated a medieval period, but what of those dome houses? Surely this greater level of construction pointed to a higher level of intelligence? I immediately dismissed this comparison, I was sure that medieval masons had the skills and knowledge to build a dome structure if they wished. Just take a look at the churches and cathedrals that still exist, all gave evidence to the abilities of medieval human builders. And that is not taking into consideration what the Romans built in their heyday. No, the use of dome structures must just be indigenous to this land, I could not use this argument to establish the era in which I found myself.

'There is nothing to understand Secuutus,' I answered finally. 'I am alone in myself with no memories to aid me. I follow Janiz and ride beside you because I don't know any different.' I quickly raised my hand to halt his interruption, quickly explaining my statement before I offended him.

'I may not know any different but I do know that I value the friendship you and the riders have shown me, I would be lost, and most likely dead, without you. At first, I followed to survive, but now I follow as part of the group, tied by bonds of friendship and camaraderie. Your goals have become my goals, your life is as valuable to me as my own. That is why I ride with you, Janiz and the others.'

It seemed I had said the right things for Secuutus fell silent, not for long I admit, but enough to show he was considering my words. After a few moments and still without uttering a word, Secuutus reached out one massive hand and gave my shoulder a gentle squeeze, a gesture recognised in any world, a gesture that spoke of understanding, support and friendship, even loyalty. I was touched, deeply touched by this small action performed by an animan who normally would choose a tirade of words. I was also secretly grateful he had not squeezed my shoulder too hard, with hands that size, I feared my bones would break. Normal service resumed within moments and Secuutus reverted to his usual chatty self, talking about anything and everything as we rode side by side behind Janiz and his growing band of riders. That brief snatch of emotion and truth now laid behind us, now we were riders, outlaws and mercenaries once again.

Chapter Eleven: Trapped!

The next few days of travel proved uneventful and the rider's suspicion of me ebbed, not entirely but enough to engage in conversation again. Janiz remained thoughtful and more distant than before. I put this down to the stress of leadership and the battles he alone must face. We had managed to hunt fresh meat to restock our supplies, and consumed in one of the best stews I had ever tasted, the rest was salted and dried before being distributed amongst the riders as provisions. Ventor and Piscator managed to bring down a couple of good sized antelope, or deer, I was not sure and cared less. Whichever it was, the meat tasted delicious!

    Journeying onwards under a clear sky with full bellies and no one trying to kill us was a situation I feared would not last long. Already our solitary shadow had been observed, once more at a distance, stalking us. After the incident at the pond, it was decided our shadow was no threat as long as we could still see him. If we lost sight of him, then we would start to worry. Along the way, we had come across small communities and the odd town but we received the same response, no help was offered. We had not seen any more patrols for a while, a fact that worried us, surely the search for us was still on? The lack of patrols and the constant presence of the shadow gradually began to grate on our nerves, the threat of battle being outweighed by the fear of the unknown. A visible enemy filled our desire for certainty, and nothing is more certain than someone attempting to lop one's head off in a fight.

As our journey carried us nearer to the palace and the city of Urbem Regium, farms, homesteads and communities began to increase. Instead of travelling days without seeing or meeting another animan, now it was almost every day. Most of the communities we now avoided, not wishing to be betrayed or slaughtered in our sleep by royal supporters or those with reward on their minds. On occasion, Janiz sent small groups of riders into homesteads and farms to purchase supplies and obtain any information available. Only once were the riders chased from the property, the farmer, his sons and farmhands mistaking the riders for bandits, but most were happy for the chance to earn coin.

I wished for a Premier Inn, Travel Lodge or even a youth hostel, sleeping on the hard ground had lost any idealistic appeal it may once have had. Now I wished for a soft bed, a meal that did not consist of reheated dried meat, roots and berries. The thought of a full Sunday roast hinged on insanity in its intensity. I was not alone, several of the riders had also begun to express their need for basic creature comforts once again. Finally, Janiz listened and plans were made to take rest at the first suitable and safe location.

Finding a safe and secure location proved harder than we thought. Most places of habitation we encountered were either too small for such a large group, or not safe in which to hide. The majority were small homesteads, lone cottages or farms, what we needed was a town. Janiz assured us we would find a suitable place as we neared the city of Urbem Regiam. In any land and any country, people always flock towards the seat of power, in this case, the palace. In my own worlds medieval times, homes, businesses and trades all conjugated around castles and churches. They became the focal point of the population and many grew into cities. It appeared the same applied here, people gravitated towards a common central location, with a dense population in the centre and rippling out into smaller settlements and towns before thinning out to farms and smallholdings. It was through this outer band of farms and smallholdings we travelled on our route to the city and the palace.

Janiz knew this area very well, he grew up here and, in his eyes, he was coming home. The riders and I trusted his local knowledge and were content to follow him, it was clear he had a destination in mind. We rode at a steady pace, only losing time when soldiers were seen in the vicinity. We all expected the number of soldiers to increase as we neared the city, so none were surprised. It quickly became obvious that we would have to continue our journey in stealth, keeping away from fields of farmworkers, animal herders and other travellers. We avoided the main routes and roads that could lead to an encounter with the king's soldiers or local militia, smaller groups of armed animan who enforced the king's law in the outlying areas. We rode, travelled and acted like the outlaws we were.

We had travelled on, twisting and turning across the countryside, following a course set out by Janiz. We placed our trust in him and eventually we were proven correct. We had camped in a wood, thick with undergrowth and hidden from all but the most inquisitive eyes. The fire was kept small to avoid its light revealing our presence and all talk was muted and whispered. We all knew the danger in being this close to civilisation, albeit still some distance from the city itself. When the evening meal was finished and all riders settled, Janiz stood and indicated we should listen.

'Tomorrow we will reach the settlement of Tutique Receptus. Those that live there are ordinary people living their lives in peace. We will not be welcomed but nor do we want to be. We must try to blend in and raise no suspicions. Ordinary folk want ordinary lives and a large group of outlaws entering their quiet town will inevitably be reported to the local authorities, bringing soldiers down on our heads. We must be very careful here, I know we all need rest from riding and fresh supplies but we must remain hidden within sight.'

At this remark, many of the riders looked at Janiz in confusion, the question clearly written on their faces. How can one hide in plain sight?

Janiz sought to clarify, 'I mean we must merge into the population, pose as traders, work seekers, pretend to be visiting relatives perhaps? But no, that may give rise to some awkward questions. Best stick to something that can't be tied to someone who actually lives in the town. Traders like I said, or farmhands looking for work and in some cases,' Janiz looked directly at me, 'perhaps even travelling mercenaries seeking coin. Use whatever you feel best suited to you but *do not* draw attention to yourselves. Understood?'

Most of us nodded or grunted in confirmation, but one of the younger riders spoke up with a question I had not even considered. A huge fact I and no doubt most of the others had overlooked.

'Um. How can we not raise suspicion or be hidden?' The young rider paused to sweep a hand round at the large group of riders. 'If we all ride into the town, I'm pretty certain someone will notice.'

Janiz grinned, I got the impression he had been waiting for this very question to arise. Moving further into the circle of riders, Janiz drew his dagger and squatted within the light of the fire. He brushed a small area of the ground clear of leaves and detritus before using his dagger to make marks in the hard soil.

'Tutique Receptus is situated on a crossroads, in fact you could say that it *is* the crossroads. It's a walled settlement with four gates, these gates give access to each of the four roads, and travellers must pass through the town in order to journey on these roads. Yes, one may circumnavigate the outskirts but it's a big town and would add unnecessary time to a journey. Most road users travel through the town, it is safe and one can purchase items along the way. Anyone seen taking the long route around the town would immediately arouse suspicion.'

Janiz paused to examine our faces, making sure we were paying attention. 'We will enter the town in ones and twos, perhaps some of our younger riders may form a group up to three, but no more. Once in the town, it will be everyone for themselves. Find lodgings, stable your mounts, refresh your supplies and rest. On no account join other riders unless the situation gives an excuse, in a publican for instance. Otherwise, stay away from each other, stay with the rider who you entered the town with, do not seek out any others.'

'How will we communicate? We will need to know when it's time to leave and learn of any plans made,' asked Secuutus with a frown.

'Good question. Fidelis will circulate amongst you and keep all informed. I'm afraid I am too well known and will have to remain hidden much of the time. Do not look for me, I will find you.'

'If you're so well known, and I suppose you would be, being the prince and all, where will you stay? It's not as if you can walk into a hostelry or inn without being recognised.'

'Ah Secuutus, trust you to be the one with all the questions. I will rest your mind, I have friends in the town, not many sadly but one or two that will hide me. I will head for one of these friends and beg for shelter. I will be safe and hidden so I might rest also. Does that answer you, Secuutus?' queried Janiz as he looked at the huge Ursidae with raised eyebrows.

Having received a nod from the huge rider, Janiz continued outlining his plans. We were all to find our own accommodation the best we could. Janiz stressed that we must not divulge any information about ourselves, the riders or our objective to anyone, not even a pretty barmaid. Here Janiz paused and stared knowingly at Fidelis, who had the grace to look away sheepishly. Janiz told us we were to stay in the town for three days, enough to recuperate ourselves and our horses. On the third day, if we had heard nothing to the contrary, we were to ride out the south gate and meet up an hour later along the road. Janiz himself would leave town at dawn and find a suitable place to regroup, so all we had to do was ride along the road until we met up with him. A simple plan, what could go wrong? In conclusion, Janiz made sure we all understood the plan, reiterating it for those whose minds operated at a slower speed than the rest.

The next day the riders travelled as a group until Janiz decided we were close enough to Tutique Receptus but far enough away from prying eyes. Apart from our shadow of course, and most of us had pushed him to the back of our minds by then. From there we set off in stages, one or two riders leaving and riding towards the town at half hour intervals. Secuutus and I decided to travel together as we had for much of the journey so far. We were relaxed in each other's company so it seemed obvious. As we both looked the part, we were to pass ourselves off as mercenaries seeking work. To be honest, we would not have to act much as we were both huge, heavily armed and fearsome, a fact that amused me. A fierce science lecturer, whatever next? If only my students could see me now. If they did, I suspect their behaviour in class might just improve somewhat. Our time came and Janiz sent us off along the southern route into Tutique Receptus.

Tell-tale signs in the sky indicated we were nearing the town, a haze of wood smoke hung visibly in the air, long before the town itself came into view. Eventually, we came to the first, or northern gate that offered entrance to the town. The gates stood about ten foot high and were elaborately constructed of metal, iron I assumed. A wall of some fifteen foot encircled the whole town with periodic towers that looked over the surrounding landscape. The towers appeared in need of serious repair and I suspected they had not been used in anger for many years. A comforting thought as it gave proof to the lack of security in the area. No one questioned us as we rode through the gates, though guards in makeshift uniforms stood idly beside what I took to be a guardhouse.

At first, Secuutus and I rode past orchards and areas planted with vegetables along with small paddocks containing livestock. I certainly got the impression that this town bordered on self-sufficiency, a useful state to be in if a wandering army decided to lay siege to the place. We had passed farms and fields that covered the land surrounding the town on our way to the gates, food it seemed, would not be in short supply here. Leaving the orchards and paddocks behind, we began to enter the town itself. The first homes were large with manicured gardens, huge white dome structures that shouted wealth, obviously the rich quarter of the town.

Next came smaller but still well maintained houses of suburbia a few streets before the mad jumble of the town burst into confusion. Houses and businesses appeared to spring up randomly. Streets both wide and narrow shot off from the road upon which we travelled, heading off in all directions. Soon the main street itself began to fill up with businesses one would expect in a prosperous town. There were stables dotted about, blacksmiths hammered out their trade, shoemakers, bakers, clothing stores, hardware, publicans, inns and a whole range of businesses plying for trade. This continued from what I could see, along each of the two main roads that quartered the town. The one on which we rode stretched north to south, the other main road cut east to west. At the very centre came the crossroads itself.

Behind the frontage of business premises, dome houses dotted amongst the back streets like goose pimples. For me, being used to ugly square buildings, the sight of so many domes proved delightful. I still wondered why the animan chose to build domes instead of boxes but I enjoyed the change anyway. Somehow it was easier on the eyes than the blocky grime covered office blocks and business premises of my world. The town was alive with activity, animan rushing here and there, small groups chatted on street corners, customers went in and out of the shops and children scampered everywhere. I was at once frightened and enthralled by the feeling of pure life given off by the town. I admit the fact that all the inhabitants I saw looked like animals; lions, tigers, bears and wolves all dressed in clothes, all talking to each other and all behaving like . . . humans!

As the town was situated on the junction of two main routes, establishments offering room and board were plentiful and it did not take us long to find a clean looking boarding house a couple of streets back from the main thoroughfare. The place was run by an elderly couple of Leomen, strange but even animan grow old and need a retirement plan, this boarding house was theirs. Secuutus and I were made very welcome and offered rooms that were clean, tidy and comfortable. Luxury compared to what I had experienced so far in this land. Two other guests were also staying at the guest house, two Lupus salesmen, staying over to ply their trade in the town for a week. Polite introductions included the obligatory questions; where are you from and what do you do. The two salesmen didn't ask what Secuutus and I did for a trade, I assumed they considered it obvious, based on our attire. In turn, the two explained they were travelling through, assessing the town for their joint business of linen supplies. We wished them luck but privately I felt they would be wasting their time in this town, the locals appeared to have every possible form of business catered for.

Locking on to the subject, our host joined the conversation, adding history to the explanation given by the salesmen. Our host, Capit, explained that the town had built its very existence on trade at the crossroads. Many years ago, a local landowner noticed the volume of traffic passing along the two roads and meeting at the crossroads. Seeing a means of profit, the landowner closed off the crossroad junction and began charging a toll to allow travellers through. The result of people accumulating at the crossroads waiting to pass through lead to the building of inns and hostelries, soon followed by eating places and stables. The landowner first took rent from his tenants but died as the town grew. No one could decide who should now own the land as there were no heirs. Finally, a committee of townsfolk took over and that was how the town of Tutique Receptus was born. Capit finished his tale by gesturing at the two salesmen before adding, 'All these years later, passing trade is still our biggest source of income, as indicated by our two friends here. Though others now also pass through our town,' he finished with a smile in our direction.

We stayed in the boarding house for two days without any trauma, taking walks around the town during the day, and enjoying a huge cooked meal and quiet conversation with our hosts in the evenings. Neither Secuutus nor I felt the need to visit a publican, we were too concerned that drink might land us in trouble from which we could not escape. Anyway, to be honest, we were both just enjoying the good food, comfortable beds and good company, the time spent travelling with Janiz had been stressful, to say the least. But sadly all good things come to an end, sometimes rapidly.

On the evening of our second day in the town, we had just finished supper and made ourselves comfortable in front of the fire, when the sound of hammering on the door tore into our peace. Our host shot to his feet and ran to the door, his hand barely turning the handle before the door burst open. Immediately upon seeing our late visitor, Secuutus and I rose to our feet and began strapping on our weapons, we knew the presence of Firmus meant trouble. We were poised and ready before he had caught his breath enough to speak.

'We've got to go, now!' he gasped; 'It's a trap. The soldiers are here.'

Though Secuutus and I were ready to leave, neither of us expected that news. How many soldiers? How did they know we were here? Questions flooded my mind as we grabbed our few belongings and with a brief word of appreciation and a handful of coin to our hosts, we followed Firmus out into the evening air.

'How did they find us?' I asked as we ran.

'We don't know, maybe someone from the town seeking a reward or maybe our faithful shadow. It doesn't matter, we need to find a way out of this town before the troops move in and corral us together for slaughter.'

'Where are we meeting the rest of the riders?' I panted, desperately trying to gain a grasp on the situation.

'I don't know, it's every animan for himself. Janiz told me to find you and head for the south gate the best way we can. That's where we're going now but for all our sakes, watch out for soldiers, they're everywhere!'

Following Firmus, Secuutus and I turned into a side road, staying away from the main thoroughfare and attempting to hide in the shadows as we ran. I considered that as long as we headed in the general direction of the south gate, it would not matter how we got there, just as long as we did. Firmus appeared to have an idea of the route as we darted from one back street to another, our weapons ready, our eyes and ears alert. Shouting could be heard now, as the soldiers moved in on the town. Local animan cried out in alarm as the troops searched for us, manhandling locals out of their way. Those who objected were dealt with quickly, and fatally. Torches began to light up the streets as soldiers peered into every nook and cranny. Inns and hostelries were invaded and ransacked as the search intensified. All too soon we could hear screams amidst the shouting, giving evidence that some riders had been discovered and cut to pieces.

The road ahead of us suddenly lit up as a group of soldiers with torches began to search the alleyways and back streets where we hid, ordering all to open their doors and allow their homes to be searched. The three of us dived behind a large garden shrub, lying flat on our bellies with fearful eyes watching the torches come ever closer. I glanced around for an escape, looking for roads or streets that remained in darkness, hoping that would indicate no soldiers. I spotted one off to our left and gestured to Firmus and Secuutus that we should head in that direction. The two other riders followed me as I crouched as low as my tall frame would allow and scampered off to hide in the darkness. We remained unnoticed and moved from cover to cover while creeping along the still dark road. It was then I realised one major drawback with dome houses, there were no corners. Our only cover was the odd shrub or tree in what was the suburbs of the town.

An idea then formed in my mind, whoever had given us away to the authorities must know we would head towards the south gate. Therefore I suspected the largest number of soldiers would be congregating in the southern section of the town, and even more, I realised the south gate would by now be heavily guarded. Another escape route was required. Pausing and panting in a gateway, I whispered my plan to the other two. At first, Firmus was against it, stating we had to stick to the orders given by Janiz, but Secuutus agreed with me and between us, we convinced him that heading south would be fatal. The plan was simple and obvious, we would head for the east gate and use the open countryside as cover while making our way around the outskirts to meet Janiz and any others who survived. Strangely the thought of Janiz not being there never crossed our minds.

However before we could act on our new plan, a flicker of light gave warning that soldiers were approaching. It was too late for us to get away so we stayed in our limited cover and prayed we would not be seen in the darkness. Our senses on high alert and our bodies tense, we listened to the soft voices as the soldiers neared. I could only make out two or perhaps three voices but that meant nothing. For all I knew, a hundred more soldiers could be in a non-talkative mood. We remained as still and as low as possible as the sound of voices was now accompanied by footfalls, coming nearer with each step. The fear and tension were palpable as the light from the torches grew, casting shadows along the street on which we hid. I realised I was sweating again, a fact that repeatedly surprised me but I gave it no more thought as the soldiers were but paces away.

Within moments the soldiers were upon us, four of them heavily armed but not attentive, luckily. Firmus gestured to let them pass before we moved on, but Secuutus disagreed, indicating with that strange sign language understood by warriors anywhere. Secuutus wanted to strike while we could, else these same soldiers might finally wake up and find us, raising the alarm to our whereabouts. His argument won, Secuutus pointed at me, then at the soldier nearest to us, and gesturing that he and Firmus would deal with the remaining three. Suits me I thought, one to one I could manage, two against three were not odds I would bet on.

Every fibre in my body screamed for action as we remained still, waiting for the soldiers to move past us. As soon as we could see their backs we attacked. I took no chances and simply lunged forward with my staff held out like a lance. Before my opponent even knew I was there, I had pushed the blade of my staff deep into the base of his skull, angling upwards into his brain, killing him instantly. As I withdrew the blade I could hear the sound of scuffling beside me. Firmus had dispatched one soldier in much the same way and was now chopping down on the second soldier, Secuutus standing ready in case he made a mistake. Secuutus's chosen victim already lay dead on the ground. All four soldiers now lay twitching in death, our attack had been silent and effective. Quickly I stamped out the torch flames and once more we were in darkness. We dragged the bodies into the garden where we had hidden, hoping they would not be discovered too soon. Then without a word, we set off towards the east gate again.

As we crept through the suburbs I noted that not a light showed nor a curtain twitched as we moved silently past rows of dome houses. I was not surprised however, anyone being too nosey would most likely lose their head. None of the residents wanted to be involved in a fight that did not concern them. A very wise choice I had to agree. We were now moving at a reasonable pace, remaining as stealthy and as low as possible and it became evident that as we neared the east gate, so the presence of soldiers decreased. I felt some relief but could not help but ponder on the short-sightedness of the commanding officer. Reason stated that we would try for another gate when we discovered the south gate was heavily guarded. All four gates should have been guarded thus trapping us in the town. Hell I thought, we haven't reached the gate yet so I had better stop counting my chickens before they hatched. I was soon to find out, one way or another.

I found out. The east gate was lit up like the Blackpool illuminations and there were guards everywhere. Secuutus, Firmus and I had made it safely to the vicinity of the gate, we had even picked up a couple more riders along the way, but now we were trapped again. Behind us lay the town and the searching soldiers, all eager to collect our heads. In front of us stood the heavily guarded gate, we had nowhere to go. Sounds of fighting and screams of pain still ripped through the night air, torchlight twinkled, sending yellow patterns over the white dome houses. Shadows flickered and danced in wild pursuit as they chased the lambent yellow sprites throughout the town. The five of us hid in the darkest of shadows while contemplating possible an avenue of escape. We could not risk heading for either of the remaining gates, it would be a good guess that those too were protected by soldiers and guards. We had one option left, a daunting route out of the town that none of us favoured. We had to go over the wall.

Keeping to the shadows and avoiding those flickers of light that foretold the presence of more soldiers, we crept away from the gate and again traversed the backstreets. It did not take long to find a suitably unguarded section of the wall, as it surrounded the whole town, guarding all of it would have required a substantial number of troops. I offered up a prayer of thanks for those derelict and disused guard towers. If they were still in use, our escape would be nigh on impossible. As it was, we only had to avoid any attention from search patrols inside the town and any that may lie in wait on the other side of the wall. Good thing they didn't appear to use dogs in this land I thought, otherwise we would have stood even less chance of success. There was still the wall standing tall and strong in our way. Figuring the section of wall with the least guards would be in the middle between the east gate and the south gate, it was in that direction we headed. I had no idea how we were going to scale the wall itself and judging from the silence of my fellow riders, no one else did either.

We had negotiated several dark streets without encountering any patrols, though the fear remained on us. It was fear that brought us to a sudden halt when a light was spotted at the far end of the road on which we now stood, transfixed. One of the buildings ahead emitted light through open windows and door with no regard to the fighting going on throughout the town. Not knowing what to expect, but forced to take that route to the wall, we crept forward, using all the shadowy places along the quiet street. We had left the suburbs some time ago and now found ourselves in the poorer section of the town. The proximity of the wall did little for the property market and the homes reflected the lack of wealth. As we stealthily moved further up the street, I suddenly realised what type of establishment would most likely ignore all the fuss and fighting going on around them. Sounds coming from the building gave evidence of my assumption, it was a publican, a bar, a pub, and none of its clientele gave a single hoot for the problems of a bunch of outlaws and pursuing soldiers.

The sight of a publican doing a roaring trade amidst all our troubles brought a grin to my face. How I envied its customers, blind to the world in their brightly lit haven of alcohol induced camaraderie and good cheer. That gave me an idea, a light bulb moment. Swiftly I signalled to the other riders to follow me. None questioned and I led them right past the publican, standing tall and in full view of the door and windows as we walked straight past. I was right, no one took a blind bit of notice and most did not even see the group of five animan walking past in the night. Once past the front of the bar, I darted down the alleyway I had prayed for, the others followed. We were once more in darkness as no light showed from the rear of the publican, just one light gave off a feeble glow from a small building set some distance from the main building. A narrow and well-trodden path leading from the back door of the bar to the much smaller building made its purpose obvious. It was the toilet, a necessity for any bar or pub. Hoping the toilet was not presently in use and any occupants would not vacate the seat of all power and find us loitering about outside, I searched for the main ingredient for my idea. It was beside the back door that I found what I was looking for.

Quickly and quietly I outlined my plan to the others, receiving a mixture of responses in return. Secuutus nodded in agreement, Firmus frowned in thought while the two other riders made it plain they thought I was mad by the expression on their faces. One of the riders I knew from our original band but the other was a young animan we had recruited on our journey. A strapping young Lupus called Audacia. His face showed misgivings at my plan but an eagerness to make the attempt anyway caused confliction in his body language. My plan was simple, stupid maybe but simple. We would use the empty barrels that stood stacked outside the publican to build steps of a sort that we could climb up to get over the wall. Like I said, simple but stupid. The older of the two riders that had joined us stated in a whisper that he thought my plan was absurd, one could not climb on ale barrels as they would roll away. I patiently explained that we would stand them on their ends, not on their sides, accompanied by muted sniggers from the others.

With all now in agreement, we quietly carried the barrels over to the base of the wall, two riders carrying one barrel each. We could not risk rolling them because of the noise. Being the biggest animan apart from me, Secuutus stood beside the rear door of the publican, ready to render unconscious anyone who chose that moment to either relieve themselves or throw out a rowdy customer. We stacked three barrels tight against the wall, then placed two more barrels on top of them. Eventually, the last barrel was balanced on top, effectively making a structure that we could hopefully climb. As the tallest I was sent first, though Audacia readily volunteered. Once on the wall, I would reach down and help each of the other riders up and over the wall. Anxiously I climbed the barrels, they were not firmly placed on level ground and wobbled noticeably. Nonetheless, neither I nor the barrels fell and soon I was perched on top of the stone wall. Before calling up the next rider, I took several moments to scan the surrounding area, both inside and outside the town wall. It would have been a pointless exercise if we had scaled the wall only to land in the lap of a patrol.

Once I was sure no one was near, I reached down a hand and immediately felt another hand grasp mine. It was Audacia of course, with typical disregard for safety or fear, the young animan quickly climbed up beside me. He too took the time to scan the area before dropping quietly over the other side. A slight thud indicated he had landed and the absence of a cry suggested he had survived without injury. 'Clear!' he called softly. I reached down and a hand grasped mine once again. Suddenly I felt as if my arm was being wrenched from my shoulder and I knew who the next rider was. It was Secuutus, the huge Ursidae who had become my friend. He clambered rather than climbed, his great bulk making the barrels wobble violently. The operation continued until we all sat huddled against the outside of the wall. We felt no urge to move at that moment. Following the stress and fear of our escape from the hunting soldiers and the town, a moments rest was a relief.

'What if the soldiers discover the barrels?' questioned Firmus quietly.

'Doesn't matter,' I replied. 'There's nothing we can do about that now. If we had kicked them over, the noise would have certainly alerted someone to our presence. Anyway, I suspect any soldiers coming this way will head straight into the publican, no soldier can resist the opportunity for a sly drink or three.' The others nodded in agreement before Secuutus added his own thought.

'I would love to be there in the morning when the publican comes out and sees six of his barrels stacked up against the wall. He'll be in for a surprise!'

We all grinned at this, the small touch of humour lifting our spirits enough to face the perils still to be confronted and conquered. We knew Janiz would be waiting somewhere near the south gate, but it was a certainty he would not be in plain sight. We would have to find him without being discovered by any of the king's soldiers. Any mistakes would be fatal.

Setting off away from the wall, we sought whatever cover we could find and luckily there was plenty. Like any town or city, the outskirts had attracted farmers, stockmen and traders who plied their trade to all who entered or left the town. It was, I noticed, the first time I had encountered buildings with four walls. Admittedly they were only ramshackle temporary structures, squat and flat-roofed and looking as if the first gust of wind would blow them away. The sheds, as I now considered them, were sparsely located amid paddocks enclosing stock animals, plots full of vegetables and yards with stacks of assorted lumber and other building materials. Remaining silent and watchful, we crept on towards the area of the south gate, staying vigilant as one would expect there to be guards out here as well as in the town. Occasionally we did come across patrols but here it was easier to avoid them. Sometimes crawling on our bellies, sometimes sprinting across open areas, and sometimes taking refuge in a shed. We did all we could to remain undetected and alive.

Nearing the south gate, we could hear the sounds of fighting off to one side of the south road. Immediately we headed in that direction, intuition telling us that was where we would find Janiz. Sure enough, there he was, swinging his sword and jabbing at two soldiers that had him cornered against a flimsy structure just off the road. Around him other riders fought with a superior number of soldiers, our arrival would certainly even the balance. Without hesitation we entered the fray, our weapons flashing as we came thundering out of the darkness.

Now there was even more urgency to the battle, if the soldiers inside the town heard the fighting, they would surely come to the aid of their comrades and if they did, we would be in dire trouble. With the boost given by our arrival, Janiz and the riders moved up a gear, slashing and stabbing in a wild frenzy of killing. All the riders fought with a desperation not shared by the soldiers, after all, they fought for coin. We fought for a cause. In truth, I fought for my life but even that was a cause, mine. The fight ended soon after our arrival, those soldiers still alive that tried to head for the town and warn their colleagues were swiftly cut down.

The fight over, all the riders, including me, stood panting, our weapons remained ready while our eyes darted towards the town gate in case more troops emerged. Janiz was not standing panting, he was already moving off, gesturing us to follow. I shared his concern, now our presence was known, we were in terrible danger. We had to get away as fast as possible before the whole damn army descended on our heads. Unfortunately, our horses were still stabled in the town and out of our reach. Janiz already had a plan and led us to a fenced off area that held a stock of horses in readiness for sale the next day. It was with some reluctance I helped myself to a replacement mount. The paddock containing the horses also stored saddles and all the rider paraphernalia we would need to replace what we had lost. I would miss Fred but retrieving him would most certainly cost me my life and I would rather miss him than me. I decided to call this horse Fred as a mark of respect, though in truth, it was the only name I could easily remember.

Leading the horses at first, until they grew accustomed to their new owners, we followed Janiz away from the south gate, putting distance and darkness between ourselves and the town. We avoided the road itself, instead we travelled through the countryside parallel to the road. We had lost much due to our rapid evacuation of Tutique Receptus, having left bedrolls and extra supplies in boarding houses and inns where we had stayed. However, the items lost could be replaced, our lives could not. After a half mile or so, we swung up into the saddle and rode at a fast trot. I soon discovered my new horse was not as forgiving as Fred number one had been. Once or twice I had to hold on as the animal made its displeasure apparent. Any loss of concentration on my behalf would inspire the irritated horse to buck, kick, anything to remove me from the saddle. I clung on, the fear of embarrassment in front of the riders far outweighing any fear of being thrown from the saddle. Another mile and the horse had settled to its fate, it appeared to accept me as its new rider, though I was not fooled, I knew the damn thing would throw me off at any opportunity. I was new to horse riding but I was no fool.

It was then that my attention was drawn to the riders around me. Doing a rough headcount I realised with shock that we had lost around half our number. Many had not survived the fight in Tutique Receptus, our desire to rest under a roof and sleep in clean sheets on a soft bed had cost our group dearly. I peered through the light of the awakening dawn and could see that Janiz felt the loss strongly. The riders had followed him, put their trust in him and now they were either dead or captured, the end result would undoubtedly be the same. Most of the original riders had survived, though a few familiar faces were missing. The greatest number of losses were among the young animan who Janiz had recruited from towns and villages on our travels, young strong animan with their whole lives ahead of them, now dead. The sadness of the loss weighed heavily on all the remaining riders, but it weighed heaviest on Janiz.

Chapter Twelve. A Warning

Daylight found us many miles from the town, a town from which many of our group would never leave. Janiz had finally called a halt and we took time to rest the horses and relieve ourselves. We had no blankets to lie upon and no supplies or rations to cook so no fire was made. Our smaller group of riders simply sat on the grass or paced about, no one wishing to talk, the silence one of gloom and sadness. Even Secuutus had no words to say as we waited while the horses rested and breakfasted on the grass.

Eventually though, the silence had to be broken and it fell on Janiz to break it. He called for all the riders to gather around him, his intention to plan our next move, how to gain entry to the palace of King Fastus. Janiz explained for those riders who did not know the area, but mainly directed at me, that there were no more towns between us and the city of Urbem Regiam, the Royal city at the centre of which stood our goal. Janiz stated there would be farms and smallholdings on our route where we may be able to purchase new supplies, but he also warned against complacency. The king had known of our presence in Tutique Receptus and it stood to reason we were under close observation. At this remark, each and every one of us glanced around the landscape for signs of our shadow, but there was none. Janiz's plan was simple he said and I was surprised at his honesty. The only plan he had at this time was to reach the city of Urbem Regiam. After walking into a trap once, he did not intend to do it again. So no further plans would be made until we had at least gained entry to Urbem Regiam. All the riders agreed to this, we all now fully understood we were being tracked, even the few remaining younger riders finally got the message that we had to be alert and watchful, our lives depended on it.

However, as the saying goes, an army marches on its stomach, and ours were empty. Janiz declared we would camp where we were and allow our two hunters, Piscator and Ventor to find us some food. Hunger was upon us so several more riders offered to help out, Secuutus volunteered both of us. What the hell did I know about hunting? A question I asked him as soon as we were a distance from the camp.

'Hunting is easy,' he replied with a grin. 'Either you catch something or you go hungry. Anyway I'll guide you, all you have to do is stay quiet.'

Off we both set, Secuutus leading the way. I wondered how we were going to ever get close enough to an animal to kill it armed with only a staff and a sword. Personally, I thought Secuutus had set his hopes too high but I was happy to play along.

The land around us consisted of areas of woodland interspersed with grass clearings, there was certainly plenty of game visible in the distance, a fact that did not escape the human part of me. Sadly, humans were responsible for depleting serious numbers of wildlife back in my world. Seeing this amount of animals roaming free would be a very unusual sight at home. Then again, watching the animals and capturing and killing one seemed an impossible task to me, I wondered if my friend had an idea. Did he intend running down a fleet of foot beast with his bulk? Was he going to use my staff as a spear? So far he had given no explanation of his plans and I began to worry this would be a wasted trip.

Motioning for me to remain as quiet as possible, Secuutus led me to a lea that edged the woods, picking up any twigs and small branches he found along the way. When he finally had a good armful, he headed off towards the treeline, his eyes glued to the ground. I was about to ask if he knew what he was doing when he suddenly stopped near a small hole in the ground. Secuutus then pushed one of the longer twigs into the ground, marking the hole. Without explanation, he set off again, found another hole and once again left a twig marking the spot. The next few holes he came across he blocked with earth and stones. I was puzzled but an inkling of what he proposed was being born in the recesses of my mind. There's not much call for poachers in Manchester city.

At last, with as many holes as he could find blocked, Secuutus led me back to the first one we had found.

'Sit there,' he said, gesturing to one side of the hole, 'draw your knife and have your staff ready.'

'Ready for what?' I asked.

'It's easy, just hit or stab anything that pops out of that hole. Make sure you're quick though, otherwise it'll get away.'

'What will get away?' I asked, beginning to feel a tad like a simpleton, repeating everything he said.

'Well hopefully it'll be a rabbit, but one can never be sure. Just hit whatever comes out. Have patience because it may take a while, and stay just behind the hole. If it sees you lurking about, it won't come out. Now stay there, keep quiet and still but ready. I'll be over by that hole,' he said pointing.

So I sat, my staff held short in my hands to achieve the greatest possible control and force. Now I realised what he was going to do. I had probably seen it on the telly, I was certain I had never witnessed it in real life. Soon I could smell the distinct aroma of wood smoke and looking over to Secuutus, I saw him sat crouched over a small fire. He was piling green leafed branches on the flames, producing enough smoke to hide a battleship. I watched as he then began flapping his arms and waving a leafy branch, obviously attempting to direct a good portion of the smoke down the hole. He had built the small fire right up against the burrow and fanned the smoke towards it. I readied myself, my staff poised above the exit hole in front of me as I quietly wished Secuutus luck in his plan. There was a flaw or two of course, if he had missed any holes then it reduced the chance of anything trying to escape through the one I guarded. Also, animals often hide from grass and forest fires underground, so a bit of smoke may not bother them enough to warrant an escape. I hoped Secuutus managed to get enough smoke down the hole to fool the residents that the fire was close.

All of a sudden something darted from the hole, scampering away and catching me completely on the hop, so to speak. Ashamed at missing the first escapee, I focused all my attention on the burrow, willing another animal out. My luck was in for at that moment a small grey head poked out from the hole, sniffing the air in readiness to bolt. With all my speed and strength I brought the heavy wooden staff down upon its head with a thud.

Quickly I reached down and pulled out the luckless rabbit, I did not want to frighten off any others that may be following. Once I had ensured the animal was dead, I readied myself for the next. I then thumped two more rabbits in quick succession, wondering if I would be this fast in human form. I doubted it. No more rabbits committed Hari Kari so after a while I waved to Secuutus and signalled the fact. Carrying the three unfortunate rabbits, I went over and joined him as he kicked the small fire out. I knew three rabbits would not feed all the riders, but at least we would not return empty handed.

As we approached the camp we could see a cooking fire already ablaze, at least someone had faith in us. My grin faded somewhat when I saw our two hunters also returning, a plump deer slung over Ventor's shoulders. It seemed we would eat well tonight after all. Not having a clue how to do it, I left the rabbits with the others, they knew how to butcher a carcase and within moments both the deer and the rabbits were skinned, butchered and prepared for either cooking or drying for future use.

Evening was now falling and several others had made beds of sorts from bundles of tall grass and leaves. I set about copying them, it may be a cold night without blankets but at best I would have something reasonably comfortable to sleep on. Night fell and the riders sat as near to the fire as the heat and spitting meat would allow. Still no one sat staring into the fire, other than the day's designated cook, Firmus. Most of the riders held their weapons or lay them close to hand. It was apparent that they expected more trouble and prepared themselves as much as possible. My staff, as always, was close to hand though I did check that the evil looking knife was also within easy access, just in case. Finally, the meat was ready and we feasted in the darkness, a nearby stream provided nature's wine. Sleep came upon me quickly as I settled down on my grass mattress with a full stomach, noticing moments before my eyes closed that Janiz, Fidelis and a few other riders remained seated by the red glow of the fire. I wondered what they discussed as I drifted off to sleep.

Morning arrived all too soon, reminding me of my poor alarm clock and the battering it suffered every weekday morning as I rose for work. Of travelling in the cold and rain of the British climate, sitting on smoking rattling buses before facing a class of hooded teenagers who wished to be there as much as I did. Here though, the day dawned bright, promising to be warm and dry. My bed of grass had worked and I had slept well, if I had attempted this in my human form, my body would be wracked with aches and pains. Not my new body as I thought of it. I awoke refreshed and full of energy, rising from my bed without a crack of bone or a squeak of muscle. Janiz of course was already awake, prodding the low fire back into life. One by one all the riders awakened and following a breakfast of cold meat, we gathered the rest and stored it best we could. We had left the saddles on the horses as we all feared the possibility of a night attack requiring a rapid escape. When all were mounted we set off on the next part of our journey, our destination, the palace. If we survived.

We rode south once again though the journey was prolonged due to the lack of water bottles. This meant we had to drink whenever the opportunity of water presented itself, stream, river, lake or pond, we took advantage of them all. I did notice, with some amusement, that those riders who had witnessed the *burning water* still approached lakes and ponds with apprehension. No matter how I tried to explain, the riders would have none of it. As far as they were concerned, I had fought off a demon and drank the burning water, I was just as magical in their eyes as the sorcerer himself. Janiz was the only animan that had doubts about me, he seemed to sense I was different than any other Tigris, but he appeared to trust me all the same. I was astonished with myself. Here I was, in the body of a huge feline, with the strength, speed and stamina of a magnificent tiger. I now rode a horse like an expert, I had fought in battles and I had killed. My new life was about as far from my old one that if written in a book, I would still not believe it. Thoughts of my home, such as it was, brought me back to that jade box. I knew both Sophos and I had the same experience of finding and opening a small green jade box, resulting in our physical transformation and our arrival in this strange land. I knew I had to find another in the hope of returning home. But, did I really want to go back to my dreary life? I could not be sure.

We travelled for four days, putting as much distance between ourselves and the soldiers of Tutique Receptus as we could, always alert for other patrols of soldiers and our ever faithful shadow. He had reappeared not long after we ran from Tutique Receptus and had remained ever since. Janiz and Fidelis had discussed leaving someone behind, hidden and armed, to stop the shadow following us permanently. At last, they agreed there would be no point, whoever sent our shadow would most certainly send another. It was not worth risking the life of another rider in such a pointless exercise.

Travelling with no supplies other than what we managed to hunt and kill was a hindrance, stopping constantly to drink ate into our travelling time. Water was relatively easy to find but without the means to carry it, thirst had to wait until we encountered a water source. Having no blankets was not a huge discomfort in the general scheme of things, but sleeping on rough beds without some form of protection from the cold of the night led to many a disturbed rest. Janiz determined to purchase or steal more water bottles, blankets and dried food at the first opportunity. Towns were now out of the question, none of the riders had any wish to be trapped or betrayed again. Towns were out but farms and small pockets of populous were little risk, now instead of avoiding all signs of habitation, we actively sought one out, finding one the very next day.

It was only a small collection of six domed buildings, surrounded by pens of livestock and small cultivated plots of fruit and vegetables. The six domes were situated in a loose ring with a courtyard at the centre. Janiz deemed the risk worthwhile, the visual aspect of the area was good and with so few buildings, we would see any threat heading our way from miles away. Nevertheless, that did not mean we dropped our guard, we approached the buildings cautiously, fully alert for signs of danger. Just outside the hamlet, Janiz instructed the riders to split into groups, one moving to the east, the other heading west. Fidelis, Secuutus and I were chosen to escort Janiz into the central courtyard. So far we had not seen a single animan, only wandering chickens, the odd goat and penned livestock indicated the presence of inhabitants. As the four of us came to a halt in the middle of the settlement, a wizened old animan, white haired with a gently stooped back and clothed in a homespun grey smock walked slowly out from behind one of the buildings. The ancient Tigris may have appeared harmless but the heavy well maintained sword hanging low at his side suggested otherwise. The old animan came to a halt directly in front of we four riders, not an ounce of fear on his lined faced.

'Greetings Janiz,' said the aged figure in a quiet and confident voice.

What happened next surprised the heck out of me. As soon as the old animan spoke, Janiz leapt from his horse and engulfed the white haired figure in his muscular arms.

'It is good to see you again Magister my old friend,' grinned Janiz when he finally released his grip on the old animan. 'I am glad to see you alive, truly you appear very well. Life must be good for you.' Janiz paused a moment before adding, 'I see you still carry your sword, but can you still swing it?'

In answer, the old animan swept his sword from its scabbard and with impressive speed, the weapon stopped with its point resting gently at the throat of Janiz. Instantly we all reacted by pulling our swords, fearing Janiz was in danger. But with a laugh, the Leo carefully brushed the blade aside. 'I see you have lost nothing Magister, your skills are still as sharp as your blade. But enough of this, tell me, what are you doing here? How do you fare?'

The old animan sheathed his huge broadsword with a smile before reaching out and firmly grasping the outstretched arm of Janiz. 'I am well Janiz and it is good to see the infamous outlaw I have heard so much about.' Janiz returned the smile but waited for the one he called Magister to continue. 'I have retired from my service to King Fastus. I now live here with my few remaining family members. I left not long after you were banished, my old stomach could not tolerate your father's behaviour or that snivelling so-called sorcerer any longer. In a final demonstration of his old self, the king endowed me with enough coin to see out my remaining days in relative comfort.' Magister swept an arm around to indicate the six buildings. 'But come, bring in your animan and rest. Please, enter my home and we will talk.'

Janiz ordered me to ride out and gather the other riders on guard outside the settlement. The old animan turned to one of the buildings and clapped his hands loudly twice. Immediately others began to show themselves as they exited from their hiding places. All were of the Tigris Cast and well armed, none showing any fear. Their bearing radiated confidence and I was thankful to be accepted as a friend. I suspected this small group of animan would make dangerous opponents, even the females and children grasped weapons. Now their features softened and we were ushered into the largest of the buildings, a structure I took to be a communal barn, judging by its contents of hay and animal feed. Our horses were taken from us and placed in stalls so that we could unsaddle, feed and water them. Once the animals were cared for, we were offered refreshments which we all thankfully accepted. We were given the choice of resting in the barn or were welcome to stroll about the settlement, the choice was ours. All of us took the opportunity to grab some rest following a snack of bread, cheese, fruit and water.

Following a short snooze, the riders were refreshed enough to venture from the barn and take stock of our hospitable refuge. The residents were all busy, working on minor repairs around the buildings or with the livestock or weeding and caring for the crops. As we wandered about the place, we were greeted with smiles and a welcome. Talk soon began between the riders and the residents of the small community. It quickly became apparent that Janiz and Magister were indeed old friends. Magister had been the king's swordsmith and had taught Janiz his weapons lore from an early age. Janiz had grown up under the guidance and instruction of Magister, their time spent together forming a relationship akin to that of father and son. Janiz's father King Fastus was often away from home and even when he was in residence, his time was taken up with the duties of ruling his kingdom. His mother had died at an early age, leaving Janiz the sole responsibility of his father. Consequently, Janiz was raised by nurses, governesses and teachers, his father only occupying short periods of his life. Magister had become the closest of the army of animan instrumental in the care of the young prince and the two became quite inseparable until Janiz had been exiled from the kingdom. The parting had been sorrowful, but Magister was too old to ride off into adventure with the young Janiz and so, after many years, they had parted.

We stayed at the settlement for three days, sleeping in the barn under blankets donated by the residents. We were fed and watered and in return, we offered coin to those helping us. They happily accepted our payment, we were, after all, eating their food and laying on their blankets. This arrangement appeared to suit all and no hostility or disagreements ruined our stay. Magister even offered lessons in swordsmanship to myself and some of the riders. It did not come as a surprise when Magister concluded I would be better off with my staff. Of course, he could not know I was not from this land where swords were commonplace. I did not have the underpinning knowledge about such weaponry as the inhabitants of this land had from birth.

My antics on the weapons field left no one in doubt that a sword in my hand would be as effective as me swinging a leg of mutton. In my past life, so long ago it seemed, I had practised martial arts, including Kenjutsu. This is a form of martial arts that centres around 'stick fighting' similar to Kendo.

Though I only spent a short time studying this form, the time spent certainly aided me now. Perhaps I should have chosen Kendo. I had no idea my future would involve trying to cut someone's head off in a sword fight. Hindsight is a wonderful thing, but foresight would be more useful.

During a break in the weapons training, Magister showed us into a small room within his home. In it were arranged dozens of swords he had collected over his years as swordsmith to the king. Some of our riders had lost their main weapons during the frantic escape from Tutique Receptus and Magister offered them the choice of a replacement. We were told that we could have our pick of any sword except one. Immediately our interest was aroused. Which sword was it and why was it special? Amid the clamour of questions, I saw it, hanging from the wall above the array of weapons that some were already examining. Magister caught my eye and gave a slight nod. I reached up and brought the magnificent weapon down, holding it in my hands for all the riders to see. It truly was a work of art, a huge blood red ruby adorned the pommel, set above the pure silver hilt. The hilt, in turn, was beautifully engraved with scenes of battle and war, the pictures so intricate that I wondered on the skill of the engraver. The sword blade was long and sleek, not as long and heavy as a broadsword but longer than the simple weapons most of the riders carried. The blade itself also sported engravings at the point where the hilt or handle joined the blade. As I held it in my hands I could feel its perfect balance, the blade seemed to cry out for battle.

At a gesture from Magister, I reluctantly handed the weapon over to him. I knew I would never have the skill to wield it, the sword was such a magnificent product of craftsmanship, everyone present would give much to own it, including me. Magister received the weapon from my hands with reverence before holding it aloft for all to see. Many gasps of appreciation uttered from the mouths of the riders at its beauty but Magister held onto the blade, refusing all offers for the weapon.

'This one must stay here,' began Magister as his arms lowered and he stared at the sword. 'I came across this many years ago and it has not left my side since. It was told that a famous warrior sorcerer once owned this blade, having had it forged by the spirits of the land. It is reputed to puncture any armour and give the user unbelievable strength and skill in battle. It is a magical sword, perhaps possessing a warrior's soul. I will not part with it until the time is right.'

Immediately following his words, all the begging hands withdrew, fear and awe visible on the faces surrounding Magister, except mine. My expression of disbelief was noticed by both Janiz and Magister and they both turned to face me.

'You are not convinced Harry? Please share your thoughts, I wish to know why you failed to be impressed with this fabulous weapon,' growled Janiz.

'I'm sorry but I don't believe in magic, you all know this fact. I admit the blade is the result of masterful craftsmanship and its fine balance and construction would no doubt assist whoever held it in conflict. But as for magical powers? I'm afraid I can't agree.'

The other riders stared at me in disbelief, the sword was unmistakenly magical, how could it not be? Mutterings and growls were directed at me then and I feared my scientific mind had finally landed me in deep poo. Neither Janiz nor Magister had responded to my confession, both simply stared at me with poker faces. I grasped my staff tightly as the atmosphere in the small room grew tense, the riders now resembling a lynch mob selecting a victim, me.

The voice of Magister cut through the growls, 'You are right Harry,' he said. 'This sword is not magical, I doubt it was forged by the spirits of the land. It has no supernatural powers.'

The room fell silent, all within it bewildered at Magister's words, all silent apart from my exhaled sigh of relief. 'You know this? Yet those were your very words when we first glimpsed the blade. Why would you contradict yourself now?' I wanted to know as all eyes now turned to Magister.

'I believe I said it is a magical sword, I did not say the sword was magical, meaning it possesses magical power. However, with its superb balance, fine blade and ease of use, it is indeed a magical blade,' replied Magister with a twinkle in his eye.

'So do you not believe in magic Magister?' questioned a puzzled Janiz. 'Not even after all the sorcerer has done? And you Harry, you have seen magic and banished demons. How can you not fear the magical arts?'

'I don't fear magic because it doesn't exist,' I stated, 'Magic is simply an explanation for what one doesn't understand. I believe in science, science can explain all that happens in the world. Through physics, biology, chemistry . . .'

I stopped talking because I could see by the expression on the faces of the riders that they had no idea what I was saying, and fear accompanied by suspicion began to emanate from their eyes. I realised, in a land where science had probably only reached the stage of basic alchemy, my words would appear a foreign language. I shrugged and finished by merely stating once again that I did not believe in magic. The room was quiet, the riders peered at me, their thoughts in confusion. I had ridden with them, eaten with them and fought with them, but their suspicions remained. In their eyes I was an enigma, I appeared as a Tigris but, they thought, I had no memory of my life, so what were these words I was speaking? Why did I not fear the burning waters or the demon in the night? I had better watch what I said in future, else I may just find myself tied to a post with flames licking up my body. To my relief, Magister broke the silence.

'Thank you Harry. No, the sword has no magical powers, perhaps I should have described it as the perfect weapon. That would not have raised your fears so. The sword is an heirloom, owned by kings of the past. If Janiz here does become king, then I will present the sword to him. By being king, he will have proved his courage, his valour and his right to own it. This beautiful weapon was crafted for kings and only a king should wield it. It was I who initiated the fable that the sword was magic, I did so to discourage all those who may seek it for themselves. The fear of magic has kept it safe all these years.'

'Why was the sword not given to my father? He is a king and therefore has the right of it?'

Magister turned to look Janiz directly in the eyes. 'I was entrusted with the blade by my old master as his life ebbed. His last words instructed me to trust my deepest instincts and not to part with it lightly. Even before the arrival of the sorcerer I realised, and I am sorry for what I am about to say Janiz, but I realised your father would never wield this blade. I know not how I knew this, but my instincts were proved correct. By allowing himself to be controlled by such a charlatan as the sorcerer, he forfeited all rights to this magnificent weapon, a sword of true kings. But now I believe I have found the new owner of this fabulous weapon. But we shall see.'

Anymore discussion was curtailed by a shout of warning from outside. All thoughts of the bejewelled blade were thrust aside as we followed Janiz from the room, our weapons ready. Once out in the sunshine, we saw a couple of Magister's family grasping a tattered and dirty member of the Lupus Cast, it appeared the animan was too weak or ill to stand on his own two legs. Slowly the Lupus lifted his head and stared around until his eyes fell upon me.

'Harry! At last I have found you. Help me!' cried the exhausted animan.

Immediately I recognised the figure, it was Sophos. 'You know of this wretch?' growled Janiz. 'Yes I do. It . . he is Sophos. He is the sage we spoke of on our first meeting, least I think we did. It seems so long ago I can't be sure.'

I moved to help the Liverpudlian from the grip of his guards and gently lowered him to the ground. Magister ordered water to be brought as we all gathered around the prone wretch, now sat with his head in his hands. One of the riders helped Sophos to drink as another produced a chunk of bread which Sophos eagerly snatched from his hands. I stared down at my countryman, or should I say my planetman. The figure I saw was even more dirty and dishevelled than I remembered, the wiry body was now thin and covered in cuts, scrapes and bruises. I recalled Sophos was not overly keen on personal hygiene but this was taking things too far. The sage bolted down the bread and swallowed the water in a single gulp. More water was given and after another huge drink, the little Liverpudlian began to recover. At a command from Janiz, myself and Secuutus carried the frail figure into the barn and laid him to rest on a straw bed. We left him there to rest.

The morning passed with all the riders busying themselves with personal chores. Some of us, though not nearly enough, had taken a bath of sorts in a nearby river. A couple of riders lay in the water fully clothed, doing two jobs in one they said, washing themselves and their clothes at the same time. I considered this but decided on the more conventional method. Magister's people had supplied some rudimentary soap and for the first time since finding myself here, I felt clean. Some of Magister's relatives had gathered a selection of old clothes for us to wear while ours dried in the sun. It appeared they were none too keen on a bunch of rough outlaws striding about completely naked. My ablutions finished, I set to checking and brushing down my new horse, a bonding exercise I called it. I would need the trust of this animal in our attempt to reach the palace, so a pampering session may just get the damn thing to like me. Somehow I didn't believe my theory.

Sophos awoke just as I was finishing brushing the new Fred, his groans, moans and creaking bones signified his return to consciousness. I allowed him time to gather his wits before asking, 'Come on then,' I began, 'Why are you here?'

'Huh! It's good to see you too,' came the growled response.

'Okay so I'm happy to see you again, but how the hell did you find me? What are you doing here? On that point, how did you get here so quickly?' I fired my questions at the poor wretch as he struggled up from his bed. Finally, with an overly dramatic sigh, Sophos made himself comfortable in a sitting position and began his tale.

'I have news, information about a weapon the sorcerer has in his possession. A weapon not seen here before, but you and I know it. I discovered it by chance. A wagon full of supplies came through my village not long after you'd left. I met the wagon driver in the publican later that day and we got to talking. He was telling me about his secret load which was bound for the palace, but to be received only by the sorcerer himself. He was under strict instructions not to reveal his cargo to anyone but the sorcerer. Of course, I became curious, what could the secret cargo be, and you know me, I had to find out.' I nodded in agreement with his last statement, knowing full well that Sophos would use any method possible to enhance his life here, and if he could discover a secret that no one else knew, perhaps he could make a coin or two by selling the information.

'The wagon driver liked his drink so I naturally helped him in his pursuit of happiness. It worked and later, with the driver sleeping it off, I snuck out to his wagon and took a peek.' Sophos paused to grin at up at me, obviously proud of his actions. But I still didn't know why he had sought me out and prodded him to continue.

'Ok, so I looked into the wagon and saw it held several waxed parchment packages. I thought this was odd. There was nothing else, just the packages. I had to have a closer look, it was very odd for a wagon to carry such a tiny load and to find waxed parchment being used as wrapping paper. So while all was quiet and most animan already in bed kipping, I used my knife and made a small slit in one of the packages. Guess what I found? Come on, take a guess. You'll never get it, not in a million years.' Sophos was almost beside himself with glee at his little secret. His face was split into the widest grin I think I have ever seen, certainly on him.

'Look! The others will be in here soon so damn well hurry up, we haven't got time to play kid's games. Just tell me what you found.' I growled at the impish face of the small Liverpudlian Lupus.

'Alright mate, keep yer hair on! So I cut a small slit in the package, and a black gritty powder spilt out. I recognised it immediately, not just from its appearance but also the smell. So, have you figured it out yet?' then came that stupid grin again.

'No. Just tell me for hell's sake!'

'It was gunpowder! Gunpowder in a land that hasn't invented it yet. About four or five packages or parcels of the stuff. I figured each parcel weighed about a pound. Five pounds of gunpowder. What the hell is the sorcerer going to do with that?' Sophos exclaimed, moments before my own exclamation.

'Gunpowder! How the hell did he get gunpowder?' I cried in shock. I knew the sorcerer was a tricky bastard, using basic chemistry and hallucinations, but gunpowder was a whole new ball game.

'Five pounds of the stuff you say?' I queried again before continuing, 'That's nearly enough to blow up a whole bloody army. What the hell is he planning now?'

'I dunno,' said Sophos as he reached into a small pouch hanging from his excuse for a belt. 'But whatever it is, he's now an ounce or two short.'

This said, Sophos handed me a small package. I knew what it contained immediately. I looked down on the small figure with a questioning expression as I hefted the package in my hand, feeling its weight but suddenly being very afraid of its contents.

'I figured you could use some as well, you know, just in case?' grinned Sophos.

'But why travel so far just to give me a handful of gunpowder? I asked.

'Ah well I admit I had an ulterior motive,' he began. 'I had to leave town in a hurry anyway, so I decided I would track down the only other person I knew who shared my experiences and came from a city not forty odd miles away from my own. Plus the fact you are the only one who may be pleased to see an old friend.'

I was about to utter a retort but ate my words as we heard footsteps coming our way from outside. Other riders had heard our voices and now curiosity drew them into the barn, each waiting to hear Sophos explain. I quickly hid the packet under my shirt and stood back, not wishing to draw suspicion on either Sophos or myself. Janiz and Magister appeared last and quietly pushed their way to the front of the group. I noticed Janiz had a hand on his sword, suspicion apparent in his posture. He was the only one who appeared concerned, as the scrawny wreck in front of us would stand little chance against so many riders and a swordsmith. I remained quiet, eager to hear Sophos's explanation while knowing he couldn't admit the real reason.

'What brings you here sage? And how did you travel so fast? I would hear your tale before we decide what to do with you,' growled Janiz. 'We are burdened with danger and cannot risk a snake in our midst. Explain yourself.'

'My Lord,' greeted Sophos to Janiz, 'I am not your enemy, I came to find my friend Harry and to warn him of a danger that awaits him, and you.'

'What danger do you speak of sage? Tell us now or we will waste no further time on you,' Janiz commanded as he lifted his sword an inch from its scabbard.

Sophos paused before answering, I knew he could not mention the gunpowder as none here would understand. Finally, he had his story straight in his mind and began his answer.

'There are two reasons I fled my village, my lord. The first being a disagreement with a husband over his wife and a very real threat to my life. The second reason was my discovery that the sorcerer has come into possession of a magic powder. A magic powder that can destroy anything. A powder that can reduce a boulder to rubble in a second. A powder that can reduce an animan to little pieces.'

Gasps of fright came from the riders at this news, only Janiz, Magister and myself remained quiet. Then voices were raised in question. What was this powder? What demon had given such a weapon to the sorcerer? How could we fight such a powerful magic? The questions rained down in a torrent before Janiz held up a hand for silence.

'This is news we did not expect to hear. How did you make this discovery? How do you know of this powder?' whispered Janiz, drawing his sword further from its scabbard.

'Lord, I overheard the wagon driver talking while at his drink. He even showed me the magic powder in his wagon. As soon as I discovered this I knew I had to warn Harry.'

'Why Harry?' demanded Magister.

'I knew he travelled with you lord, it is common knowledge in the gossip of the land. I also knew you travelled to the palace. It took little to deduce you wished to regain your royal position at the palace, but everyone knows the sorcerer plots against you. Therefore in order to save my friend Harry, I had to seek you out.'

'Very loyal of you, but how did you reach us so quickly? We have ridden fast to get here. You could not possibly have caught us so fast,' asked Janiz, still not convinced at Sophos's tale.

'Oh, that part is easy. First I was being chased, and that always adds speed to one's riding. Secondly, I did not stop at any of the towns or villages as you did. I was too afraid, I know nothing of these parts and had no idea of the dangers. You ride in a group of tough and armed animan, I rode alone. I avoided all other animan and skirted around any populated areas, riding my horse almost to death in my efforts to catch you. I barely rested or ate, only stopping to rest my horse and to refresh my water. I was scared my lord, that's all.' Sophos lowered his eyes at this statement, indicating his shame at admitting his fear.

I knew better, I knew Sophos wasn't scared. His cunning little mind decreed he acted in a way that would be expected of him, cowering before the animan warriors. The small Lupus even gave a tiny sniff, reiterating his lowliness and dread. The animan believed him, growling quietly at his lack of courage. The devious little bugger played his part well. Low muttering began amongst the riders, not caring how Sophos had caught us, their concerns lay with the magic powder the sorcerer had conjured. Even Janiz and Magister were in deep whispered conversation. Suddenly Janiz looked down at Sophos.

'Did you see any other on your remarkable journey to find us?' he asked.

'No, no I spoke to no one. Like I said I avoided all contact with animan as I travelled. I saw no one,' replied Sophos.

'No one at all?' pushed Janiz.

'No one my lord, no . . . well I did see one I remember, but I kept my distance.'

'What did he look like? Did he seem to be following our path?' continued Janiz.

'Well now you mention it, yes, yes he did appear to be heading in the same direction as you,' admitted Sophos.

'Well what did he look like Sage?' growled Janiz with a rising temper.

'Oh sorry. I didn't get close enough to see his features, but from what I could see, he looked an evil individual. Not someone I would approach lightly. I did notice he was a Leo though. More than that I can't say. I'm sorry.'

'That is enough. Thank you. Now back to this powder. How do we protect ourselves from it? Can we fight it?' Janiz questioned as all present listened intently.

'I don't think so, I . . actually if it gets wet it becomes useless I think, but you can't fight it. Your only choice is to keep well away from it. Well away.'

Janiz fell silent as his mind pondered on this news. A magical powder was yet another threat placed on us by the sorcerer. I could see both Janiz and Magister were deeply concerned at Sophos's news. The riders whispered and shuffled as they talked in muted tones, discussing this new magic. They were frightened, fearful of this unknown magic and the sorcerer's power in conjuring this evil powder. I was scared too, I knew what gunpowder could do. And I had a bag full of the stuff up my shirt . . . .

The meeting over and all curiosity concerning Sophos satisfied, Janiz, Magister and the others filed out of the barn to continue whatever activity they had been engaged in before the confession of the sage. I remained, there were still some matters I wished to discuss with the only other person who would understand. Sophos had regained his composure and now lay back on the straw, peering up at me.

'You've changed,' he stated after a brief pause. 'When I last saw you, you were lost and afraid. Now you bear an aura of confidence and your Mancunian ways are no longer evident. So what happened to you Harry?'

'Where do I start? I have been through more exciting, dangerous and confusing adventures here than an action movie back home. I've fought and killed, encountered so-called magic and been hunted. Yeah, I'd say I've changed. Anyway, I want to know what action caused you to run from your village. You mentioned a husband?'

'Ah well, yes a husband. Erm . . , as you know, my title of Sage brings all sorts of folk to my home in search of guidance and wisdom,' he paused until I had stopped laughing. 'Yes, thank you. Now, are you going to listen or laugh?'

I nodded that I would listen so he carried on with his tale. 'Well, one day a young female animan came to my home. She suspected her husband had discovered her infidelity with another and sought an excuse or persuasion that would calm her husband and save their marriage. So I gave her a couple of suggestions and she went away to try them. Anyway, one of them must have worked because she returned the next day for more advice. Soon she was coming to see me regularly and, well you know, one thing leads to another and things happened. I don't need to tell you what, I can see on your face. All went well and very pleasurable for both of us until one day the husband followed her to my home. He had become suspicious of her daily visits to me and decided to check up on her. It was what he found that caused my sudden departure from my home and village. The husband was a powerful man locally and set assassins and bounty hunters after me. So I ran, I ran after the only person I could trust, you.'

'Well that's a hell of a story but, it doesn't surprise me one little bit. You typical randy scouse git!' I laughed. 'But what are you going to do now? No one knows you out here and you risk life and limb by being associated with Janiz and his riders. You may be better off facing the husband.'

'Yes, I see that now, but it's too late. I'm here, I can't go back home so I may as well risk my life for a noble cause as any other.'

I was not sure if I believed the little Liverpudlian but I had to admit, I was pleased to see him again. Having someone to talk to who came from my world, my land and my country would be helpful. I decided I would still keep an eye on the little bugger though, just in case.

Chapter Thirteen: A Friend in Need

We left Magister and his settlement on the morning of the fourth day, laden down with food supplies, blankets, extra clothing and weapons. Our horses were well fed and rested and eager to go, but the same could not be said for the riders, especially Janiz. We had been made so welcome by Magister and his folk that leaving was difficult and made all the harder by the knowledge of where we rode. Our final destination was now growing very near, the city of Urbem Regiam. There we would face the might of the king and the cunning of the sorcerer, and most likely, our deaths.

    Sophos rode with us, which surprised me. I had never thought of him as a fighting man but he insisted. As we rode, and when my constant companion Secuutus left us to answer a call of nature, Sophos confessed his real reason for joining us. The little Lupus sage from Liverpool had decided he wished to return home, to his home in England. Sophos, like myself, hoped the small jade box would send him back and travelling with Janiz and myself was likely to be his only chance. As for myself, my goal to acquire the jade box remained, however the thought of returning to the cold and rain of Manchester and my lonely life as a lecturer was rapidly losing its appeal. I found I liked this land and the animan, I found the adventure stimulating even if terrifying at times. Also, my curious mind longed to discover more about the evolution of what are still predatory animals on my world. Other questions remained such as why the tectonic plates had not moved apart here, and why the single landmass still existed? And of course the biggest question of all, how had evolution affected other creatures with no oceans to act as borders? Did the kangaroo still exist? These questions filled my mind when not fighting for my life of course, so could I return to the polluted world? I was not sure.

We rode on with all our senses alert, this close to the king's residence meant military patrols were increasingly frequent. On several occasions over the next few days we had to dodge into cover or make lengthy detours to avoid being seen or captured, or worse. I now rode as part of a trio, myself, Sophos and Secuutus. It did not take long for my two chatty friends to break the ice and, it seemed to me, talk incessantly all day. It still struck me as surreal, a tiger, a wolf and a bear riding horses while conversing. Even more unbelievable was the fact that a Mancunian, a Liverpudlian and an Animan rode together over this strange land. Sophos had lived here much longer than me, so felt more at ease holding a conversation with Secuutus. He knew the gossip of the day and the ways of the animan. I still had to check my words before speaking, making sure I used no references from my past life.

The other riders were not so accommodating toward Sophos at first and generally avoided him. Janiz however, did not seem to mind his presence, providing the little Liverpudlian didn't talk too much in his company. Any animosity did not last long, Sophos used all his skills to overcome their attitude towards him and gradually won them over. At night whilst camped around the cooking fire, Sophos came into his own, entertaining the riders with tales and anecdotes that helped disperse the fears and anxieties of our future. Even I found some of his tales amusing, though most were beyond my understanding, they related to matters closer to the animan.

Amidst the jokes and chatter, one serious subject returned to the conversation frequently, that of the sorcerer. How would we fight a being with the ability to control the magical arts? All too often for my liking, the eyes of the riders turned to me when the sorcerer was mentioned. It was obvious they saw me as their saviour against magic, after all, I had drunk of the burning waters and faced down a demon. My reputation grew with each telling of the tales. To my annoyance, Sophos joined in with the riders, even though he certainly understood that nothing magical had occurred. The little bugger derived great amusement from watching me squirm as my legend blossomed.

On our fifth night of the journey, Janiz called a halt to the antics of the sage and insisted we make plans on how to gain entry to the palace. Janiz ordered that we all give the matter our full consideration and offer up suggestions on how to achieve our purpose. I could contribute little to the schemes as I had not yet seen the palace or the royal city. My input would have to wait until I had a clear understanding of what we faced. I told this to Janiz and the riders and received nods of understanding in return. As I was the magical 'legend', it was finally decided we would not settle on any plans until we were within sight of Urbem Regiam. A decision that I approved of, though some riders felt we should plan now. I admit I agreed with them to a point, some form of plan should be initialised before we reached the stage of no return. Some agreed structure to underline any plans we may make should be laid now.

'It seems to me,' I interrupted quietly, 'that we make plans for dealing with the sorcerer prematurely. First, we have to reach the city in one piece, then we have to gain entry. Two very important factors that will decide any further actions.'

My comments struck a chord with Janiz. 'Ah, Harry is right. First, we must get to the city itself. For those who do not know, the city of Urbem Regiam is protected by huge walls, far higher and stronger than those of Tutique Receptus. We will not be able to scale them for entry. We must gain access via the city gates, and for that to happen, we will need a very good plan. Perhaps our wily sage can offer suggestions?'

To my great amusement, suddenly all eyes were on the Liverpudlian, who appeared to physically shrink under everyone's expectant gaze. The moment did not last long before the showman accepted the spotlight. Sophos drew up his slight frame and theatrically placed his head to one side and closed his eyes, indicating to all that he was deep in thought. I didn't believe him.

'Perhaps some form of disguise?' came his first suggestion, 'or perhaps there is another way past the walls, drains, sewers or waste outlets? One does not necessarily need to enter by an obvious route.'

'Now those ideas are worth considering,' agreed Janiz, 'nonetheless, once inside the city walls we will still have to reach the palace without detection. What we need is a form of deception that will aid us reach the very heart of the palace.'

My brain kicked into gear as I had an idea. 'Who would have free access to the gates, the city streets and possibly even the palace?' I asked in general.

Immediately all sorts of answers and theories bubbled up as the riders gave voice to their thoughts and suggestions. Janiz watched me intently, his mind working to follow my thoughts. A sly grin of understanding spread over the wolf like features of Sophos. While the others discussed and argued, I pondered over my idea, digesting it before tearing it apart again, making sure my idea was strong before revealing it. After the discussion bounced back and forth for a while, Janiz called a halt to all the babbling and turned to face me, curiosity and hope conflicting on his features.

'Well?' he growled.

I considered my words carefully, not sure of the reaction to my plan. 'Yes, we can seek another entrance to the city but that is only one obstacle conquered. We need a plan to enter the gates, move through the city safely and possibly allow us to gain entrance to the palace. We need to be soldiers.'

'What?' came the cry from several surprised animan. 'Soldiers? How can we be soldiers, we're outlaws, not soldiers!'

'Explain!' ordered Janiz while signalling for quiet.

'Alright, here goes. We could never hope to sneak into and through the city without causing suspicion or Janiz being recognised. Our group of riders would have to split up as we could not travel together. This would present more difficulties in communication and the ability to deal with any unknown situation that might arise.'

'No, we need to remain as a group, separating will put us all at risk. And before you start shouting, I know we would not get but a few yards as a group, the military would be down on us in an instant. So, our main challenges are avoiding being recognised and getting past the king's soldiers.' I paused to allow my reasoning to be digested by the riders. 'However, if we too were soldiers, riding as a patrol or small troop, who would even notice us?'

My last question was greeted with a thunderous silence. Every single animan stared at me in mute shock as what I had suggested penetrated their minds. I knew my plan held risks but the fact was that we intended entering a royal city, in a land from which Janiz had been banished, to invade the palace of the king and kill the royal adviser and close confidant to His Royal Majesty. Not too difficult, surely? I realised I was kidding myself, perhaps I had watched too much television back in my world, I must have done something weird to come up with a plan such as this.

'I see the potential of your plan Harry, but one wonders how we are to obtain uniforms and pass ourselves off as soldiers?' said Janiz as he waited or a response from the others. Predictably none came forth.

'I admit I haven't thought the whole thing through yet, it was just an idea that came to mind after your comment, you said we needed a deception. Entering the city dressed as soldiers seems to be the only possible solution.'

Janiz and several others nodded at my reasoning. 'Perhaps we could steal the uniforms from a barracks? Are there any in this area?'

'No, the only army base with supplies such as uniforms is inside the city. The barracks, armoury and headquarters are all situated in a section of the city, between the north and east gates. We would have to first gain access to the city before we could raid the military stores,' Janiz answered with a frown.

At that point, our devious and cunning sage decided to interject with a possible solution, one that was already on my mind and I could see Janiz and others had reached the same conclusion, it simply fell to Sophos to give voice to it.

'There is only one way to obtain uniforms from the soldiers,' he said. 'We will have to take them.'

'That's no good,' muttered Secuutus. 'The uniforms will be torn and bloody, we need clean uniforms if we are going to get away with this plan.'

Again nods and words of agreement confirmed the general misgivings of the riders until Janiz silenced them. 'Then it would be prudent not to mark the uniforms when we take them.' This statement brought an end to the discussion and the camp settled down for sleep.

As we were nearing the city and the likelihood of increased patrols, Janiz had ordered a guard set through the night. Fidelis was charged with organising a rota. Three riders would share this night's guard rota, each standing guard for a couple of hours each. Nights were short and we rose early, so three could cover the night. From then on, three different riders would be on guard every night, meaning each of us would be on watch once every four or five days. A sound arrangement I thought, as no single animan would become so tired that they became a liability. Luckily for me, tonight was not going to be my night so I settled down and tried to sleep. But sleep did not come easy that night, the conflicts and worries of my previous and new life played upon my mind.

The next day found spirits high, we had an initial plan, and we had an objective. We were very near the city of Urbem Regiam and win or lose, we would give our best. I suspected this excitement would not last long, the grim threat of death could always be relied upon as a party spoiler. The day passed uneventfully with riders discussing and dissecting our plans. We encountered no threat and saw no patrols, it was a pleasant day, one of a very few I realised. The day passed into night and under a clear starry sky, bursts of light could be seen in the sky over the horizon in the direction of the city.

Although we were too far away to see clearly, the sight still unnerved some of the riders and several drew their weapons closer as they settled into their blankets. I was intrigued, the sight appeared familiar and then I had it. 'Fireworks,' I muttered and received a nod of agreement from Sophos, though neither of us bothered attempting to explain my comment to the frightened riders. The sorcerer was using some of his gunpowder to either frighten or demonstrate his powers to the populous of the city. By adding substances such as copper or iron filings to gunpowder, it was relatively easy to construct a colourful firework to shock the denizens of Urbem Regiam. The riders nonetheless, feared the sorcerer was casting spells over the city and I doubted any explanation would suffice. I huddled down under my blanket and fell asleep, the fireworks forgotten.

We continued to avoid any larger villages, but as Janiz had promised, there were no large towns between us and Urbem Regiam. The mood of the riders grew steadily more solemn, each rider retreating into his own thoughts. All except Sophos, he remained annoyingly cheerful and even more irritating, he continued to chat endlessly. Trouble continued to avoid us and on the third day, our objective came into view. A haze of wood smoke hovered on the horizon, underlined by the black shape of the city. Now our eyes and fears were constantly drawn to our destination, as it grew steadily larger in our vision. The city was still some distance away and it would take at least another week before we reached it, travelling by horse alone making the journey so much longer than if taken by a motor vehicle of my world. Now in sight of the city, Janiz decided we should acquire our uniforms. A challenge I did not look forward to with glee.

It was the next day before we saw a patrol of soldiers in the distance heading in our direction. They appeared to number about eighteen, more soldiers than riders but Janiz assured us we would triumph by ambush. We chose a section of the road that was lined with enough undergrowth and trees to hide us. A fallen tree was dragged across the road to halt the soldiers long enough for our attack. The soldiers came closer, sweat once more adorned my brow as I clenched tightly on my staff, its blade still hidden. As we didn't want the uniforms marked, each rider was armed with a stout cudgel instead of a sword. I could see many of them felt naked without a sword in their hands, but I was content with my trusty staff. The troop of soldiers were now in plain sight and I risked a furtive glance each side of me, seeing others filled with the anxiety and dreadful excitement of what was to unfold. None of the riders moved or even breathed it seemed. I wondered how many were having to clench their buttocks as tightly as I was. We waited like coiled snakes as the soldiers approached, and we waited for a signal from Janiz, we waited to either live or die.

We lay hidden, spread out in the undergrowth beside the road until the troop of unsuspecting soldiers came level with us and Janiz signalled the attack. We flew out of hiding and fell upon the soldiers with such speed and ferocity that most never even managed to draw their weapons before receiving a crashing blow to the head. A good number of the soldiers lay unconscious on the road within seconds, those that remained stood fighting for their lives. I played little part in the fight, apart from smashing my staff down upon the head of a soldier nearest me. He dropped to the ground like a stone and I spun to assist the others. However, I found myself redundant, with the numbers now securely in favour of the riders, the remaining soldiers each faced at least two riders against them.

Suddenly one of the soldiers broke free from the melee and charged straight at me, screaming like a banshee as he wielded his sword; whirling it in circles above his head in readiness to bring it down on mine. I stood as he ran towards me, I stood until his sword began to descend upon my head. I stood until I could feel his breath on my face, and then in a blur of speed, I sidestepped. Positioned at the side of the now unbalanced soldier, I brought my knee up level to my hip, then with my toes pointing forward, I drove my foot around and kicked into his solar plexus with all the force I could muster. His headlong charge came to a sudden halt, his sword falling from his grasp as he bent forward, his breath rushing from his body as he collapsed to the ground. A blow to the solar plexus will stop even the biggest foe. As my victim fell I whipped up my staff and prepared to cave in his head as he lay at my feet, curled and gasping in pain on the ground.

'Hold!' commanded Janiz as he ran towards me, a hand held up in a gesture to reinforce his verbal instruction. My staff halted barely inches from the soldier's bare head and there it stayed until I knew what I was supposed to do, I was taking no chances of my opponent recovering and resuming the attack. Janiz stopped beside the fallen soldier and gently but firmly lowered my staff with his hand then gestured for me to move back. What the hell was going on I wondered? Janiz crouched over the figure at his feet and placed a hand under one of the soldier's arms and began helping him to his feet. I stood ready, not sure what Janiz intended. I quickly glanced at the soldier's uniform and could see from the insignia that he was an officer of some sort, what exactly I had no idea but I was certain he was not a simple grunt. The soldier was of the Leo Cast and had a bearing of importance about him, his posture once he straightened, was solid and confident, his gaze showing no fear, only acceptance. His eyes glanced over me with disdain before coming to light on a fellow Leo, Janiz.

'Greetings Ductor. I am pleased to see you, though different circumstances may be more favourable,' hailed Janiz as he placed a hand on the soldier's shoulder and peered at his face.

'Ah Janiz, I hadn't expected to see you again,' whispered the soldier as he fought against the effects of a solar plexus kick. 'What are you doing here? If you're discovered breaking banishment, you'll surely be put to the sword.'

'Yes, of that there is no doubt. However, I don't intend to be caught, at least not until I'm ready. But enough, sit and recover a while. I will not apologise for my friend Harry, but perhaps I sympathise with your pain. Harry has a somewhat different but very effective method of combat.' Janiz gently helped the soldier down to the ground again, his actions not what one would expect between foes.

'My men. Do they live?' queried Ductor through clenched teeth.

'Rest yourself Ductor, your men will live, perhaps with sore heads when they awake, but they will live,' replied Janiz. 'We have need of them yet.'

With that, Janiz ordered the riders to carry out our plan. Immediately the soldiers were stripped of their uniforms, backpacks and even their boots. Every item that would aid our disguise as soldiers was taken from their unconscious bodies, leaving them still prone on the ground in an assortment of military and personal undergarments. One or two did cause a raised eyebrow or snigger regarding their choice of underwear, but this was quickly forgotten as the riders sought uniforms that fit.

'What are you doing?' Exclaimed Ductor. 'What torture do you plan for us now?'

'We need your uniforms is all Ductor, no need to fret, nothing else is to happen. Now, if you will kindly strip?' Janiz asked the still shocked officer. 'We or I need your uniform also, luckily we were always of similar size. I believe you are of a rank to command these animan?'

The soldier began unbuttoning his tunic, bewilderment evident on his face. 'Yes, I'm now a captain and these are my animan. I warn you, whatever you plan will fail. If I live I will hunt you down personally. I don't agree with the king's orders to kill you on sight but now you affront myself and my soldiers. I will seek atonement.'

'Do not threaten me Ductor, or should I say Dux . . ? I leave you and your animan alive because of the close bonds we once shared, but I could change my mind,' growled Janiz as he pointed his sword at the captain menacingly.

'Wait. What is it you plan? Perhaps I can be of assistance? I'm no traitor but we were once close and there has always been trust between us. I admit I have no love left for your father and despise his sorcerer. He is the evil behind what is happening in the kingdom I'm sure. I am, like many, disturbed at what is happening in the palace. I fear the sorcerer means to remove your father from the throne and take it for himself. I'm still a king's officer and my duty remains with the king, but as a soldier loyal to his country, I cannot stand by and let evil descend upon our animan.'

'Huh! A fine plea Ductor, but there is the little matter of, as you say, trust. It has been some time and I wonder if that trust still lives,' replied Janiz, his eyes glinting like yellow steel as he stared thoughtfully at his almost naked past companion. 'Why would you help us, me? You are a soldier of the king and therefore your first loyalty will be to him. My friend you have been, but that time is past. Why would you offer help and why should I trust you? Tell me this before you are gagged and bound along with your patrol.'

Ductor paused, considering his words carefully. His reputation may depend on them. 'I know your spirit is pure Janiz, as friends and companions I grew to know your mind. I know inside me that any plan you have will be for the good of this land. I may also remind you that despite your banishment, you're still the heir to the royal throne. Perhaps you're the only animan who could rid the palace of the disease that has riddled it since that sorcerer arrived. You're the only animan that could achieve this without being called a traitor or conqueror. You fight for your kingdom, you fight for your inheritance and you fight for your right to rule. You're the only one who could restore justice to the throne. That is why I would help you.' Ductor paused again and looked over to his prone and semi-naked solders before continuing. 'However, I cannot speak for my soldiers, they may not share my trust in you. They may betray us, but as their captain, I would not see them harmed.'

'I will consider you words Ductor,' replied Janiz thoughtfully.

Janiz left me guarding the captain while he wandered off to check his riders had stripped and secured the still unconscious soldiers. Fidelis had administered a few further bumps on the head of any unfortunate soldier stirring to wake. Janiz ordered that the riders maintained the state of unconsciousness while he considered Ductor's request. Each rider was now dressed in a stolen uniform, most looked presentable but with his huge frame, Secuutus's bulging form strained the largest uniform he could find. Janiz decided it would be wise for Secuutus to travel amidst the other riders, thus hiding his bursting uniform from suspicious eyes. Finally, he reached a decision and, ordering a uniform to be found for himself, he returned to where I stood watch over a now shivering and embarrassed Ductor.

'Get dressed,' growled Janiz to the captain. 'We can use you in the fulfilment of our plan, but know that your life will be forfeit at the first sign of any treachery. Harry will be your guard but beware, he is far more dangerous than he appears.'

Ductor stood and replaced his clothing with a few muttered words of gratitude as Janiz continued. 'Your animan may be a problem, though all appear unconscious, there might possibly be some feigning to avoid another blow from Fidelis. I agree you could be useful, but only if no one suspects.' Janiz's voice dropped even lower, he had not spoken loud enough to be heard by any conscious soldier but he refused to take the chance. 'When you are fully attired, stand and pretend to take flight. We will stop you and any watching will believe you taken as a hostage. It will help our plans if you appear innocent, if we fail and are caught, no blame or accusation will befall you. Make it look real!'

With that said, Janiz began to walk away and Ductor took his chance. He sprang to his feet and launched a massive blow at my surprised jaw. Down I went, the blow knocking me senseless for a moment. Even though I knew what was to happen, I had not considered it happening to me. In an instant Janiz whirled, his cudgel still in his hand and swung it round to smash against Ductor's head. The captain went down as hard as I had, though Janiz hit harder and Ductor was out for the count. I struggled to my feet with embarrassment glowing on my face under the grins from the other riders. No one but Janiz and I knew of the farcical escape attempt, so the other riders assumed I had been outwitted by the failed escapist. To be honest, I had. At a gesture from Janiz, a couple of riders tied and gagged the still unconscious officer, with opportune timing as some soldiers were awakening and witnessed the events. A fortunate occurrence and a necessary one for our plan to work. Finally, Ductor was flung unceremoniously over a horse as we mounted and rode off, leaving the bound soldiers to escape by whatever means they could devise and firmly believing their officer a captive.

I could not fathom the level of trust Janiz had placed in allowing Ductor to accompany us, he was after all a king's soldier and loyalty to the throne had been ingrained into his very being, as proven by his rise to the rank of captain. Whatever the reasoning of our leader Janiz, the now captive Ductor rode on his belly over a horse, trussed up like a turkey. Secuutus, my constant riding companion held onto the reins and Ductor journeyed sandwiched between us. I secretly wished Ductor would attempt another escape, I had a desire to share my painful jaw with the captain. Sadly there would be no chance for him as Secuutus also kept a vigilant watch over the prisoner, and I could see he had no intention of allowing the prisoner to get free. I did have one small sense of satisfaction when I saw Ductor's red and grimacing face, riding belly down on a horse's back can never be described as pleasant.

We travelled on, riding parallel to the road that would lead to our final destination, Urbem Regiam. The road itself had grown increasingly busy with traders, merchants, travellers and soldiers constantly moving along its surface. Not wishing our plans thwarted, we avoided contact with all others. At times we rode under a silent canopy of thick forest, other times we had to increase our distance from the road as the landscape opened up. This close to the city, we frequently passed farms and other such communities that customarily sprout up in the peripheries of a city. Close enough for trade and protection without actually being in the city itself. Moving furtively slowed us down, it would have been far easier and faster to travel along the road, but it was a luxury we could not afford. Janiz wanted to be certain of Ductor before he released him.

It was while under the cover of a small wood that Janiz called a halt to allow the horses to rest and drink. Ductor was finally untied and the plan outlined to all the riders. It was simple, as we now resembled a troop of the king's soldiers we would need an officer.

Someone who understood the present military procedures and command structure. Ductor would travel at the lead of our group, just as he would be expected to, however, both Janiz and Fidelis would ride beside him, watching for any sign of treachery. I was relinquished from my duties while we rode, for which I was grateful. Some of the riders expressed concern at having a military captain in our midst but Janiz assured them Ductor would die at any discretion. Following Ductor's orders, confirmed by Janiz, we formed up in pairs and moved off, this time risking the road itself. If anything was to go wrong with our deception, then better it happened in the countryside than in the confines of the city.

We joined the throng moving towards the city, merchants, travellers, traders and farmers herding animals all travelled the road in search of wealth or a future. The nearer we came to the city, so the traffic along the road increased to a stage where Ductor had to order other travellers out of our way. It was an action expected of an officer in charge of a troop of soldiers, and although we received many muttered comments of defiance, all still moved to the roadside and allowed us to pass. At no time did Ductor give any indication of betrayal or escape. It became apparent that the two had once been firm friends, a friendship that had stood the test of time and the gulf between a loyal soldier and a wanted outlaw was no barrier. Soon all the other riders, including myself, grew to like the quick-witted and capable captain, our mistrust dissipating over the time spent in his company. Janiz remained in overall command but the riders no longer scowled or resisted any instructions given by Ductor. In a short time, he was accepted as a member of our group, though trust remained to be achieved.

Now travelling along the road we made good speed and the city grew in our vision and it was not long before our deception was put to the test. We had only journeyed some distance along the widening road before we encountered a real military patrol. Ductor called a halt as we came close, the other officer signalling his intention to question our business. The opposing patrol outnumbered ours but not by many. However being this close to the city, more troops would quickly come to investigate any disturbance. Fighting our way past was not an option. The real patrol came to a halt in front of our fake patrol and the two officers greeted each other formally. Both appeared to be of similar rank, though I could not be sure, I had no idea of the insignia used here. Formalities over, the real officer demanded to know our purpose. He too was a Leo, his arrogant manner and ramrod posture indicated a dedicated soldier, proud of his position and wanting all to witness his warrior heritage. Ductor also drew himself up, facing off the other officer in a show of his own. I readied my staff and noticed several of the riders doing the same. Janiz kept close to Ductor, ready to strike him down if he showed any attempt to betray us. Following several tense minutes, the meeting was a success. Ductor had been recognised and his explanation of a returning patrol was accepted. We were allowed on our way.

Nearing the city, we began to pass through the shacks and patched tents of the poor sector, animan sheltering in whatever form of structure they could assemble from whatever they could scavenge. The smell was bad as it is in all *shanty towns* in any land, rotting vegetation, unwashed bodies and animan waste combined into a rich aroma of poverty. It reminded me of the infamous shanty towns of South America in Brazil and Rio or those in Africa and even the Bahamas. Notably, the materials used here consisted more of patched cloth, leather and wood; corrugated iron and sheets of plastic did not exist but would have seemed a luxury here. Nonetheless, whatever materials were used, the place was still recognisable for what it was.

Gradually the shantytown was replaced with the small domed homes of the not-so-poor, those working families who toiled long hours just to survive. The smell had lifted but not yet completely gone as we plodded along the dirt streets, moving deeper into the city. The domes of the not-so-poor were intermixed with simple wooden structures that consisted of four walls and a roof. Alas in this great land, square buildings were the residence of those on the bottom of the ladder and considered fit only for animals or storage. To live in such a building labelled one in society, being on a par with the shantytown slums. I could see no reason for the fashion of dome buildings, I had been warned about the strength of the wind here, but as yet I had not witnessed it. Yes, there had been a storm while I hid in a publican with Sophos, but that was only a minor storm, nothing like the big ones I had been told occurred here. However, I will admit the dome was logically far better at coping with all sorts of weather conditions than a square. But old preferences still came to the fore. Riding through this mixture of alien buildings, shacks and sheds, reminded me of how far away from home I was, and of course the relative safety of civilised society. Here, danger lurked constantly.

So far no one had sought to question us, though we were eyed with suspicion and mistrust. Dressed in uniform, we represented the rich and powerful and therefore to be avoided by all who's social class could not afford to pay bribes. Our journey proved uneventful and we finally reached the city gates. Hordes of animan attempted to gain admission into the city while just as many wished to exit. Most were merchants carrying their wares on donkeys or pulling tiny handcarts. Others were farmers riding oxen or horse pulled wagons laden with produce or driving livestock before them. Amid this confusion, wealthy individuals strode purposefully, their private guards battering animan out of their way. Many in the throng had the appearance of travellers, those wishing to make a better life in the city or simply visiting. All flooded through the gate in an orderly procession, kept under control by the city guards.

We were quickly allowed through the gates, the guards holding back the crowds to make way for us. Ductor called to one of the guards whom he recognised and received a cheery comment in return. A display of familiarity that unwittingly reinforced our deception. In truth, the guards were more concerned with filtering out known petty villains, thieves and cutthroats, no one even considered a threat to the palace or the king.

Once inside the gate, the cries and shouts of street traders indicated we had entered the trading or commercial part of the city. Janiz ordered that we leave the horses in one of the cleaner looking stables, all of us doubting we would ever see our mounts again. Once the horses were safe, we formed up as a troop of soldiers and continued our journey through the streets. All the while our ears and eyes were berated by the sounds and sights of the city. Traders hoping to cash in from the large numbers of animan passing in and out of the gates. Here one could buy or sell anything, even the impossible. From a trinket for a lady to a loaf of bread for the table, from an item of clothing to an elaborately decorated dagger, an assassin to sex, everything was for sale.

The scene appeared familiar until I realised the same had occurred on my world and still did in many countries. Street markets full of temporary stalls, all decorated in an explosion of colour, smell and sound. Traders shouted and touted for business, each vying to be heard above the calls of their neighbours. Sole traders carrying trays of trinkets or food plied their trade along the street itself. Whores called suggestively from alleys created between the stalls, though where they gave their services escaped me. A blanket on the ground behind a stall I suspected.

As soldiers no one bothered us as we marched through the crowded streets, no one apart from the whores, of course, they always recognised potential customers. With Ductor leading, traders and customers alike quickly made way and allowed us through. No one wishing to be on the receiving end of a sword from an irate soldier. All we had to fear as we marched along was stepping in something nasty, and believe me, there were a lot of nasties littering the streets. More than one rider was sent skidding off balance after treading in something unidentifiable. As in the third world countries of my home, the poorer sectors are not readily provided with sewers, waste of all kind was dumped in the streets. At that stage, we were more at risk of catching something horrible than we were of being discovered as infiltrators.

In due course, Ductor led us from the street markets into what I would describe as suburbia, small dome homes began to appear, ringed by little well kept gardens. The streets were clear so our progress increased. We marched on, barely noticing the few local residents who in turn, gave no more than a fleeting glance as we passed by. I concluded that soldiers passing through was a common sight, the residents well used to a military presence. I could not believe how easy it had been for a group of outlaws posing as military to penetrate all the cities defences and guards. Surely it could not last I thought.

But it did and before long we had reached deeper into the city and found ourselves in the business and retail sector. Here large dome structures advertised a variety of goods and services. Real shops sold everything one would expect of a town centre. The smell of the poor sector now replaced with the aroma of fresh bread, cooked meats and scented animan. There were even several large publicans and it was towards one of these that Janiz and Ductor now led us. We had travelled quite a distance from the south gate and we were in need of a rest and refreshments. A publican was ideal, for where do soldiers from any race, creed or world head straight for? A publican.

Chapter Fourteen: A Plan

We did not linger long in the publican, afraid of arousing suspicion. It would be unusual for a patrol of soldiers to spend too much time in a publican whilst on duty, all we needed was time to regroup. Ductor ordered no alcohol to be consumed, an order backed up by a glare from Janiz. Instead, we chose to refresh ourselves with a strange hot drink that tasted like hot chocolate. I suppose it was not impossible, no land borders would mean products such as cocoa could be widespread. I gave up thinking and simply enjoyed the beverage as Janiz and Ductor informed us we were within a few streets of the main palace gate. A planning session ensued amongst the senior riders, a group including Janiz, Fidelis, Secuutus, Firmus, Ductor and myself. Though why I had been included I had no idea. We huddled around a table to discuss strategy while the other riders provided a security circle around us, ensuring no eavesdropping could occur.

The plan began simply enough. Led by Ductor, we would march in through the palace gate on the pretence of returning to barracks. Once inside the perimeter wall, one group would split off and attempt to enter the palace by the main entrance. Ductor was to gain entry by declaring he had caught Janiz while on patrol and intended taking him to the king for sentencing. This group would be led by Janiz who would remain very close to the captain, a dagger held concealed against treachery. Once Janiz and his group were inside, they would act and plan accordingly as they searched for King Fastus.

Another group led by Fidelis would make their way to the rear of the main palace building and create some form of distraction. It was hoped that this distraction would draw the attention of the palace guard and reduce the risk of Ductor's subterfuge being challenged. The last group would seek entry into the palace via a servant's entrance that Janiz informed us was to the right of the building. I was to be included in this group under the command of Firmus, though Janiz reminded him to take note of any suggestion Secuutus or I came up with. Firmus readily agreed, his features suggesting he was not happy with being in charge and any excuse to follow another's lead would suit him just fine. We were to be the assassins with the main objective of hunting down and dispatching the sorcerer. Sophos was to accompany us as Janiz considered our 'strangeness' may combat the powers of the sorcerer. He would never know just how strange Sophos and I were. A plan agreed, we left the publican and not long after I received my first look at the palace, the home of Janiz; the den of the sorcerer, and the climax of my quest to obtain that damn box.

As we stood posing as a patrol of soldiers at the huge gate, I stared in awe at the massive structure in front of me. A huge white shinning dome reached as high as the only other palace I have ever seen, Buckingham Palace. Its white walls curving smoothly up into a giant white hemisphere. I could only marvel at the construction skills required to achieve such a structure. Windows situated around the dome glittered in the sun, the four levels of windows indicating the considerable interior space. Each window fitted perfectly to follow the curve of the dome. Most dome structures I had encountered in this land had windows, but none to this level of craftsmanship. Every window shone like a jewel, reflecting the daylight in a way reminiscent of the mirror balls often seen in the old discos and dance venues. Facing the gate at which we now stood, one of the windows was much larger than the others and incorporated a curved balcony. I noted even here, kings and queens liked to wave at the populous that gathered on special occasions. Around the towering hemisphere, much smaller domes ringed the main structure like petals on a flower, a daisy to be precise. Each dome appeared to merge into the next, linking all the domes into one large building.

    Lastly, the magnificent structure sat in fabulous gardens, gardens that featured plants, shrubs and trees from across the world. Even I recognised some of the colourful species. Capability Brown himself would have been proud of this immaculate landscape. Trim lawns stretched out, blanketing the ground in a green carpet interspersed with splashes of colourful flora. Shrubs bloomed and scattered trees offered shade from which to view the magnificent gardens. Narrow white gravel roads radiated out from the palace, dissecting the gardens. Each road followed a point of the compass, north, south, east and west. Each direction coming to an end at a similar but smaller version of the main gate.

Once I had overcome the beauty of the building and its gardens, I began to notice things that may possibly have a bearing on our hasty plan. Soldiers littered the grounds. Soldiers stood guard beside each gate and encircled the palace. Ramrod stiff troops lined the main road leading to the great entrance door, dozens of soldiers standing at attention on each side of the gravel road. A guard of honour that would explode into action if any threat should arise. Other guards could be seen patrolling the boundary wall which encircled the vast grounds and the giant daisy at the centre. The heavily guarded palace would be the death of us if our deception did not work. We would not stand a chance against so many and would be cut down in moments. A thought that dampened the beauty of the place in my eyes.

I trembled slightly as I waited for Ductor to convince the gate guard to allow us in. I estimated the road from gate to palace door as being some eight hundred yards, just over seven hundred metres long. A mad dash to the palace door would be out of the question, we would never reach it before the lines of soldiers closed in on us. Janiz and Ductor's deception had to work or our quest ended here. At last, Ductor convinced the gate guard and we were allowed in. As soldiers, no one sought to take our weapons, our task would have been seriously challenged if we were unarmed. Oddly, my staff caused some concern to the guards until Ductor explained I had received a knee injury during a skirmish, and that the staff was a walking aid. I immediately began limping.

The march along the white gravel road was the most nerve-wracking action I have ever undertaken in my entire life, either in the land of humans or here amongst the animan. While doing my very best imitation of a soldier marching, limp included, I quickly realised our initial plan would not work. The grounds were so open that if any of our group split off, they would be seen immediately. Aside from the trees dotting the gardens, there was no other structure or feature large enough to provide cover for fleeing riders. There were not even corners we could hide behind, every inch of the palace was visible to the many guards that patrolled the grounds. My terror grew as the futility of escape became apparent. It appeared that Janiz would indeed come face to face with his father, but as a prisoner rather than an invader.

The hairs on the back of my neck stood on end as we marched stiffly through lines of soldiers, each and every one staring menacingly at us as we passed. Every soldier was heavily armed and from their stances, I judged them to be extremely well trained. A missed step or a wrong look from anyone of us could cause the soldiers to react instantly and fatally. I prayed none of the other riders would concede to his fear and start a chain reaction that would result in my demise. After the tensest eon of my life, we ultimately reached the main door. A huge pair of doors standing twice my height and constructed of thick oak planks, held together with wide iron bands and massive iron hinges. Ornate scrolls of wrought iron decorated each side, adding visual design alongside further strength to the doors. Here we were met by two guards, both officers, who issued an order for Ductor to halt before taking up position in front of him at the head of our 'patrol'. To my consternation, we were instructed by the lead guard to make a ninety degree turn to our right. Realisation hit me then, a troop of soldiers bringing a known outlaw to the king's palace would not be expected or allowed to enter by the front entrance. We were being marched to another door hidden from sight of the main gate. No witnesses!

    Trying to show no reaction, all the riders turned and marched behind Ductor as the palace guards led us around the building. We marched past several smaller nondescript doors spaced around the palace exterior, including what I took to be the servant's entrance. My conclusion was based on the number of buckets, mops and rags stacked on wooden shelving just outside the door. We continued on round to the rear of the palace before coming to a halt. The guard ordered us in through yet another sturdy and guarded pair of doors. I could not help but wonder why the main and rear entrances were so well guarded while the servant's door was left insecure. A point to remember I pondered. Once inside we were faced by even more guards. Some stood at a large desk while others lounged on chairs or leaned against walls. It was obvious this was the guard's station. Tables with food and drink, some form of playing cards and the evitable handful of coins suggested our arrival had interrupted the soldier's favourite pastime of gambling. All snapped to attention as we were led through the guard room and into a narrow murky corridor. No words of instruction came from the leading guards, they simply marched ahead and expected us to follow. Any thoughts of attack so far from their minds as to be non-existent.

We turned into another, much wider and brighter corridor, large curving windows on one side provided the illumination. The walls were as white as the exterior and beneath our feet lay a fine mosaic of tiles, polished to a high sheen. Doors leading to an assortment of rooms stood along the corridor, lit from the daylight pouring in from the beautifully crafted windows opposite. Some doors were open, showing corridors into the heart of the building. Narrower doors allowed views of a wide range of room contents. From storerooms to empty ones, from sewing rooms to armouries, from rooms piled high with wooden crates to some that were dark and cobweb filled.

I was slightly surprised that there were so many rooms which would serve as hiding places left unattended and unguarded. It appeared at this stage that the majority of guard presence was outside the palace. A lack of foresight indicated no plans had been made by the security forces for intruders within the palace. No doubt the vast number of guards outside would never allow a threat into the palace itself. An oversight that may prove to be costly to the inhabitants of the royal residence. We marched on in silence until we came to a flight of elegant stairs leading up to the next floor. It was as we approached the stairs that Janiz gave a discrete gesture, warning us that the time to act was near.

We had climbed halfway up the stairs when Janiz suddenly reacted, so swift was his action that he not only surprised the guards but also most of the riders. In a blur the huge form of Janiz whirled, slashing a blade across the throat of the lead guard before spinning to push his now bloody blade deep into the eye of the second. The riders nearest to Janiz quickly recovered from their momentary shock and leapt to catch the guards as they fell. Janiz ordered the lifeless bodies to be carried down the stairs and hidden in the last empty room we had passed. He wanted no bodies lying around to give warning of our intentions.

As soon as the bodies were safely stored and the room door closed, Janiz led us up the stairs again, signalling us to remain quiet. Upon reaching the next floor we were ordered to split into our prearranged groups and follow the plan as best we could. All the riders scattered, some turning right, some turning left, Fidelis and his group headed off down the stairs. I paused for just a moment as I had forgotten what I was supposed to do and with whom. Janiz turned to glare at me. It was a tug on my arm that reminded me of my orders. 'Come on,' whispered Sophos as he dragged me after Firmus and the others in our group.

As our job within the plan was to enter via the servant's entrance and seek out the sorcerer, we were now all slightly befuddled. Where were we and where the hell was the servant's entrance anyway? Following a moment's thought, I realised that because the sorcerer was held in such high esteem by the king, surely his quarters would be in the vicinity of the royal chambers. I voiced my assumption to the others and once more we climbed those damn stairs. On the next level, we were faced with yet another corridor. This one similar to the last, running around the circumference of the building, again dotted with doors on one side, windows on the other. There was no sign of Janiz so Firmus decided we would turn left and follow the corridor round in hope of discovering some clue as to the whereabouts of our target. One thing was for sure, we could not get lost, providing we did not turn into any of the larger doors, because it was evident each outer corridor ran the circumference of the building. If we kept running we would eventually end up right back where we now stood. Off we set, with weapons now drawn and ready, luckily as it turned out.

We had only proceeded a few steps along the corridor when a door opened and several guards stepped out. A moment of frozen time passed before both the guards and riders reacted. Our drawn and ready weapons had instantly given away our intent. With a shout, the guard leader drew his sword and lunged for Firmus, the other guards quickly followed his action. Suddenly we were fighting for our lives, a fight made more difficult as we all wore the same uniform. A guard rushed at me, his sword swinging in a slashing motion at my head. I ducked below the weapon to avoid my head being swept from my shoulders. Following my defensive action, I continued down into a crouch and rammed the butt of my staff into the belly of the guard. As the guard doubled up in pain, I shot upright, whipped up the butt of my staff again and cracked it under his jaw with the duel strength of my legs and arms. The guard collapsed to the floor as another sprang at me.

I whirled to face his attack, his army issue sword held out low in front of him. Quickly stabilising my balance, I kicked out across his body, deflecting the blade away with my foot before swinging my staff round to crash against the side of his head. The blow was not hard enough to render him unconscious but it gave me a split second to charge in with another attack. I had no time to release the blade hidden within the staff so I again whipped the heavy staff up and smashed it down upon his head as if I was bringing down an axe on a stubborn wooden log. The sound of a sickening crunch suggested a broken skull as the guard dropped to the floor, landing in a heap on top of his colleague.

I spun to face the melee of riders and guards, each busy trying to end the life of their opponent. I saw Sophos almost overcome by one burly Ursidae guard and rushed to his defence. This time I pressed the stud that released the blade and now I had a spear. As the guard's full attention was on the cowering figure of Sophos before him, I ran straight at him, projected my staff forward and penetrated the guard's side, just below the rib cage. Immediately the guard let out a roar and swung to face me. In one smooth motion, I withdrew my blade and as the guard turned his face towards me, I stabbed upwards and sank the blade deep under his chin. The huge guard dropped his weapon, both hands flying up to his torn throat in a vain attempt to stem the bubbling blood that erupted from the fatal wound. His falling weight freed my blade, allowing his lifeblood to pour even faster. Ignoring the dying guard, I reached down and hauled Sophos to his feet and pushed him behind me. With a bloodlust upon me that I had never thought possible, I searched for my next opponent, only to find the floor littered with bodies of the palace guards. The fight was over and we had not lost a single rider, many nursed cuts and bruises but none were seriously wounded. As for myself, I didn't have a single scratch. I was amazed!

Regrouping and regaining our breath, we bundled the bodies back into the room they had exited from. Bare shields hung from the walls while others lay flat on a table. Pots of paint and brushes suggested the king's coat of arms was painted on the shields in this room. As we laid out the bodies on the floor, I noticed something off to one side of the room. Something huge that prised recognition from the depths of my adrenaline fuelled brain. Instructing Firmus and the others of our group to wait, I stepped over to the focus of my interest. It was covered in a cloth sheet so I pulled it away and stood transfixed in amazement.

'What is it?' questioned Firmus as I stood staring down at a contraption of iron and wood. I looked over at Sophos, seeing an expression of enlightenment on his Lupus features.

'I know why the sorcerer had the magic powder delivered to him,' I muttered with an explanation I knew only Sophos would understand, 'and I know what he intends it for. This is a cannon!'

Sophos stared in shock while Firmus and the others in our group simply stared in confusion at my statement. Of course, they would have no idea what a cannon was or what it could do, Sophos and I did. With this weapon, the sorcerer could wreak havoc on the land, no animan had any idea of its destructive abilities. Sadly we humans have advanced this killing machine to the ultimate level and I feared for the animan race if gunpowder weapons were to be introduced here. I moved closer to get a better look at the cannon but my examination was abruptly interrupted by shouts coming from the corridor. I would not have the chance to satisfy my curiosity. I hurriedly threw the sheet back across the cannon, I did not want anyone knowing that I knew of its existence, yet. That done we fled from the room and back into the corridor. The sound of voices were behind us so off we ran again, keeping as quiet as possible as we searched for any indication of the sorcerer or his rooms. Running through the curving corridor, I was struck by the similarity between this corridor and the ones seen on the Starship Enterprise in a Star Trek episode. Unfortunately, Captain Kirk and Mister Spock would not be dashing to our rescue.

The voices behind us were growing nearer despite our speed of travel. They had no reason to remain quiet, nor did they need to be wary of each door they passed. Our group led by Firmus had no idea where we were going or what we might encounter along the way, so stealth was our travel companion. It was not long before we came across another flight of stairs, surely this would lead us up to where the sorcerer had his rooms?

Annoyingly, our feet had barely touched the first step before another group of palace guards spotted us, coming from the opposite direction to those we were fleeing. Now we were trapped between two guard patrols, both with the intention to do us harm, fatally. Sophos ran lightly up a few steps out of our way as the riders turned to do battle. It soon became evident that these palace guards had been trained more in palace etiquette than combat and the riders and myself slashed our way through body after body with relative ease.

The guards outnumbered us and now I held both my staff and knife as I slashed and stabbed, smashed and jabbed with a blood fury utterly alien to me. My body twisted and turned, ducked and spun as both blades sought soft flesh to tear. My thoughts were almost non-existent as I fought automatically, my actions reacting to the actions of others. But I was faster and more deadly, not so much through superior skill but pure fear. Adrenaline pumped around my body, giving strength and speed to my limbs. I fought for my life in the most vicious way possible, no Queensberry rules here. My staff spun, striking enemy soldiers with butt and blade. Those who unwittingly came inside the reach of my staff discovered a long vicious knife embedded deep in their bodies.

More guards could be heard making their way to join the fight, we would stand no chance against more fresh opponents, we were all tiring and flight became our only option.

I shouted over to Firmus, 'We have to get away, more guards are coming. What should we do?'

Poor Firmus was busy fighting two guards at once so his normally slow thinking became even slower. 'I . . . don't . . . know,' he ground out between sword thrusts.

'Up the stairs, this way. Quickly! We must take the higher ground and the stairs will help.' This advice came from Sophos, his shouted order quickly acted upon. The riders nearest the staircase fought their way to the foot of the stairs and began to make their way up, striking down at the guards with the advantage of height. Soon we were all fighting our way upwards, all praying there would be no more guards waiting for us on the next level. Now fortune began to favour the riders as the strategic move helped gradually overpower the unskilled guards.

'Move!' I shouted to those riders still able, 'I'll hold them back as long as I can. Go!'

'Don't be stupid Harry. Come on, now,' commanded Firmus but I had yet another advantage, my staff. With its long length and wicked blade protruding from one end, I could outreach the remaining guards, keeping them back while the riders scrambled to the top of the stairs. My plan was great for a hero, not so good in real action as I soon discovered. At first, my swinging staff had deterred the guards, but not for long. My staff was quickly knocked aside by one burly guard, allowing the others to charge at me. I could not pull the staff back quickly enough to defend, I was helpless.

Relief flooded into me as, from the corners of my frightened eyes I saw the flash of two swords, one on each side of me as Secuutus and Firmus rushed forward and plunged their weapons hard into the oncoming guards. The two riders had not believed my boast about holding back the enemy and had come to my aid. Just in time I realised. With added confidence, I drew back my staff and stabbed forward at a new opponent. My blade pierced deep into his eye, killing him instantly. If I had learned anything since arriving in this land, it was that the eyes were the best place to stab at when using a long staff. Bodies now littered the bottom of the stairs, hampering our foes and slowing them down.

The news of fighting had alarmed the whole palace and shouts from reinforcements were drawing closer, so the three of us did not stop to congratulate each other. We turned and fled up the stairs after the other rapidly disappearing riders led by a scampering Sophos. Glancing around while running, I saw that this corridor was more opulent than the one we had left in a gory mess. Although here the basics remained the same, windows on one side, doors on the other, I realised we were now running over a rich red carpet. No hard tiles underfoot here, though I did have the fleeting thought that the deep red of the carpet would better hide bloodstains.

Sophos and the leading riders disappeared as Firmus, Secuutus and myself ran full tilt to catch them. A moment later we were none too gently grabbed and bundled into a vacant room, Sophos closing the door behind us. I always knew that little Scouser would come in handy. The room was in total darkness, only the faint light glittering around the door frame allowed me to orientate my position. The room was too dark to make out any of my companions, the only reason I knew I was not alone was the sound of rapid and rasping breathing coming from the other riders. I too was gasping for breath as I stood trembling and clutching my staff, waiting for more guards to burst through the door. We gasped in fear, the sounds of pursuing guards could be heard approaching the room in which we hid. We listened as they drew level to our room, and then to our disbelief, the guards continued on their way, the sounds into the distance. We had survived, for the moment, but what next I wondered while wishing I was back in the classroom with only students to face.

The sounds of pursuit faded into the distance as the guards ran on in search of us, not knowing we hid in the blackness of the room. None of the riders moved as each fought to regain their breath and composure, myself included. Soon the sound of heavy breathing subsided and silence surrounded us. Still no one moved. We had survived a hard fight and none were keen to push our luck again so soon. Nonetheless, we could not stay hidden in this room forever, we had to make a move and continue our search for the troublesome sorcerer. I hoped Janiz and the other riders were having more success. By now the internal guard numbers would have been boosted by the skilled veterans from outside. Our little groups faced an insurmountable challenge to achieve our objectives. A really good plan was needed if we were to succeed but at that moment, in that dark room and amongst my fellow animan, I could not think of one damn thing.

Finally ending the long silence, Firmus eased the door open and peered outside. He took his time, checking both directions while listening intently for any approaching threats.

'Come on, let's go,' commanded Firmus as he led the way out from the safety of the dark room and turned to continue our way along the corridor. The thick carpet helped muffle our footfalls as we moved stealthily past more rooms, the light from the windows opposite had begun to dim as the day neared its end. I pondered on the possibility of remaining hidden until darkness fell but quickly decided against it. We had no idea where the others were or if they were even alive, waiting for darkness may delay our plan and put the other two groups at more risk. We had to move now, we had to find that sorcerer before it was too late. On we crept, I could not help but thank whoever or whatever was responsible for making me a cat, a tiger, as I moved effortlessly and silently through the corridor.

After a short distance, we finally encountered what was obviously the entrance to the king's residence. The rows of small rooms had ceased and now the walls were adorned with huge portraits of past royalty, family members, stunning landscapes and small children, all encased in ornate golden frames. Pedestals supporting delicate vases, busts and artwork stood sentinel between each wall hung picture, and between each of the now huge windows. I was amazed and pleased to discover that even in a land ruled by evolved animals, art still held its place of beauty and prestige. All too soon my attention was dragged away from the stunning works of art, to the heavily armed and numerous guards that blocked our advance. Sophos had spotted them and alerted us before any caught sight of us. Just in time as one more step would have placed us in plain view and most likely sealed our fate in the bloodiest of ways. Still, it would not be long before we were discovered, we had nowhere to run. We were trapped.

Chapter Fifteen: The Palace.

I looked enquiringly at Sophos, then Secuutus and Firmus but each, in turn, shook their head, no one had any ideas that could save our skins. It looked like I would end my life by the sword and in the body of a Tigris, an Animan. 'Crap!' was the word that sprang to mind while despair washed over me. However, it appeared my time was not yet ended. All of us spun with wide eyes as the sounds of fighting abruptly echoed along the corridor. I risked a peek and saw all the guards nearest our position head off in the opposite direction. The cause of their sudden departure became immediately evident as shouts and clashes of metal reached our ears.

'I think Janiz has arrived,' I called to the others before erupting into movement.

Quickly I made my way around the corridor and arrived at an ornate pair of doors that had until very recently, been guarded by soldiers. I carried on past with the others in pursuit behind me, and soon reaffirmed the cause of our timely distraction. Janiz and his group had arrived from the opposite direction and were now fighting furiously outside an even more richly decorated pair of doors. Janiz and his group were busy fighting their way forward, a look of grim determination on the Leo's face. Though his stolen uniform was splattered with blood and gore, the skill of his sword arm and his fierce intent cut a path through the guards like a scythe through wheat.

I realised that Janiz was heading for what could only be the king's chambers. I stopped abruptly, the significance of the doors we had just passed dawning on my adrenaline filled mind. Firmus and the others ground to a halt around me as they too realised where we were. Unfortunately, we had no time to retrace our steps, as the guards finally noticed us, several leaving the attack on Janiz and charging at us. Our enemies numbered greater than us but in defiance, we charged at them.

As the first guard approached at a run, I stole the initiative by running straight at him, my staff with its protruding blade aimed right at his gut. The guard lunged to my right, away from my blade, only to feel the hardwood of my staff whip round and smash into his jaw. The blow robbed him of his senses for just a moment, but that was all Secuutus needed to slash his sword down across the guard's neck, almost decapitating him with the force of the strike. I had little time to admire the handiwork because I was faced with another opponent, equally intent on spilling my life's blood. Up swung my staff again as I blocked his chopping blow aimed at my head. As I blocked I took a step forward, slamming my staff against his nose in a two-handed strike. The guard reeled backwards as one hand shot up to his ruined nose, leaving a gap in his defence that cost him his life as my blade sunk deep into his throat.

I readied myself for the next attack but saw with some surprise that the remaining guards were backing away from us. We were easily outnumbered so why the retreat? A shout from behind us answered the question. Fidelis and his group had finally joined us, arriving on the scene and swelling the numbers of our small group. I did not know if Fidelis had managed to cause a distraction as his part in the original plan, but I was thankful for the arrival of him and his group now. Regrettably, it didn't last long, the palace guards quickly regained their composure and attacked again.

I briefly wondered how Janiz fared before my attention was forced to focus on the muscular frame of an Ursidae guard who rushed towards me with a growl. I would not be so lucky this time as the guard had more sword skills than my last opponent. A flurry of strikes buzzed about me while I frantically wielded my staff in defence. Despite his size, the guard moved with alarming speed, his sword penetrating my defence repeatedly and leaving me with numerous small cuts and stab wounds. With one mighty blow, the guard smashed the staff from my hands, leaving me defenceless. It was his first and last mistake. With my staff lying out of reach, the guard took a step backwards and raised his sword for the killing blow. With the speed of desperation, my hand flashed to my knife and I lunged forward at him. My actions caught the over confident Ursidae completely off guard as the knife slammed into his undefended body. The momentum of my attack combined with the force of my blow buried the evil blade so deep into his gut it almost passed right through him. With a snarl, the guard grabbed my hair, determined to take me with him to whatever afterlife the animan believed in. My karate training rushed to the fore as I struck with a *Taisho-uchi*, a palm heel blow at his solar plexus while in a counter-reaction, I dragged back the hand that grasped the knife. The action took but a blink of the eye, freeing my knife and knocking the guard away. The guard stumbled back a couple of paces before falling to the floor, his wound fatal, and his fight over.

I quickly retrieved my staff, not stopping to wipe the blood and guts off the knife. Now armed once again with staff and knife, I flung myself back into the melee in search of another victim to feed my bloodlust. A small figure faced me, his sword held out in front of him in shaky hands. This guard was of the Lupus Cast and I towered over him. The fear upon his face and his terrified stance leant compassion to my soul. In one swift movement, I blocked his feeble sword thrust and crashed the butt of my staff down hard onto his head, rendering him unconscious immediately, unconscious but alive.

The sounds of fighting were dying around me as the riders slowly gained the upper hand. Guards lay sprawled about the corridor, the plush red carpeted floor slippery now with the red of blood. Riders also lay prone but a swift almost subconscious headcount indicated many more guards than riders had fallen. Those surviving riders stood hunched over as they fought to regain their breath, only a few still battled against the last of the guards.

Peering around I saw the little Liverpudlian backed against the wall by a Tigris guard virtually as big as me. Poor Sophos stood no chance, a fact he knew himself laid witness by the sheer terror crumpling his face. With one bound I placed myself behind the Tigris guard and before he realised my presence I whipped my staff across the back of his knees. Immediately he fell to his knees in front of the petrified Sophos. With absolutely no thought of chivalry, I thrust the staff blade into the base of the guard's skull, severing his spinal cord and windpipe in one blow. The guard remained kneeling for a brief moment as if in prayer, before toppling sideways to the floor, stone dead.

The fight was over for now. Bodies littered the floor while gasping riders stood or sat in exhaustion. Suddenly pain flooded my body as my mind became aware of the numerous cuts and wounds inflicted upon me. I sank to the floor beside Sophos who sat with his head buried in his arms. I noticed the small Lupus was quietly weeping, the fright of the battle being succeeded by the relief of being alive. I left him to his emotions and looked about me. I saw that Janiz along with Firmus, Fidelis and Secuutus had survived and for that I was grateful. But then I saw the huge ornate doors of the king's residence defenceless and unguarded. Several yards around the curving corridor, the less ornate doors which I assumed would be the sorcerer's apartments also stood undefended. Our revised and somewhat fortuitous plan had worked and we now rested within feet of our goals. Janiz could confront his father King Fastus, while Sophos and I tackled the sorcerer. I was about to stand when I felt a light touch on my arm. Glancing down I saw Sophos gently bandaging my wounds with strips of linen from his bag. Though still red-eyed and with the occasional sniff, Sophos had dried his tears and set about my wounds. I felt grateful to the little Liverpudlian and was pleased that he had not sought to run from the battle, even though he was no fighter. He had proven his courage and overcome his fears to stay with the riders, a choice that almost cost him his life.

'We must move,' commanded Janiz. 'More guards will arrive soon and I don't think we have the strength for another fight just yet. Harry? Take Sophos, Firmus and Secuutus back to the sorcerer's chambers and finish him. The rest of us will go and visit my father but take care, more guards may linger within the chambers. I had expected a greater number of guards between ourselves and my father but, whatever the reason, we must make best use of it. Go.'

'Ductor?' I queried.

'He got away, now go!'

Following Janiz's orders, the group split once more. I forced myself up from the floor and turned back down the corridor, accompanied by the other three. I realised I ached all over and prayed we would not encounter any more resistance between us and our objective, the sorcerer. It was at that point I remembered the jade box, I needed that box to return home. I had been told it was in the king's chamber but how was I to obtain the damn thing now? But there was nothing I could do, I first had to find that accursed sorcerer and end it. Then perhaps I could persuade Janiz to let me have the box as payment for my help or even for my loyalty. Now though, we neared the sorcerer's chambers.

I reached for the door when Secuutus suddenly grabbed my arm. 'Wait, just wait a moment,' whispered Secuutus, 'we have no knowledge of what to expect inside, we are to enter the residence of a powerful sorcerer and care must be taken. He can't fail to know we're here, the noise of the fighting would surely have warned him. He's had time to prepare but we have no way of knowing what he plans.'

Though I held no belief in sorcery, Secuutus's command made sense, walking straight into the abode of someone so devious could be dangerous, especially to the first animan through the door. A scan to ensure the others were in position about the huge doors, I reached forward and carefully turned the handle. Not a single squeak issued from the well maintained mechanism as I slowly opened the door just enough for me to check no threat awaited behind it. I pushed a little more but still no cries of alarm rose from within the room. Then with a quick glance at my fellows, I gave the door a mighty shove and leapt into the room, my staff held out in front of me. My eyes flittered about the place as Sophos and the other two riders burst in behind me. The rooms were empty. No one rushed to attack us and no traps sprung to kill us.

Quickly we searched the apartment, the sorcerer lived in luxury to a very high degree. The apartment was full of rich trappings, elegant furniture and the décor gleamed in cream and gold. I suspected the gold colour of the columns, the beams across the slightly curved ceilings and all the wooden door frames was indeed real gold, gold leaf perhaps but gold all the same.

Silk and lace covered the deep plush chairs and chandeliers of candles illuminated the apartment, the yellow light flickered in the reflections from the golden surroundings. I simply stood and stared for a moment. Rarely had I seen such opulence, the place outshining any other living quarters of an employee. Only a stately home or palace in Britain or Trump Towers could compare with the abundance of pure luxury in this place. I wandered into a bedroom and found the same level of decadence all around me. A huge circular bed, again covered in the finest silks, dominated the centre of the room, accompanied by all the fixtures and fittings associated with the richest of sleeping chambers. This sorcerer lived in the height of luxury I thought, a thought that caused the hate, and a large degree of envy, inside me to grow. Just then, Sophos shouted for my attention, beckoning me to investigate yet another room that led off from the main living quarters.

Sophos's call was not in alarm so I walked across the deep pile and intricately patterned carpet, fully expecting yet another display of wealth and luxury. As I entered the room I was first mildly surprised at how dim the light was, the other rooms had glared in their brightness. As my eyes adjusted another surprised awaited me as the items contained in the small room came into my vision, confirming my suspicions regarding the so-called the sorcerer. The room was unfurnished apart from tables and shelves that lined every wall. No chandeliers here, solitary candles scattered about the room gave a dim flickering light, fighting a desperate battle against the gloom. Writing materials were strewn all over the tables and the floor. Looking around I saw an Aladdin's cave of alchemy items, equipment and colourful substances. Glass wear, bottles, brass instruments and powder in boxes filled the shelves, some coated in dust, others gleaming with use. A gasp from behind me announced the arrival of the others into the room.

'This is the den of magic,' muttered Secuutus in awe.

'A place of evil more like. This is not the work of an ordinary animan, demons must abide here. Let us leave this instance, before the evil devours us!' cried Firmus.

'No,' I said quietly while reaching out to grasp the arm of Firmus as he turned to run from the room. 'No, there are no demons here. Nor is there any magic, this is science, alchemy.'

'Strange words Harry. What evil is this science, this alchemy you speak of?' whispered Firmus.

'Man . . . Animan-made tricks to frighten us. Nothing more.' I quickly corrected my slip of the tongue. 'The sorcerer is using substances, plant materials and metals to make poisons and devices to scare us. It is not magic. This is science, the ability to use those things we find about us and turn them into something different. That is all.'

'Magic,' muttered Secuutus in a tone of defiance.

I would have liked to linger and investigate what was happening in this room but other matters still required attention. We needed to find the sorcerer and from what I saw about me, we needed to find him quickly. Whoever he was, his knowledge was far superior to the abilities of this time period in animan history. Alchemy did not reach Europe until the 12th century, though it is believed to have begun in Egypt sometime earlier. I concluded that knowledge at this moment in time corresponded with that of the early Middle Ages in my history. The contents and the reason for this room should not be here in this era. The sorcerer was either way ahead of his time, or he was not of this age.

Moving back into the extravagant living quarters, I peered around for any clues as to the sorcerer's whereabouts. There were none, none other than perhaps some evidence of a rapid departure. A half-finished snack rested on an ornate table, a chair pushed back at an angle that suggested the diner left his seat in haste. A napkin lay crumpled upon the floor.

'It's obvious our quarry is no longer here. He must have heard the sounds of fighting outside in the corridor and has fled. We must continue our search but we will check on Janiz before heading off to find our elusive sorcerer.' I instructed before moving towards and through the large doors and back into the corridor. The others fell in behind me, all but Sophos were relieved to be leaving that strange room behind. But once back in the corridor, all of us wished we had not left the sorcerer's chambers. I had failed to note the sounds emanating from outside the rooms, but now my eyes brought me to an abrupt halt. There were more damn guards rushing towards us. The alarm had been heard and reinforcements had arrived while we were enjoying the beauty of the royal guest room. A glance told me Janiz and the others were fighting desperately, they had not managed to gain entrance to the king's residence before being set upon once more. Now it was our turn.

Returning to fight mode took but an instant as up came my staff in readiness to defend and survive. A guard leapt at me with a cry of triumph, almost without thought I whipped his legs out from under him and slashed the staff blade across his face. The others erupted from the empty chambers and pushed eagerly into the struggle, I swear Secuutus was even grinning as his sword flashed.

'Clear a path to Janiz!' I shouted as I leapt straight at another opponent, batting his sword aside before jamming my blade deep into his gut. Immediately I was faced with a barrage of armament all pointing in my direction. I whirled and slashed, stabbed and smashed my way through the soldiers and guards, battling my way towards our leader. I could hear Secuutus shouting incoherently at my back as I sliced and diced all who stood in my way. A momentary thought crossed my mind. Perhaps my choice of weapon was proving to be provident as the guards were trained in sword skills but not for the extra reach and versatility of my staff.

Soon we had made a bloody path littered with torn bodies as we forced our way forward. Our tough lives on the road, on the run, had hardened us to a peak of fitness, sadly the same could not be said for the guards, the comfortable palace life-sapping their strength and stamina and making them almost easy prey for the battle hardened riders. Not as tough perhaps, but still very deadly and in greater numbers so we still had to fight hard to stay alive. Janiz saw our small band of reinforcements striving to reach his side and shouted encouragement to his riders.

In truth, I would have expected every guard and soldier in the palace to be on our backs, not just patrol sized groups. At that moment I feared I would be an extinct Manchester lecturer with my hide hanging from a wall somewhere. Do they use animan skins as rugs here like we do at home I wondered? I too was somewhat baffled at the small numbers of guards that faced us. Perhaps the design of the palace restricted the movement of larger numbers? Possibly another threat to the security of the palace had occurred outside the building itself, occupying the guards? I certainly did not know or care, fewer guards meant an increased chance of survival and I was all for that.

We had almost reached Janiz as he fought viciously outside the king's chambers. A few more steps and he would be at the doors, ready to gain entrance. I briefly wondered where the sorcerer was but assumed he had escaped in the uproar of our onslaught. Just then a shout was heard from those around the doors to the royal chambers, a shout that became a cry of fear. Suddenly all the fighting stopped as guards and riders paused to stare in disbelief at a cloud of green smoke that seeping out from under the doors. Then came a shouted warning from inside the chambers.

'Flee! Flee now or be consumed by devils. I have commanded the Devil to my aid. See the smoke of Hell rising. Flee or die!'

As we watched, the smoke gradually turned red, a colour that all associated with the fire and brimstone of Hell. Least that's what human's believed, unfortunately for the individual who called the warning, the animan were not so easily fooled. Though the superstitious belief of magic and demons frightened the animan, the concept of the Devil and Hell requires a religion, and the animan had none. Demons could scare them as I had discovered, but none understood the notion of a devil or Hell. Their only response was to stare mystified at the increasing cloud of red smoke issuing from under and around the ornate doors of the king's rooms.

I also failed to run screaming hysterically from the palace, though in all honesty, it would have been difficult anyway. The tangle of riders and guards surrounding the doors blocked the corridor and impeded any routes of escape. Another fact played a major part in my lack of fear was my scientific background. I recognised the simple trick of burning substances to produce coloured smoke. I had done it myself on several occasions in the classroom, sometimes even deliberately. Nonetheless, the smoke did achieve one thing, it proved to me that the sorcerer had not fled, he was in the king's chambers.

I took advantage of the momentary lapse in the art of killing and leapt beside Janiz, my staff held in readiness for the next attack. With startling reflexes, the others in my group followed suit and before the guards could react, we stood together. All the riders now controlled the area immediately outside the doors, facing the guards that hemmed them in. Then the fight restarted. All appeared to overcome their surprise caused by the smoke that still bellowed out, causing some coughing and stinging eyes but no fear. All too soon I found myself fending off another guard as he swiped his sword through the smoke. Now the riders were together, we managed to form a defensive line against the pressing guards and soldiers. I stood shoulder to shoulder with Janiz, his sword and my bladed staff slashing, chopping and stabbing at the uniformed figures before us. Fidelis managed to manoeuvre up to us, and now the three of us fought with our backs against the doors.

'What took you so long?' I grunted at him between thrusts of my staff.

Fidelis quickly glanced at me to ascertain humour or criticism before replying through gritted teeth. Blood poured from a wound on his arm indicating he had not had an easy time completing his diversion.

'Well I had to reduce the numbers for you, there's no way you would have managed without me otherwise.'

'What did you do?' I shouted back at him between defending and attacking those that came at me. Talking was difficult and many pauses and gasps for air punctured our conversation.

'Not much else I could do, I set fires wherever I could,' growled Fidelis through clenched teeth as he fought off another attack.

'A building such as this has many dusty dry and empty rooms. It was the only thing I could think of, my group was too small to create an armed distraction, we would have been cut to pieces in no time.'

'Brilliant idea!' shouted Janiz as his sword pierced the heart of a Tigres guard, 'I wondered why we were not besieged by much larger numbers of soldiers.'

I remembered thinking the very same thing earlier. Starting fires about the palace would certainly keep a large number of guards and soldiers busy. I suspected one could not call the fire brigade here, so it would be a case of all hands to the buckets. I agreed with Janiz, it was an act of genius. I only hoped Fidelis had not lit fires too close to our position, I was sweating profusely already, I didn't need any more heat.

A burning sensation in my side made me wonder if the flames had reached us until I realise a sword had gotten through my defence, I had been distracted by my thoughts and Fidelis's explanation. I could feel blood wetting my skin but I would not let my attention wander again. Putting my injury aside, I gave all my concentration to the guard with the blooded blade in front of me. The urge to kill resurfaced and my new found animan instincts leapt to the fore. Up came my staff to swipe away his sword before snatching at my knife and ramming it into his chest. The evil blade went in just below his breast bone and angled up into his heart. Suitable revenge for the painful wound in my side.

The battle in the corridor showed no immediate signs of relenting. As some fires were brought under control, those soldiers were sent to reinforce the defence of the king. Out of the corner of my eye I caught sight of someone small slithering along behind us, staying pressed hard to the wall as the figure moved towards the doors. I was beset by two guards at once so the figure moving behind us would have to wait, my life was important to me and I wished to retain it for as long as possible.

We had lost several riders and our numbers were shrinking noticeably. With nowhere to run and no help on the horizon, our plight was becoming desperate. I fought with the fear of death clinging to my shoulders, its cold breath on my neck. I managed to dispatch one of the two guards that had singled me out for the afterlife but in doing so I had left myself open to the second guard. I need not have worried as Janiz took but a moment to aid me by ramming his sword through an ear of the second guard, its blade reappearing on the opposite side of his head. In a blur, Janiz pulled the guard to him before slamming his palm into the head to withdraw his blade. From out of nowhere rose the memory of those party hats with a fake arrow seeming to pierce right through the head. I managed a brief nod of thanks to Janiz before my next opponent reared up in front of me. Up shot the butt of my staff, striking the uniformed figure squarely in his most vulnerable of places. As he bent over in pain I spun the staff so I could use the blade. The blow never landed because I suddenly flew backwards, a huge paw pulling me from behind. A moment later I stood bewildered and shocked inside those very doors I had fought so hard to reach.

Chapter Sixteen: Face to Face

I stared at the inside of the doors for a second, wondering how the hell I got here before spinning round to face the room, realising I may still be under threat. I found myself standing beside Janiz, Secuutus and Sophos in the king's chambers. Sounds of furious fighting continued outside the doors, but in the chambers, a strange and deafening quiet descended on me. My eyes darted to and fro, seeing everything but seeing nothing until my gaze settled on the scene before me.

There stood the magnificent figure of a Leo. The resemblance to Janiz was astounding and I immediately realised I was standing before King Fastus. Even if I had not recognised the family similarity I would have known him as the King. His ruby red gown displayed golden trim and a roaring lion's head motif lay over his right breast. A gleaming and heavily decorated scabbard hung at his side, the golden hilt of a sword giving evidence of a magnificent weapon lying within. No crown adorned the golden mane of the King, in its place a heavy and ornate gold chain lay around his neck. Similar but way more expensive than a Lord Mayor's chain of office back in Britain. There could be no mistaking the regal figure as the King.

The King did not stand alone, close beside him stood another figure. A Lupus animan had hold of the King's shoulder while the other hand grasped a long thin tube of metal. The Lupus figure stood at least a head shorter than the King, his wolfish features set in a snarl. He was covered in long black robes that swamped his thin body and fell over his feet, tied at the waist by a deep red sash. This has got to be the alleged sorcerer I thought, though I did wonder where the pointy hat was. Greying hair or I should say fur, topped the head while yellow eyes held us all in a steady gaze. Confidence shone in those eyes, portraying proof that the sorcerer knew he was in charge. Janiz immediately made to move towards the King but I grabbed his arm to hold him back as the Lupus spoke in a calm and controlled voice.

'I would advise you not to come any closer Prince Janiz. This device in my hand is a powerful magic and would kill your father before you even managed one step.'

'What madness is this Sorcerer?' demanded Janiz while his body shook with fury, 'How dare you lay hands on the King! This is treachery, treason! You will die for this.'

I held on to the bulging bicep of my friend and leader, my brain desperately searching for a solution to the scene before me. I glanced over to Sophos and received a nod of understanding in return. He too recognised what the sorcerer held in his hand. Neither Janiz nor Secuutus could know, it was the word magic that stayed their hands but I wondered for how long. I retained my grip on Janiz while Sophos stood close to Secuutus, in case the huge Ursidae attempted to rescue the King.

'I will not be the one dying Prince Janiz, my magic is powerful as you have no doubt already experienced. Did you not see the demon I sent for you? Did I not make the pond water burn? My magic is strong and what I hold in my hand is the strongest. Don't make any rash moves my young Prince, or you will die alongside your father. A simple flick of my finger can send both you and your father straight to Hell!' The sorcerer was enjoying himself, convinced of his invulnerability.

So far the King himself had not uttered a word, but now he growled out in answer to the sorcerer. 'You will not live Sorcerer, kill me and my men will see you slain. I have given you wealth, power and respect that no ordinary animan could dream of. But this is how you repay me? Let go of me now Sorcerer and I promise your death will be quick.'

'Ah my King, I have planned and schemed for this day ever since I arrived here. You and yours will die and I shall be King. A new King who will lead armies forward and crush anyone in my way. My magic will be the death of all and I will conquer this land, all of it. You are but my first step. I shall rule this land as is my right. I have the power and the magic that simple swords cannot stand against. Even as we speak, your very own blacksmiths toil to make more magical weapons of the like this land has never seen. Your time has gone, now it's my time, my time to rule.'

The King began to struggle, his fury crumpling his face, Janiz tensed in my grip but the sorcerer pressed the metal tube harder against the King's cheek, staring hard at Janiz, daring him to make a move. Both Sophos and I held the animan back, we knew what was happening, after all, we had both watched TV, we were in a hostage situation and I could see no end to the plot. I had my staff and my evil looking knife but these weapons could not match that which the sorcerer held.

Randomly, I then remembered the small package that Sophos had given me so long ago on our travels, perhaps I could use that. I looked around the chambers and found what I needed everywhere. Candles and oil lamps illuminated the room, just what I would need to ignite the package. Just how I was to achieve this without blowing myself and everyone in the room to kingdom come eluded me at that moment in time. At least I had some 'magic' of my own, an advantage possibly, I just needed a plan. The question was, could I think of a solution before the sorcerer executed the King.

As I pondered, two soldiers entered from another room, they had remained out of sight but chose this moment to appear. Two Tigrismen, heavily armed and taciturn moved to each side of the sorcerer, their swords held ready. 'As you can see, I am not alone. Many of your soldiers and guards have chosen to be on the winning side. When you are dead, I will take command of your entire army, those loyal to me are already waiting outside, remaining hidden while your soldiers and ragtag band of outlaws kill each other.'

'You have been busy, but you will fail,' growled Janiz, 'No Lupus will ever be accepted as King in this land. The other Casts would not allow it, the Leo Cast has long been the rulers and so it will remain.'

'No, I am sorry Janiz. Now is the time for change. None of your Casts will be able to stop me. My army will be armed with my magic, magic far greater than the sword. The Casts will bow to me or perish, it is as simple as that. However, you do have a choice that your father does not. Join me Janiz, and rule at my right hand. I would have need of your skill and leadership, you may even keep your riders. Join me and I will give you more power than you could ever imagine.'

With a roar, Janiz made to charge at the sorcerer, his desire to rip the Lupus limb from limb clear in evident his snarl. I lunged at him, holding him with all my strength as the two soldiers moved to defend the sorcerer. 'Never will I bow to you traitor,' shouted Janiz. 'Never will I be your right hand, I will see you dead and fed to the Hyaenidae, you and your so-called army!'

'As I expected,' replied the sorcerer, 'perhaps I will make you my prisoner. With your father dead and you held captive, none of the other Casts would dare defy me. Now I think upon it, the idea has much appeal. But now, place your weapons on the floor. Quickly else my patience will end.'

No one moved to lay down their weapons, the sorcerer was greeted with stony faces and defiant stares. 'You will have to use your magic if you believe we would surrender to you, Sorcerer. You may kill my father and me but we will never bow to you.' Janiz growled in reply.

'It is true,' interjected the King, 'we will never allow you to take our land. My son is strong and I was unwise to listen to you. Your words upon my ears fooled me and your warnings and threats have proved fruitless. My son is welcome here, I recant the banishment with a glad heart. Despite my foolishness, my son has come to my aid, to free me from your bonds. Janiz will be King in my place, not you!'

The sorcerer shouted, his temper rising. 'Hah! You were a fool and I had you totally in my control. You were easy to convince and I have used my skills and my position to gain much wealth and through bribes and threats, I have gathered many followers in your army. I have won and you both will die, along with your troublesome riders. This kingdom will be mine. I am a powerful sorcerer and none can stand against me. Drop your weapons now!'

Okay I thought, this has gone on long enough. All this soul-baring and male blustering were getting on my nerves. I glanced across at Sophos and with a slight gesture, I reminded him of the package that remained hidden upon my person. I received an almost imperceptible nod in return. Having a Liverpudlian on my side greatly increased my chances of survival, if anyone can be devious and cunning, it would be a Liverpudlian.

None of us had relinquished our weapons and the sorcerer once again demanded that we drop them. This time, at his signal, the two guards edged forward, their swords held out before them threateningly. This alone would not have persuaded me to lower my staff, however, that black narrow tube in the sorcerer's hand could overcome my reluctance. All the riders held onto their weapons, not afraid of the two menacing guards. We had fought our way here and were not to be stopped by a couple of mongrel guards. Seeing his threats ignored, the sorcerer raised the tube and suddenly there came a loud bang and a vase across the room exploded.

The sound erupted around the room, bouncing off the walls before echoing into the distance. A smell of cordite hung in the air as every animan other than the sorcerer reacted with alarm and fear. I was the first to regain my senses and my hearing, with Sophos a close second. All the others, riders and guards alike stood transfixed. My suspicions proved founded, the sorcerer had constructed a crude gun. All eyes turned in fear to stare at the shattered vase, its pieces scattered over the table it had rested upon. That's it I thought, he can only have one shot in that homemade gun, now is the time to move. Sadly I was too late reacting for the sorcerer had dropped the discharged weapon and pulled another from his sash with a speed that belied his appearance. Everyone, the riders along with the King and even the sorcerer's own guards remained standing in shock and dread. Sophos was crouched down with his arms wrapped around his head. Like me, he knew a gun when he heard one.

'See my power,' shouted the sorcerer, 'witness my magic. I can kill without a blade, without even touching you. I have more of these magical tubes and as I speak, more are being made. Drop your weapons now!'

The power of the sorcerer's magic shocked all into submission. This time the sound of metal clattering upon the floor gave evidence that his command had been obeyed by all, except me. Foolishly, he did not consider my staff as a threat. The sorcerer was delighted and uttered a statement that begged a response. 'I will conquer this Kingdom and the entire land of Totus Terra. No one can stop me now.'

'Huh! I bet Hitler said those very words.' I muttered.

With pure delight, I saw a look of disbelief freeze the face of the sorcerer. He turned to stare at me, puzzlement mixed with apprehension showing in his eyes. I knew what he was and I knew where he came from. All the pieces were fitting into place. Janiz had told me the sorcerer had suddenly appeared as I had. All my assumptions were proven by the simple fact that, apart from Sophos who had risen to his feet once more, no one else in the room could possibly understand my short statement. Only someone from my world and my time would know, only a human would understand. As realisation dawned on the sorcerer, the second gun in his hand slowly moved in my direction.

'What did you say?' he whispered.

'I said, I bet Hitler spoke those very words. What's up mate, you deaf as well as stupid?'

Oh crap I suddenly thought, have I said too much? I could see rage slowly overpowering the shock as his face turned from a pale white to that of beetroot red. I think I may have pissed him off. All the others were staring at me in bewilderment, what was I saying? What were those words I had spoken that caused such a reaction in the sorcerer? Only Sophos showed no astonishment, a slight smirk lifted his lips. I was taunting a nutter with a homemade gun. I glimpsed Sophos edging sideways, away from the riders and myself, but my attention stayed on the sorcerer. The room stood shocked into silence, not noticing as the little Liverpudlian crept unnoticed to the side of the chamber. From the corner of my eye, I watched him move and saw his eyes flicker to where the small package was hidden within my tunic. I knew what he intended to do.

'How do you know of Hitler?' asked the sorcerer still in shock.

Unwisely I was so greatly amused by the look of shock and bewilderment on his face that with reckless abandon I laid into the sorcerer. An armed trickster from my world of violence and hate. Stupid!

'Ah, I know many things that may surprise you. I know you are no damn sorcerer. I know you use feeble party tricks. I know you are a fraud.'

'How dare you! You, a killer for hire, a Tigris whose only skills involve death. What do you know about magic? You are the fraud!'

'I know how to make sodium.' I whispered at his angry face.

Everyone in the room watched as my bombshell once again twisted the sorcerer's features. His mouth opened but he could not speak, his eyes widened for a moment, then closed down into slits as the consequences of my statement penetrated his astounded brain.

'No,' he gasped, 'you can't possibly know such a thing. No one in this entire world would know how to do such a thing. You lie!'

'I also know how to make potassium.'

At this, the sorcerer almost choked in his amazement and the gun shook in his hand, though it remained pointed in my direction. 'You can't,' the sorcerer repeated in a stunned voice, 'it's not possible. Who told you these things? Explain now, or die. It's your choice.'

With perfect timing, the doors to the chambers abruptly opened and the remaining riders squeezed into the room shouting. 'The soldiers are attacking the guards!' shouted Fidelis.

'What?' came a chorus of bewildered voices.

'Ah. That will be those loyal to me,' confirmed the sorcerer. 'Soon they will finish the palace guards and then I shall deal with you. But first my dear King, you shall lead the way.'

The gun moved from me back to the King and I tensed to pounce as soon as he fired the shot. I intended launching my attack before he had a chance to drag yet another gun from his person, information which he had unwittingly given me earlier. To my disappointment, the sorcerer gestured to the two guards, 'I will retain control of the rest. You two send the King on his last journey - I see you,' shouted the sorcerer with a look in my direction, 'whatever your name is. And no, I'm not foolish enough to use my magic on the death of your King. My Tigrismen will have that pleasure.'

Immediately all those riders who had just entered the room made ready to rush the sorcerer and his two willing assassins. Seeing the danger Janiz whirled to face them, shouting at them to stop as the knuckles of the sorcerer's hand whitened around the gun. Instead, he ordered them to secure the door so no more treacherous animan could enter and swing the balance further in favour of the black robed figure.

The room was now filled with animan from both sides, making it difficult to notice a small figure still edging his way nearer to the sorcerer and his hostage. Sophos caught my eye before his eyes flicked towards a candelabra sat on a large sideboard behind the two guards who in turn, stood just a pace behind the sorcerer. I knew what he was going to do. I needed to stall for more time.

'Hey. You with the gun,' I called and was once again met by a look of surprise from the sorcerer. 'I know how to make sodium but how the hell did you achieve that procedure in this land?'

'You appear to know much about alchemy, or perhaps chemistry,' replied the sorcerer as suspicion replaced surprise. Clearly you also have knowledge of guns.

Where do you come from?' His voice had risen as realisation dawned on him as it had me. Now he had grasped the implication of my questions. Again the barrel of the crudely made gun moved to point at me, the tension between us transfixed all in the room, halting the two assassins ordered to dispatch the King.

I answered with a question of my own, an infuriating habit many have in my world and I knew it would irritate him even more. 'I was wondering, how did you manage to separate sodium, and potassium for that matter? I assume those two substances were behind that amateurish burning water prank?'

'I am a powerful sorcerer, I . . . .' he began.

'Oh give it a break!' I interrupted with a sigh of frustration. 'Just tell me how you did it without the theatricals.'

A snarl appeared on his face, indicating his anger at my rude interruption. His hand shook with the desire to end my impertinence. But then, his ego quickly regained control and with a superior air, he began to explain, safe in the knowledge that he held the upper hand. Or gun actually.

'As you obviously have some experience in chemistry, unlike these retarded animan, I will explain my genius, though no other in this room will understand. It does not matter, only I and my animan will exit here alive and no one else will ever know.' The sorcerer thought for a brief moment before drawing himself up with pride. 'It was very simple. I used a rough and ready Downs Cell, constructed by my talented blacksmith for the electrolysis. A simple fruit battery supplied the power, though I did use a lot of fruit to obtain the voltage I required.'

'I had considered the Castner Process but I was unsure sufficient quantities could be manufactured in that way. I had to make several adaptions and numerous trial runs, but eventually I achieved a suitable amount. I stored both metal substances in oil-filled jars and used small amounts in my . . .,' the sorcerer paused to look round the room, noting all were staring dumbstruck at our conversation. ' . . in my magic.'

Having finished his gloating explanation, I urged more information from him. There were two reasons why I did this, one was to give my sneaky friend more time, and the second was purely out of professional interest.

So I asked, 'What about the gunpowder and the cannon?'

'That is a fairly stupid question I feel,' he replied. 'In a world where the sword is the mightiest weapon, anyone with the force of gunpowder behind him would be victorious in every battle. I will use my gunpowder, guns and cannon to defeat all these stupid animan and take control of the entire land. I will rule as my right!'

The others growled at this statement, even the two traitorous guards. Insulting your supporters is never a good way to go. Suddenly the King grabbed for the gun, Janiz made to lunge at the sorcerer and I made ready to do the same. The sorcerer's animan acted even faster, one of them crashed his sword butt down onto the back of the King's head, momentarily stunning him. The sorcerer used this opportunity to strengthen his hold on the King, once again pressing the gun into the royal neck. The scene could very quickly turn ugly, I feared we had pushed the sorcerer too far. It was time to calm him down with a further distraction.

'So what did you do when you were human?'

My simple question caused yet another a reaction in the sorcerer. His shoulders sagged and his head bowed, though his eyes remained on me.

'I was a laboratory technician in a university,' he finally responded, now convinced our pasts had originated on the same world.

He now understood my knowledge of his so-called magic, and he knew I was his biggest threat. A hard gleam came to his eyes, his head lifted and his shoulders straightened. I may be a threat but he still retained the upper hand in the scenario that was being played out in the King's chambers. Thuds could now be heard against the doors, outside the chambers the guards loyal to the sorcerer were hammering to get in. The guards or soldiers, I had no way of knowing, were shouting out support for the sorcerer. A dead giveaway I thought. I knew if things didn't change soon, we would lose any chance of surviving this.

'So how did you end up here, in this land, on this world?' I asked, already knowing the answer.

'I don't really know. The last thing I remember was finding a small green box outside the post office. I picked it up and . .'

'Opened it!' I finished.

His mouth fell open as he stared at me, motionless as comprehension lit in his eyes. 'A small green jade box?' he finally croaked out.

'Yes.'

'Ah now I understand,' muttered the sorcerer as his mind worked on the possibility of two humans in this land of Animan. I didn't let on about Sophos, he was now in position and nodded gently to let me know he was ready.

'That cursed jade box is the reason I manoeuvred my way into the King's graces and favour. I needed to find the only known jade box in this land, and it's in the possession of the King here.'

The mind of the sorcerer could almost be seen working, contemplating his journey to this particular moment in time and space. Now he knew he was not alone. I realised then that no one had interrupted us during our conversation. I could tell from his body language that Janiz had laid his faith at my door. He had little idea of what we spoke but he understood there was a strangeness about the sorcerer that I matched. Janiz and the riders impatiently awaited the outcome of this baffling confrontation.

'It appears you must also die alongside the King and his son then. I can't have another with my knowledge wandering this land, disrupting my plans. It's been very easy to fool these animan into fearing magic, and until now it had worked very well. Nevertheless, you and I know that all my tricks are simply science, tricks used to keep unruly children quiet in the classroom. These animan have no science to speak of, no understanding of chemistry or physics. They don't even have religion! I used their lack of knowledge and determined to climb the social ladder, though there is little class distinction here. Instead, they all follow their Casts as would be expected when lions, tigers, wolves and bears rule the world.'

Here the fake sorcerer paused for a moment before adding. 'Unless, unless you join forces with me. With our combined knowledge we could rule in absolution, no one, none of these creatures could withstand us. We would be like Gods to these beasts.'

Once again growls from the animan followed the sorcerer's pejorative words. The sorcerer appeared not to notice or more likely did not care what the animan thought, in his mind they were merely animals. Many parts of our conversation were unfathomable to the animan, but nonetheless, some words had been understood.

As the sorcerer concluded, the King himself interjected before I could frame a response. 'You talk of a small green box sorcerer, and you are right, I do have such a trinket. But what is the lure of this box, it is but a gewgaw, it has no value. I do not even recall how it came into my possession. Take it and leave if you wish, but you will never rule my Kingdom.'

'Oh I will,' scorned the sorcerer, 'and I will take that box. Where is it?'

Crap! If that damn sorcerer bloke got hold of the box, I would never escape this world. I had to make my move soon but as yet the sorcerer's attention had not relaxed on the gun. A glance at Sophos confirmed his concerns matched mine. I had to do something.

'The trinket is in my desk, I will fetch it if you let me go for a moment?' offered the King.

'Oh no. I'm not letting you go until you are dead!' growled the sorcerer. 'Just tell one of those witless outlaws that followed Prince Janiz like sheep, but not him,' ordered the sorcerer with a nod in my direction. 'Another rider can get it and bring it to me. It's mine and mine alone.'

At this statement his eyes bored into mine, his meaning clear. The hammering on the door and shouts of support continued, it would not be long before those loyal to the sorcerer gained entrance. An urgency overtook me, I had to stop him in his mad quest or I would never get access to the box. I would never get home. My sense of urgency grew to an almost unbearable level, I had to get that box or I was trapped. Janiz nodded at Fidelis and following the King's directions, he walked across the room to a beautifully carved and constructed walnut desk that stood against the wall directly behind the hostage group. He opened a draw as instructed and withdrew the small insignificant green jade box. Everyone in the room watched as Fidelis held the box in his hand and stared down at it. His other hand came up and moved towards the object of interest.

'Don't open it!' shouted the sorcerer and me in unison.

Our combined voices carried such alarm that Fidelis was startled into nearly dropping the box, fear suddenly lining his face. Now holding the box gingerly out in front of him, he slowly walked back until he was between the loyal animan and the hostage group. Adrenaline coursed through my body as I realised all eyes were on Fidelis and the green box. All eyes save mine and Sophos. I nodded and he acted.

As I dragged the package of gunpowder out, Sophos took three rapid steps that placed him in position to execute our plan. I threw the package to Sophos, causing all eyes to unwittingly switch to me. With a small leap, Sophos caught the package and threw it at the burning candles of the candelabra. Immediately it exploded. Not in a huge blast but the resulting flash of light was followed instantly by a resonating bang and finally a large cloud of pale grey smoke billowed out. The blast was enough to send the two assassins stumbling across the room, coming to a halt under a hail of sword blows from the riders.

As the package of gunpowder left my hand, I hefted my staff and launched it with as much power as I could muster butt first at the sorcerer. The shock of the blast had struck him, causing his grip on the King to release and sending the King to the floor. The sorcerer buffeted by the explosion, staggered forward and my staff hit him smack on the forehead. The double blow from the blast and staff knocked the sorcerer unconscious instantly, and as he crumpled to the floor, his hand liberated the gun. I dived towards the weapon and wrapped my hand around it as uproar ensued within the room. Janiz and his riders rushed to encircle and protect the King, Fidelis had also been caught out when the gunpowder erupted and now he lay flat on his face, the all-important box a few feet from his outstretched hand. Being the fighter he was, Fidelis immediate began to climb to his feet, one hand reaching for the box that had been in his care.

Suddenly a hand shot down and snatched the box from his fingertips. Secuutus had dived at the sorcerer and now sat upon the prone body, his massive bulk trapping the sorcerer firmly on the floor. I stood with the homemade gun in my hand as the room fell calm once more. Janiz and his father were hugging each other in a show of affection that belied their previous estranged relationship. The two assassins were dead, lying in a pool of blood from the multiple wounds about their person. The smoke from the explosion was dissipating to show the obliterated remains of the desk amidst a huge circle of black on the wall that gave evidence of the blast area. The riders and guards loyal to the King stood about, unsure of what had happened but relieved to be alive. Some still shook with fear at the explosion, others stared vacantly as their minds sought to come to terms with the 'magic' they had witnessed. I noticed that Firmus had entered when the riders burst into the room and felt pleased that my friends had shared in our success.

The pounding on the doors has stopped, apparently, those treacherous guards outside had also been shocked by the sound of the blast. Soon the battlefield humour began to arise in all who had known the fear of war. Riders and guards alike began congratulating each other with back slaps and manly hugs galore. I found myself at the centre of the riders' attention, all wishing to praise my actions in fighting the dark magic of the sorcerer. Some however, still eyed the black metal tube in my hand and chose to keep a safe distance.

As soon as I could, I peered around the packed room for my small Liverpudlian friend. Finally, I saw him, crouched in a corner away from the celebrations. What I saw caused me some concern. Sophos held the jade box and was staring at it with indecision frowning his face.

Chapter Seventeen: The Green Jade Box

Seeing Sophos safe, for a brief moment all became surreal as relief flooded my mind. The sorcerer was safely stored under Secuutus, Prince Janiz was reunited with his father the King, and I had found the jade box. I looked about the room at the characters who had been my life since I arrived in this strange land and I knew them all. From the strength and determination of Janiz, the friendship of Secuutus, comrades Firmus and Fidelis, and of course, Sophos the Liverpudlian. Sophos, in the guise of a Lupus, the wily sage who had survived on his wits since finding himself amongst the animan. Sophos who now held the jade box. I began to worry once more.

My attention was caught by Janiz and I momentarily ignored the sage as the King and his son released their embrace. The King looked around at the remnants of his chamber, before turning to hold each of us in a brief but intense gaze. After a few moments of consideration, he gave a slight nod and turned back to Janiz.

'These animan have proved their courage and loyalty and in their actions they have shown the true strength of you, my son,' the King reached out, placing his hands upon the shoulders of his son.

'I was wrong to be swallowed in the deceitful words of that creature,' he gestured dismissively at the prone but now conscious sorcerer. 'I shall not make that mistake again. I have realised that my age has left me vulnerable to the lies and falsehearted whispers of others. If not for the love and persistence of the son I banished, I would be but a puppet, controlled by another. But now, I have recovered my wits and will do what must be done.'

As if to demonstrate his return, the King walked to the doors of his chamber, the sounds of hammering had paused with the explosion but now began again. Before any of us could object, the King wrenched open both doors and roared at the sorcerer's supporters outside.

'Get out of my palace! Your sorcerer is defeated, your cause is lost. Flee this place now, flee this land now or be put to death!'

The King then slammed the doors closed once more, the enemy at the doors too startled to react. The hammering ceased.

As one, all the riders voiced their loyalty, relief in their voices at the return of the good King they had known. Even I joined in the adulation for a King I didn't know, hell I didn't even know what I was doing here, but my voice accompanied the others just the same. Janiz stepped forward once again to hug his father, watery eyes and a huge swallow betrayed his emotion. The King also struggled to contain his feelings as he pulled himself taller and squared his shoulders, determination in his features.

'I will put right my mistakes,' he said. 'My Kingdom will return to peace and stability before any of our neighbours see an advantage in our weakness, and attempt to take what is ours. My first duty will be to judge and condemn this evil creature for his crimes, not only against me and my family but also against the very land in which we live. Get him to his feet please.'

The sorcerer was hauled unceremoniously to his knees by Secuutus who, to be fair, had appeared quite comfortable sitting on the accused. The once mighty sorcerer knelt dejected and very frightened, a slight shiver ran through his body as the King stared down into his face. Without a word the King held out his hand and a sword was placed in his palm. The demise of the sorcerer was imminent and his eyes told of his fear.

'Please! Please spare me your majesty, I was a stranger in this land, I did what I did to survive,' whimpered the sorcerer.

'Rubbish! Lies!' the King shouted, his huge Leo head now only inches from the cowering Lupus. 'You would be King in my place. You would see me and my kin dead. You wanted power, the power to rule in my stead. Now you stand accused of assassination and treachery, of attempting to steal the crown.'

The King stood tall again, looking down on the sorcerer with no mercy in his face. His decision made, he now prepared to pronounce judgement. Slowly the King raised his sword, ready to administer justice.

'Beg your permission your Majesty,' I interrupted, 'there are some answers I desperately require from this creature before justice is done. May I seek this information?'

The King's glare turned on me, a snarl beginning to form on his lips as an angry retort readied to issue forth.

'Your Majesty, father,' said Janiz while laying a soft hand on his father's sword arm. 'Please, I ask you to allow Harry the opportunity to gain the knowledge he seeks. I owe my life and yours to this animan and he has proved to have a strong heart. His ways are strange to me but I know him enough, if he needs answers from this creature, I beg you to stay your arm.'

The King glared in turn at Janiz and me before finally lowering his arm slightly, his sword now pointing directly at the sorcerer's heart. With a nod, he signalled his permission. I stepped nearer to the sorcerer, my eyes boring into his. I fought to hold back all my fear and shock, my dread and loss as I stared down at this wretch from my world. I had no idea how or why I got here, I could not fathom why fate had ripped me from my dull but familiar life and dumped me helpless in this world of animan. I knew the sorcerer could not provide the real answers to my questions, but I had a choice to make and his answers might indicate which route I should take in my future.

'What is your name, your real name?' I demanded for starters.

A brief flash of defiance glinted in the sorcerer's eyes before futility returned. He knew his time was ended. With a sigh, he finally responded. 'My full name is Arthur, Arthur Stultus. I used to live in London. I lived alone, all I had was my work. I had no future until I found that damn box, lying unclaimed on a bench in Hyde Park.'

'Keep going,' I instructed as Arthur stared at the twitching blade in the King's hand.

'I thought I could sell the box for a few quid so I snatched it and put it in my pocket until I had left the park. I walked to a secluded corner. Then I opened it and everything went black. I awoke to find myself here, I had nothing except the clothes I was wearing and a few quid in my pockets. I tried my phone but there was no signal, none at all. I was scared. Eventually, I was found wandering in confusion by a trader and I'm afraid to say, the sight of him on top of what had happened finally drove me mad.'

'Yep I can empathise with that, but keep talking. What do you know about the box, have you studied it since you had access to it?' I questioned further.

At that moment Janiz interjected with a question of his own. 'Where did you learn this magic? What is Hyde Park and London? What are these words you speak, words that only Harry understands? Explain what you say or you will suffer in ways you could not imagine. Now speak!'

The sorcerer called Arthur Stultus saw the grim expression on the face of Janiz and shivered. He paused for a second or two while he gathered his thoughts, fearful that a wrong word would end his life there and then.

'I know nothing of magic, what I did were just tricks. I used my knowledge from my previous life to use things from nature and make them into something else.'

Like myself, he had to give his answers in such a way that the animan might understand, or at least accept. Science was unheard of here so what we knew as school classroom science appeared as magic to the animan.

'I came from another land, another world not like this one. I don't know how I got here or why. I am not a warrior or a farmer, I know nothing of trade or even bakery. I only knew what knowledge I brought with me. My knowledge lies with the understanding of what I find around me. For example, I made the iron cylinder shoot a small ball of lead by mixing three substances. I obtained a substance called saltpetre from the droppings of birds, sulphur from your so-called demon holes and charcoal from burnt wood. That is all, there was no magic.'

'But you conjured a demon!' exclaimed Secuutus.

'No, I did not,' explained the sorcerer, 'I . . . .'

'I can and have explained that my friend. It was nothing more than mushrooms that make you dream and those items placed around that tree,' I interrupted. 'It was the idea of a demon that grew in your minds after you had eaten those mushrooms. There are no demons and no magic.'

I was relieved no one asked about the 'burning water' we had witnessed on our journey. I was not sure how that could be explained. How could one explain electrolysis to those with knowledge on a par with the medieval age on my world?

All the rider's attention was glued to the questioning of the sorcerer, broken suddenly when calls for the King could be heard from outside in the corridor. Judging these calls to be friendly, Janiz moved to the chamber doors and opened them. Immediately a group of guards led by Ductor rushed into the room, weapons held in readiness to face any threats. There was no sign of the disloyal guards that hammered on the door earlier, though in truth, I couldn't identify who they were anyway. Though I was sure Janiz and the captain Ductor would have an idea.

Janiz calmed down the anxious guards, instructing them to remain stationed outside the door until our business with the sorcerer was concluded. I let out a quiet sigh now that we were once again surrounded by loyal soldiers. The sorcerer understandably, did not appear too happy at this turn of events. He was now truly on his own, facing the wrath of the King with no one to come to his aid.

During this distraction, the King had not once removed his gaze from the sorcerer, his sword never wavered. With the guards in place, all focus returned to the kneeling sorcerer and as silence fell once more, I asked one final question.

'Why didn't you use the box to get home again? You had plenty of access to it while the King was under your influence. And how did you manage to control the King? Some form of mind drug?'

'Why would I want to go back?' the dejected sorcerer muttered, 'I had everything I wished here, power, wealth, all I could eat and drink. Why should I return to my non-existence at home?' replied the sorcerer in a low voice.

'As for the King, yes I did use a form of drug, cannabis actually, amongst other things, to help pacify him and make him open to persuasion. Nonetheless, he too made it easy for me, I simply played on his own desire for power. Power to defend his kingdom and my magic to conquer one of the nearby kingdoms and make it his own. Having a powerful sorcerer at his side would go far in keeping the surrounding kingdoms from thoughts of invasion and conquering this land. I played to his ego and spoke what he wished to hear until he was convinced he could no longer live without my wisdom and my support.'

The sword, now at his throat, quivered as fury and shame overtook the King. Janiz laid a calming hand on the King's arm while nodding for the sorcerer to continue.

Looking directly at me, the fake sorcerer, Arthur Stultus continued. 'I believe it is similar to those feelings hostages feel for their abductors. I convinced him that Janiz wanted his throne, that his son was an enemy of the Kingdom. I wanted him gone for good, but as the King's only son, I could only achieve banishment for Janiz. I never expected to see him again. Once Janiz was out of the way, I had full control over the King and the kingdom. It was a power I could never gain at home. I never opened that jade box. I wanted to stay.'

The room fell silent as those who witnessed the confession took time to digest the information. Some nodded as they remembered how strange the King's behaviour had become, others found their suspicions confirmed. As for myself, I felt shame, shame that a countryman of mine who, finding himself in a new land, would immediately contrive to rule that land. I suppose it's a human trait, I only had to remember all the wars, troubles, meanness and cruelty of my world to realise the fact. Out of the three in that room who were from a modern Earth, the law of averages suggested there would be at least one bad apple. I glanced over at Sophos, no one knew he shared the birthplace of me and Arthur, I intended to keep it that way if possible.

Following the admission of Arthur Stultus, the onetime sorcerer, the King was filled with self-loathing at the ease in which he had been controlled. Fury rose at the fake sorcerer for his deeds and shame that he had willingly abandoned his only son. His face resembled a true snarling lion as he slowly bent down face to face with the fake sorcerer and growled, a growl so ancient and savage it sent a shiver of fear down my spine.

'So you would be King?' he snarled. 'You like to talk and use your power of persuasion to control others? Well, that is something I can cure. Janiz, have your riders remove the tongue of this serpent.'

The sorcerer stared in horror at the King's words, his face portrayed the disbelief at what was to happen to him. A low keening sound crept from his lips, building rapidly into a scream as Firmus and Fidelis grabbed his arms, Secuutus moved in behind and restrained the sorcerer's head in a grip of iron.

Janiz drew a dagger and stepped close, grasping the sorcerer's jaw before prising his mouth open with the blade. The fake sorcerer struggled and screamed from behind clenched teeth, his eyes wide, sweat pouring freely down his face. With a grunt, Janiz forced the jaws open, grasped the tongue and with a sawing motion, began to cut through the tissue. In moments Janiz held the bloody body part in his hand and stepped back. The other riders released the sorcerer who fell to the floor, his mouth working in a moaning whimper that bubbled in the blood that poured from his mouth. In a final insult, Janiz bent and wiped his dagger on the black robe of the now mute sorcerer.

'Let's see how you work your word magic now sorcerer,' sneered the King. 'No more will you sap the will of another, never again will your words be heard. Stand up Sorcerer, and look me in the face, I wish to witness your torment.'

Firmus and Fidelis jerked the sorcerer to his feet and held him upright in front of the King. I stood along with the others, no compassion or sorrow emanated from any of us. The judgement would have been classed as cruel in my world, but I was here not there and I understood the necessity of the King's actions. To become King, one had to be strong, one had to make choices that others could not, and one had to be cruel. As I watched the quaking sorcerer stand weakly before the

King, a sound caught my ear. Looking around I spotted Sophos, his hand clamped over his mouth in a vain attempt to avoid spewing on the King's plush carpet. He failed. A guard moved quietly into the room and without a word, began clearing up the mess. The little Liverpudlian moved over to stand near me, embarrassment moving him away from his deed.

'Harken to me Sorcerer. You will not die for your crimes, you will be chained forever to the main door of my palace. You will serve as you open the doors for all, a reminder to everyone of the dire judgement that will befall any who challenge this kingdom. There you will remain until the new King tires of your presence at his door.'

The King fell silent after making this decree, a small smile on his face as he waited for his words to sink in.

I began to smile and soon all the riders and even the guards joined me as Janiz stood dumbfounded, his jaw falling lower and lower. 'What?' was all he could say.

'Yes my son,' began the King, 'these recent events have shown me it is time I retired. I have been fooled and controlled by that wretch,' he pointed at the sorcerer. 'I must also be held accountable for what befell my kingdom, for your banishment, for allowing this false sorcerer to beguile me.'

'Therefore, I accept my time has come to abdicate the throne in favour of you, my son. I will stay at your side as is my duty as your father, but you will be King. I charge all those present to witness my last proclamation.'

'Father wait! Are you sure? This is your kingdom, you won it and you rule it and everyone in it. You are the King and must remain so. My time will come sadly, but it is not now, not this day,' implored Janiz, shock still evident on his face.

The King drew himself up in a stance of confidence and pride. 'I am sure my son. I have ruled for long enough. I am not a young animan and the weight of the crown has become heavy.'

The King's shoulders slumped again as if a weight had been removed as he continued. 'You will be King and I will enjoy my retirement. I will go fishing, hunting, I may even find a new wife, or two or . . . But I wish to enjoy my remaining years and have no wish to do so with the strain of the whole kingdom on my head. Enough now Janiz, I proclaim you are King!'

The old King paused, took a deep breath and roared, 'All hail King Janiz!'

'All hail King Janiz,' shouted all in the room. A shout that echoed through the palace, taken up by all who heard the cry. 'All hail King Janiz!'

I shouted along with everyone, amused by the face of Janiz, a face that portrayed varying degrees of sadness, joy, embarrassment and pride as this new chapter in his life began to dawn on him. I looked happily about the room, sharing in everyone's joy until my eyes fell upon Sophos. He was stood silently staring at the green jade box in his hands, he did not hail the new King, he did not return my gaze. He simply stared down at that box. I moved closer to him, understanding the turmoil within his mind. Now he could return home, go back to his city of Liverpool in Britain. Once more he would see friends and family, familiar places and a world he knew. But I was mistaken. Looking up from the box, Sophos's eyes met mine.

'I don't want to leave,' he said quietly, 'I like it here. I have a home, friends and I'm held in favour by many, even the new King. I had nothing at home, no wife or children, few friends and I lived in a small rented bedsitter. What have I to return home for? This place, this land is now my home.'

For a moment I was stunned into silence. I was convinced he wished to return to his human home, but it seems I was wrong. So what did I feel? Would I take this opportunity to return to my small flat in Manchester and continue to squeeze education into the unwilling minds of teenagers? At that instant, I could not answer my own question. Suddenly another thought entered my mind, one I had not considered before.

'Sophos,' I began, 'do you believe the box will take me home again? Or is it possible it won't send me home at all? Is it possible this was a one way trip?'

The small sage pondered this for a few moments. 'To be honest, I'm not at all sure. Why would it send us here, with no hope of return? It is a question neither of us can answer, I doubt if even Arthur can answer that question. It will be a chance you'll have to take if you open that box again.'

Sophos and I held each other's gaze for a moment, he was content to stay here but was I? I had assumed the box would return me to my small flat but now I realised I did not know. The shouting and congratulations continued around us as I mulled over the significance of what Sophos had said. Could I be sure I would return to the life I once knew? What if it didn't? What if I woke up each day as I am? Would I want to know the definitive answer? I honestly did not know.

With myself and Sophos deep in thought, and all the riders, guards, retiring King and new King were all celebrating the rise of Janiz to King, no one noticed the sorcerer. The first I knew of his subtle plans was when a bloody hand shot out and snatched the box from the hands of Sophos. I shouted in alarm and all those in the room turned to look at me, before switching their attention to the voiceless sorcerer. No one moved as the creature once known as Arthur

Stultus gripped the box tightly, staring about the chamber. His eyes finally settled upon the old King and as he held his gaze, the sorcerer gently opened the box, lowered his eyes and peered in, and promptly disappeared.

Uproar ensued as riders and guards alike rushed about the chamber searching for the sorcerer, all believing he had pulled yet another and perhaps final trick in a bid to escape. Janiz roared for the guards in the corridor to immediately search the vicinity, offering double pay for whoever found the false sorcerer. I did not move, nor did Sophos. We knew what had happened, the sorcerer had indeed escaped. Where to we couldn't know, but his final trick proved to be his best yet. I reached down and retrieved the box that had dropped as the sorcerer disappeared. The lid had closed when it landed on the thick carpet and, as I grasped it, I kept my hand firmly around the box to ensure it did not open again.

'Harry,' called Janiz, 'what happened? Where is the false sorcerer?'

I sighed. 'He is gone Janiz,' I said, forgetting his new title and added in an apologetic tone, 'Your Majesty.'

Janiz ignored my slip, 'But where has he gone? What strange magic has he conjured this time? We need to catch the creature and make him pay for all that he has done to my father and our kingdom. You two are wise in his ways, where has he gone?'

'I am sorry your Majesty, the sorcerer is no longer on this land I fear. I cannot be sure but I suspect he is not even on this world.' I replied.

Janiz peered at me for a moment before issuing further commands. I had said the sorcerer was no longer anywhere in this kingdom, but he needed to be sure. Secuutus came over to stand close to me as the new King moved away. He stood looking at me for a minute or two, then he grabbed me in one of the strongest hugs I have ever endured in my entire life.

'We are free,' he whispered, 'our new King has pardoned all the riders and we are now to serve as his personal guard and companions. No more sleeping on hard ground or crapping behind bushes, no more saddle sores and no sorcerer to battle. All we have to do is keep King Janiz safe, not an easy chore I suspect, but at least we will have a palace as our base.'

'I'm pleased for you Secuutus, for you and all the riders. You'll have to mind your manners though, no farting or scratching your private bits in public. You'll even have to wash daily.'

I returned his massive hug, my mind was made up though sadness filled me. I had never known such friends as I had gained amongst the animan. My home could never match the feeling of belonging I had here, but I did not really belong. Now the object of my search was in my hands I felt dejected. What would I do if I stayed here? Would I be a palace guard like Secuutus, Firmus and the rest? Was that really what I wanted in my life?

I looked long and hard at Sophos and Secuutus before turning my gaze on each of the other riders. I coughed loudly to interrupt the chaos, I had to cough a few times before I caught everyone's attention. When everyone was looking at me in puzzlement, I said my last words.

'Thank you for being my friends, I will miss you.' I could not delay the inevitable any longer. Sophos smiled while Secuutus looked confused. I looked down at the green jade box, and opened it.

I awoke flat on my back once again, from the breeze on my body I knew I was alive. I did not move as I stared up at a blue sky, while my hands brushed through the grass on which I lay. The cry of an eagle in the distance caught my attention and I sat up to stare in that direction. I found myself on the very edge of a huge forest, trees stretching away as far as I could see. The air still smelt clean and the only other sound to reach my ears was the chirping of birds in the trees. With resignation, I knew I was not back in Manchester. I had not returned home at all. Yet again I had awoken to a strange world. I peered down at my body to see it remained covered in a light brown fur and my limbs were still strong and lithe. I still held my staff and that evil looking knife, a fact I was grateful for.

I looked around at the countryside and suspected I was no longer in the Kingdom of Janiz. It seemed I was still on Totus-Terra but exactly where I had no idea. I sighed, here we go again. My Manchester flat had never felt so far away as it did at that moment. I stared at the land around me, wondering which direction to travel. To be honest, I didn't really care, the disappointment of not waking in my own kitchen lay heavy on my soul. I lay back on the grass in despair, not sure if I would ever get home.

Suddenly I heard a groan very close behind me. I sat up and swung round, once again ready to fight, or run like hell. To my total shock and surprise, I saw a huge body lying on the grass only a few feet away from me. I leapt to my feet expecting the worst and turned to face the prone figure. It stirred, groaned again before slowly and ponderously it raised its head, farted and stared back at me.

'Hello Secuutus,' I said.

Finis.

Printed in Great Britain
by Amazon